# THE
# CAPTAIN'S
# ORDER

Part 4
of
The Windsor Street Family Saga

By
VL McBeath

**The Captain's Order**
By VL McBeath

For more about this author please visit
https://valmcbeath.com

For permission requests, write to the author at:
https://vlmcbeath.com/contact/

Editing services provided by Susan Cunningham at Perfect Prose Services
Cover design by Books Covered

ISBNs: 978-1-913838-22-5 (Ebook Edition)
978-1-913838-23-2 (Paperback)

Main category - FICTION / Historical
Other category - FICTION / Sagas

## Legal Notices

This story was inspired by real-life events but as it took place over one hundred years ago, parts of the storyline and all characterisation are fictitious. Names have been changed and any resemblance to real persons, living or dead, is purely coincidental.

## Explanatory Notes

### *Meal Times*

In the United Kingdom, meal times are referred to by a variety of names. Based on traditional working-class practices in northern England in the nineteenth century, the following terms have been used:

*Working Class*

**Dinner:** The meal eaten around midday. This may be a hot or cold meal depending on the day of the week and a person's occupation

**Tea:** Not to be confused with the high tea of the aristocracy or the beverage of the same name, tea was the meal eaten at the end of the working day, typically around five or six o'clock. This could either be a hot or cold meal.

*Upper Classes*

For members of the aristocracy, the upper-middle classes, and in the first-class saloon of the ship, naming conventions differed:

**Luncheon:** The meal eaten around midday. This would usually be a hot meal.

**Afternoon tea:** Taken at around four o'clock, this would typically consist of sandwiches, cakes, and a pot of tea.

**Dinner:** The meal eaten at the end of the working day, typically around seven or eight o'clock. This would usually be a hot meal.

### *Money*

In the nineteenth century, the currency in the United Kingdom was Pounds, Shillings and Pence.

- There were twenty shillings to each pound and twelve pence to a shilling.
- A crown and half crown were five shillings and two shillings and sixpence, respectively.

For further information on Victorian-era England visit:
https://vlmcbeath.com/victorian-era

Previously in
**_The Windsor Street Family Saga_**

Part 1: _The Sailor's Promise_
Part 2: _The Wife's Dilemma_
Part 3: _The Stewardess's Journey_

Set in Liverpool (UK), _The Windsor Street Family Saga_ was inspired by a true story and it is recommended that the books are read in order.

For further information visit my website at:

https://valmcbeath.com/windsor-street/

**Please note:** This series is written in UK English

# CHAPTER ONE

*Liverpool, September 1882*

Number three, Princes Park Mansions. Despite visiting monthly for the last six months, Nell wondered how she'd become a regular visitor to such a magnificent address. Not that she'd been inside the house beyond the entrance hall. Gazing up, she shuddered at the imposing four-storey building with its stuccoed facade and rows of Georgian windows. It was impossible to approach without being watched by the curious eyes peering from behind numerous sets of curtains. Taking a deep breath, she climbed the front steps and knocked on the elaborate door-knocker. *I hope Miss Ellis is ready.*

As usual, the butler opened the door within seconds.

"Good afternoon, Mrs Riley. If you'll step in, I'll tell the mistress you're here." He closed the door behind her before making his way up the ornate wooden staircase, his grey hair an attractive contrast to the black of his morning suit. Nell ran her eyes over the now familiar portraits hanging on the wood panelling, but Miss Ellis broke her concentration.

"Mrs Riley! How marvellous to see you again." She skipped down the stairs. "Did you have a good voyage?"

"I did, thank you, but I'll tell you about it later."

"You didn't go into New York again, did you?" Miss Ellis's eyes widened.

"Sadly, it wasn't that good. Are you ready to go out?"

Miss Ellis screwed up her face. "What's the weather like?"

"It was trying to rain, but it should hold off for the next hour or so."

Miss Ellis's shoulders slumped. "Would you mind if we don't walk today?"

"Would you like me to come back tomorrow?"

"Silly. I don't want you to leave. I just thought we could stay here. The sitting room's on the first floor and Mother's taking a lie-down so we'll have it to ourselves. You'll see the view of the park I've been telling you about, too."

Nell tried to smile. *Why didn't I put my better dress on?*

The butler took Nell's cloak and, with the promise of afternoon tea, Miss Ellis led her up the staircase.

"What a splendid house." Nell ran a hand along the solid oak handrail. "Have you always lived here?"

"Yes, Father bought it before I was born. Now, here we are." She ushered Nell into a large square drawing room filled with two oversized settees, several elaborate chairs and an occasional table. A set of four chairs, with gold effect legs and green velvet cushions, surrounded a matching table in the central window.

"We can sit here and admire the view." Miss Ellis offered Nell a seat.

"It looks too good to sit on."

"Don't be silly. We've used them for years. I hope you've known me long enough to make yourself comfortable."

Nell perched on the edge of the seat. "How've you been while I was away?"

A grin split Miss Ellis's face. "I had some good news. I wasn't going to tell you until tea arrived, but I can't wait." She bounced on her seat. "I got a cheque from my publisher last week. It's for more money than they've ever sent me before. Father's delighted."

"That's wonderful. I presume it's because Mr Rodney didn't get his share."

"I imagine so. We've not heard a word from him since New York."

"Maybe he stayed out there."

"I do hope so."

Nell smiled at the grin on Miss Ellis's face. "Have you seen any more of Mr Hewitt?"

"Not since you were last here." Miss Ellis pouted. "He wrote to say he'd finished his business in Liverpool and he and Mr Cavendish were going back to London. I don't expect to see them again. I suspect they only called in the first place to visit Father and make sure he was happy with the arrangements with the publisher."

"That's a shame. I enjoyed having them around."

Miss Ellis sighed. "So did I, but they were out of our league. You knew that."

"It would still have been nice to say farewell."

"It would, but enough of them–" Miss Ellis's eyes narrowed "–what about Mr Marsh? Was he still checking up on you?"

"He wasn't there!" Nell's face lit up. "That's why the voyage was so good. I hadn't realised how much of a relief it would be."

"I still think he liked you."

"He had a funny way of showing it. He always made me feel inferior, even compared to Mrs Swift. As far as he was concerned, I couldn't do anything right, especially around other men."

"He was jealous."

Nell rolled her eyes. "I doubt it. More of a moral judge, I'd say. Anyway, hopefully, I've seen the last of him. Word has it he stormed off the ship shortly after I left the previous voyage and he's not coming back."

"Was it to do with you?"

"I don't think so, although he was short-tempered with me on the morning we disembarked."

"Perhaps it was because you accepted a ride home from that new steward, Mr Hancock."

"Well, he's a fool if it was." Nell's cheeks flushed. "Mr Hancock only offered because he was travelling to Toxteth."

"Did Mr Marsh know that though?" Miss Ellis sat forward. "That may be why he was upset."

"I'm not getting involved in this story-making. Mr Marsh was nowhere to be seen when we made the arrangements."

Miss Ellis cocked her head to one side. "Perhaps it was because he didn't want to work in steerage any more, and Mr Price told him the only way to do that was to change ship."

Nell shrugged. "That would make more sense. I'd hate to spend a whole voyage in steerage, let alone six months in a row. I'd be leaving myself."

Miss Ellis paused as a maid brought in a tea tray and she waited for her to close the door as she left. "Have you decided whether you'll carry on next year?"

Nell sighed. "Not yet. I can't deny the money's welcome and now things have settled down with the stewards and chefs, I enjoy it. The trouble is, the girls are missing me, and Maria's constantly moaning about me going away. She wasn't happy about me coming out this afternoon."

Miss Ellis's face dropped. "I'm sorry. I shouldn't take you from your family when you're only home for a few days."

"Oh, you don't. It's my choice. When we left New York, I promised to introduce you to the local parks, and I enjoy our walks far more than doing chores. She only wants me to stay at home as some sort of punishment."

Miss Ellis picked up the teapot. "I've enjoyed going out over the summer, too. I must admit, I feel incredibly mean keeping you indoors today."

"You needn't worry." Nell grinned. "It's very pleasant to sit and have tea poured for me. Maria needn't know we didn't go for a walk." She accepted a slice of Victoria sandwich cake before Miss Ellis settled in her chair.

"I must look forward to you coming home almost as

much as your sister. If you decide against going to sea next year, could we go out more often? Twice a week, perhaps?"

"That would be nice, although I can't make any promises. I've not spoken to Maria, but I may still need to earn some money. At least my brother-in-law, George, is working again, but he won't be earning nearly as much as he was when he was at sea."

"What will you do if you stay in Liverpool?"

Nell shrugged. "I've not decided. I may try to get a position in one of the shops. Female assistants are becoming popular nowadays, and I'll have more experience than most."

"I hadn't thought of that." Miss Ellis gazed through the window as spots of rain began sticking to the panes.

"What's the matter? You don't look very happy."

"I'm sorry, I'm being selfish. I hoped you'd be my key to freedom..."

"What do you mean?"

"I'm probably being silly, but since we've been going out, I've realised what I've been missing. I wondered if we could venture further afield if you were here all the time."

"We could still do that. I don't know whether I'll need to work, but even if I do, it won't be every day."

Miss Ellis's face brightened. "And your sister won't mind?"

"It's not up to her. I've been thinking about this, and it's time I stood up to her."

Despite the rain, Nell took the long way home, but as she arrived outside the house, she stared at the door. *What sort of mood will she be in now?*

Rebecca jolted her from her thoughts as she opened the front door.

"Thank goodness you're here." She stepped outside and closed the door behind her. "You're in trouble."

Nell groaned. "What have I done now?"

"Nothing. That's the problem. She wants some help."

"I've been out for two hours..." She gritted her teeth. "I should turn around and walk away again..."

"Please don't. If you go in now, she'll forgive you. Besides, George is still here, so she's less likely to shout."

"You're right." Nell let her hand settle on the doorknob. "I'll see you tomorrow." She watched her sister disappear into her own house across the road before letting herself in.

Maria planted her hands on her hips as Nell walked into the living room. "What time do you call this? I thought you said you'd only be an hour."

"Miss Ellis wanted to talk, and I couldn't walk away."

"Doesn't she realise you have family who like to see you? A bit of help around here wouldn't go amiss, either."

"Leave her alone." George pushed himself up from the chair by the fire. "Is tea nearly ready? I need to be at the alehouse shortly."

"It is thanks to me. I have to do everything myself." Maria disappeared into the kitchen and returned with a plate of sausages and boiled potatoes coated in butter. "Here you are."

Nell sighed. "Stop complaining. I'll do the tidying up." *And she wonders why I want to go away...*

"I know you will..."

Nell poured the tea and pushed a cup to George as

Maria returned to the kitchen. "It's as well you're working now. Do you enjoy it?"

"I do. I thought I'd miss the sea, but I don't. Not much, anyway. I just wish this job paid the same as the last one."

Maria scowled as she brought in some fruit cake. "They probably can't afford to pay you more with all the ale you sup while you're there."

"I can't stand behind the bar all night with nothing in my hand. Besides, if the customers tell me to take one for myself, it would be rude to say no." He winked at Nell. "It saves me some money, anyway."

"How's the leg? Can you stand on it for long?"

"I manage, and I've a stool for when it's quiet." He took a slurp of tea. "Have you decided what you'll do next year?"

"She's staying at home." Maria put the plate on the table.

"Let her speak for herself."

"The answer won't be any different. Will it?" She glared at Nell, then bustled back to the kitchen, but George patted Nell's hand.

"Don't let her upset you."

"I try not to."

She watched him clear his plate, and once he'd finished his cup of tea, he stood up.

"I'm off to work. Don't wait up."

Nell waited for him to leave before carrying his plates to the kitchen. "Is there anything you want me to do?"

"You can top the teapot up. Alice will be home with the girls in a minute, not to mention Billy and Vernon."

Nell had no sooner carried the teapot to the kitchen than the front door opened and Leah ran to her.

"Mama." She reached for her skirt and wrapped her arms around her legs.

Nell smiled down. "Where've you been?"

"The ducks. We gave them bread."

"Did you now? That's nice. Go and ask Alice to wash your hands while I get tea ready. Is Elenor with you?" Nell peered into the living room. "Aren't you coming to see me?"

"I'm helping Alice."

*Oh.* Nell's shoulders slumped. "All right, I'll be out in a minute. You wash your hands, too."

Billy and Vernon were at the table when the girls arrived downstairs and Nell joined them, sitting between her daughters. She ran a hand over Elenor's hair.

"Have you had a nice afternoon?"

Elenor nodded. "Alice does nice things with us."

"You must have been good girls then."

"We're always good."

Alice's cheeks coloured. "They are, but we went to the park because we had some stale bread. I thought we might have seen you there with Miss Ellis."

"Oh ... we, erm ... we walked up to Sefton Park."

"I'm not surprised you were out for so long, then." Maria scowled, causing Leah to scramble onto Nell's knee.

"My like the ducks."

"I know you do. If you're a good girl, we can go again tomorrow."

"Not before you've helped me, you can't."

"Will you give me a minute? I've got all morning to do housework. I'd like to spend some time with my daughters."

"You'd have more time if you weren't leaving on Saturday."

"You're going again?" Elenor folded her arms over her chest. "I want you to stay here. The girls in the street all laugh at me."

The colour drained from Nell's face as she glanced at Alice. "Why? Other mams have jobs, too."

Alice shrugged, but Elenor continued. "You never come home."

"I'm here now." She put an arm around Elenor's shoulders, but she pushed it off and moved closer to Alice.

"I want you home all the time."

Nell bit her lip. "That's enough. I'm only away once more this year, then I'll be here for Christmas and we can spend lots of time together."

Maria couldn't keep the smirk from her face. "And she won't be going again after that. Will you?"

Nell glared after her sister as she went into the kitchen.

"Don't worry, Aunty Nell." Billy flinched as a pan crashed into the sink. "James should be home for Sam's wedding next month. Will you be here for it?"

Nell's heart sank. "If we stick to our roster, I'll be leaving the day before. I'll have to pray James arrives a few days earlier."

## CHAPTER TWO

The sun was warm the following afternoon as it peeped out from between the clouds. Nell stood beside Rebecca and pointed to a bench in the shade of a large elm tree that overlooked the lake.

"Over there."

Rebecca grinned. "Marvellous. We'll be able to watch the girls feed the ducks."

Leah tried to climb from her pram as Nell positioned it on the side of the footpath.

"All right, give me a moment." She lifted her down as Elenor ran to the edge of the water with her cousin Isobel.

"You two be careful. And keep an eye on Leah and Florrie. We don't want any of you falling in."

"We won't." Elenor planted her hands on her waist. "Alice lets us put our hands in the water."

"Alice doesn't usually have the four of you."

Rebecca unwrapped a sheet of brown paper. "Here you are. A piece of bread each. Break it up into small pieces for the ducks."

Each of the girls took their bread and crouched by the lake.

"It should keep them quiet for five minutes. It's so nice to sit and watch." Nell sat back, but Rebecca raised an eyebrow.

"You could do that all the time, you know."

"Don't you start."

"I'm sorry, but I miss you, and as much as I like Alice, walking out with her isn't the same."

Nell studied Elenor. "Does she really let them put their hands in the water?"

"Only if she's with them, holding their other hand."

"I'll have a hard act to follow if I stay at home. I'm not sure I have the patience."

Rebecca cocked her head to one side. "What will Alice do if you stay?"

"I've not asked her. I assumed she'd go back to making waistcoats."

"She won't like that now she's used to looking after the girls. She picks Isobel up from school for me, sometimes."

Nell sighed. "That's part of the problem. I'd be happy for her to carry on, but if I'm not working, I can't pay her. I tell you, Maria will miss the money. For all her moaning, I've kept her going this year."

"You wouldn't know it." Rebecca clasped her fingers on her lap. "I can't remember the last time I saw her happy. If it's not you she's complaining at, it's someone else. It's usually Jane, but we all get our share."

"Even you?" Nell raised her eyebrows.

Rebecca nodded. "She's been quizzing me again about why I haven't had a son yet. She said I owe it to Hugh."

"You've not told her it's him who doesn't want one?" Nell watched as Leah threw her last piece of bread to the ducks, but jumped from her seat as Elenor pushed her sister.

"Leah, you've thrown it in too quickly."

Nell grabbed Elenor as she raised her hand. "Don't do that. She's not as old as you. She has to learn."

"Well, she's not having any of my bread." Elenor clasped the pieces she'd broken into her hand.

"Well, let her watch and don't be so bossy."

Rebecca waited while Nell retook her seat. "Hugh can't deal with the girls when they fight, which is more often now Florrie answers back. The last thing he wants is another one."

"I can understand that, but I'm surprised it's not just happened."

Rebecca rubbed her eyes. "There's no chance of that. He barely looks at me these days."

"Oh." Nell patted her sister's hand.

"You'd think he'd want a son, but all he cares about is going to work, or the alehouse. When he's at home, he wants peace and quiet, and for me to be at his beck and call."

"Is that why you put the girls to bed so early?"

Rebecca stared out over the lake. "It makes life easier..."

"He was like that when you were first married, but I thought he was better now."

"He was for a while, but not any more. Many's the time I wish he'd go straight from work to the alehouse and not bother coming home." Rebecca let out a gentle sob. "I'm sorry. I shouldn't burden you with my problems."

"It's not a burden. If you can't tell me..." Nell squeezed

Rebecca's hand but jumped up as Elenor pushed Leah to the ground.

"Elenor Riley, stop that this minute." She picked Leah up and carried her to the bench, but she struggled free.

"My want to see the ducks."

"You can see them from here. Sit on Mam's knee."

"No. It's Elenor's fault."

Elenor threw her last piece of bread into the water and ran along the edge, scaring the ducks as she did.

Nell plonked Leah onto the bench and stood up. "Elenor, come here this minute. You'll fall in."

She balanced on the edge. "Alice lets me."

Nell grabbed hold of her daughter's hand. "Alice wouldn't let you fall into the water. Now, come along, we're going home."

"We don't want to."

"I don't care what you want, and if you don't walk nicely, you'll be going in the pram with Leah."

"No." She stamped her foot.

"Right, that's it. You're being a naughty girl." She picked her up and sat her in the pram before turning round for Leah. "Come on. You show Elenor how to be a good girl."

"She's naughty."

"I'm not." Elenor bawled and hit out at Leah as Nell sat her down.

"Stop that noise, now." Nell took a deep breath and released the brake on the pram. *I know what Mr Grayson means.* "I'm not cut out for this."

"It's because you've not been here. She thinks she can get away with behaving like this." Rebecca sat Florrie in her pram and called to Isobel. "She wouldn't do the same with Alice."

"Well, if she thinks that having a tantrum will make me want to stay at home, she's sadly mistaken. Alice can have her."

Nell stormed along the path as Elenor screamed. "You wait until we get home, Elenor Riley. You're going straight to bed."

"No!" Elenor's cries split the air, but Nell kept on walking. By the time they reached the park gates, the crying had quietened, and Nell stopped to watch Rebecca gasping to catch her up.

"I didn't know you could walk so fast."

"I'm sorry. A fine sister I've turned out to be, rushing off when you're telling me your problems."

"I expect I'll still have them next time I see you."


Elenor had cried herself to sleep before they reached Merlin Street, and Leah sat by her feet, banging her ankle. Nell nodded down towards them.

"I'm sorry they spoiled the afternoon. If you ever want to talk, you know where I am. I can always come over one evening, if you prefer."

Rebecca nodded. "Next time you're home. I've a feeling Hugh will stay at home tonight. He does it from time to time so I can't make any arrangements."

"What would you do with two children to look after?"

Rebecca grimaced. "He probably worries that I'll have someone round and enjoy myself. Anyway, don't you need to pack your bag tonight? You'll be leaving early tomorrow."

"It's already packed. I need to leave about half past six, so I don't want to do anything at the last minute. Will I see you in the morning?"

Rebecca nodded. "I expect so, even though I hate saying goodbye. I can't deny I'd be happy if you didn't carry on next year."

Nell gave a weak smile. "I can't promise, but we'll see."

Leaving Elenor in the pram outside the front door, Nell picked Leah up and took her inside.

"It's only me." She took off her cloak but stopped before she could take Leah's off. *That's Jane's voice. But there's no shouting.*

She pulled Leah's coat from her arms and lay it on the console table as she headed for the living room.

"Jane. I thought it was you. What are you doing here?"

"I've got some news." Jane beamed at Maria. "Betty's young man, Mr Crane, has proposed marriage to her."

"Oh, that's lovely." Nell took the seat beside Maria. "Is this the one Vernon introduced her to?"

"That's him. A nice man, and shipbuilding's a good steady trade."

"Have they set a date yet?"

"They need to speak to the vicar first, but we hope it will be in June next year. I don't know where we'll have the wedding breakfast, though."

"Why not?"

Maria picked up the teapot. "I'll top this up."

Nell's brow furrowed and she lowered her voice. "Won't she let you have it here?"

"I've not asked yet. I'm hoping she will, because my

landlady won't let me use her house, and it's too hectic at Sarah and Tom's."

Nell creased the side of her lips. "That makes it awkward."

"It doesn't help that I don't have the money for anything else. What will Mr Crane's father think if we can't put on a good spread?"

Maria returned and put the refilled teapot on the table. "Can't he help with the expense?"

Jane gasped. "Hardly."

Nell cocked her head to one side. "Could we ask George if we can have it here?"

Maria shot her a glance. "We don't have the money, either."

"Shouldn't George be the one to decide?" Jane clasped her hands in front of her. "Betty wants Alice to be her bridesmaid and I doubt he'd refuse to host the wedding breakfast when his own daughter's part of the ceremony."

"I'm sure he won't mind..." Nell flinched as Maria banged a hand on the table.

"George *never* minds, that's why everyone always expects so much of him. Haven't you realised? He doesn't earn the same money as he used to. Even if we let you use the house, we're not paying for everything."

"Perish the thought." Jane put a hand to her chest. "We'll all have to chip in. I'm earning a little now, with the mending I'm taking in."

"That's good. I'll help too." Nell beamed at Maria's scowl. "All we need now is the date and we can start making arrangements."

# CHAPTER THREE

The first rays of morning sun crept over the horizon as Nell stepped out of the front door and placed a kiss on Leah's forehead.

"You be a good girl."

Leah wrapped her arms around her neck. "My come with you."

"Not this time." She pulled herself free and handed her to Alice. "Look after her for me."

"Of course I will."

Leah cried and reached out as Nell hugged her sisters.

"I'll see you all soon."

Billy put an arm around her shoulders and ushered her away.

"Come on, we'd better go."

She nodded and linked her arm through his as they set off down Merlin Street. As they approached the corner of Windsor Street, she turned to give a final wave. Rebecca was standing with Maria, while Alice held Leah, who had both arms outstretched.

"Still no sign of Elenor." She dabbed her eyes with a handkerchief.

"She's upset, that's all. It was better that she stayed inside."

"As if that makes me feel any better. I'm doing this for her and Leah as much as anyone else. Why is it so hard to make them understand?"

"They're still young. They'll appreciate all you do, one day."

"I hope so." She tucked her handkerchief into her pocket. "I'd hate Leah to turn out like Elenor when she's older."

"Will they make you change your mind about going back next year?"

Nell sighed. "I don't know. There are so many good reasons to work, but is it worth it if the girls won't speak to me?"

They walked in silence down Parliament Street and Nell sighed as they turned onto the dock road, where gas lamps highlighted the masts of the ships as they waited for the workers to return.

"The mornings are drawing in. It was already light when we were here last month."

"The nights are, too. It was dark when I went to the alehouse last night. Another year nearly gone."

The crowds heading towards the docks increased as they approached the landing stage and Nell clung to Billy's arm.

"I'd swear it's getting busier down here."

"There are more ships than ever coming in, so it won't get any better. Still, we should be grateful."

"Oh, I am, but it's rather disconcerting." Her stomach fluttered as she stared up at the ship that filled her vision. "Here we are again. Will you follow me with my bag?"

She glanced up at the top of the gangplank and stopped, causing Billy to walk into her.

"What's the matter?"

Nell took a deep breath and gripped the handrail as the tall, slim frame of Mr Marsh stared down at her. *Stay calm. You can do this.*

"Aunty Nell?"

"I'll be fine." She put her head down and continued to the platform at the top.

"Mrs Riley. Welcome back."

Her mouth was dry, and she turned to Billy. "M-Mr Marsh. This is my nephew, Billy; Billy, Mr Marsh."

Mr Marsh offered Billy his hand. "Pleased to make your acquaintance."

"Same here." Billy indicated to Nell. "You will keep an eye out for her, won't you? You'll have me mam to deal with if anything happens to her."

"It will be my pleasure."

Nell closed her eyes. *That's all I need.*

"Come on, Aunty Nell. Cheer up. We'll look after the girls for you." After giving her a peck on the cheek, he handed her bag to Mr Marsh.

"I'll see you in a month."

Nell watched as he walked down the ramp and waved when he reached the bottom. When she finally turned around, Mr Marsh was by the door.

"I didn't expect to see you on board. I heard you'd left."

His face was stern. "I needed to go up to Cumbria and

there wasn't time to be there and back before the last voyage."

"Oh."

He ran his eyes over her as he ushered her onto the ship. "After you."

Nell hurried along the corridor. "Do we have a meeting this morning before we start?"

"At half past seven. Mr Price wants us all in the dining room. He has some updates for us."

"Anything major?"

"I don't think so." They stopped as they reached Nell's cabin, and he put her bag beside the door. "I'll see you over there."

Nell groaned as she stepped into the room, but was surprised to find it empty. *Where's Mrs Swift? It's not like her to be late.* She checked under the bunk for her bag. *Nothing. I didn't think I was early.* She set about unpacking her clothes and had almost finished when the door opened.

"Where on earth have you been?"

Mrs Swift stumbled into the room and sat on the settee. "I'm sorry. Mother had a turn last night, and I needed to fetch the doctor before I left."

"Is she all right?"

"I don't know. I didn't have time to wait around." Mrs Swift caught her breath. "I practically ran all the way here."

"Oh dear. I'm sure Captain Robertson would have understood if you'd been late."

"I don't doubt it, but Matron wouldn't. Anyway, I'm here now. My sister will have to take charge. Mother seemed better this morning, so hopefully it's nothing serious. I asked her to write if it was. We should be in New

21

York long enough for a letter to reach me." Mrs Swift stood up and unfastened her bag. "I'd better get a move on. Mr Cooper ushered me onto the ship and said we have to be in the dining room in ten minutes."

"Mr Cooper did? They don't usually have more than one steward on the door."

"Why? Who brought you down here?"

"Would you believe, Mr Marsh?"

"Gracious." Mrs Swift straightened up. "Did he say where he'd been?"

"Only that he'd had to go home to Cumbria and there hadn't been time between voyages. I hope he's in steerage again."

Mrs Swift retrieved her dresses. "Give me another minute and we can go over to the dining room and find out."

Nell's pulse raced as they entered the foyer outside the first-class dining room. Judging by the noise, most of the stewards had already arrived, and she peered through the door to check on the whereabouts of Mr Marsh. *At least he's not waiting for me.*

She followed Mrs Swift to their table, where they joined Matron and Mr Ross, who was delivering a pot of tea. The front of his dark brown hair fell over one eye as he set down the tray.

"I was beginning to think you weren't coming."

"I'm sorry, I was a few minutes late." Mrs Swift's cheeks flushed.

"And we were talking."

"About Mr Marsh I shouldn't wonder."

"N-no." Nell hesitated. "Not especially..."

"Give over. It's written all over your face." Mr Ross smirked as he nodded towards the door. "He's here now so I'll leave you to it." He disappeared into the galley.

"I don't know why you're still bothered about him." Matron huffed as she reached for the milk. "He's not given you any trouble in months."

"Because he's been in steerage."

"Well, you need to get used to him. He's a perfectly reasonable man, and very good at his job."

"Yes, Matron." Nell's cheeks flushed as Mr Price rang the bell for quiet and introduced Captain Robertson.

"Good morning, ladies and gentlemen, and welcome to our penultimate voyage of the year." The captain stood with his arms outstretched. "We've made several changes this month. Firstly, you'll have noticed Mr Marsh is back with us. He'll be working in first class this voyage, alongside Mr Price. Mr Cooper will also move from steerage to first class, while Mr Hancock will take charge downstairs. We also have a new steward, Mr Cunningham, who'll work downstairs with him."

A short, balding man with a round face and stomach to match stood up and acknowledged his new colleagues. Nell gave him a cursory glance, but turned to Mrs Swift.

"What's Mr Marsh doing in first class? Mr Price promised he'd stay in steerage."

Mrs Swift shrugged. "Don't ask me."

"I need to have a word..."

Captain Robertson clapped his hands for silence. "If I may remind you that with winter approaching, the weather will turn choppy over the next few weeks, meaning Dr

Clarke is likely to be occupied by those with seasickness. We're fully booked in steerage, so please, if anyone asks for the doctor's services, or even Matron's, ask yourselves if it's urgent. As much as we appreciate our first-class passengers, we know that they often want medical attention for the most minor of ailments, so you need to assist them yourselves, if you can."

Nell grimaced at Mrs Swift. "That sounds like fun. At least we're not working in steerage. It sounds to me like Mr Hancock and his new helper are going to bear the brunt of it." Nell flinched as Matron tapped her on the arm.

"Shh."

"Sorry." She mouthed the words as the captain looked at them.

"Right, that's all from me. Have a good voyage, everyone."

Mrs Swift nodded towards Mr Ramsbottom, who was waving from his seat in the middle of a group of stewards. "They didn't move him down to steerage."

Nell groaned but gave a discreet wave. "It's as well I've got used to him."

"I hope you have. He's coming over."

Nell forced a smile. "Good morning, Mr Ramsbottom."

"Good morning, ladies, and what a lovely day it is, seeing you both here. The ship was rather dreary without you."

"We were only gone three days. Did you stay on board?"

"I did. It wasn't worth going home. I'd only have been there for half a day before I needed to leave again."

"I assumed you lived in Liverpool."

"No, Birmingham. It takes almost a day to get there and I've only a couple of brothers to see. If I had a wife, it would be different…"

Nell shuddered as he leered at her. "I'm sure."

He ran a hand through his curly hair. "Did you hear that Mr Cooper's in first class?"

"We did. I'm surprised he's not been over to stop you talking to us." Mrs Swift glanced over towards the stewards, but Mr Ramsbottom laughed.

"He'll be fine. We've come to an understanding. I told him the best way to stay in people's good books is to relax more. He's finally got the message."

*And what exactly does that mean?* A shudder ran down Nell's spine and she looked at Mrs Swift. "If we're finished here, we'd better go. The staterooms won't clean themselves."

# CHAPTER FOUR

N ell kept her head down as she and Mrs Swift walked to their table at the far side of the first-class dining room. They'd no sooner sat down when Mr Ross joined them.

"Luncheon, ladies. A nice piece of cod, today."

"Lovely, thank you." Nell picked up her knife and fork. "Did we miss anything while we were ashore?"

"Not a lot. Other than the problems with Mr Marsh."

Nell's brow furrowed. "What do you mean?"

"The way he turned up, expecting his job back."

The creases in Nell's forehead deepened. "He gave me the impression he took time off from the last voyage for family reasons."

Mr Ross shrugged. "That's news to me. And Mr Price. We had too many stewards yesterday when they all turned up. Fortunately, one was new and there's a ship due in tomorrow, so he's waiting for that."

"How strange."

"It most certainly was. Mr Marsh got quite angry when

Mr Price said he hadn't been expected. He offered to give him his old job in steerage, but Mr Marsh was having none of it."

"So that's why he's in first class?"

"It is. There was quite a to-do, but in the end, they had to promote Mr Hancock to head of steerage, so he'd agree to swap roles. That's why Mr Cooper's up here. He wouldn't work under Mr Hancock." Mr Ross glanced back to the galley. "I'd better go. I'll bring your desserts shortly."

"It seems like we missed a lot." Mrs Swift studied Nell as she flaked off a piece of fish. "What's the matter with you?"

Nell sighed. "I don't know. Something doesn't sound right. Mr Ross's story is very different to Mr Marsh's."

Mrs Swift shrugged. "Mr Marsh probably forgot to tell anyone what he was up to."

"But you wouldn't forget something like that. And why insist on moving to first class after what happened?"

"The incident in Central Park was over six months ago. Maybe he thinks he's been punished enough. It can't have been easy working down there all that time."

Nell gritted her teeth. "That's beside the point. Mr Price promised he'd keep him in steerage so we wouldn't be together."

"As long as he doesn't trouble you, you'll be fine."

Nell creased the side of her lip. "We'll see."

Once luncheon was over and the staterooms prepared, Nell wandered to the saloon. She poked her head through the door, but stopped when Mr Ramsbottom grinned at her.

"Don't be shy, you can come in."

Nell glanced at the half dozen stewards cleaning the tables. "I was looking for Mrs Swift."

"Can't say I've seen her. She mustn't have finished her rooms yet."

Nell hovered in the doorway. "I'll see if she wants any help before we start in here."

Mr Ramsbottom shrugged. "As you like."

She turned to leave but straightened up as Mrs Robertson joined her in the foyer. "Good afternoon, madam."

"Good afternoon, Mrs Riley. Has afternoon tea been served?"

"I'm afraid it hasn't … with there being no passengers yet."

"Ah. I should know these things, but I'm losing track of the days. I miss having guests around."

Nell tried not to stare at Mrs Robertson's unusually wide skirt. "Should I order you a pot of tea? It's no trouble."

"That would be lovely. I'm not stopping you from anything, am I?"

"Not at all." Nell opened the door and ushered her inside. "Mr Ramsbottom's already started in here." She escorted her to a section with polished tables and held out a chair. "If you'd like to wait here." Nell hadn't taken two steps when Mr Ramsbottom joined them.

"May I help, ladies?"

Nell smiled. "Could Mrs Robertson have a pot of tea?"

"Certainly. Shall I bring two cups?"

"If you would." Mrs Robertson watched him leave.

"Please, take a seat, Mrs Riley. I've been hoping I might have a word with you."

Nell's heart skipped a beat as she perched on the edge of the chair.

"Don't look so worried. I wanted your advice on a rather *delicate* subject."

"My advice?"

Mrs Robertson rested a hand on the bump beneath her skirt. "Forgive me for talking about such matters, but I'm currently with child."

"Oh." Nell's cheeks coloured. "I had wondered..."

Mrs Robertson held up a hand. "I know it's highly irregular to talk about such things, but I've no idea what to expect."

Nell shifted in her chair. "Shouldn't you ask Dr Clarke or Matron?"

"I've tried, but neither will talk to me. Dr Clarke's rather embarrassed by it, and all Matron says is that I'll find out in due course. But find out what? How will I even know when the baby's ready to be born?" Mrs Robertson kept her voice to a whisper, but the tone was distressed.

"You'll just know."

"But then what?" Mrs Robertson put her hands to her face. "Mrs Riley, you're the only one of the crew who's had a baby. Why will nobody talk to me about it?"

Nell sighed as an image flashed through her mind of Maria standing over her, while a midwife delivered Elenor. "When's the baby due?"

"It can't be long off. I can feel movements inside and sometimes they're quite strong."

The skin across Nell's shoulders prickled. "You should

have started your confinement. I really don't think you should be walking around the ship."

"But my husband and I only have the one room and I don't want to be on my own all the time."

"But you need to make your own space, and not in the *marital* room. We have a couple of staterooms that aren't being used. Perhaps you could move into one of them?"

"Did you do that?"

"There isn't enough room in our house, but ladies of your standing..."

"If you managed without locking yourself away, then I can, too. But..." she leaned forward, her voice barely audible "...how does the baby come out?"

Nell gave an involuntary shudder. "Going into the details won't help. You need to make yourself comfortable and let everything happen naturally."

"Will I need any help?"

Nell's eyes flicked to the stewards who were close by. "We can't talk here."

Mrs Robertson followed her gaze. "I wasn't thinking. I've another question, though. You've got children. How do you manage being at sea?"

"I live with my sister and her family, and they look after the girls."

"That's right. I remember, now. I've become so forgetful lately. It's really quite embarrassing."

"I expect you'll be glad to get home and settled before the baby arrives."

"I might if we had our own house, but we've been at sea for so long, we let it go. I've been wondering how easy it would be to look after a baby on a ship."

Nell grimaced at the thought of all the washing they did when the girls were babies. "It would be a challenge, not least with the laundry ... and being able to soothe the baby when it cries."

"So, you don't think I should travel while the baby's small?"

"Probably not. Do you have someone you could stay with while it's young?"

Mrs Robertson shook her head. "I've no sisters and my parents have both passed."

"That must be hard." *However bossy Maria is, I wouldn't want that.*

"I've got used to it, but with the baby I'm at a loss."

Nell paused as Mr Ramsbottom arrived at the table. "Here you are, ladies."

"Thank you. I hope you don't mind me keeping Mrs Riley from her work. It won't be for much longer."

"We can manage." Mr Ramsbottom gave a slight bow before he disappeared.

"A pleasant man."

"I suppose so." Nell bit her lip. "Have you spoken to Captain Robertson about having a baby on board?"

"Oh, I've not troubled him with the details. He's carrying on as if nothing will change."

*As they all do.* "He won't realise how different life will be for you."

"I don't think I do, either." Mrs Robertson fidgeted with her fingers as she watched Nell pour the tea. "Will it really change everything?"

Nell pursed her lips as she nodded. "I'm afraid so. Not

that it won't be worth it. It will. But it's different. Very different."

Mrs Robertson was about to respond when Mrs Swift joined them. "Good afternoon. Am I missing something?"

Nell jumped to her feet. "Not at all, we were just talking."

"Oh."

Mrs Robertson's cheeks coloured. "It was a rather delicate matter, I'm afraid."

Nell nodded at her friend before indicating to the other side of the room. "If you want to start, I'll join you in a minute."

"Ah, right, I'll leave you to it."

Nell sat down as Mrs Swift left. "I probably should help her. I hope you don't mind."

Mrs Robertson sighed. "How can I, when I'm stopping you from doing your job? Could we talk again, though?"

"It might be difficult to find the time over the next few days. We have passengers joining tomorrow, and then we need to settle them in, but I won't forget."

Mrs Robertson smiled. "Thank you, Mrs Riley. I really need a friend at the moment."

Nell finished her tea and was about to join Mrs Swift when Mr Marsh strolled into the saloon, his dark hair greased back more than usual.

"Mrs Riley." His eyes took in the cup and saucer at the same time as he acknowledged her. "I didn't realise we were serving afternoon tea."

"Mrs Robertson asked if I'd keep her company. Will you excuse me? I need to get on." She hurried over to Mrs Swift.

"He's doing it again. How does he always know where I am?"

"Being in the saloon at this time of day isn't unusual, and you must have sat with Mrs Robertson for the best part of half an hour. What did she want?"

Nell rubbed a hand across her forehead. "It's rather personal, but..." she lowered her voice "...she's with child and I'm the only one on the ship who's given birth before. She wants to know what to expect."

"I wondered why she was wearing wider skirts."

Nell's cheeks flushed. "Quite, but I can't talk to her about things like that. It's private."

"I'm afraid I can't help. Did anyone tell you what to expect before you had yours?"

Nell paused. "Maria tried to explain things, but I'd no idea what she was talking about. I'll have to try and remember what she said, although whatever it was, it bore no resemblance to what happened on the day." Nell let out a deep sigh. "The thing is, I can't tell Mrs Robertson the truth. It will frighten the life out of her."

# CHAPTER FIVE

The following morning, with the saloon already set out for morning coffee, Nell once again stood in the foyer with Mrs Swift while Captain Robertson greeted the guests. He extended a hand as the first arrived.

"Good morning, sir, madam."

A middle-aged man with greying black hair and a bushy moustache took his hand. "Good morning, Captain. Mr Hampson, and this is my wife."

A timid woman of slight build stepped up from behind her husband.

"Mrs Hampson. How nice to meet you." The captain gave a half bow.

"It's the first trip we've taken in over ten years." Mr Hampson's voice boomed around the foyer. "When you build up your own business from scratch, you can't afford to take time off. Not that I've had a choice this time. My brother emigrated years ago, and he insisted we visit."

The captain smiled. "I'm sure you'll enjoy it when you're there."

"I'd better. I had to leave the foreman in charge. Cotton, you know. Made a tidy bob from the stuff, but you'd be amazed how many men would thieve a finished roll to sell on the market. This trip will be no rest for me. I'm worried sick there'll be nothing left when I get home."

"Well, I hope to make the voyage as pleasant as possible." The captain ushered him to one side and indicated to Mr Cooper to show him to his stateroom.

"Once you're settled in, you'll find tea and coffee being served in the saloon."

The captain raised his eyebrows to the first mate as Mr Hampson disappeared, but Nell watched his wife. *The poor thing looks like she can't get a word in edgeways.* Her attention returned to the foyer when an elegantly dressed couple arrived.

"Good morning, Captain." The gentleman, with slicked-back brown hair and a neatly trimmed moustache, shook Captain Robertson's hand. "May I introduce my wife, Mrs Askwith?"

The woman appeared to be of similar age to Nell, and her hat perched within the boundaries of a dark brown chignon. The captain accepted her hand. "Welcome. I hope you'll be comfortable on your voyage."

"I'm sure we will." Mrs Askwith tittered. "Tell me, are any members of the aristocracy travelling with us?"

"I'm afraid not."

"Not to worry. We'll find other guests to sit with, won't we, dear?" She turned to study Nell and Mrs Swift. "Could one of your maids help with my unpacking? We foolishly let ours stay at home."

"We can manage that." The captain summoned Nell over. "Mrs Riley, would you escort Mrs Askwith?"

"Certainly." Nell stepped forward and offered to carry Mrs Askwith's small hand baggage. "If you'd walk this way."

"Steady on." Mr Askwith pulled on his wife's arm. "I hope I'll still get a steward." He gave an apologetic smile to the captain. "My valet isn't with us, either. We didn't think it was worth them travelling for such a short period of time."

"That's no problem." The captain beckoned to Mr Ramsbottom. "Would you show Mr Askwith where the amenities are?"

"Yes, Captain."

Nell walked with Mrs Askwith, while Mr Ramsbottom followed with her husband.

"So, you're not staying in America for long?"

"Only a month." Mrs Askwith stifled a yawn.

"We have to be back, you see." Mr Askwith stood behind Nell as she opened the door. "If we didn't have the ancestral home..."

Mr Ramsbottom raised an eyebrow at Nell as he followed Mr Askwith into the stateroom. "An ancestral home? I thought only lords and ladies lived in them."

Mrs Askwith tutted at her husband. "Now look what you've done. The entire ship will hear about it." She smiled at Nell. "Sometimes it's such a burden having a title. We prefer to travel as plain Mr and Mrs. You won't tell anyone, will you?"

Nell shook her head. "Not if you don't want me to, Your Ladyship."

Mrs Askwith flicked her hand. "Oh, please don't call me that. People are bound to overhear."

"I'm sorry. I'll try not to." Nell's cheeks flushed as she extended her arm around the room. "I hope it's to your satisfaction. Let me show you where the facilities are." She led Mrs Askwith along the corridor. "Everything's on hand, and if you need any help, just let me know."

"Thank you, my dear. Now, did I hear the captain mention coffee?"

Mrs Swift had disappeared when Nell returned to the foyer, and she took her usual spot by the wall as a man and woman spoke to the captain. Two younger women stood behind them. One was dressed in the finest clothes, but the other was clearly a maid. Nell tried to picture the guest list. *This must be the Fothergills. The wife had a maid, if I remember rightly.* She chewed on her lip. *That's right, we made up the room to include their daughter. I wonder if the maid will attend to both of them.* Her musings were cut short when the captain called her over.

"Would you see to Mrs and Miss Fothergill, and show Mrs Fothergill's maid to her room?"

"Yes, Captain."

They walked in silence to the stateroom and Nell smiled as she pushed on the door. "We've set the room up for three, with a single bed where the settee would usually be."

Mr Fothergill nodded. "That should be satisfactory." He stepped past her, lifting his chin in the air. "Come along, Marjorie."

Mrs Fothergill gave a weak smile as she scurried past Nell, but Miss Fothergill hesitated in the corridor.

"I'll walk with you to Elsie's room ... so I know where she is."

"It's this way." Nell hadn't taken half a dozen steps when Mr Fothergill reappeared from the stateroom.

"Where do you think you're going?"

The young woman froze and stared at Nell before edging towards her father. "I-I thought we should know where Elsie's room is."

"I'll go. You stay here."

Mr Fothergill kept his chin aloft as he spoke to Nell. "Lead the way."

Nell took them to the end of the corridor and around the corner to the maids' rooms. "I'm afraid we have an uneven number of maids on this voyage and so Elsie has a room to herself."

Elsie shuddered as Mr Fothergill glared at her. "I don't expect you to talk to any of the crew, is that clear?"

"Yes, sir."

Elsie scurried into the room as Nell held the door open and followed her in. "You should be comfortable, but I suggest you turn the key in the lock when you're in."

The girl's eyes widened. "Isn't it safe?"

"It's just to be sure. You can't be too careful." Nell's smile faltered. "If you need anything, let me know. I'm usually in the dining room or saloon, depending on the time of day. Or cleaning the staterooms on this side of the ship."

"Thank you." Elsie hesitated at a knock on the door.

"What are you doing in there?"

Nell opened it. "We're coming, sir. I'll show Elsie where the facilities are, then I'll be right with you."

Mr Fothergill was waiting for her when they returned.

"My family and I like to keep to ourselves. We'd like a private table for mealtimes and no interaction with the crew unless asked for."

Nell gulped. "Yes, sir. I'll see what I can do."

The last of the guests had boarded by the time Nell got back to the foyer and she found Mrs Swift serving morning coffee in the saloon.

"Have you got any interesting passengers?"

"Not really, but there's an elderly lady called Mrs Turner who I showed to her room. She's on your corridor. She arrived walking with a stick, and wearing a bright orange hat, if you like."

"Is she travelling alone?"

"She is. My guess is she's a widow and comes on ships like this to meet people."

"It's nice if you can afford it. I hope she doesn't want to mix with the Fothergills, though. A right funny bunch they are."

"I must have missed them."

"Think yourself fortunate. Mr Fothergill doesn't want them talking to anyone unless they're *worthy*."

Mrs Swift tutted. "We've not had one of those for a while. Full of their own importance, they are. Still, it makes life easier if we don't have to pay them any attention."

# CHAPTER SIX

N ell stood with Mrs Swift as the stewards escorted the guests to their tables for their first luncheon. Mr and Mrs Hampson were the first to arrive and were shown to a long table. They hadn't taken their seats when Mr and Mrs Askwith joined them.

Nell nudged Mrs Swift as they sat down. "They should really be Lord and Lady Askwith. They only put Mr and Mrs on the passenger list because they don't like people knowing they have a title."

Mrs Swift's forehead furrowed. "I've never met a member of the aristocracy who didn't want to broadcast it across the ship. They've left their maid and valet at home, I presume."

"They have, as it happens, because they didn't want to draw attention to themselves."

Mrs Swift nodded towards them "They may change their tune now they're sat with the Hampsons. If Mr Hampson doesn't stop talking, they'll pull rank and ask to be moved."

Nell laughed. "Oh, here are the Fothergills. Let's see where they sit. He asked for a private table, but we don't have any in the mixed section."

"Judging by Mr Fothergill's face, he's already got the measure of Mr Hampson. Wait a moment." Mrs Swift straightened up. "He wants to sit in the ladies' section."

"He can't do that. Unless he wants his wife and daughter to sit there while he joins the men?"

Mrs Swift shook her head. "He's sitting down. The rest of the ladies don't seem best pleased."

"I should think not. Did you see the look Mrs Turner gave him?" Nell shuddered as the woman, who still wore her orange hat, glared at the table in the corner. "I hope she doesn't think she's too close to the Fothergills or we'll be moving her next. Not that I can worry about her. I need to serve the Askwiths first with them being a lord and lady."

Mrs Swift grimaced. "I doubt Mrs Turner can wait. Shall I serve her for now?"

"Would you mind? I'll introduce myself later."

Nell strode across the room to Mrs Askwith. "Good afternoon, madam. I trust the stateroom is to your liking?"

"It's very pleasant, thank you."

"Splendid. I'll be along after luncheon to help with your unpacking. In the meantime, may I get you a drink?"

"A sherry, please."

"Very good. Mr Askwith, would you care to order from me or wait for a steward? I'm sure our head steward, Mr Price, would be happy to serve you. He's the one with the lighter brown hair, if you see him around."

"I don't mind who serves me as long as they get on with it. A whisky and water, please."

"Yes, sir." She was about to leave the table when Mr Hampson summoned her over. "Is this a private service or can anyone get a drink?"

"I'm sorry, sir. I was coming to you."

"I'll have a pint of ale, then."

Nell forced a smile. "I'm afraid we only serve it by the bottle."

"You'd better make it two, then. If it's more than a pint, I'll finish the rest with the next one."

"Yes, sir. And for Mrs Hampson?"

Mr Hampson studied his wife. "She'll have a lime cordial."

"A-actually..." Mrs Hampson stuttered as her husband stared at her "...might I have a sherry ... like Mrs Askwith? I-it is our first meal, after all."

Mr Hampson looked from his wife to Nell and back again. "Why not? A sherry for my wife."

Nell scurried from the table, and Mr Brennan, the barman, looked up as she approached. "Do we have any drinkers?"

"We do. Two sherries, a whisky with water, and two bottles of ale poured into a pint glass."

"Splendid." He nodded to the Fothergills. "What are they doing over there?"

Nell shrugged. "I presume it's because there was a spare table, and he doesn't want to mix with anyone."

"The rest of the passengers should be glad. They don't look a barrel of laughs."

"You're not wrong. I expect they'll either be on tea or elderflower cordial."

"Typical." Mr Brennan stared at them as he poured the

ale. "I might slip a shot of vodka into his to see if it cheers him up."

"Be my guest." Nell waited for him to pour the rest of the drinks, then carried the tray to the tables. "Here you are, ladies. And for you, gentlemen."

"Let's see what this is like." Mr Hampson picked up his pint. "I'm used to Yorkshire's finest from the brewery at the end of our road. Not this bottled stuff."

"We carry a selection of spirits, if you prefer, sir."

Mr Hampson spluttered on his drink. "At this time of day? I need to keep my wits about me. I didn't get to where I am by drinking spirits at one o'clock in the afternoon."

Mrs Askwith cocked her head at him. "Well, you won't be working on the ship, so perhaps you could treat yourself."

Mr Askwith patted his wife's hand. "Excuse my wife. Did we hear you say you were in cotton?"

"You did and a fine business I've built up, too. I only hope it's there when we get home. I'm not happy leaving the foreman in charge."

Mr Askwith took a sip of whisky. "You need to relax, dear chap. There's nothing you can do about it on here."

"It's all right for you to say. Do you run your own business?"

Mr Askwith smirked, causing Mr Hampson's cheeks to redden. "After a fashion."

"What's that supposed to mean...?"

Nell cleared her throat. "If you'll excuse me, I need to go. Will that be all?"

Mr Askwith sloshed the dregs of his whisky around his glass. "You can bring another one of these, next time you go to the bar. Don't make a special trip, though, I can't be too extravagant." He nudged Mr Hampson. "Will you take another *ale*?"

"Don't talk nonsense. I've hardly started this yet..."

Nell grimaced as she left the table. *That's an interesting pairing.*

"Good afternoon, Mrs Fothergill. Sir." She inclined her head to the pair. "Luncheon will be ready shortly. May I get you any drinks while you're waiting?"

Mr Fothergill studied the surrounding tables. "What's everyone else drinking?"

"A variety of things. A lot of ladies enjoy a sherry..."

"As I thought. Marjorie, you need to have something different."

Mrs Fothergill put a hand to her chest. "Well, I really don't know. Is it too early for cocktails?"

"I don't think so. It is a special occasion, after all. Do you have any recommendations, Mrs Riley?"

Nell pursed her lips. "It depends on what you like, but many of our more *refined* passengers like a Manhattan. It's very popular amongst those who know about such things." Nell bit her lip as she watched Mr Fothergill's expression change from puzzlement to delight.

"Yes, it's been a while since I had one of those. We'll have two ... and do you carry fresh oranges? My daughter has a taste for the juice."

Nell's cheeks flushed. "I couldn't say, sir. I'll check with Mr Brennan, if you like. Is there anything else I can get her if we don't have any?"

Miss Fothergill glanced at her father. "May I try a Pimms? It is considered something of a health drink."

Mr Fothergill studied her. "Why not? We are taking a holiday."

Nell hurried to the bar, unable to contain her grin. "You'll never guess what they ordered."

Mr Brennan studied her. "Not cordial, by the looks of it. Don't tell me they both want sherry."

Nell chuckled. "Perish the thought, only the common or garden passengers would drink that. They want two Manhattans and a Pimms."

"Good grief. I'm surprised they've even heard of them."

"Whether they have or not, when I told them the more refined passengers often ordered them, they didn't hesitate."

He winked at her as he reached for the whisky. "You're learning. I presume the Pimms is for the daughter."

"It is. Her father originally ordered some freshly squeezed orange juice, but when I doubted whether we had any, she asked for a Pimms. I think she'd prefer that."

Mr Brennan grinned. "Pimms it is, then. I'll pretend to look for some oranges in a minute, to keep him quiet."

Nell flinched as Mr Ramsbottom arrived by her side.

"Afternoon. May I have a whisky for Mr Askwith? He's already got the water."

Nell put a hand to her mouth. "He asked me for another one, too. Perhaps I've been too slow."

"We can both take him one. That should keep him happy."

"We can't do that. He'll be drunk before luncheon."

Mr Brennan tutted as he rejoined them. "There was me thinking you were getting the hang of things. Of course you take him one each. The more he drinks, the more he's likely to order."

"And the more he'll appreciate us, and the more tips we'll get!" Mr Ramsbottom beamed. "You know that."

Nell lowered her voice. "He told me he didn't want to appear extravagant."

"Why's he announced that he's Lord Askwith, and not Mr, then?" Mr Ramsbottom grinned. "It sounds to me like he wants to flash his status around, not to mention his money."

"He's a lord?" Mr Brennan's eyes widened. "Why did they put Mr and Mrs on the guest list then?"

Nell sighed. "They said they didn't want any fuss."

"You knew?" Mr Brennan's mouth dropped open. "You're not supposed to keep stuff like that to yourself."

"I only found out an hour ago, at the same time as Mr Ramsbottom, and we've been rather busy since. Anyway, you know now." Nell's forehead creased. "Should we carry on calling them Mr and Mrs?"

Mr Ramsbottom nodded. "I would, until they tell you not to. To their faces at least."

Mr Brennan placed a whisky on Nell's tray. "Take this to His Lordship, then come back for the Fothergills' drinks."

Mr Hampson had barely taken the top off his ale when Nell returned to the table. "Here you are, Mr Askwith. Sorry for the wait."

"You're just in time." He handed her his empty glass. "You'd better take this. We don't want you running out."

"We have plenty, sir. If you'll excuse me..." Nell hesitated as Mr Fothergill glared at her, then raced to the bar. "I need to take these Manhattans. Is the Pimms ready?"

Mr Brennan sighed. "Give me a minute. Take these first."

Mr Fothergill rounded on her when she arrived at the table. "I expect to be served before those dreadful people, not to be kept waiting."

"I'm sorry, sir." Nell served the Manhattans. "Our barman says the oranges are reserved for meals, so he's preparing a Pimms."

Miss Fothergill's face brightened.

"It wasn't quite ready, but I'll get it now." Nell headed for the bar, but stopped and took a deep breath as Mr Marsh beat her to it. *Keep going. He won't say anything in front of everyone.*

She smiled at Mr Brennan as she joined them. "Is it ready?"

Mr Brennan handed her the glass, but Mr Marsh stood in her way as she turned to leave.

"We don't serve much of that."

"No."

"It says a lot about people, don't you think? What they drink." A smile flicked across his lips. "Do you have a favourite tipple, Mrs Riley?"

"Erm ... not especially. I don't drink much. Other than tea."

"Ah, tea. One of my favourites. What a coincidence."

# CHAPTER SEVEN

N ell stood with Mr Price by the door to the dining room as the guests arrived for their evening meal. He bowed as Mr and Mrs Askwith joined them.

"Good evening, sir, madam. I trust you've had an enjoyable afternoon."

Mrs Askwith smiled. "It was delightful to sit on the deck as we sailed past the Welsh coast. Such lovely weather for the time of year."

"It certainly is. According to the captain, we can expect it to last for the next few days."

"Splendid." Mr Askwith rubbed his hands together. "Perhaps we can take morning coffee out there tomorrow."

Mr Price nodded. "I'll see what I can do. We dock in Queenstown overnight, so there'll be a wonderful view of the cathedral."

"I'd quite forgotten about that." Mrs Askwith smiled at Nell. "Thank you for unpacking my trunk. We really should have brought our own staff. Still, we'll know for next time."

"You're welcome, madam. If there's anything you need, just ask."

Mr Askwith winked at his wife, then smiled up at Nell. "Are you free to take our drinks order or must we wait?"

Nell looked at Mr Price, who answered for her.

"I can manage here. Please, Mrs Riley, make Mr and Mrs Askwith comfortable."

Mr Askwith led the way to the table. "We've beaten the Hampsons."

"They won't be long. Would you like to wait for them before you order?"

"Good grief, no. The man made his ale last for the whole of luncheon. I'd rather go at my own pace."

"Very good, sir. Will it be a whisky and water?"

"Indeed, but could my wife try one of those cocktails the table over there had at luncheon?" He pointed towards the Fothergills' table, which was still unoccupied.

"A Manhattan? Certainly, sir. I'll order it straight away."

Nell acknowledged Mrs Swift, who was taking orders from the next table, and hurried to the bar, where she grinned at Mr Brennan. "The Askwiths have upped their order. Mrs Askwith wants a Manhattan."

"That's more like it." His brow furrowed as he reached for the whisky. "The guests at the other tables are late. I hope they're not going to eat in their rooms."

"I've not been told to take any trays, so they must still be getting into their routine."

"I hope so." He nodded towards the woman still wearing the orange hat. "That Mrs Turner likes a tipple. Have you spoken to her yet?"

"Not yet. Mrs Swift dealt with her at luncheon."

"She's a widow." He gave Nell a knowing look. "I reckon she's got a bob or two."

Nell picked up the tray with the drinks. "We'll find out soon enough."

The Fothergills had arrived when Nell returned to the table, and after delivering the Askwiths' drinks, she joined them.

"Good evening. Did you enjoy your afternoon?"

"We've been unpacking for most of the time." Mrs Fothergill gave an apologetic smile. "We've brought too many dresses, so it was quite a squeeze hanging them up."

"That will be because there are three of you in the stateroom. I could see if you could use a wardrobe in another room if that would help."

"We've managed now, thank you."

Mr Fothergill sat up straight, halting the conversation. "I notice the woman over there is drinking a Manhattan. I thought they were a restricted order."

"Oh, no, sir. Anyone can order them, but only those with a refined palate seem to appreciate them."

"I fail to see how people like them have such taste."

Nell pursed her lips. "Actually, sir, I believe they're more sophisticated than their entry on the guest list suggests."

"Really?" He turned to study them. "That surprises me. What's their background?"

"I'm afraid it's not for me to say, sir. They don't want a fuss."

"That makes me even more suspicious." He smoothed down his moustache. "Will the chef be able to spare any of those oranges you found? We'd like two champagne cobblers but they need orange peel."

"I can ask, sir."

"Splendid. If it's possible, we'll have the cobblers, and a Pimms for my daughter. I presume the barman knows how to mix one."

*We'll soon find out.* "I'm sure he does, sir."

Mr Brennan was finishing an order for Mr Ramsbottom, but he looked up when she arrived.

"What are you looking so worried about?"

"This drinks order."

Mr Ramsbottom laughed. "Why? Couldn't you spell it?"

Nell rolled her eyes. "They want a Pimms and two champagne cobblers, with orange."

Mr Brennan grunted. "Why can't they have plain champagne?"

"Do you know how to make it?"

"I've made cobblers before, but there's not much call for them made with champagne. I need to check the quantities." He bent down behind the bar. "Here we are. *The Bartenders Guide.* If it's not in here, they'll get my adaptation."

"I suspect Mr Fothergill could tell you the ingredients, if you'd like me to ask him."

Mr Brennan raised an eyebrow. "Don't you dare. Why don't you serve Mrs Turner while I sort these out?"

Nell was about to leave the bar when Mr Marsh arrived at her side.

"You're busy this evening."

"Aren't we always? Especially on the first day when guests haven't settled into their routines."

"Indeed." His eyes lingered on her face. "I've been watching you, and you seem a lot more relaxed than you were. I'm glad."

Nell edged away. "I'm on my ninth voyage, so I should be. Now, if you'll excuse me, I need to get on."

Mrs Turner glanced up from her menu as Nell approached. "Good evening, dearie. We've not had the pleasure yet." She extended her hand. "Mrs Turner. Widow of the late Cecil Turner."

Nell hesitated. "Pleased to meet you. And I'm sorry for your loss. I presume you're no longer in mourning."

"Not any more. It was nearly ten years ago. A charming man who thankfully left me well-provided-for."

Nell studied her rings, studded with gems of every colour. "You're very fortunate in that respect. May I get you a drink?"

"I heard your barman mention champagne, so I'll take a glass of that."

"On its own or made into a cocktail?"

"Gracious no, on its own. It doesn't do to look flashy."

Nell bit her lip as she glanced at the orange hat. "Very good, madam. I won't be a moment." Before she made it to the bar, Mr Askwith called her over.

"Yes, sir?"

"The same again for us, please."

"You enjoyed the Manhattan, Mrs Askwith?"

She laughed. "I'll get used to it if I have enough."

"Waste of money if you don't enjoy it." Mr Hampson pulled out a chair for his wife as they joined them. "You should stick to sherry. You seemed to like that well enough, earlier."

Mrs Askwith twisted a piece of hair around her finger. "I like to try new things. Will you be sticking to your ale again?"

"I'm going to keep my wife company and have a sherry, if you must know."

The champagne cobblers were waiting by the time Nell got to the bar. "They look nice. I see you managed to get an orange."

Mr Brennan shook his head. "That's dried peel, not fresh."

"It still looks nice. Perhaps I'll try one at our next dinner."

"You'll need to remind me."

"I will, assuming you have enough. Mrs Turner saw the champagne, so she'd like a glass too. On its own, not mixed."

Mr Brennan grinned. "It looks like we're shaping up for a competition as to who can order the most expensive drinks. I'd better get the cognac out for when they finish their meals."

Nell picked up the tray. "Tell me what you have, and I'll let them know when we serve coffee."

Nell was still smiling when she returned to the bar, and Mrs Swift joined her. "You're in a good mood this evening."

Nell cocked her head to one side. "We're having some fun with these passengers. Mr Brennan's teaching me how to get more money out of them for drinks."

"Well, be careful about being over friendly with him. Mr Marsh has hardly taken his eyes off you."

Nell tutted. "That's all Billy's fault. He told him to

watch out for me and he's taken it literally. On the plus side, Mr Ramsbottom's on his best behaviour."

"I'd make the most of it, if I were you."

Nell glanced across the room and caught Mr Marsh staring at her. "I'm not sure which I dislike most, Mr Ramsbottom being overfamiliar, or Mr Marsh giving me the creeps."

Nell's feet throbbed as she and Mrs Swift made their way to the sitting room that evening.

"I'll be glad to sit down. These new passengers certainly know how to drink."

Mrs Swift chuckled as she took a seat. "There may be a few sore heads in the morning if they carry on like that when they're in the saloon."

"I can't believe the Fothergills drank a whole bottle of claret between them, after having those cocktails, too. I don't even think the daughter had any. She seemed quite taken with the Pimms."

"They're dark horses, that's for sure."

Nell took the seat beside her friend. "I'm glad I won't be the one to help Mr Fothergill back to his stateroom later."

"That's the price for being a steward rather than a stewardess, although Mr Ramsbottom won't mind. He'll see it as a way to make more tips."

"Won't he just." Nell paused as Mr Potter joined them.

"Here you are, ladies. Oxtail stew, tonight. I imagine you're ready for it."

"We are indeed." Nell lifted the lid from the plate. "That smells nice."

"It should be tender, too. I've had it in the oven all day." He raised a hand as he left. "I'll see you tomorrow."

Nell licked her lips as she picked up her knife and fork. "I wish all the men were as nice as Mr Potter. He never outstays his welcome, either."

"Maybe that's what working in steerage does for you. He won't have time to stand and talk."

"Possibly. He doesn't seem to mind, though. I get the impression he wouldn't join Mr Ross in first class, even if he could."

"I think you're right." Mrs Swift reached for a piece of bread. "Are you going to say anything to Mr Marsh about him following you around?"

Nell sighed. "What is there to say? The fact he makes me feel uncomfortable is hardly a crime."

"I suppose not. Did you ask why he wasn't on the ship last month?"

Nell shook her head. "I didn't want to encourage him."

"We'll have to hope Mr Ross finds out."

"I'm not really bothered. I'm more concerned about why Mr Price gave him his job back."

"You'll need to ask Mr Price that."

"I know." Nell set down her cutlery. "I just need to find the right time."

# CHAPTER EIGHT

Nell never failed to be impressed by the splendour of Queenstown's cathedral, but it looked particularly attractive this morning with the sun shining on it.

Nell sighed as she paused by the handrail. "What a lovely view."

"It is. It will be a change serving morning coffee on the first-class promenade, too."

Mrs Swift stared over the side. "There won't be many more nice days once we hit the open sea."

"I hope it clouds over by this afternoon. I still don't like being outside when we pass Mizen Head."

"They'll have had enough of being out here by four o'clock. As soon as we leave Queenstown, they'll come indoors." Mrs Swift put a hand on Nell's shoulder. "Come along, let's get breakfast started."

The galley was empty when they arrived, and Nell picked up the list of trays that needed delivering.

"Nothing for us." She flinched as Mr Ramsbottom breezed in behind them.

"Good morning, ladies. Any on that list for me?"

Nell stepped to one side. "Not that I can tell. We've not seen Mr Ross yet, so it may need updating."

"He was in the store. He won't be long."

Nell pursed her lips as the pause lengthened. "How was Mr Fothergill last night? Did you escort him to his stateroom?"

Mr Ramsbottom laughed. "I wish I had. There might have been some money in it for me. For someone so highbrow, he knows how to hold his drink. He walked out of the saloon as straight as you like."

Mrs Swift raised an eyebrow. "Did he let his guard down before he left?"

"Not at all. Mr Askwith tried to befriend him, but he was having none of it."

Nell cocked her head to one side. "I'd have thought he'd enjoy being in the company of a lord."

"Mr Fothergill probably doesn't know. I didn't hear it mentioned last night."

"Perhaps not, although when he was complaining about the Askwiths yesterday, I suggested they may be more sophisticated than he imagined. Not that he was impressed." Nell studied the list again, but put it down when Mr Ross joined them.

"Sorry to keep you. Do we have passengers waiting?"

Mrs Swift poked her head through the door. "A few of them. In fact, talk of the devil, Mr Fothergill's here. He's on his own, though."

"That's strange, although it wouldn't surprise me if he wanted to get out of the way while the ladies get ready. It can't be easy having three of them in one room."

57

Mr Ramsbottom guffawed. "You've clearly not been down to steerage. It's a lot more cramped than three people to a stateroom."

"In case you'd forgotten, we're not allowed..." Nell stopped as the galley door opened and Mr Price joined them.

"What are you all doing in here? There are guests outside who need serving."

"Yes, sir." Nell darted through the door, with Mrs Swift close behind her. "What's up with him?"

"I've no idea. You were going to ask about morning coffee, too."

"Mrs Askwith can ask. He's less likely to bite her head off."

Neither the Askwiths nor Hampsons had arrived in the dining room and Nell headed towards Mr Fothergill.

"Good morning, sir. Will you be taking breakfast alone?"

"No, although my wife and daughter may be some time yet."

"May I get you a pot of tea while you're waiting?"

He glanced up at her. "Why not? They'll have to order a fresh pot when they arrive."

Mrs Turner waved to Nell as she crossed the room.

"Are you ready to order, madam?"

"Some tea and toast, please. I've never had much of a stomach for rich food in the morning."

"Did you sleep well last night?"

"Like a top. I only woke when the ship docked."

"I must admit, there was rather a thud. That's the last time until we reach New York, though."

"And the last day before we're on the open ocean. I never like being too far away from land, either."

"Have you travelled much?"

"I've a sister in New York who I visit most winters. They seem much more bearable than those in Manchester."

Nell's smile disappeared as Mr Fothergill stared at her. "I don't doubt it. Now, let me get this tea."

Once she'd delivered the tea, Nell crossed to the couple's section but hesitated as Mr Price stood talking to Mr Askwith. *Is he taking their order?* She glanced at Mr Hampson, who was listening in. *No, he won't be.* She strode to the end of the table.

"Good day to you both." She smiled at Mrs Hampson. "How are you this morning?"

"Very well, thank you." Mrs Hampson spoke as her husband glared at Nell before returning to his eavesdropping.

"Would you like to order breakfast, or shall I bring the tea while you look at the menu?"

"Tea would be lovely, but we're creatures of habit, so I can order now. We'll both have two fried eggs on fried bread."

"That sounds nice. Shall I bring extra toast?"

"You'd better, otherwise I'll be in trouble."

"What are you in trouble for now?" Mr Hampson joined the conversation as Mr Price left.

"I'm ordering extra toast to go with your eggs. I don't want to be accused of starving you."

Mr Hampson pulled on the lapels of his jacket. "I should think not. Did you order two eggs?"

"And fried bread."

Mr Hampson grunted as Nell moved on to the Askwiths.

"Good morning, sir, madam." She resisted the urge to bow. "Did Mr Price take your order, or may I get you something?"

Mrs Askwith smiled. "I'll go for kippers this morning. Mr Price was inviting us to the captain's table this evening." She beamed at her husband. "The cat is well and truly out of the bag now, and to think we didn't want any fuss."

"It will be worth it, Your Ladyship. What may I get you, sir?"

"Kedgeree, please, with bread and butter."

Nell hovered by the table. "Would you prefer the crew to call you Lord and Lady Askwith, now the captain knows?"

Lady Askwith pursed her lips as she studied her husband. "What do you think?"

"Why not? The stewards will hear soon enough, so what harm can it do?"

"My thoughts exactly." She smiled up at Nell. "If you wouldn't mind telling the stewards. Oh, and would you come to the stateroom at around six o'clock this evening to help me dress? I need to make an effort for the captain."

Mr Price was in the galley when Nell returned, the smile still missing from his face.

"Did the Askwiths mention they'll be joining the captain's table tonight?"

"Yes, sir. They seem rather pleased."

"Why they couldn't put Lord and Lady Askwith on

their reservation, I don't know. I've had to rejig the whole rota to accommodate them."

"I suspect it was nothing more than a game. Mrs Askwith, I mean Her Ladyship, seemed delighted their secret's out."

"Well, if they try anything like that again, they'll get no special treatment. The time I've wasted..."

Nell gulped. "Have you remembered we're serving morning coffee on the promenade?"

"That was her idea, too. Doesn't she realise I've other things to do?" He picked up a breakfast tray and headed to the door.

"Will it be in the saloon, then?"

"I've already planned to have it outside, and I'm not changing it again. This is the last time, though. If she asks for anything else, tell her no."

Nell let out a deep breath as she turned to Mr Ross. "What's upset him this morning?"

"I've no idea, although my guess is that it's something to do with Mr Marsh."

Nell rolled her eyes. "What's he done now?"

"Nothing that I know of, but they've not been on the best of terms since Mr Marsh rejoined us. There's bound to be something."


The ship was still docked in Queenstown as Nell and Mrs Swift collected the cups and saucers from the tables on the promenade.

"Mrs Robertson looked to be enjoying herself when she was on the deck. I've not seen her smiling for a while now."

"It certainly put some colour in her cheeks. She's been in her cabin for too long."

Nell sighed. "I feel sorry for her. It can't be easy being on board in her condition."

"She's only herself to blame. She needn't have come."

"Perhaps, although she told me yesterday she has no family in Liverpool. At least she has Matron here."

"She won't have once we leave here. Tomorrow will be one of the worst days for seasickness." Mrs Swift's frown turned to a smirk. "You may get called in as her companion."

"I hope not!" Nell shuddered. "She still wants to talk to me about *things*–" she pointed to her abdomen "–but I don't know what to say."

"Well, if you don't..."

"I'm not going into that sort of detail." Nell's cheeks coloured. "If she insists on knowing, it should be Matron..."

"I doubt you'll persuade her to say anything." Mrs Swift began straightening the deckchairs. "If I were you, I'd start thinking about what you're going to say."

## CHAPTER NINE

M r Price was repositioning the cutlery on the Askwiths' table when they arrived in the dining room.

"Ah, you're here." He indicated to the table. "I've pulled a couple of chairs away to give the Askwiths more room. Will you adjust the rest of the table to match?"

Mrs Swift watched Mr Price walk across the dining room with one of the spare chairs. "Is all this because the Askwiths are members of the aristocracy? I've never seen him worried about it before."

"Maybe they've complained about something."

"He should be used to it. It's not uncommon." Mrs Swift moved the cutlery further along the table as Mr Price returned for the second chair.

"That's better. Let's hope they're happy with that."

"Have they complained about the seating?" Nell's voice squeaked.

"No, but I don't want them to." He straightened a knife

Mrs Swift had just positioned. "I'll take over serving them as well. Mrs Riley, you focus on the Hampsons."

"Yes, sir." Nell watched him leave. "He'll need to be at the table before me if he wants to serve their drinks. From what I saw yesterday, Lord Askwith doesn't much care who serves him."

Mrs Swift led the way to the galley. "I expect Mr Price will meet them in the foyer and escort them to their seats."

Nell nodded towards the door. "That might have been his plan, but they're here already."

Mrs Askwith waved to her.

"Do I go over?"

"You can't ignore them..."

"I know." Nell's heart pounded. "She's asked me to help her get ready tonight. I'll talk about that until Mr Price arrives." She wandered to the table. "Good afternoon, Your Ladyship. You're early today."

"Being on deck has given us an appetite. What a lovely morning it was."

"I'm glad you enjoyed it." Nell's eyes flicked to the other end of the dining room. *Where's Mr Price?* "Would you still like me to help you dress later?"

"Oh, please. I've been planning my outfit..."

Lord Askwith sat forward. "It would be even better if you served us a drink first, then you can talk about it."

"I'm sorry." Nell stared at the far corner of the room. "Our Mr Price will serve you from now on, and he'll probably want me to wait."

"Well, I don't." There was a twinkle in his eye, but Nell shuddered.

"I'm sure he'll understand. What may I get you?"

Mrs Askwith leaned forward. "We're hoping you can tell us. I saw you taking some marvellous-looking drinks to the Fothergills' table yesterday evening, and I'd like one of those. What was it?"

Nell grinned. "Champagne cobblers."

"Splendid." She smirked at her husband. "Won't you try one?"

He shook his head. "A whisky and water for me, as well you know."

"Yes, sir." Nell hurried to the bar as Mr Price reappeared.

"He won't be happy with me."

Mr Brennan peered around her head. "Why not?"

"He wanted to serve them, but Lord Askwith didn't want to wait."

"That's hardly your fault."

Nell sighed as she glanced towards the table. "I know, but he was already in a bad mood. This will make it worse."

"He seems to be talking to them happily enough. What do they want?"

"The usual whisky and water, but Lady Askwith spotted the champagne cobblers yesterday and wants one of them. She didn't even know what it was until I told her."

"There you are, then. Mr Price would have had to ask one of us what they had, which he wouldn't have liked. You've saved him from himself."

"Well, you can tell him when he comes over. He'll probably want to serve the drinks himself, so I'll see to Mrs Turner."

Mrs Turner smiled up at Nell when she arrived.

"It's quiet today."

"Oh, I don't mind. It's nice to talk occasionally, but I'm perfectly content with my own company."

Nell nodded. "I know what you mean. Not that I get much time to myself."

Mrs Turner studied her. "Do you have a husband, Mrs Riley?"

"I'm a widow."

"Ah. That explains it. I wondered what sort of man would let his wife work at sea."

Nell gave a wry smile. "Had he not died, I'd have travelled as a captain's wife instead."

"What a shame." Mrs Turner folded her hands on the table. "Life can be cruel. I'm sure you'll meet someone else when you're ready."

Nell studied her. "Did you meet anyone else?"

"Oh, I'm far too old, but you. You're an attractive woman..."

Nell's cheeks coloured. "Thank you. Maybe one day..."

"Well, don't leave it too long. I was widowed when I was in my early fifties and kept telling myself it was too soon, then suddenly... Well, here I am with a cane and my memories."

Nell nodded. "I'll remember that. Thank you. May I get you a drink?"

"The champagne I had yesterday was rather nice, so if you have any more."

"We do. Mr and Mrs Fothergill seem to have started something. Lady Askwith wants to try it, too."

Mrs Turner's eyes widened. "So, they *are* members of the aristocracy?"

"They are. They said they didn't want a fuss, which is why they didn't tell anyone."

"Well, you'd never guess." Mrs Turner peered through the flower partition. "They struck me as quite common."

Nell bit back a smile. "Members of the upper classes don't have to try as hard to impress as those who strive to be amongst them."

"Wise words, Mrs Riley. I shall remember that. Now, I'd better let you go. Mr Fothergill is trying to attract your attention."

Nell nodded as she stepped away from the table and waited for Mr Fothergill to take his seat. "Good afternoon. Have you had a pleasant morning?"

"We did until we came in here."

"Oh, I'm sorry. Is it anything I can help with?"

Mr Fothergill nodded to the Askwiths. "That woman. Every time we order a cocktail, she has the same at the next meal. What's she up to?"

"That's Lady Askwith." The frown fell from Nell's brow. "She said she liked the look of your drinks yesterday, and asked for one herself. I don't believe there's any malice to it."

"Lady Askwith?" Mr Fothergill peered at them with renewed interest. "They're described as Mr and Mrs on the guest list."

Nell fixed her smile. "They didn't want a fuss, but accidentally mentioned it in passing, so now the whole ship knows." *Or at least I hope they do. I'm sick of telling everyone.*

"I need a word with *His Lordship*."

Nell flinched. "Would you like to change tables?"

"Not now, later, in the saloon. Preferably when that dreadful woman isn't with him."

"Actually, she's very nice..." Nell's voice trailed off as Mr Fothergill glared at her. "May I get you a drink?"

"You may, but we're at a loss as to what to order now." He turned to his wife. "A gin cocktail?"

Mrs Fothergill's eyes lit up. "Ooh, yes. And a Pimms for Rachel. She's developed quite a taste for it."

Miss Fothergill shifted in her seat. "I'd be happy to try a gin cocktail instead, if the barman needs to make any quantity of it."

Mr Fothergill's face straightened. "That's enough. You'll have a Pimms and be glad."

Nell was pleased to see Mrs Swift by the bar.

"Have you been to the Hampsons yet?"

Mrs Swift shook her head. "No, I've not. Why don't you go now while you're waiting?"

Nell handed her order to Mr Brennan and hurried to the far table, smiling at the Askwiths as she passed. "Good afternoon, Mr Hampson, madam. I'm sorry to keep you waiting."

"Don't worry, we've only been here a minute. Mrs Hampson mislaid her jewellery."

The colour drained from Nell's face. "Did you find it?"

Mrs Hampson put a hand to her chest. "I did, thank you. I'd hidden it in the wardrobe and forgotten where I'd put it."

"Don't tell her that," Mr Hampson hissed through the side of his mouth. "She'll know where you keep it, now."

"Your wife's jewellery will be perfectly safe with me." Nell pulled herself to her full height. "Even if I wanted to take it, which I don't, what would I possibly do with it on a ship? I couldn't disappear with it, and if anyone found it in my room, it would be more than my job's worth."

"I didn't mean you'd take it, but you can't be too careful." Mr Hampson's jowls wobbled as he spoke.

"I have my reputation to think of." Nell's cheeks burned as she imagined Lord and Lady Askwith's eyes on her. "Now, may I get you a drink?"

"A sherry for my wife, and I'll take another of those bottles of ale. Just the one, this time."

Mrs Swift had left the bar when she returned, and Mr Brennan looked up from the gin cocktails he was mixing.

"What's up with you?"

"Mr Hampson. He thinks I'll steal his wife's jewellery, because Mrs Hampson mentioned where she keeps it."

Mr Brennan's eyes twinkled. "Where is it?"

"In the..." Nell stopped with a groan. "I'm not telling you."

"So, you think I'd take it?"

"No, but I'm not repeating a word of it. If she's any sense, she'll move it. In fact, I'll tell her she must. That's the last thing I need, to be accused of stealing."

## CHAPTER TEN

Lord Askwith opened the stateroom door as Nell knocked that evening.

"Mrs Riley, do come in. My wife's waiting for you."

Nell stepped inside as His Lordship spoke to his wife.

"I'll wait for you in the saloon, darling. Don't be too long."

Mrs Askwith waited for her husband to close the door before she reached into the wardrobe. "I was planning to wear this. What do you think? I wasn't expecting to dine with the captain, so I didn't bring my finest gowns."

Nell studied the peacock blue dress. "It makes a change to see understated gowns. They stand out more."

Mrs Askwith's face fell. "Do you think it's too plain?"

"Not at all. It's lovely." Nell took the dress from her. "There's nice detail around the buttons at the back."

"Exactly. That's what I thought."

"A necklace or brooch will set it off, nicely."

"Oh, I don't wear jewellery. I find it so vulgar." Lady Askwith slipped out of her robe and cast it onto the bed.

"Would you tighten this corset for me before we put on the dress? My husband doesn't like me having it too tight, but one has to keep up appearances."

Nell smoothed down her unflattering uniform as her eyes were drawn to Lady Askwith's already slim waist. *If only.* She took hold of the laces at the back of the corset. "Tell me when it's tight enough. I don't want you coming over all faint."

"Oh, don't worry about me. I've had them tighter than you're likely to pull them. Before I met Mr ... Lord Askwith." She tittered. "I'd forgotten we'd given up our pretence."

Nell's hands were red as she pulled on the cords. "It must have been thrilling to marry a lord."

"Oh, it was, but no more than Mama expected of me. We met at a debutante ball. It was very romantic."

"It sounds it." Nell grimaced as she fastened a knot at the bottom of the corset. "There we are. Shall we get your dress on?"

Lady Askwith stood with her hands on her waist. "Is that as tight as you can make it?"

"I'd say so. Can you still breathe?"

Lady Askwith nodded. "It will be fine."

"Good. Now, stand still while I lift this over your head. It will take a while to fasten all these buttons."

Captain and Mrs Robertson were standing in the foyer as Nell escorted Lady Askwith to the saloon.

Mrs Robertson welcomed them. "Good evening, Lady Askwith. How lovely to meet you."

"Likewise." Lady Askwith smiled at the captain. "I presume you've seen my husband."

Captain Robertson accepted Lady Askwith's hand. "I'm afraid not, we've only just arrived." He turned to Mr Price. "Would you ask Lord Askwith if he'd care to join us? We might as well go straight downstairs."

"Yes, sir."

Nell stepped towards the door. "I'll leave you with Mrs Robertson. Have a nice evening." She hurried into the saloon, where Mr and Mrs Hampson looked up.

"Good evening, sir, madam."

"You're late." Mr Hampson's voice growled.

"I'm sorry, I've been helping Lady Askwith, and it took longer than expected."

"They're dining with Captain Robertson, I believe. Not that they've told us."

"They are, sir. Didn't they mention it at luncheon?"

He rolled his shoulders. "It would appear we're not good enough any more. Not that it bothers me. There are other people to meet."

"There are indeed. May I get you a drink before dinner?"

"Two sherries, please. *We've* no need to show off."

Nell pursed her lips as she headed to the bar. "Two sherries."

Mr Brennan tutted. "Can't you get them onto cocktails. Everyone's drinking sherry, tonight."

Nell watched as he emptied another bottle. "The Fothergills haven't arrived yet. They'll keep you busy when they do."

"I hope so. I've even found extra oranges for them."

"Who wants oranges?"

Nell flinched as Mr Ramsbottom bounded up beside her.

"You gave me quite a start."

"Keeping you on your toes." His eyes twinkled.

"You're in a good mood tonight." Mr Brennan polished a glass.

"And why not? We've a generous group on this voyage. I'm already looking forward to getting my tips."

"At least you're happy. It's not exactly a barrel of laughs on our side." Nell's gaze flicked towards the Hampsons.

"Keep the drinks flowing; they'll soon cheer up. Even if they don't, the tips will."

Nell rolled her eyes as she picked up the sherries. "Is that all you think about?"

"It's not all..."

"Mr Ramsbottom...!"

He winked at her as she turned to leave, but Nell gasped as Mr Marsh arrived beside her.

"Is he annoying you again?"

"No, I'm not, I'm only teasing, and she knows it."

Nell stood up tall. "Yes, I do. Will you excuse me?"

Mr Fothergill was in the doorway surveying the tables when she arrived at the Hampsons' table, and he indicated for her to follow them to a table in the far corner.

"Good evening, sir. What may I get you?"

"We'd like two champagne cocktails, please. Not to be confused with the cobblers we had the other day. The cocktails use lemons rather than oranges, although I would hope your barman knows that."

"I'm sure he does. Would Miss Fothergill like her usual Pimms?"

The girl smiled as she nodded. "Please."

"I'll be right back." Nell grinned as she returned to the bar. "I hope you found some lemons with the oranges. They want champagne cocktails, tonight."

Mr Brennan groaned as he shook his head. "I've only got one up here. Let's hope they move downstairs quickly."


As the last of the ladies left the dining room, Nell helped Mrs Swift clear the tables.

"When the Hampsons leave, would you do their table? Mr Marsh has been staring over here all evening, so I'd rather not work in the middle on my own. He's bound to join me."

"I can manage that."

Nell spun around at the sound of voices behind her but relaxed as Captain Robertson led the Askwiths from his private dining room.

"Thank you for a wonderful evening, Captain." Lady Askwith clutched her hands in front of her chest. "I do enjoy lobster."

"We're fortunate to get the best ingredients." The captain's smile looked strained. "Now, forgive me, but I need to be on the bridge." He put an arm around his wife's waist. "Come along, my dear."

Mrs Robertson stopped. "One moment. I've left something in the dining room." She smiled at Lady Askwith. "Please go without me. I may be a few minutes."

"What is it?" Captain Robertson hesitated, but his wife gave a coy smile.

"It's only my handkerchief, I must have dropped it. I'll nip and get it." She wandered back to the captain's dining room but stopped at the door and watched the Askwiths leave the room. As soon as they disappeared, she turned and headed towards Nell.

"Mrs Riley, might I have a word?"

Nell glanced at the captain. "Well, I…"

"It's all right, Mrs Riley. I suspect my wife's up to something. As long as she doesn't take up too much of your time…"

"I won't, I only want a minute." Mrs Robertson pulled Nell to one side. "I'm sorry for all the deception, but I wondered if we could have that talk tomorrow. It would make me feel better."

"I … erm … I'm not sure if I'll have time. We often see a lot of seasickness the day after Queenstown."

Mrs Robertson's face dropped. "I'd quite forgotten … but if you have a minute, I'd appreciate it. I'll probably spend most of my time in the saloon."

Nell nodded. "I can't promise, but I'll come and find you if I get the chance."

"Thank you. You don't know what it means to me."

Nell smiled. "Did you enjoy the evening with Lady Askwith?"

"It was pleasant enough." She looked around. "If you'll excuse me, my husband's waiting."

Nell raised an eyebrow at Mrs Swift as she rejoined her. "That didn't sound very convincing."

"What didn't?"

"She said she'd had a nice evening, but I got the impression she was lying."

"Perhaps she's feeling uncomfortable with her *condition*."

"Maybe. She still wants to speak to me about it."

Mrs Swift grimaced. "You'd better start practising what you're going to say."

"Let's get these tables ready for the morning first. If we're quick, Matron may still be in the sitting room when we get back."

Matron was finishing a jam sponge when they arrived at their quarters, and she looked up as they arrived.

"You're early tonight."

"The passengers were eager to move to the saloon." Mrs Swift took the seat beside Matron while Nell sat opposite her.

"I also wanted a word with you."

"If it's about Mr Marsh, I've told you what I think."

Nell flushed. "N-no, it's not. It's Mrs Robertson."

Matron's head shot up. "What about her?"

"Well ... she's told me about her *condition,* and she wants to know what to expect ... but I don't know what to say."

"You say nothing." Matron's voice was sharp. "I've already told her she shouldn't be here. She should be at home enjoying her confinement and having pleasant thoughts about the child. How's she going to deliver a tranquil baby when she insists on gallivanting around the ship?"

Nell gulped. "I tried to tell her that; I even suggested she use one of the empty staterooms, but she didn't like the idea."

"It's not a matter of liking it. I've told her she may harm the baby if she doesn't rest."

"What about Dr Clarke? Could he speak to her?"

Matron's voice softened. "Dr Clarke's a busy man. He shouldn't have to worry about such matters. Besides, he isn't used to dealing with women's conditions after working on ships for the last twenty years. Captain Robertson should never have let her on board."

"But he won't know what to expect either, and she has no family to stay with."

"She must have friends..."

"I don't think she does with being away at sea for so many months."

"Then she should have thought of that. A ship is no place to have a baby."

Nell bit her lip. "She won't know that, though. Shouldn't I tell her something?"

"No, you shouldn't. Before I started on the ships, I worked with our local midwife, and the less these women know about giving birth, the better. Their minds need to be calm, not frightened."

Nell nodded. "Yes, Matron."

"If she asks again, tell her that everything will be fine, and encourage her to stay in bed."

## CHAPTER ELEVEN

There was no sign of Mrs Swift when Nell finished her staterooms the following morning. *Where is she? I can't go downstairs on my own.* Her stomach churned as she headed to the far side of the ship. She was almost at the end of the corridor when Mrs Swift emerged from a stateroom door.

"There you are. Have you finished?"

Mrs Swift picked up her bucket. "Just. Let me get rid of these and then we can go to the dining room." She grinned at Nell. "Are you hiding from Mrs Robertson?"

"Is it obvious?"

"Not really, but I know you too well."

Nell groaned. "I wish I hadn't said anything to Matron. If I'd spoken to Mrs Robertson beforehand, Matron might have grumbled at me, but now she's told me not to say anything..." She sighed. "I don't know what to do."

"Tell Mrs Robertson that you don't want to confuse her and it's for her own good."

"But she thinks that not knowing is more likely to do the baby harm."

They started down the stairs to the dining room. "Then do what Matron told you. Talk about preparing a room for her confinement so she can make herself comfortable."

"I will."

Mr Price was wrestling with a table as they walked in. "Don't just stand there. I'm going to need this set in a minute."

"What are you doing?" Nell picked up a tablecloth as he pulled a square table away from the longer set-up.

"We've had to rearrange the furniture so the Askwiths can dine on their own. Apparently, they arranged it with Captain Robertson over dinner last night."

Nell raised an eyebrow. "Mr and Mrs Hampson won't be pleased."

"Neither am I, but there's not much we can do about it. That should be the last of the changes, though." Mr Price looked at his pocket watch. "You'd better get those places set. They'll be here shortly."

Nell was positioning the glasses on the Askwiths' table when the Fothergills arrived. Mr Fothergill stared at the new arrangement as he ushered his wife to their seats.

"What's going on here?"

Nell flicked a speck off the starched white tablecloth. "We've rearranged a table for Lord and Lady Askwith. They prefer to sit on their own now everyone knows who they are."

"I can understand why they wouldn't want to stay with the Hampsons. Far too common, I imagine."

"They're actually very nice..." Nell didn't finish her sentence before Mr Fothergill moved on and the Askwiths arrived.

"Ah, Mrs Riley. This looks splendid." Lady Askwith beamed. "I suggested to Captain Robertson that we should have our own table, and here it is." She glanced over to the Hampsons' table and seemed disappointed that they hadn't arrived, but her smile reappeared as Mr Price joined them and held out a chair for her.

"May I get you both a drink?"

"The usual whisky and water for me. What would you like, my dear?" Lord Askwith looked to his wife, who stared up at Nell.

"The drink the Fothergills had the day before last. It looked rather splendid. What was it?"

"Hmm. Now you're asking. I'm not sure I can remember. I'll tell you what, why don't I ask?" Without waiting for a reply, Nell hurried to the next table.

"Ah, Mrs Riley..." Mr Fothergill glanced up, but Nell interrupted.

"Forgive me, sir, but before I take your order, would you remind me which cocktail you ordered the day before last, at luncheon? I remember you had the champagne cocktail last night, but my memory's failing me."

His eyes narrowed. "Why do you want to know?"

"Lady Askwith thought it looked nice and asked what it was."

"Did she now?" Mr Fothergill raised an eyebrow to his wife. "It was a gin cocktail."

"Oh, yes. Will you excuse me for a minute? I'll be right back."

Lady Askwith looked up expectantly as Nell returned. "It was a gin cocktail, Your Ladyship."

"Ah, lovely. I'll try one of those, thank you."

Mr Price had stayed by the table. "I'll take the order, Mrs Riley. If you'd like to see to our other guests."

Nell went straight back to the Fothergills. "I'm sorry about that, sir. What may I get you?"

"Could you tell me what Lady Askwith ordered in the end?"

"She went with the gin cocktail."

"Really? How interesting. Perhaps you could introduce us later." He stared over to the Askwiths. "We'll have the champagne cocktails, again. So much nicer than the cheaper, gin option."

"And a Pimms for Miss Fothergill? Yes, sir." Nell headed to the bar but made a detour as Mrs Turner waved her over.

"Good afternoon, madam. What a marvellous hat you have on."

"Thank you, dear." She held her hands to either side of it. "I must admit, I was ready to put it back in its box earlier. I couldn't get the hatpin in and ended up stabbing myself." She showed Nell a bloodied finger.

"Oh, I'm sorry. It's very fetching, though." Nell admired the navy hat with plumes of peacock feathers. "If you ever need help again, feel free to ask."

"I may do that, although I only have one hat that I haven't worn yet. It's a little less extravagant than this one, but I'll save it until I dine with the captain. One needs to make an effort for him, I always think." She glanced at the Askwiths' table.

"Indeed. Would you like a glass of champagne with your meal?"

"Please. I've developed quite a taste for it."

"And why not? I imagine I would if I was given the chance."

Nell hesitated as she approached the bar. *Stop being silly. He needs to order drinks the same as you.* She took a deep breath and carried on, but her step faltered as Mr Marsh watched her approach.

"You look busy, Mrs Riley."

"I am rather. Do you mind if I give Mr Brennan my order? I still need to see to the Hampsons. They were late."

He stepped to one side. "After you."

With her order delivered, Nell bustled over to the Hampsons.

"Sorry to keep you, sir. May I get you a drink?"

"You can tell me what's going on first." He pointed to the single table.

"Lord and Lady Askwith asked if they might sit on their own."

"So, we're not good enough for them now?"

"I'm sure it's nothing like that, sir."

It was as if Mr Hampson hadn't heard. "She was quite rude yesterday afternoon, too. I thought she'd be interested in how we make our cloth, especially with her being a woman, but she told me to be quiet."

"I'm sorry, sir. Perhaps it's as well they're on a separate table. It will give you a chance to mix with some of the other guests."

"I'm not sure who. Those Fothergills don't look like much company, and there aren't any other couples our age."

Nell pointed to the ladies' section. "The lady in the fancy hat is very nice. Mrs Turner, her name is. She's a widow. She may enjoy the company."

Mr Hampson nodded. "I'll ask her to join us in the saloon. It will give Mrs Hampson someone to talk to. Once she's settled, I'll join the gents. They seem to be enjoying themselves. Would you arrange some introductions?"

"I'll arrange for a steward to bring over your drinks, and you can speak to him. Would you like a bottle of ale?"

"Please, and a lemonade for the wife. If she has a sherry with luncheon, it sends her to sleep."

Mrs Hampson sighed. "I did it once."

"But this is only our third day." He patted her hand. "I'm sorry, my dear, but we'll save the sherry for evenings."

She shook her head but smiled at her husband. "I don't know why you worry about me having a snooze. We've not much else to do."

Mr Marsh was still at the bar when Nell returned, and he gave a broad smile.

"Is that all the pre-luncheon drinks ordered?"

"It is, but may I ask you a favour?" She indicated to the Hampsons' table. "Mr Hampson would like some introductions to the male passengers. Would you take their drinks and talk to him?"

"Certainly. Let me deliver these first." He picked up a tray and marched to the men's section.

Mr Brennan looked up at her. "What do they want? An ale and a sherry?"

"A lemonade instead of a sherry. It seems Mrs Hampson

can't take her drinks in the middle of the day. Are the Fothergills' cocktails ready?"

He flourished a strip of lemon over the top of each one. "Yes. At least they keep me busy."

"You'd better have one of these ready for Lady Askwith this evening. Not that Mr Fothergill likes it when she copies them. He'll want something completely different tonight. Having said that, now he knows they're lord and lady, he wants to talk to them."

"Ah, they're not beneath him any more."

She chuckled. "It appears not. Poor Mr Hampson doesn't stand a chance."

# CHAPTER TWELVE

Nell scraped the last of the custard from her bowl before sitting back in her seat.

"That's better. There's nothing like apple pie to finish a meal."

Mrs Swift followed suit. "You're not wrong. Let's get tidied up here and we can go out on deck for half an hour." She collected up the dishes and carried them to the galley.

"Thank you, Mr Ross, that was lovely."

"Always a pleasure." He looked at Nell. "Mrs Robertson was looking for you earlier. Did she find you?"

"No, she didn't." Nell's stomach flipped as he rested his hands on the counter.

"What's that all about, then? It's not often the captain's wife hobnobs with one of us."

"Ah … it's a private matter. She wants some advice."

"Now I'm intrigued."

Nell tutted. "You'll have to stay that way. I'm saying no more. We'll see you later."

They headed for the door, but as they approached, Mrs Robertson joined them.

"Mrs Riley, I thought I'd find you here. I'm not disturbing anything, am I?"

"Not at all."

Mrs Swift looked between the two of them. "I'll leave you to it, then."

Mrs Robertson accepted the seat Nell held out for her, but as she took her own seat, Mrs Robertson waved to Mr Cooper.

"Might we have a pot of tea? We may be here for some time."

"Certainly, madam."

The blood drained from Nell's face, but Mrs Robertson appeared not to notice.

"That was a stroke of good fortune. Now, Mrs Riley, will you tell me what to expect with this baby?"

Nell fidgeted with her fingers. "Your situation's quite different to mine, so I can't say for sure."

"But you must have an idea."

"All right, probably the main thing is you're going to struggle sleeping for the next few months. That's why you should consider your confinement. You should be relaxing and taking naps, or perhaps reading poetry. You shouldn't be worrying about anything."

"But the baby's not due yet. I spoke to Dr Clarke last night, and he assures me it won't be born on this voyage. It seems pointless disturbing a stateroom."

"But the baby will get distressed if you keep walking around and entertaining. You'll regret it once he's born and won't settle."

"Is that what you did?"

"I-I'd have loved to, but our house is too small. My sister took over most of the chores though…"

"And was your child restless?"

Nell opened and closed her mouth several times before she spoke. "I struggled to get her to sleep. Especially at night. It would have been nice to avoid that."

Mrs Robertson paused. "I heard brandy's good for soothing them."

"It is, but it gets expensive." Nell bit on her lip. "Where will you have the baby?"

"That's part of the problem. I don't know. I told you we let our house go several years ago, and we've not made any new arrangements. It didn't seem real to start with…"

"So that's why you're still on the ship?"

Mrs Robertson nodded, but paused as Mr Cooper delivered their tea. "Here you are, ladies. Let me know if you'd like anything else."

"Thank you, Mr Cooper." She returned her attention to Nell. "We've not looked for a house yet, because I'd like to stay with my husband until the baby arrives. I'd also like you and Matron to be on hand."

Nell squirmed in her seat. "The problem is, you won't know exactly when the baby will be born. I may not be here."

"I'll wait until you're back."

"If I'm at home, you won't be able to."

"Oh." Mrs Robertson rubbed her bump.

"Don't forget, you'll need to stay in bed for about four to six weeks after the baby's born. That may be over Christmas when even Matron isn't here."

Mrs Robertson gasped. "I hadn't thought of that."

"That's why I suggest you start your confinement now. It will keep you calm and stop the baby being born before we get back to Liverpool."

"I spend most of my mornings in bed, as it is. Won't that be enough?"

Nell bit her lip. "You'll need to spend a lot more time in bed over the next few weeks, and ... well..." Nell lowered her voice so much she could barely hear herself speak. "You won't want to have the baby in your marital bed."

"Why not?"

"Because ... because you won't. You'll want your own space."

"Couldn't I move when the baby's due?"

"You need to be comfortable before then."

Mrs Robertson's forehead creased. "How will I know when it's coming?"

"You'll ... erm ... you'll feel it moving."

"It's moving already!" Mrs Robertson's eyes bulged. "Might it come now?"

"Not yet, calm down." Nell poured the tea and put an extra spoonful of sugar into Mrs Robertson's. "Here, take some deep breaths and drink this."

"But it might be coming... I can't relax..."

"Please, Mrs Robertson, you must stay calm. Think of the baby."

"Yes, think of the baby." She took a deep breath and closed her eyes. "Deep breaths."

"Why don't we think about your confinement room? Stateroom nineteen, at the far end of the corridor, is empty. You could use that."

"Yes." Her eyes remained closed. "I need to make a room for the confinement. And stay calm."

"That's it. We don't want Matron seeing you like this."

Mrs Robertson opened her eyes. "Is this why she wouldn't tell me anything?"

"Perhaps..." Nell squeezed Mrs Robertson's hands but let go when she spotted Mr Brennan. "I won't be a minute." She raced to the bar. "May I have a glass of brandy for Mrs Robertson?"

"At three o'clock in the afternoon?"

"S-she has a bit of indigestion."

"Nothing to do with Mr Ross's cooking, I hope." He poured a generous measure into a rounded glass on a short stem. "Here."

"Thank you."

Mrs Robertson's breathing was rapid when Nell returned. "Here we are. Take a sip of this."

"What is it?"

"Brandy. It will calm your nerves."

She took a gulp of the amber liquid but coughed as it hit the back of her throat. "Urgh!"

Nell stroked her hand. "It will do you good, but sip it next time. And carry on those deep breaths. We want to keep that baby healthy."

"We do." Mrs Robertson took another mouthful, but Nell jumped as Mrs Swift joined them.

"Oh, it's you."

"That's a nice welcome. I was beginning to wonder where you were."

"We were talking."

Nell didn't miss Mrs Swift eyeing the empty brandy

glass. "She had indigestion. I was about to escort her to her quarters, then I'll come and join you."

"We need to set up for afternoon tea now."

Mrs Robertson stood up. "I'm sorry. I didn't mean to keep Mrs Riley for so long, but, well..."

Nell offered her an arm. "It's all going to be fine. In a few weeks' time, you'll wonder what all the fuss was about."

Mrs Swift raised an eyebrow as Nell grimaced.

"You start upstairs; I'll be right back."


The night was dark with clouds covering the moon as Nell and Mrs Swift walked to their quarters. Nell's heart pounded as they went.

"I don't know what to do. I'm frightened I've upset Mrs Robertson. I should never have spoken to her."

"You had no choice. She found you."

"But I should have been vaguer. Or told her to speak to Matron." Nell shook her head. "Matron will be so angry with me."

"Only if she finds out, and I doubt Mrs Robertson will tell her."

"I hope you're right. I wouldn't forgive myself if anything happened to the baby after all this."

Mrs Swift held the outer door open. "It will help if you can prepare a room for her confinement."

"I know, but I can't just take over a stateroom. Someone needs to talk to Mr Price about it ... and it can't be me."

"No." Mrs Swift stopped as they arrived at the galley. "Good evening, Mr Potter. Do you have anything for us?"

"I do, indeed. Shepherd's pie tonight."

"Ooh, lovely."

"It is, even if I say so myself." He ran a hand over his jet-black hair. "You get yourselves downstairs and I'll follow you."

Matron was nowhere to be seen when they reached their sitting room, and Nell plonked herself onto the settee.

"That's a relief. I couldn't face her tonight."

"You'll have to speak to her soon. She's the only one who can speak to Mr Price or the captain about preparing a confinement room."

Nell nodded. "I know."

"I wouldn't worry about it, though. Yesterday, when you asked her what to say, she was angry that Mrs Robertson wasn't already in confinement. If you tell her you encouraged her to do it, she should be pleased with you."

Nell bounced in her chair as she turned around. "Do you think so? Oh, that would be such a relief. I'll plan what to say and hope she's in a good mood in the morning."

## CHAPTER THIRTEEN

There was no sign of Matron when Nell and Mrs Swift arrived for breakfast the following morning. Mrs Swift tipped a cup to one side.

"It looks as if she's been and gone."

"Why would she leave so early? Oh my goodness..." Nell put a hand over her mouth. "Mrs Robertson! You don't think something's happened?"

"So quickly?"

"It may have done." Nell's heart pounded as she flopped onto the settee. "What if she's having problems because I upset her? I'll never forgive myself."

Mrs Swift sat down beside her. "Let's not jump to conclusions. It might be nothing more than someone with seasickness."

"But what if it's not?" Nell's eyes widened. "What if I've caused the baby to be born early?"

"Then she'll have a baby by this evening. Now stop worrying and eat your breakfast." Mrs Swift served out two bowls of porridge.

"How can I eat at a time like this?"

"Force it down. We're not walking to the dining room until that bowl's empty."

The porridge had settled like lead in Nell's stomach as they walked across the deck to the first-class rooms.

"I can't believe even Mr Potter missed her. What's she up to?"

"We'll find out soon enough."

Nell peered through the billowing sails to the grey clouds scurrying across the sky. "I hope it's nothing bad."

"Why are you so worried? It's not as if women haven't had babies before."

"But I'd unsettled her. What if it disturbed the baby? It could cause any number of problems." Nell took a deep breath as Mrs Swift held open the door.

"She'll be fine. Matron knows what she's doing." Mrs Swift took Nell's cloak and hung it up. "Hopefully, doing a bit of work will occupy your mind."

Mr Ramsbottom's hazel eyes twinkled as they arrived outside the dining room.

"Good morning, ladies." He pushed a loose piece of hair from his face as Nell stopped.

"Where's Mr Price?"

"That's not much of a welcome. I thought you'd be pleased to see me."

"Please, Mr Ramsbottom. Where is he?"

"He's with the captain; he didn't say why."

"Have you seen Matron this morning?"

Mr Ramsbottom shrugged. "I don't usually."

"Well, if you do, would you tell her I'd like a word with her?"

"Only if you give me a smile." He winked at her, but Nell stamped her foot.

"Will you be serious, for once? I need to speak to Matron, and it's urgent. Will you pass the message on or not?"

"All right, calm down. Of course I will."

"Is there a problem here?" Mr Marsh appeared at the door, his eyes cold as they bored into Mr Ramsbottom.

"Nothing that needs your attention."

"Mrs Riley?" Mr Marsh searched her face, but Nell turned away.

"Everything's fine. I'm looking for Matron. Have you seen her this morning?"

"I can't say I have. Would you like me to go onto the bridge and see if she's there?"

"Please don't trouble her. She may be with a patient... Oh, actually, if you'll excuse us." Nell grabbed Mrs Swift's arm and dashed to the galley. "Why is it always those two?"

"Is that why you rushed off?"

"No, I had a thought." She pushed through the door, startling Mr Ross, who nearly dropped the pan he was carrying.

"Steady on. What's the rush?"

"Has anyone taken Mrs Robertson's tray this morning?"

Mr Ross's brow furrowed. "Mr Price did. Why?"

"So, the captain didn't cancel it?"

"Why would he?"

"Oh, no reason." Nell allowed herself to breathe. "Have you seen Matron?"

"Not this morning. She was in here late last night with Dr Clarke, though."

"Matron was?" Nell gaped at Mrs Swift. "What time?"

"Ooh, it was late. Even the stewards had left. I came in to turn off the lights and disturbed them."

"How unusual." Mrs Swift's forehead creased. "She's usually in bed early because of the time she gets up."

"Well, not last night. Have you checked her cabin?"

The two women glanced at each other before Mrs Swift spoke. "We didn't, but it looked as if she'd had breakfast and left. We assumed someone must be ill."

"They may be, then. That might have been what she was talking to Dr Clarke about, although why they needed to sit so close together..." He grinned at them. "You could check the hospital room."

"Mr Ross, I hope you're not suggesting..." Nell's eyes were wide as she and Mrs Swift stared at each other.

"Not Matron. She'd had a cup of tea. I saw the tea leaves."

"Maybe she's not, then. I'm just saying she could be."

Nell's mouth fell open. "There must be a perfectly innocent explanation." She jumped as the door opened and Mr Marsh joined them. "Have you found Matron?"

"Unfortunately not, but several of your guests are in their seats and I thought you should know."

Nell let out a deep sigh. "We'd better go." She stepped into the dining room but stopped when she saw the Askwiths. Mrs Swift bumped into her.

"What's up now?"

She nodded across the room. "What do I do with them?"

"You serve them. You can't leave them waiting for Mr Price. We don't know when he'll be back."

"I wish he'd hurry up. If he's with Captain Robertson, he'll have heard if there's a problem with Mrs Robertson."

Mrs Swift tutted. "Stop worrying about her and put a smile on your face. They're looking at you."

Nell did as she was told and strode to the Askwiths' table. "Good morning. I'm afraid Mr Price has been called away. May I take your order?"

"You may indeed." Lord Askwith smiled up at her. "We'll take the eggs this morning. Two softly boiled ones each, with bread and butter."

"Certainly, sir. And a pot of tea?"

"Naturally." He leaned towards her. "What do you know about this chap Fothergill? Have you any idea what he does for a living?"

Nell scrunched her forehead. "I'm afraid not. He likes to keep to himself, so I've not asked. He was asking after you yesterday evening."

"Not him too." Lord Askwith tutted. "It's one reason we wanted to travel *incognito*. You get so many people wanting to talk to you because of the title."

"I can see that, sir. If I find out what he does, I'll let you know."

Nell moved to the Hampsons' table. "Good morning, sir. Would you like your usual eggs on fried bread?"

Mrs Hampson leaned forward. "He could do with a glass of milk with a spoonful of soot in it."

"Oh dear."

"Quite. He had a rather boisterous evening in the saloon

last night." Mrs Hampson smirked at her unusually quiet husband. "The soot often helps."

"I can ask Chef, but I doubt he'll have any up here. We could get some from the boiler rooms..."

"I'll be fine." Mr Hampson's voice was gravelly. "I only had a few brandies. A glass of milk, without the soot, will be perfectly fine. And porridge."

"And I'll stick with my usual, please."

Nell was about to leave when Mrs Hampson called her back.

"I wanted to thank you for suggesting we make acquaintance with Mrs Turner. She and I had a lovely evening, although that's why Mr Hampson isn't so well."

"I'm glad you enjoyed it. Now, if you'll excuse me."

Nell took her orders to the galley before returning to the Fothergills' table.

"Good morning, sir. I hope you slept well."

"Very well, thank you."

"What would you like for breakfast?"

"Poached eggs on toast for us all, with a pot of tea and extra toast and jam."

"Yes, sir." Nell hesitated, waiting for further comment, but when it didn't come, she walked to Mrs Turner's table.

"Good morning, Mrs Riley."

Nell smiled at her. "Good morning. I've been hearing about your evening with Mrs Hampson. She seemed to enjoy herself."

"It was pleasant enough. I've a book I'm trying to read, but it won't do me any harm to be sociable ... as long as she doesn't follow me around all day, every day."

"I'll make a note not to encourage her…" She paused as Matron stormed from the galley and headed for the foyer.

*What's up with her?* A shiver ran down Nell's spine.

"Excuse me, Mrs Turner, something's cropped up. I won't be a moment." She hurried to the galley, where her friend was reorganising a tray.

"Did you see Matron?"

"I did."

"What's the matter?"

Mrs Swift put a finger to her lips. "Not here, I'll tell you later."

# CHAPTER FOURTEEN

B reakfast was over when Nell ushered Mrs Swift to the tables on the far side of the room.

"Did you speak to Matron?"

"I didn't." Mrs Swift shuddered. "She was gunning for Mr Ross because she said he was spreading rumours about her and Dr Clarke."

Nell grimaced. "I presume they're not true then."

"That's the thing. She didn't deny it. She was just furious that her name was being sullied."

"So, it might be true?" Nell's eyes widened.

"Who knows? All I'll say is, we're as well keeping out of her way."

"But what about Mrs Robertson? Did she mention her?"

"No."

Nell sighed. "I hope the fact she came storming in here means Mrs Robertson is all right. She wouldn't come down here if she was in the middle of delivering a baby..."

"And she'd have wanted to speak to you if there'd been any problems."

Nell puffed out her cheeks. "That's a relief. At least I can stop worrying for now, although I still need to arrange a stateroom for Mrs Robertson."

"Oh, oh." Mrs Swift stared over Nell's shoulders. "You can ask her now. She's heading this way."

Matron's face resembled thunder as she stormed towards them, but Nell put on her best smile.

"Good morning, Matron. You were up bright and early."

"No thanks to you."

"Me?" Nell's voice squeaked.

"You spoke to Mrs Robertson yesterday, and Captain Robertson sent for me at six o'clock this morning to calm her nerves."

"I-I'm sorry. I didn't mean to upset her. All I said was that she should start her confinement, and we'd find a room for her. I-I was going to talk to you about it this morning."

"She doesn't want to go into confinement and she's upset at the thought of it."

"But she must…"

"That's as maybe, but there are ways of saying these things. I've had to speak to Dr Clarke and Captain Robertson about what to do with her, and all Dr Clarke can suggest is to give her a sedative."

"I'm sorry." Nell studied the floor. "I thought you'd be pleased that she realised it was for her own good, and the benefit of the baby. I told her to stay calm."

"But that's what did it! She's now panicking so much she's hysterical. I told you not to say anything. I was only talking to Dr Clarke about the whole situation last night and we'd come up with a plan. Now she'll need to stay isolated for longer, to make sure there's no damage done."

"I'm sorry. I'd no idea."

"Well, think on in future."

"Yes, Matron."

"Thankfully, I've spoken to Captain Robertson and Mr Price about the confinement and he's decided that she'll use one of the staterooms."

Nell nodded. "I suggested that to her. Number nineteen is free."

"I'm well aware of that, and so if you give it a thorough clean this morning, you can start moving some of her personal effects this afternoon."

"Yes, Matron."

"And keep it to yourself. We don't want the details all round the ship. The only people who know, besides the captain, are the three of us, Mr Price and Dr Clarke. And it needs to stay that way." She glared at them both as she emphasised the last few words.

"Yes, Matron. I'll start on it as soon as we're finished here."

The stateroom was spotless and filled with all Mrs Robertson's personal effects by the time Nell went back to the saloon.

Mrs Swift smiled as she went in. "Are you all done?"

"I am for now, but Mrs Robertson wants me to help her move in."

"When?"

"Shortly. I'll serve afternoon tea and then leave you to tidy up. You don't mind, do you?"

"I can manage. Did you see Captain Robertson while you were moving her things?"

"No, he was on the bridge."

Mrs Swift's face brightened. "Hopefully, that means he's not angry with you. He'd have wanted a word if he was."

"I hope you're right." Nell stood up straight as Lady Askwith breezed into the saloon, with her husband close behind, and took the table nearest to her.

"Mrs Riley, how convenient. I've had my eye on this table since we boarded. We should obviously get here promptly."

"Not at all, Your Ladyship. I can reserve it for you if you'd like."

"Really? How marvellous." She grinned as her husband took the seat opposite. "We'd like it for morning coffee and afternoon tea."

"And if we could have our own platter of sandwiches on the table..." Lord Askwith winked at his wife.

"And cakes? Perhaps we could have one of each."

Nell glanced at Mrs Swift. "I-I'll need to check with Mr Price, but I'm sure that will be fine."

"Don't look so worried. I'll make it worth your while, come the end of the trip." Lord Askwith rubbed his thumb and forefinger together.

"Yes, sir. I'll see what I can do. In the meantime..." Nell collected three plates from the table and a platter of sandwiches "...if you'd like to take a selection before everyone else arrives."

Mr Fothergill walked past as they filled their plates. "What a marvellous idea."

Lord Askwith grunted. "Special service. They won't let everyone do it."

"I don't see why not."

Lord Askwith smirked at him. "Titles, my dear fellow. They mark one out for special attention."

"So it seems." Mr Fothergill lifted his nose in the air. "Make sure you enjoy them."

As soon as she'd offered the cakes around, Nell hurried from the saloon towards the bridge but slowed as First Mate Jones watched her approach.

"Good afternoon, Mrs Riley. Captain Robertson told me you'd be calling. Mrs Robertson is waiting for you."

"Thank you, sir." She headed towards a solid door set between the oak panels of the sleeping quarters and knocked.

"Come in." Mrs Robertson's voice was weak. "Ah, Mrs Riley. Thank you for coming."

"It's my pleasure. Are you all ready?"

"I think so." She remained in a chair as she surveyed the room. "It won't be the same, though, will it? I mean, this is my home."

"Your new stateroom looks very nice, and it's not far away for Captain Robertson to visit. Let me show you."

Nell led the way down the corridor and opened the stateroom door. "There we are. I hope you like it."

Mrs Robertson smiled at the shawls and cushions scattered about the room. "I'd say it's wonderful." She picked up one of the brass ornaments that had come from her own room. "It's actually nicer than the captain's quarters. Bigger certainly. I'll be having a word about why we aren't in here all the time."

Nell chuckled. "That did cross my mind, but I didn't like to ask. At least you should be comfortable." She opened a chest of drawers and pulled out a nightdress. "Slip this on, and you can get into bed."

Mrs Robertson stared at the nightgown. "But it's only five o'clock."

"Well, you can't go to bed in your clothes, and that's where Matron will expect you to be. She may let you use the settee if you do as you're told."

"To think I used to make these decisions for myself..." She sighed and took the nightdress from Nell.

"Would you like any help?"

"Oh ... no. I'll ... erm, I'll wait and do it myself."

"As you wish. Now, I should help set the dining room for dinner. I'll call back at seven o'clock with your tray. You will be in bed by then, won't you?" Nell raised an eyebrow.

"I will, I promise."

Nell walked to the door. "Good. You don't want Matron calling and finding you still dressed. Not after the mood she's been in today."

"No, I don't." Mrs Robertson shuddered. "She was cross with me this morning when I mentioned she'd been seen with Dr Clarke."

"It was you!" Nell strolled back into the room. "Who told you?"

"My husband, obviously. He said it was nice to see her and Dr Clarke getting along so well, but they really shouldn't be alone together. After all, Matron's supposed to be the one keeping men away from the ladies, not encouraging it."

"Then why didn't the captain say anything to her?"

"To be honest, he didn't want to. He'd rather not get involved with women's things and so I said I'd have a quiet word, which I did. There was no need for her to get so cross, though. She said she needed to ask Dr Clarke's advice on my confinement."

"Did you tell Captain Robertson that she'd shouted at you?"

"It really wasn't that bad."

"But she knows you need to keep calm. She shouldn't have raised her voice."

"I don't think she meant it. You won't say anything about it, will you?"

Nell bit her lip. "Not if you don't want me to."

## CHAPTER FIFTEEN

Nell steadied herself against the wall of the corridor as a wave rocked the ship. *Why did I suggest Mrs Robertson move into the room furthest away?* She balanced the tray on her arm and was about to knock when Captain Robertson opened the door.

"Oh, excuse me, sir. I didn't mean to interrupt."

"No need to apologise. I was about to leave. I only looked in to see how my wife was feeling. This storm's likely to last the day, I'm afraid."

"That's unfortunate. Is Mrs Robertson all right?" Nell swayed as another wave struck, and Captain Robertson took the tray from her.

"She's as well as can be expected. Do come in, though. She'd like a word before you go."

He put the tray on his wife's knee and left with a wave.

Nell smiled as she approached the bed. "How are you this morning?"

"I'm fine. Or at least I would be if I could get out of bed. This will be the third day I've been stuck here."

"Is Matron still insisting?"

"She is, and the trouble is, she comes to check on me at any time of the day or evening. I daren't even sneak onto the settee because I don't know when she'll call."

"The storm may have done you a favour, then. I expect she'll be busy with passengers who are not as used to it as you."

Mrs Robertson's eyes gleamed. "I hadn't thought of that. I could read the book you borrowed for me from Mrs Turner."

Nell's forehead creased. "You mean you haven't already? I thought you'd be finished it by now."

Mrs Robertson rolled her eyes. "I've had to hide it. Matron said it would excite me too much."

Nell sighed. "That hadn't crossed my mind. Shall I return it to Mrs Turner?"

"Oh, no, please don't. I promise I'll stop reading if my pulse starts racing."

"Very well, but don't tell her I know about it, or I'll be in even more trouble."

Mrs Robertson grinned. "You have my word."

The dining room was only half full when Nell arrived back, but with stewards still taking trays, she waited for Mrs Swift to return from a group of ladies at the far side of the room.

"Have you served the Hampsons yet?"

Mrs Swift glanced over at them. "I've not, but I will. Lady Askwith wants a tray in her room and asked for you."

Nell tutted. "What about the Fothergills?"

"Their maid was down earlier so they're taken care of."

"Good." Nell glanced around the room. "I might as well take the tray now."

The waves were still fierce when she reached the Askwiths' room, but with the door locked, she had to knock three times before Lady Askwith answered.

"A tray for you, madam."

Leaving the door open, Lady Askwith stumbled to the bed. "I don't know why my husband ordered it. He knew I wouldn't be able to eat a thing with the ship rolling like this." A fresh wave hit, throwing her onto the bed. "Damn weather."

Nell put down the tray and rushed forward. "Are you all right?"

"No, I'm not. Not only do I feel dreadful, I've now banged my leg." A trickle of blood ran down her shin.

"Let me get a cloth."

Lady Askwith lay on the bed as Nell dipped a facecloth into the basin on the washstand.

"There we are. It's only a nick. It should stop bleeding in a minute."

"It had better. I wouldn't have been out of bed if you hadn't come to the door."

"I-I'm sorry. I was only following orders. Shall I fetch His Lordship?"

"And let him see me like this? No, thank you."

Nell gulped, as Lady Askwith put a hand over her mouth. "A tot of brandy may help ... and a ginger biscuit. Both are good at settling the stomach."

"What are you waiting for, then? And make it a large brandy."

Nell kept a hand on the wall as she made her way to the

dining room and was too preoccupied to worry about Mr Marsh as he held open the galley door.

"Are you all right, Mrs Riley?"

"I am, but Lady Askwith isn't."

He reached up to one of the higher shelves. "I presume you need these." He handed her the tin of ginger biscuits.

"I need a large brandy, too. Where's Mr Ross?"

"I'll get it. He's gone down to the storeroom." Mr Marsh disappeared as Nell put some biscuits on a plate.

*Where's Mrs Swift?* She peered through the galley door. *Busy.*

"Have you found the brandy, Mr Marsh?"

"I'm coming." He gave her a glass with a covering of brandy across the bottom.

"She wants more than that. Would you bring me the bottle?"

"It's most irregular..."

Nell glared at him. "*Her Ladyship* asked for a large measure."

"I really don't think ladies should drink..."

"Mr Marsh, please. Now isn't the time for your thoughts." Nell's tone left no room for compromise.

"Very well." He wandered back for the bottle. "Here you are. Don't let anyone see it."

Nell grabbed the bottle and half-filled the glass before putting it on the plate of biscuits and covering it with a silver cloche. "Will that do?"

She didn't wait for a reply before she stormed from the galley, stopping only to steady herself as another wave hit the ship.

The door to the stateroom was still open when she returned.

"Here we are."

Lady Askwith hadn't moved since she'd left.

"Let's sit you up and you can take a sip of brandy."

There was a groan as Nell pulled on the pillows. "A little higher. Here you are. Take it slowly."

Brandy ran down Lady Askwith's chin, and onto her nightgown, as the waves crashed into the ship.

"Now look at me." She wiped her face with the back of her hand. "Did you have to fill it so full?"

"You asked for a large one." Nell took the glass from her. "Try a biscuit instead."

Lady Askwith struggled to swallow, and Nell offered her more brandy. "Don't take such a big mouthful this time."

"It's not easy when the ship's moving like this. Why don't you leave me to lie down?"

Nell stood up straight. "Very well. I'll speak to His Lordship and ask him to look in on you."

"Don't you dare."

Nell took a step back at the severity of her tone.

"I don't want him seeing me looking such a mess. You can lock the door on your way out and tell him not to come in until it's time for luncheon."

"Yes, madam." Without a backwards glance, Nell slammed the door and turned the key in the lock. *Stay in there and sort yourself out, then. See if I care. Lady Annabel wouldn't have been so vulgar.*

The roll of the ship threw Nell from one side of the

corridor to the other, and as she approached the dining room, she paused to catch her breath.

"Is everything all right, Mrs Riley?" Mr Ramsbottom caught hold of her arm, but she pulled it away and stood up straight.

"I'm fine, thank you. If you'll excuse me, I need to carry on."

Mrs Swift was in the galley when she got back. "Is she any better?"

"No."

"Is that it?" Mrs Swift put her hands on her hips.

"I don't know what's come over her. She's more like a common washerwoman than a lady. Don't tell me she hasn't married above herself."

Mrs Swift put down the teapot she'd just picked up. "What's she done?"

"I don't know. It's the way she was acting ... and talking. She was so rude. Well, she can take care of herself as far as I'm concerned." Nell peered out into the dining room. "I need a steward."

Mrs Swift chuckled. "That's not like you."

Nell scowled at her. "I need one of them to speak to Lord Askwith. Ah, here's Mr Price."

"Ladies." He turned to Nell. "Is everything all right?"

"Lady Askwith's not very well. I've taken her some brandy and ginger biscuits, but she asked me to pass a message to her husband. Would you speak to him for me?"

"Certainly."

"She said she doesn't want to see him again until luncheon, so can he stay away."

"She said that?" Mr Price raised an eyebrow.

"Apparently she's not up to visitors at the moment."

"But he's her husband…"

Nell shrugged. "I'm only delivering a message."

"Very well, I'll tell him now. I suspect we'll be quiet this morning."

"Actually, if we're quiet, might I have a word with you once you've spoken to Lord Askwith?"

He gave her a smile. "Give me a minute and I'll be right back."

By the time Mr Price returned, Nell had wandered to a quieter part of the dining room, and he held a chair out for her at one of the tables.

"How may I help?"

Her cheeks coloured. "I wondered if you'd tell me why Mr Marsh was brought back to first class when I thought we'd agreed he'd stay in steerage."

"Mrs Riley. Mr Marsh is a very able steward who's wasted downstairs. We couldn't leave him down there indefinitely because of an incident that happened at the start of the year."

"But I heard he left the ship in August, under quite a cloud."

Mr Price sighed. "I'm afraid you've no one but yourself to blame for that."

"Me? How was it my fault? I wasn't even on here at the time."

"Because you upset him by leaving with Mr Hancock."

Nell's mouth fell open. "How did he know?"

"He saw you. You know he cares for you, but ever since

you joined the ship, you've flirted with countless gentlemen while Mr Marsh can only look on. Mr Hancock was the final straw."

"I wasn't flirting... I've never flirted..." Nell gasped. "Mr Hancock offered me a ride home because he was going my way."

"Well, whatever your reasons, Mr Marsh was rather upset."

"Then why did he come back?"

"You'll have to ask him that..."

Nell blinked away her tears. "He said he always planned to, but from what I understand, you weren't expecting him."

"There was a misunderstanding. Nothing more. Now, if you'll excuse me..." He stood up and tucked in his chair.

"I'm sorry, but that doesn't answer the question." Nell's voice squeaked. "Why did you put him in first class?"

Mr Price shook his head. "I can't have him and Mr Hancock working together. Haven't you wondered why Mr Hancock's in steerage?"

"But ... but you could have left him upstairs and given Mr Marsh his old job."

"And favour the man who caused the trouble?"

Nell gasped. "All he did was offer to take me home. It was Mr Marsh who caused the problem. He should be the one being punished."

"I'm sorry, but I can't send Mr Marsh to steerage while Mr Hancock is there."

"Then bring Mr Hancock up here." Nell's voice croaked as she spoke. "It's most unfair when he was only doing me a favour. Mr Marsh should learn to keep his temper to himself. He has no right to dictate who I accept lifts from."

"I can't leave Mr Cunningham on his own downstairs."

"There are other stewards down there."

"Mr Cunningham is new to the role and Mr Hancock's supervising him. I can't move him mid-voyage."

Nell puffed out her cheeks. "So I have to put up with Mr Marsh creeping around, watching everything I do?"

"Now you're exaggerating."

Nell nodded towards the room divide. "Look over there."

Mr Price had no sooner followed her gaze than Mr Marsh turned on his heel and disappeared into the galley.

"Did you see him? It's the same thing, day in, day out. Maybe if he hadn't been so fixated, he wouldn't have seen me with Mr Hancock."

Mr Price sighed. "I really don't know what the problem is. Men look at women all the time. It's hardly something to be disciplined for."

"No." Nell's voice fell to a whisper, and she wiped her eyes with the back of a hand as Mr Price strode to the galley. *Why did I think it was?*

Nell hadn't moved when Mrs Swift joined her. "What was that about?"

"I asked why Mr Marsh was now in first class."

"And?"

"It was all my fault."

Mrs Swift's eyes narrowed. "How?"

"Mr Marsh got upset because I accepted a lift home with Mr Hancock. That's why Mr Hancock's now downstairs and Mr Marsh is up here."

"But why did he let him back at all?"

Nell paused. "He wouldn't say. He said I'd have to ask Mr Marsh."

"But he said it was always planned."

"He did." Nell studied her friend. "Something's not right here, and I'm going to find out what it is."

## CHAPTER SIXTEEN

Nell held onto the rail behind her as she and Mrs Swift stood outside the galley waiting for the guests to arrive for luncheon. *Five past one.*

"There should be more here by now, given we haven't taken many trays. I've only delivered Mrs Robertson's."

Mrs Swift shifted her feet as another wave hit. "If the ladies are ill, they won't want to eat."

"That's true. It's unusual for it to be all of them, though."

"Don't complain. We'll be finished early if they're not here soon."

Nell's hands tightened on the rail. "That would be nice. Ooh, look. Mr Fothergill's here on his own. Should I suggest he sits with the men?"

"I thought he didn't want to socialise."

"He doesn't usually, but he's looking over. Let me find out what he wants." Nell grabbed the backs of the chairs as she made her way towards him. "Good afternoon, Mr Fothergill. Will you be dining alone?"

"Indeed. My wife and daughter are both suffering with seasickness."

"Have they had any ginger biscuits or brandy?"

"We had both delivered to our room earlier, but unfortunately neither have had the desired effect."

"It may take time." Nell stumbled into the chair behind her. "It looks as if we'll be empty in this section. Would you care to sit with the rest of the gentlemen instead?"

Mr Fothergill studied the opposite side of the room. "Is Lord Askwith dining alone?"

"Yes, sir. Lady Askwith was rather ill when I took breakfast this morning."

"Might I possibly join him?"

Nell scoured the room for Mr Price, but when she couldn't find him, she beckoned over Mr Ramsbottom. His eyes glinted as he strode towards them.

"Mrs Riley. How may I help?"

"Mr Fothergill wondered if he might join Lord Askwith for luncheon."

"Well–" Mr Ramsbottom studied the men's tables "–I know His Lordship wanted to sit alone, but there's a spare seat on Mr Hampson's table."

Mr Fothergill's face twisted. "Perhaps I'll stay here."

"Ah." Mr Ramsbottom stared at Lord Askwith. "There can't be any harm in asking. Give me a minute."

Nell waited for him to leave. "Might I offer you a drink while you're waiting, sir?"

"A brandy cocktail. To be on the safe side, you understand."

"Certainly. If you're able to move tables, I'll ask Mr

Ramsbottom to bring it over." Nell headed to the bar. "A brandy cocktail, please."

Mr Brennan groaned. "It's going to be a quiet couple of hours if this weather doesn't let up."

Nell grimaced. "Even if it does, people won't be hurrying back. Food will be the last thing they want."

"I don't care about the food. I've enough brandy for all of them. It would be nice to serve it."

"Maybe this evening..." Nell clung onto the bar, but Mr Brennan interrupted.

"Where's he going?" He pointed to Mr Fothergill.

"He asked if he could sit will Lord Askwith and it looks like the answer was yes. If you're fortunate, they may encourage each other to order a few more drinks."

The smile returned to Mr Brennan's face. "Splendid. I'll pour another whisky for His Lordship. I've not known him turn one down."

By the time luncheon was over, and Nell and Mrs Swift had eaten, the ship was still being pounded by the wind and waves. Nell finished her cup of tea.

"I'm not going back to our quarters across the deck. Should we go through the boiler room?"

Mrs Swift grinned. "I've a better idea. Half the staterooms are empty. Why don't we make use of one? We can tidy up after ourselves once the storm dies down."

"I like that idea. Do you have one in mind?"

"Number two, on my side. It's the nearest to the saloon. Nobody should find us."

"Excellent. The less we have to walk, the better."

. . .

They spent the afternoon dozing and by the time afternoon tea was over, the waves were beginning to subside.

Nell straightened the chairs in her section of the saloon. "I expect we'll be back to normal this evening. Nobody's eaten today so now the ship's steadier, hopefully they'll be feeling a little better."

"In that case we'd better be quick here and then go and tidy the stateroom before anyone sees it."

Mr and Mrs Hampson were taking their seats for pre-dinner drinks by the time they returned, and Nell smiled at Mrs Hampson as she wandered over.

"Good evening. What a beautiful dress."

"Thank you. I put it on to brighten myself up. I look terribly pale."

"Well, it certainly works, and your cheeks have more colour than they did at afternoon tea. It saved you putting on your jewellery, too."

Mrs Hampson rested a hand on the coloured beads decorating the front of her dress. "I didn't have the energy to stand up while Mr Hampson fiddled with the fasteners."

Nell smiled at her. "I'm always happy to help if you need me to."

Mr Hampson scowled at his wife. "I wish I'd known, confounded nuisance those clasps. Now, what about a drink?"

"Certainly. What would you like?"

"Two sherries. My wife's had quite enough brandy for one day."

"Only for medicinal purposes." Mrs Hampson's cheeks coloured.

"Nevertheless." Mr Hampson nodded towards the Askwiths' table. "Where are they this evening? They're usually here before us."

"Lady Askwith was poorly this morning, and didn't want disturbing. Lord Askwith's not arrived yet."

Mrs Hampson put a hand to her chest. "At least it wasn't only me."

"Not at all." Nell smiled at Mrs Turner as she entered the saloon. "Even your new acquaintance was under the weather. If you'll excuse me, I should ask if she needs anything."

Mrs Turner had settled in her seat when Nell reached her. "Good evening, Mrs Riley."

"Good evening, madam. How are you feeling?"

"I must admit, I've felt better. I hardly ate a thing at afternoon tea. At least the storm's passed."

"Hopefully, we'll have a clear run to New York. We should be in sight of land by tomorrow, so that always helps. May I offer you a glass of champagne?"

"Not tonight. I'll have a brandy cocktail, please. I don't like to mix my drinks."

"No, indeed. I'll bring it as soon as I can."

Nell hurried to the bar, but as she was giving her order to Mr Brennan, Mr Price called her over.

"Yes, sir?"

"Lady Askwith wants a tray in her room."

Nell groaned. "Did she ask for it herself rather than her husband? After the fuss she caused this morning..."

"Don't worry, it was her. Would you ask Mrs Swift to serve your drinks? She'd like it now."

Once Nell had spoken to Mrs Swift, she headed downstairs for the tray and made her way to the stateroom. Lady Askwith was at the door when she arrived.

"Good evening, Your Ladyship. I was expecting you to be in bed. Are you feeling better?"

"I am, thank you. And may I say how sorry I am for the way I behaved this morning. It was quite unforgiveable, but I'm not at my best when I'm feeling under the weather."

Nell stepped into the room and put the tray on the table. "I quite understand. At least the wind's subsiding now."

"It was still rather fierce when I popped my head outside."

Nell's eyes widened. "You've been onto the deck?"

"Not really. I'd hoped to take a walk on the promenade to get some fresh air, but it was too cold."

"I should say so, after the day we've had. I hope you had your cloak."

"I'm afraid I didn't. It's so warm in here, I quite forgot to take it. I wasn't outside for more than a few seconds, though."

Nell lifted the cloche from the tray. "This should make you feel better. Potato and leek soup to start, followed by roast rib of beef."

Lady Askwith smiled as she pulled up a chair. "I'm sure it will. Thank you, Mrs Riley."

"Good evening, madam. I hope you enjoy it."

. . .

Mr Brennan was at the bar in the dining room by the time Nell had delivered Mrs Robertson's tray.

"Here you are. Mr Marsh was looking for you."

"Why?"

He shrugged. "He didn't say. I expect he was missing you."

"That's not even funny." She watched him polish a glass and set it on the shelf behind him. "I don't suppose you know why Mr Marsh is on the ship after disappearing last month."

"He wanted to see you."

Nell plonked her hands on her hips. "I'm being serious."

"So am I. He told me he left because he was angry with you, but realised that if he didn't come back, he'd never see you again."

"Why didn't you tell me before now?"

"Give me chance. He only told me this afternoon when we were quiet. I caught him staring at you when you were with Mr Price and asked what he was up to."

"You saw it, too?" Nell sighed. "Mr Price doesn't think it's a problem that he watches me all the time."

"You've spoken to him about it?"

"That's what we were talking about when Mr Marsh was watching. I asked Mr Price why he'd taken him back, but he wouldn't say."

"It's nothing sinister. Mr Marsh turned up, and it was an easy option for Mr Price. He'd have had to train the other chap, otherwise."

"I don't know why he couldn't have left him in steerage, though."

"Mr Marsh said he wouldn't stay unless he came up

here."

Nell's shoulders slumped. "Thank you for letting me know."

Once she'd served her guests, Nell stood by the wall and surveyed the room. She was about to go and collect some plates when Lord Askwith bounded towards her.

"Mrs Riley. Forgive me." He put a hand in his pocket. "Have you seen my wife by any chance?"

"I took her a tray little under an hour ago."

"And how is she?"

"Remarkably chirpy considering how ill she was this morning."

"Splendid. I haven't wanted to disturb her all afternoon, hence the outfit." He pointed to his dark brown lounge suit.

"I did wonder, sir."

"My morning suit's in the wardrobe. I feel rather foolish now everyone else has made the effort to get changed."

"It's not a crime, sir."

"Thank goodness." He gave her a boyish grin. "I'll finish off here, then see how the old girl is."

"Very good, sir." Nell shrugged as Lord Askwith returned to the table he was sharing with Mr Fothergill. *What a strange conversation.*

Mrs Swift looked up as Nell approached the bar. "How was she?"

"As right as rain. If I didn't know better, I would never have guessed she'd been ill."

"That's something, at least. Hopefully, the dining arrangements will be back to normal tomorrow."

"I hope so. Time passes much more quickly when we're busy. Now what?" Nell groaned as Mr Ramsbottom made a beeline for them.

"Good evening, ladies. You're in for a quiet night, tonight."

Mrs Swift sighed. "We are. We should make the most of it."

Nell looked up at him. "I notice Mr Fothergill's dining with Lord Askwith, again. How are they getting along?"

Mr Ramsbottom sneaked a glimpse at them. "It's funny you should ask. Lord Askwith's his usual drunken self, but Mr Fothergill's constantly interrogating him. Did you ever find out what he does for a living?"

"I didn't. Why?"

Mr Ramsbottom shrugged. "I just wondered. He's acting as if he's the police or something."

"Really?" Nell gazed over to the other side of the room. "As soon as he's back in my section, I'll see what I can find out."

# CHAPTER SEVENTEEN

M r Marsh was by the door to the dining room when they arrived the following morning.

"Good morning, ladies."

"Mr Marsh." Nell forced a smile. "Are there many trays to deliver today?"

"Not many for the ladies. Mrs Robertson obviously..."

"What about Mrs and Miss Fothergill?"

"Their maid's already been to collect their trays."

"So they're still not well? That surprises me."

"Perhaps they enjoyed breakfast in bed." Mrs Swift smirked. "Or being without Mr Fothergill."

"That's a possibility." Nell grinned. "Do you know if the Askwiths have requested a tray?"

"They hadn't when I looked."

"So Her Ladyship will join us for breakfast?" Nell's eyes narrowed. "It sounds like I'll have Mr Fothergill to attend to, then." She strode over to the galley with Mrs Swift on her heels. "I'll take Mrs Robertson's tray before we get started."

Captain Robertson was leaving his wife's stateroom when Nell approached and he held open the door for her.

"Good morning, Mrs Riley."

"Good morning, Captain. How's Mrs Robertson today?"

"She's waiting for you. Before you go, may I thank you for everything you're doing for her. I'm glad she has someone to talk to."

"You're welcome, sir. Although it's not really a chore."

"Maybe not, but it's still appreciated. Carry on, Mrs Riley."

Mrs Robertson was sitting up in bed when Nell walked in. "Good morning. How are you today?"

Mrs Robertson grimaced. "This baby's determined to make me uncomfortable. I hardly slept last night."

The smile fell from Nell's face. "Have you seen Matron since yesterday?" She placed the tray on Mrs Robertson's lap.

"She called with Dr Clarke last night, but I've not seen her since."

"I'll ask her to visit, then. You shouldn't be in any pain."

"It's not pain as such, but if you wouldn't mind speaking to her, I'd appreciate it."

"Not at all. We can't be too careful."


The dining room was filling up as Nell returned, and she raised her eyebrows at the sight of Mr Fothergill sitting with Lord and Lady Askwith. *They must get along better than Mr Ramsbottom thought. I'll have to make do with Mrs Turner.* She wandered over to the table.

"Good morning, madam. Has anyone taken your order yet?"

"Not yet, but I've only been here a minute. It's nice to see so many people today."

Nell glanced around the room. "Isn't it? It makes life easier too, not having so many trays to take."

"I don't understand why people take meals in their rooms. It's so much nicer watching what's going on."

"There are some who like their privacy."

"But if they're well enough to eat, they should eat in the dining room, wouldn't you say? I bumped into Lady Askwith walking the corridors yesterday afternoon, and yet she still didn't come down for dinner."

"You did?" Nell raised an eyebrow. "She was poorly yesterday morning, and so perhaps walking was as much as she could manage."

"You may be right. I shouldn't judge."

After taking her order, Nell walked to the galley. "Has anyone been to the Hampsons yet?"

Mr Ross checked the pieces of paper in front of him. "It doesn't look like it."

"Give me a minute." Nell turned on her heel and smiled at the Hampsons as she approached. "Good morning."

Mr Hampson flicked his thumb towards the Askwiths. "That pompous old fool is good enough to sit with His Lordship, then. They didn't invite me to join them when I was on my own."

"I suspect they have things to discuss."

"They're all alike. No respect for those of us who've made our own way in the world rather than having it given to us on a plate."

"I don't believe it's intentional."

"I bet it is, but to heck with them. I had a better time with the other passengers than I would have had with them."

"I'm pleased to hear it. Would you both like your usual eggs and fried bread?"

"Need you ask?"

"No, sir. I'll bring some tea over straight away."


Once breakfast was over, and the tables set for luncheon, Nell and Mrs Swift collected their cleaning equipment and went upstairs to the staterooms.

Mrs Swift smiled as they split up. "Let's see who can finish first. I'll meet you back here."

Most of Nell's rooms were empty when she arrived and she hurried to make the beds and flick a duster around the furniture before sweeping the floor. *It's so much easier when the guests aren't here. Only the Hampsons' room to do.*

She knocked on the door, but before she reached for the handle, Mr Hampson opened it for her.

"Oh, I'm sorry, sir. I'm here to clean your room and expected you to be outside. We should be able to see land anytime now."

"We hadn't planned on going out. I expect it's rather chilly."

"It is, but it's always a treat to see Newfoundland for the first time, especially if there's snow on the hills. I'd highly recommend it."

"Hmm. I suppose we could. Wait there a moment while I speak to Mrs Hampson."

"Yes, sir."

Nell only waited a minute before Mrs Hampson stepped out in her cloak.

"Thank you for giving him a nudge. I told him we'd see land today, but he's still sulking about Mr Fothergill and Lord Askwith."

Nell had no time to answer before Mr Hampson appeared in a thick woollen coat and hat. "Come on then, if we're going. It had better be worth it."

Nell waited for them to leave before carrying her bucket inside. The bed had already been made and so she quickly dusted the surfaces and swept the floor. *That should do it.*

She picked up her things and was giving the place a last look around when the door flew open and Mr Hampson stomped in, followed by his wife.

"Oh! I wasn't expecting you so soon."

"You need binoculars to see any sight of land. A waste of time."

"I'm sorry. I thought we'd be closer."

Mrs Hampson tried to smile. "I expect we'll see more this afternoon."

"You will. Perhaps you could join us for morning coffee instead. I'm about to go to the saloon to set it out."

"We'll follow you there when we've taken off our outdoor clothes."

Nell stepped into the corridor and pulled the door closed behind her, but stopped as Matron walked towards her.

"There you are." Nell waited for her to stop. "I was looking for you earlier. Have you called on Mrs Robertson this morning?"

"Of course." Matron glared at her.

"That's a relief. She was in some discomfort when I saw her."

"It's nothing to worry about. All part of the normal process."

Nell breathed a sigh of relief. "Thank goodness. You were out early this morning. Did you have another emergency?"

"Some lingering seasickness. Now, if you'll excuse me, I need to be in steerage."

*A likely tale.* Nell didn't wait for Matron to disappear before she hurried back to the foyer to find Mrs Swift waiting for her.

"What kept you?"

Nell tutted. "Not much, except the Hampsons were in their stateroom and I had to encourage them to go out."

"That doesn't happen very often. Passengers are usually keen to get a first glimpse of land."

"He's not usual. He was only outside for five minutes and came back complaining the land was too far away. I don't know why I bother with him." She followed Mrs Swift to the cupboard and put away her equipment. "He'd better not still be grumpy at luncheon or he can serve himself."

Mrs Swift chuckled. "I'd like to see that. Come on, let's get it over with, and then we can go out on the deck and find out what he was complaining about."


The sun peeped from between the clouds as Nell and Mrs Swift stood on the first-class promenade peering into the distance.

"Land's getting closer. It's a shame the snow hasn't arrived, though."

Mrs Swift shuddered. "I'm not sorry. It's cold enough."

"I suppose..."

"Ah, Mrs Riley, there you are."

Nell turned to see Lady Askwith approaching. "Good afternoon, Your Ladyship. Were you looking for me?"

"I was. I wonder if you'd help me dress this evening."

"Is it a special occasion?"

"Not at all. My husband has agreed to host a table with those ghastly Fothergills, and despite my reservations, I'd like to look my best."

"Certainly, madam."

"Splendid. Come to the room at half past five, so we've time for a pre-dinner drink."

"I'll be there."

"She sounds determined not to enjoy tonight." Mrs Swift turned back to the railings.

"She'll probably make sure nobody else does, either." Nell sighed. "It might be awkward."

"Let's hope so. We've not had any decent gossip for days." Mrs Swift smirked. "Come on, we'd better go. It will be time for afternoon tea soon."

## CHAPTER EIGHTEEN

It was precisely half past five when Nell arrived at the Askwiths' stateroom, and Lady Askwith opened the door to her.

"That was well-timed. My husband has just left."

"I passed him in the corridor." Nell closed the door behind her. "Have you decided what you're wearing tonight?"

Lady Askwith held up an emerald green dress. "This. I know I needn't try too hard, but I can't help myself."

"I'm sure Lord Askwith appreciates it." Nell waited for her to slip out of her dressing gown and undid the bow on the corset. She pulled the cords until her fingers were red. "I hope that's not too tight."

Lady Askwith took a deep breath in. "That should be fine. The dress I've chosen for tonight is a little slimmer than the others and all the food doesn't help."

"I don't doubt it. Let's see how we get on."

After several minutes of struggling, Nell fastened the last of the buttons down the back. "There we are. All done."

Lady Askwith's face looked pained as she put her hands on her hips. "I knew it would still fit. Now, where did I put that stole?"

Nell peered into the wardrobe and took out a long fox-fur wrap. "Is this the one?"

"It is."

Nell placed it across her shoulders before Lady Askwith adjusted it on the front of her dress.

"There we are. I just need my gloves."

The Fothergills were seated with Lord Askwith when Nell escorted Lady Askwith into the saloon.

"I'm sorry I'm late." She feigned a smile as the gentlemen stood up. "Mrs Riley couldn't find my brooch, so I had to put on my stole instead."

Nell raised an eyebrow as Lord Askwith helped his wife into a chair.

"Think nothing of it. We were making some introductions, but we can do it again."

"Splendid." Lady Askwith clasped her hands together. "Before we let Mrs Riley go, we should order some drinks."

Mr Fothergill retook his seat. "You've tried most of the cocktails we've been drinking. Do you have a favourite?"

"Now, there's a question. I'd probably say the gin cocktail."

"Really?" Mr Fothergill's eyebrows inched up. "I'd have thought someone in your position would prefer the champagne."

"Oh ... well ..."

"She likes to make her own decisions. Don't you, my

dear? Not follow the crowd." Lord Askwith squeezed her hand.

"Exactly. I like to stand out."

*You certainly do that.* Nell smiled as she took out her notepad. "So, will it be three gin cocktails, a Pimms, and a whisky and water, then?"

Lord Askwith waited for agreement. "Well done, Mrs Riley. And please don't dally, some of us have been sitting for far too long without a drink."

Nell rolled her eyes at Mr Brennan as she approached the bar. "This should make for an interesting evening."

"What have they ordered?"

Nell handed him her piece of paper. "Mr Fothergill seemed surprised that someone of Lady Askwith's standing drinks gin."

"Did he say that to her?"

"In a roundabout way. She looked rather flustered, and Lord Askwith had to step in."

"Hopefully, that means they'll switch to champagne when they move to the dining room."

"You can hope." Nell watched Mr and Mrs Hampson arrive, and once they'd taken their seats, she strolled over to greet them.

"Did you go out on deck this afternoon?"

"Oh, we did." Mrs Hampson's rosy cheeks beamed. "How wonderful to see land again. We were so busy admiring it, we were late getting changed. I didn't even have time to put my jewellery on."

"That would have taken another ten minutes." Mr Hampson glared at the Askwith and Fothergill table. "I'd like a drink before dinner. A glass of whisky, please."

"With water?"

"No, as it comes. And make it a large one."

"Yes, sir." Nell made a note of the order. "And a sherry for Mrs Hampson?"

"That's the one."

Nell kept her head down as she walked to the bar, aware of Mr Marsh's eyes on her.

"You're looking nice tonight, Mrs Riley."

She shuddered as he peered down at her. "Oh ... I've not done anything different."

"Maybe it's because you always do."

"T-thank you." She stepped closer to the bar. "Are the Askwiths' drinks ready yet, Mr Brennan? I've a feeling we'll be getting a complaint if I don't take them soon."

Mr Brennan placed the final drink on the tray. "There you are. I can pour His Lordship another one at a moment's notice if he doesn't want to wait for the others."

Nell grinned. "I don't doubt it."

Lady Askwith looked up with a sigh when Nell returned. "Ah, Mrs Riley, thank you. I'll take a gin cocktail here."

"Certainly." Nell handed the drinks around. "Will that be all?"

"For now." Lady Askwith raised her glass as her husband took a gulp from his. "To this evening. I'd like to ask Mr Fothergill where he gets his ideas from for cocktails. It would be fun to try something else later."

"I'll have another one of these whenever you're passing." Lord Askwith raised his half-empty glass.

"Yes, sir."

Nell stepped away and signalled to Mr Brennan, but

hovered beside the table as Lord Askwith spoke to Mr Fothergill.

"What is it you do?"

"Well, I need to be discreet, but in the broadest terms, I'm a solicitor. I tend to the estates and other matters, for several members of the aristocracy."

Lord Askwith choked on his drink and Nell turned as he slammed down his glass.

"Are you all right, sir?"

He coughed to clear his throat. "My drink went down the wrong way."

Nell picked up the glass. "Let me get you another."

"One moment." He snatched it off her. "This one's not empty yet."

"Oh, I'm sorry." Nell hurried to the bar as Mr Brennan put down another glass of whisky.

"What was all that about?"

"I'll tell you later." Without a pause, she collected the new drink and returned to the table.

"...Lord and Lady Hamilton. Do you know them? They're out near Chester." Mr Fothergill didn't register Nell as she put the fresh glass in front of him, but Lord Askwith immediately leaned forward and added a spot of water.

"I can't say I do. I know of them, obviously, but our paths haven't crossed."

Mr Fothergill's brow furrowed. "That's strange. They're a rather sociable couple, host several balls a year. What about Lord Carmichael, near Prescot?"

"Erm, yes. We did meet him. Nice chap." Lord Askwith

finished his whisky. "Before you go, Mrs Riley…" He turned to his wife. "Would you like another drink?"

Lady Askwith glanced at her near full glass. "Not yet, but perhaps we could arrange to have some fresh drinks ready for us downstairs when we move. What would you suggest, Mr Fothergill?"

Mr Fothergill's moustache twitched as he took a sip of his own drink. "Champagne cocktails, please, Mrs Riley." He didn't pause for breath before he leaned towards Lord Askwith. "You get along with Carmichael? Most people think he's a dreadful fellow."

"Well, yes, he is. I was being polite. I see you have no such qualms."

"I speak as I find…"

"So it seems." Lord Askwith patted his wife's hand. "We need to watch what we say, my dear. We don't want Mr Fothergill speaking badly of us."

"No." She looked up at Nell. "May we have the champagne cocktails here? This gin won't last long."


Nell breathed a sigh of relief as the last of the guests left the dining room.

"What an evening." She collected up the dirty tablecloths as Mrs Swift unfolded the clean ones.

"What did I miss?"

"Not a lot, once they came down here, but the atmosphere was tense in the saloon. I got the impression the five of them won't be sitting together again."

"What was the problem?"

"I don't know. Mr Fothergill seems to be on good terms with a lot of people he expected the Askwiths to be acquainted with, but when they weren't, they were rather embarrassed."

"That's no reason to be embarrassed."

Nell shrugged. "I'm only telling you what I saw. Anyway, it's over. All I've got to look forward to now is Mr Hampson grumbling about how he wasn't included."

Mrs Swift laughed. "You get all the best guests."

# CHAPTER NINETEEN

Nell groaned as she pushed herself up from the breakfast table.

"Do I really need to serve the Hampsons again? He did nothing but complain yesterday. As if it was my fault the Fothergills had dinner with the Askwiths the night before last."

"Well, they didn't last night, so hopefully he'll have cheered up."

Nell raised her eyebrows. "I wouldn't bank on it. Come along, let's get it over with."

The wind was brisk as they hurried across the deck, and Nell straightened her hat before hanging up her cloak.

"The land's supposed to stop it being so windy."

Mrs Swift grimaced. "It doesn't work like that."

Matron was waiting in the foyer when they arrived. "Mrs Riley, might I have a word?"

Nell glanced at Mrs Swift before looking back at Matron. "Is it Mrs Robertson?"

"She's fine, but Captain Robertson wants to speak to you."

"Captain Robertson. Why?"

"It's not for me to say, but if you'd follow me."

"I can take myself..."

"I've been told to escort you, now, if you wouldn't mind." Matron caught hold of Nell's arm as they set off down the corridor towards the bridge.

"What have I done?"

"I'm not here to discuss anything, Mrs Riley. Just keep walking."

The office door was open when they reached the bridge and Captain Robertson beckoned them in. "Good morning, ladies."

Nell didn't have time to respond before Matron interrupted. "She hasn't left my sight since I passed on your message, Captain."

"What's going on?" Nell stared between the two of them.

Captain Robertson cleared his throat. "I'm afraid I've had a complaint from Mr Hampson."

"I'm sorry. I didn't mean to be rude to him." Her cheeks flushed. "He just wouldn't stop complaining about being ignored by Lord Askwith. I had to be blunt with him..."

"That's not what it was about. Unfortunately, someone has stolen Mrs Hampson's jewellery ... and he believes it was you."

Nell's mouth fell open. "Stolen?" She reached for the nearest chair. "I-I've never taken anything in my life."

"And yet some valuable jewellery's gone missing."

"But ... but it could have been anyone."

"According to Mr Hampson, his wife always took care to hide it, but he said you knew where it was."

"I didn't." Her eyes were wide as she stared between the captain and Matron.

"Mr Hampson said his wife had inadvertently let slip where it was, and then the day before yesterday you insisted they leave their room."

Nell's brow creased. "Only so they could get a first sight of land. Please, sir, I wouldn't steal anything. What would I do with it if I did?"

"That's precisely what Matron is hoping to find out. She'll search yours and Mrs Swift's belongings and if she finds the jewellery, I'll have no alternative but to dismiss you."

Nell pivoted to stare at Matron. "You can't go through my things ... or Mrs Swift's. Not without telling her."

"If the jewellery's found, we'll interview her as well."

"It would be her word against mine."

"Do you expect us to find something?"

Nell shook her head. "No, but I can only speak for myself."

"We'll wait and see, then. Matron will check the cabin now, while I go to the bridge. I'll lock the door behind me. We can't risk you speaking to anyone before we've finished our investigation."

"But Mrs Robertson's breakfast..."

"Mr Price will take care of that." He stepped into the corridor. "I won't be long."

Nell flopped into a chair as he turned the key in the lock. *Please God, don't let Matron find anything*. Her heart raced as she sat, unable to move. *What will everyone think? I*

VL MCBEATH

*won't be able to show my face in the dining room again. Or the saloon. And what about getting home? They can't leave me in New York.* She wiped the tears that slid down her cheeks. *I'd never get home.*

Fifteen minutes afterward, she jumped to her feet as Captain Robertson ushered Matron back into the room.

"Take a seat, Mrs Riley." Captain Robertson walked to the far side of his desk. "You'll be pleased to know Matron found no evidence of the jewellery in your cabin."

Nell's shoulders relaxed. "Thank goodness."

"Did you expect her to?"

"No, but someone else might have put it there. I swear it wasn't me."

"Then why did Mr Hampson specifically tell me it was you who took it?"

"I-I've no idea."

"Very well. It still doesn't alter the fact that Mrs Hampson has lost some valuable items and I can't dismiss the accusation until we've recovered them." The captain paused as he paced the room. "I've heard you've been rather friendly with Mr Brennan and Mr Marsh on this trip. We can't discount the idea that you handed the stolen items to one of them."

"Mr Marsh! He's the one who follows *me* around. It's nothing to do with me. I even spoke to Mr Price about him and asked why he wasn't in steerage."

"You reported a fellow steward?" The captain's voice was brusque.

"I-I didn't know what else to do. I don't want his attention..."

Captain Robertson looked at Matron. "Were you aware of this?"

"No, Captain. Should I fetch Mr Price?"

He checked his pocket watch. "Yes. We need to search the stewards' accommodation and it can't wait. Ask him to join me in here as soon as he can."

"What should I do with Mrs Riley?"

The captain studied her. "I think we can assume Mrs Riley is innocent of the crime, but she shouldn't be in the dining room with Mr Hampson until our investigation is over." He smiled at her. "My wife would be delighted to have company. Perhaps you could sit with her for an hour."

Nell's back straightened as the door to Mrs Robertson's stateroom opened, and Captain Robertson joined them. His smile disappeared as he looked at his wife.

"Why are you looking at me like that?"

"How could you accuse Mrs Riley of such a thing?"

He sighed. "I didn't accuse her of anything, but when a passenger complains..."

"You can't assume they're right. Poor Mrs Riley's been in a terrible state."

He opened his arms in her direction. "I'm sorry if I jumped to conclusions, but after further questioning, Mr Hampson has admitted he has no firm evidence you were the thief. Not only that, we found no trace of it amongst the crew."

Nell's eyes narrowed. "What does that mean?"

"That you're free to go about your usual business."

"But what about the jewellery? Was the theft a hoax, all along?"

Captain Robertson paused. "What do you mean?"

"One night last week, they were late to the saloon because she'd hidden it in the wardrobe and forgotten where she'd put it. Has she done the same again?"

Captain Robertson shook his head. "They said nothing of that, but I'll ask them. They've wasted a good few hours this morning, with everything we've had to do."

"Not to mention Mrs Riley's reputation."

"Mrs Riley has nothing to fear on that score. The Hampsons have been told that she's not their thief, and most of the stewards are unaware of what's happened." Captain Robertson opened the door. "Carry on, Mrs Riley, I'll see you later."

Mr Price climbed the last few steps from the dining room as Nell entered the foyer outside the saloon.

"Mrs Riley, I heard you'd be back. That was quite an inconvenience."

"Yes, sir."

"You can continue with your staterooms later. Morning coffee's in quarter of an hour." He ushered her into the saloon.

"Is that it?"

Mr Price stared at her. "Is what it?"

"I don't know how much you were told about events this morning, but not only was I accused of stealing, but Captain

Robertson thought I was working too closely with Mr Brennan and Mr Marsh."

Mr Price continued to stare at her.

"Mr Marsh! I've been doing my best to avoid him ever since we started this voyage, but he's been following me everywhere. How is it that even the captain can see it, but you can't? Is it too much to ask to have him moved to steerage?"

"I've already explained, I can't do that."

"You haven't. You've only told me why you won't."

"Nonsense."

"No, it's not. Did Captain Robertson speak to you about it?"

Mr Price's brow furrowed. "Why would he?"

"Because I told him I'd spoken to you but you'd done nothing."

"The captain's aware of the problems we had when Mr Marsh rejoined the ship, but I can't reorganise the entire crew because of one complaint."

Nell took a deep breath as Mr Price left her. *Keep your head down and do as you're told. It's only for another two and a half weeks.*

She ran her hands over her face, but froze as a hand settled on her shoulder.

"Mrs Riley, it's good to see you back." Mr Marsh's voice sent a chill down her spine. "Are you feeling better?"

She spun to face him. "Why don't you leave me alone? I'm not interested in you; I never have been and never will be."

The smile fell from his face, but she couldn't stop.

"Why did you have to come back to the ship and insist

145

on being in first class? Twice I've asked Mr Price to move you to steerage, but he's refused. What did you say to him?"

Mr Marsh's mouth trembled, and he took a step backwards. "I-I'm sorry. I-I didn't mean to upset you."

"Then stay away from me." She stormed to the outer door, only mindful of being without her cloak, as the wind chilled her arms. Tears stung her cheeks as she gazed out over the railings. *Confound him. Confound them all.*

# CHAPTER TWENTY

H er hands were like ice when she returned to the foyer, and she rubbed them up and down her arms as she stamped her feet on the carpet. *That was a stupid thing to do.* Her eyes watered and she used her sleeve to wipe her cheeks as she squeezed into the cloakroom and wrapped her cloak around her shoulders.

*Now what? I can't see Mr Marsh again.* She waited until the blood returned to her fingers and they tingled as she pushed on the door to peer out. The voices from the saloon suggested most of the guests were already taking morning coffee. *I'll start cleaning the staterooms.*

She hung her cloak over the peg and darted across the foyer to the corridor beyond. She hadn't gone far before Mrs Swift's voice stopped her dead.

"Where are you going?" Mrs Swift stood with her hands on her hips. "Haven't I done enough this morning without serving coffee by myself?"

"I'm sorry. There was a mix-up over some jewellery."

"I was told you'd been cleared."

"I was, but I can't face seeing Mr Marsh at the moment."

Mrs Swift moved to the side of the corridor and folded her arms. "All right, you've got some explaining to do. What's he got to do with it?"

Nell sighed. "Nothing really, but I was horrible to him. I said I wanted nothing to do with him and that I wished he'd leave me alone."

Mrs Swift raised her eyebrows. "Well, you got what you asked for. He announced before the guests arrived for coffee that he'd be working in steerage for the rest of the voyage. He made the arrangements himself to swap places with Mr Hancock. It even took Mr Price by surprise."

Tears welled in Nell's eyes. "Oh goodness. He must hate me now. I didn't mean to be so nasty."

Mrs Swift sighed. "Make your mind up. I thought you wanted him to be sent downstairs."

"I did, but not like this."

"Sometimes you have to do these things. You should have said the same to Mr Ramsbottom months ago."

"I couldn't possibly do the same to anyone else."

"Come on. Stop feeling sorry for yourself. I need your help in the saloon."

Nell nodded. "Only if you deal with the Hampsons. They caused all this."

Mrs Swift grinned. "You needn't worry about them. Nobody's seen them this morning. I don't imagine they're proud of what they've done, either."

. . .

Mr Brennan looked up from drying a glass as Nell arrived to serve pre-dinner drinks.

"Who'd have thought that talking to your work colleagues would get you into so much trouble."

Nell's heart sank. "Does everyone know?"

"Pretty much. They searched our bunks."

"I'm sorry. What was Captain Robertson thinking?"

"I don't think he was, except he always puts the passengers first."

Nell pinched the bridge of her nose. "How am I going to face the Hampsons again?"

He picked up another glass. "Won't Mrs Swift serve them?"

"She will, but they'll still be in the same room. Do you know whether they found the jewellery?"

"Not that I'm aware. It'll probably turn up in the next day or two."

"Well, if it does, I hope it's in a place I don't have access to."

Nell wandered from the bar but took a step backwards as Mr Ramsbottom walked towards her. He glanced over his shoulder. "I've not had a chance to talk to you, but what a to-do that was this morning. That Mr Hampson needs a good talking- to."

She gave him a curt smile. "I expect he does, but I doubt he'll get one."

"The captain should have supported you, not found you guilty before he asked any questions."

Nell rested a hand on his arm. "Thank you, Mr Ramsbottom. I appreciate that."

His grin returned. "It wouldn't be the same if you weren't here."

"I might say the same about you." She stepped around him towards the tables as the Fothergills walked into the saloon. "I need to go."

Mr Fothergill was helping his wife into a chair as Nell approached their table.

"Good afternoon, Mrs Riley." He took his own seat and lowered his voice. "I heard there's been some jewellery taken."

"Y-yes, sir. How do you know?"

Mr Fothergill tapped the side of his nose. "I may not say much, but I listen. A very valuable skill."

Nell nodded but said nothing.

"Have the pieces been retrieved?"

"Not that I've heard, sir."

He checked around them again. "Might I suggest you look in the Askwiths' stateroom."

"The Ask–" Nell's voice squeaked, but she stopped as Mr Fothergill put a finger to his lips.

"I can't promise you'll find anything, but it would surprise me if you didn't. Now then." His voice returned to its usual level. "We'll have the champagne cobblers again. It's been a few days since we last had them, and my daughter would like to try one this evening."

"Yes, sir ... and thank you."

He nodded. "Just be discreet."

Mrs Swift was at the bar when Nell returned. "What's the matter? Has someone said something?"

"No, nothing like that."

"What is it then?"

Nell shook her head. "I can't tell you here. We'll talk about it later."

Mrs Swift grimaced. "Look who's here." She nodded towards the Hampsons.

"Trust them to choose the table next to the Fothergills. I wouldn't be surprised if they've sat there on purpose."

"Would you like me to move them?"

"You can hardly do that. Oh, wait." Nell smirked. "The Fothergills are moving."

Mr Fothergill walked towards her. "We'll take the table in the corner, Mrs Riley. The quality of guest at the other end of the room leaves something to be desired."

"Yes, sir." Her eyes flicked to the door as the Askwiths arrived. "Am I right in thinking you'd like to sit alone this evening?"

He followed her gaze. "Most certainly. Quite frankly, Lord and Lady Askwith would be better sitting with the Hampsons."

Nell raised an eyebrow at Mrs Swift, who stared after Mr Fothergill.

"What was that about?"

"I'm not sure, but he's not happy with the Askwiths."

"They're not best pleased themselves. I wonder what happened."

Nell's eyes narrowed. "I don't know, but hopefully we'll find out."

## CHAPTER TWENTY-ONE

M rs Robertson was sitting up in bed when Nell arrived with her tray the following morning.

"Ah, Mrs Riley, how are you feeling today? Have you forgiven my husband for his silliness?"

"It's the Hampsons I'm most angry with, for accusing me in the first place."

"I'm not surprised. They behaved quite inappropriately."

Nell's mouth was dry as she watched Mrs Robertson take the top off one of her eggs. "I don't know whether I should raise this with you ... with your condition and all, but would you mind if I asked your advice on something?"

"Not at all. What is it?"

Nell bit her lip. "It's about Mrs Hampson's jewellery..."

Mrs Robertson looked up from her egg. "Go on."

"When I was in the saloon last night, one of the passengers, Mr Fothergill, suggested that it might be in the stateroom of Lord and Lady Askwith."

Mrs Robertson's mouth fell open.

"Precisely, but I've no idea what to do with the information. I can't go into their stateroom alone after what happened yesterday, but if it was them who took it, we need to do something about it."

"You must tell my husband, immediately."

"I can't." Nell's voice sank to a whisper. "I clean the Askwiths' stateroom, as well as the Hampsons', and he'll think I took the jewellery from one room and put it in the other."

"Why would you do that?"

"I wouldn't, but isn't that what it would look like?"

Mrs Robertson returned her attention to her eggs. "I suppose it could."

"I'm sorry to trouble you with this, but ... well ... I didn't know who else to talk to."

Mrs Robertson finished her mouthful. "Am I right in thinking that if you ignore this information, the jewellery would remain missing and, assuming they had it, the Askwiths would take it from the ship, and nobody would see it again?"

"I expect so."

"So, why try to retrieve it, knowing it would put you under suspicion?"

"We can't turn a blind eye to stealing." Nell's voice rose as she spoke.

"Which suggests you had nothing to do with the theft. If you placed it in the Askwiths' stateroom, why tell anyone? You could put it back in the Hampsons' room as easily as you moved it, and everyone would assume Mrs Hampson had been forgetful."

"But if anyone caught me..."

"Precisely. You want to do the right thing without ruining your reputation. If that wasn't your motive, you wouldn't have told me."

"The problem is, I doubt I'll be able to speak to Captain Robertson before I need to clean their room."

Mrs Robertson took a mouthful of tea. "Will Mr Price be in the dining room when you get back?"

"I expect so."

"Excellent. Tell him I'd like to see him as soon as he's able. I'll ask him to bring my husband here. He'll know what to do."

Nell smiled. "Thank you. You've lifted a great weight off my mind."

The dining room was almost full when Nell returned, and Mrs Swift scowled as she went into the galley. "You took your time. What have you been doing?"

"Talking to Mrs Robertson."

"You shouldn't be chatting at this time of day."

"It was something that couldn't wait." Nell cleared her throat as Mr Ross joined them at the counter.

"Here you are. A kipper for Mrs Turner."

"I'll take it." Nell picked up the tray without waiting for a reply and smiled at Mrs Turner as she approached the table. "Good morning, madam."

"Good morning, dear. How are you today?"

"Better than I was, thank you."

Mrs Turner sat back as Nell placed the plate in front of her. "I sat with the Hampsons last night. Mrs Hampson was telling me about the to-do with the jewellery."

The blood drained from Nell's cheeks. "What did she say?"

"Naturally, she was upset about it being taken, but she was cross, too."

"With me?" Her voice cracked, and she coughed to clear her throat.

"No, with Mr Hampson. She said he'd jumped to conclusions about you, after she'd told him it could be anyone. She now thinks everyone's giving them the cold shoulder because they got you into trouble."

*Serves them right.* Nell took a breath. "Well..."

Mrs Turner picked up her knife and fork. "Please don't be too hard on her. It wasn't her fault."

Nell waited for the last of the guests to leave the dining room before she walked over to Mrs Swift, who had made a start on changing the tablecloths.

"Here you are." Mrs Swift straightened up. "Did you say anything to Mrs Robertson about the Askwiths?"

"I did. She was very nice about it but insisted Captain Robertson was told."

"Will you speak to him?"

"She said she would, but I don't know when. I can't service their stateroom before someone checks for the jewellery."

Mrs Swift spread a clean cloth over the table. "Could you go and ask if she's spoken to him yet?"

"I don't want to keep disturbing her. She's supposed to be resting." Nell's stomach churned as she laid out the cutlery. "Would you do my corridor until we get to New York and I'll do yours?"

"I'm not doing the Askwiths' room."

Nell let out a sigh, but yelped as Captain Robertson walked towards them with Mr Price and Mr Fothergill.

"Ladies." The captain nodded to them. "I wonder if Mrs Riley could join us in my office."

Nell's cheeks burned as she gazed at the group. "N-now?"

"If you wouldn't mind." The captain stepped to one side and extended an arm towards the door. "Mrs Swift, take over all Mrs Riley's duties, but leave the Askwiths' stateroom. We haven't finished with it yet."


The men walked in silence as they escorted Nell to the bridge. Captain Robertson opened the door to his office with a flourish and waited for everyone to enter before he followed them.

"Please take a seat." He indicated to a round table in the corner of the room, before striding across to his desk. He took a key from his waistcoat pocket, and once the centre drawer was open, he removed several boxes and carried them to the table.

"The jewellery?" Nell's eyes widened.

"Indeed." Captain Robertson opened each box and pushed them towards her. "Have you seen any of these pieces before?"

"Not in the boxes, but I've seen Mrs Hampson wearing several of them." She looked at the captain. "Did you find them in the Askwiths' stateroom?"

"We did. Thanks to Mr Fothergill."

Nell nodded. *So why am I here?*

"Lord and Lady Askwith have been informed of the

development, but they've lodged a complaint against the accusation. They said someone must have placed them there."

Captain Robertson paused as he held Nell's gaze.

"Me! But I told you... What about Mr Ramsbottom? He's in and out of their stateroom as much as me."

"We'll call him in next, but we wanted to talk to you first. You must realise you're the only one who regularly goes into both staterooms."

"I knew you'd say that, which is why I didn't want to tell you." Nell closed her eyes as the room spun.

"Lord Askwith suggested it was you who hid the jewellery in their stateroom so you could retrieve it when you packed his wife's trunk."

"I wouldn't have said anything to Mrs Robertson if that's what I'd planned." She pointed at Mr Fothergill. "He was the one who told me... How did he know?"

"We'll come to that presently. First, I'd like your version of how these jewels ended up in the wrong stateroom."

Unbidden, tears ran down her cheeks. "I-I don't know... Please, believe me."

"Very well." The captain turned to Mr Fothergill, who sat with his hands clasped in front of him on the table. "Could you explain how you knew where the jewellery would be?"

"I should begin by explaining my interest in the Askwiths. When I'm not on this ship, I work as a solicitor, managing the estates of members of the aristocracy. This means I'm acquainted with many of those who live in the north of England. When Mr and Mrs Askwith announced they were a lord and lady, it piqued my curiosity. Most particularly, because I hadn't come across them before."

"Yet you said nothing." The captain's face was stern.

"It wasn't my place, certainly not before I had any evidence."

"And now you do?"

"Nothing that would stand up in court, but over the last few days I've realised that the Askwiths are no more a lord and lady than my good wife and I."

"They're not?" Nell's hand flew up to her mouth as Captain Robertson gave her a silencing glance.

"What makes you think that?"

"The first thing that drew my attention was the way they speak. They're most uncouth, her especially, although I tried to make allowances in case *His Lordship* had married beneath himself. Something that's becoming all too common."

Captain Robertson nodded. "Indeed."

"Then there's the fact she prefers gin to champagne. No self-respecting lady would ever admit to that, even if it were true."

Mr Price sat forward in his chair. "That might be explained if she'd married above herself."

"Such women make an extra effort to acquire a taste for the finer things in life and leave their pasts behind. They also love to socialise, and yet when I've spoken to them, it's been clear they've never met anyone I'd expect them to associate with."

Mr Price shrugged. "Maybe they don't get out much."

Mr Fothergill tutted. "My dear chap, it appears you know less about the aristocracy than the Askwiths. These people live to be seen in the right places. They flaunt the balls and social gatherings they've been to, drop the names of any dukes or earls they may have met, and if they're ever introduced to royalty, that's all you hear about. They need to boost their sense of importance and secure the best possible marriages for their children, yet not once have the Askwiths alluded to any such ambitions. I doubt they even have a family."

Captain Robertson's eyes pierced Mr Fothergill. "The Lord is gracious to those he grants children. It may not be their fault."

"Maybe not, but there should be mention of nephews. No member of the aristocracy is without siblings. Neither would they marry someone who didn't have an extended family. To do so would be the end of the family line. That's all these people care about."

"And so, based on this, you concluded they were the ones who stole the jewellery? That's quite a leap." The captain raised an eyebrow, but Mr Fothergill straightened his back.

"One thing I enjoy about this sort of travel is being able to observe people. Most guests are as you'd expect, but it's obvious that these two are cheats. I fear they've fooled you and your crew, Captain, in order to receive preferential treatment."

Captain Robertson paced the room. "Whether they did or not, it doesn't prove they stole the jewellery."

"As I explained, Captain, I'm a solicitor. I'd like to speak to the guests who had staterooms on that side of the ship, as well as those who worked in the area. I don't believe for a moment that nobody saw anything." He looked up. "Do I have your permission to make discreet enquiries?"

Captain Robertson studied Mr Fothergill for several seconds before he nodded. "Very well, but you report to no one but me."

# CHAPTER TWENTY-TWO

Nell's legs shook as the captain left and Mr Fothergill took the seat opposite her. He had a large notepad in front of him, but he held her gaze.

"Please relax, Mrs Riley. I'm not here to judge, just to find out if you saw anything that may help."

Nell took a deep breath. "Yes, sir."

"You said you'd seen Mrs Hampson wearing the jewellery. Are you able to tell me the last time that was?"

Nell wiped the palms of her hands on her skirt. "I couldn't say for certain." Her mind was blank.

"Was she wearing any last night?"

"I-I don't know. I didn't serve them yesterday, not after the accusation." She tilted her head to one side. "They'd reported the jewellery missing by then, so I imagine not."

"What about the night before they reported it missing?"

"I don't think so. In fact, no, she didn't. I thought it was strange at the time."

"Did you ask her why?"

Nell shook her head. "Mr Hampson was too busy

complaining about you and Lord Askwith having dinner together."

"Really?" He raised an eyebrow. "What about the night before that?"

She closed her eyes and thought back to the dining room. "That was the night she was wearing a beaded dress. I'm fairly sure that was the first night she was without it."

"So, you've not seen her with jewellery for four days?" Mr Fothergill continued as Nell nodded. "So, they reported the theft the day before last, which leaves a narrow window for it to have gone missing."

Nell gasped. "That would mean it was taken on the day of the storm?"

"By Jove, you're right." Mr Fothergill banged a hand on the table. "That will make everyone's movements much more memorable."

"Or it might mean that nobody saw anything." Nell's shoulders slumped. "Many of the passengers stayed in their rooms that day."

"Hmm." Mr Fothergill pursed his lips. "But you were working?"

"Yes, sir. I had to take a lot of trays."

"Including to Mrs Askwith?"

Nell nodded. "She'd been poorly for most of the day and was rather rude when I took her morning tray because I'd made her get out of bed."

"What happened after you'd delivered it?"

Nell's cheeks flushed. "She banged her leg on the bed and was in such a bad mood, I had to go to the dining room to fetch her some ginger biscuits and a tot of brandy."

"Do you have anyone who can confirm that?"

Nell bit her lip. "Mr Marsh."

"The steward?"

"Yes." *Why did I have to be so mean to him?*

"Excellent. I'll speak to him later. Now, was Lady Askwith in her room when you returned?"

"She was on the bed in the same position as I'd left her."

"And did you see her again that day?"

"That evening. She was late asking for a tray and so we were halfway through dinner service when I took it to her."

"And was she still in bed?"

"No. She'd been onto the promenade for a walk."

"In that weather?"

"Yes, sir. She said she hadn't stayed outside for long, but I remember saying to Mrs Swift that if I hadn't known any better, I wouldn't have guessed she'd been ill."

"Splendid." Mr Fothergill scrawled on his notepaper. "Do you remember anything else?"

Nell stared at the table for several seconds. "Actually, I do. I was speaking to Mrs Turner that evening, and she commented how unusual it was for Lady Askwith not to come down for dinner given she'd seen her walking the corridors that afternoon." Her face brightened. "That's it, isn't it? If she was in the corridor, she could have been into the Hampsons' room. In fact, thinking about it, I saw the Hampsons in the saloon for afternoon tea. It may have been then."

Mr Fothergill smiled at her. "Let's not get ahead of ourselves. I'll add Mrs Turner to my list of guests to talk to. Well done, Mrs Riley."

.  .  .

Mr Fothergill was nowhere to be seen as Nell welcomed the ladies to afternoon tea, but his wife and daughter took their usual seats.

"Good afternoon, ladies." Nell held out their chairs. "Will Mr Fothergill be joining you?"

"We're not sure. Captain Robertson asked for some assistance, and we don't know when he'll be finished." Mrs Fothergill placed her handbag on the empty chair.

"Let me get you some sandwiches while you're waiting, then."

Nell wandered to the table where the tea was being laid out and picked up a platter. She was about to head back across the dining room when Mrs Turner arrived and signalled to her. She followed her to her table.

"Good afternoon, Mrs Riley." A twinkle lit Mrs Turner's eyes. "I've been to see Mr Fothergill."

Nell gasped and glanced around her. "We need to keep it to ourselves."

"Don't worry. He told me he'd spoken to you."

Nell leaned in closer. "Did he ask you what time Lady Askwith was in the corridor?"

"He did. It was as I was leaving my room for afternoon tea."

"When the Hampsons were in here?"

"Precisely. They were in here when I arrived, and I remember thinking that Mrs Hampson looked worse than I felt."

"Hopefully, that will be the evidence Mr Fothergill needs."

"I hope so. I've never taken to those two. They're far too brash for my liking."

Nell smiled. "A few people have said that. Now, would you like a sandwich before I offer them round?"

Mr and Mrs Hampson were taking their seats as Nell made a round of the tables. She turned away, but Mrs Hampson called to her.

"Mrs Riley, please don't rush off."

Nell's heart faltered. "I thought Mrs Swift was seeing to you. Would you care for a sandwich?"

"No, thank you. We'd like to talk to you."

"Perhaps later. I really need to carry on serving."

"Please. It won't take long. We wanted to apologise for the trouble we caused. Don't we?" Mrs Hampson stared at her husband.

"It was a simple mistake. You were the only one who went into the room."

"I'm sorry, I need to go..." Nell's cheeks burned as Mr Hampson jumped to his feet.

"It's just that we were upset about what happened."

She took a deep breath. "I'm sure you were. Now, if you'll excuse me."

"That wasn't an apology..." Mrs Hampson's words were harsh as Nell made her way towards the galley.

*Men like him never apologise.*

"Are you all right?" Mrs Swift arrived beside her.

"I will be. Would you mind serving the Hampsons? I can't face them at the moment."


The last of the guests were still seated as Nell began clearing the tables, but she froze as Mr Ramsbottom sidled up to her.

"I've spoken to Mr Fothergill, and he told me what's been going on."

"Did you tell him anything of interest?"

He glanced over his shoulder. "I didn't mean to, but I gave His Lordship an alibi."

"How?"

"I served him dinner when his wife wasn't with him."

Nell's eyes widened. "I remember that. I was walking into the dining room when he asked after his wife. He made a point of telling me he hadn't been to his room all afternoon. I wondered about it at the time, but it never crossed my mind to tell Mr Fothergill."

"I wouldn't worry. He seemed quite happy with what he had."

"Do you think he's worked out who took it?"

"I'd say so, which means we can have a celebration."

She stared at him. "Why would we do that?"

"Because we're in the clear. You realise we were both suspects."

"I knew I was..."

"It's not been easy for me either, you know. That's why I've not spoken to you for a couple of days. I didn't want anyone getting ideas."

"Ideas about what?" Nell's forehead creased.

"In case they suspected me of being your accomplice."

She plonked her hands on her hips. "So you were happy enough for me to take the blame?"

"I didn't want to add fuel to the fire."

"Well, the only way I'll be celebrating is by getting a good night's sleep."

"Maybe tomorrow then." He winked as he backed away

to the men's section. "And no Mr Marsh to keep an eye on us."

Nell groaned. *I really shouldn't have been so horrible to him.* She wandered over to Mrs Swift, who was clearing tables.

"Can we work together? Mr Ramsbottom's decided he's talking to me again."

Mrs Swift paused as she positioned the glasses on the table. "I didn't know he wasn't."

"Neither did I until he just told me. Anyway, he says I'm in the clear over the jewellery, so he's decided it's safe to speak to me."

"Lucky you. Come on, let's get a move on. We'll need to be downstairs shortly."

Captain Robertson was standing near the galley door when Nell and Mrs Swift arrived in the dining room. He smiled as they approached.

"Good evening, ladies."

"Good evening, Captain." Nell coughed to clear a squeak in her throat.

"There's no need to be nervous." He looked at Mrs Swift. "Forgive me, but I was waiting to speak to Mrs Riley and Mr Ramsbottom. Ah! Here he is."

"I'll get on, then." Mrs Swift left as the captain ushered Nell through the door. "Mr Fothergill and Mr Price are waiting in my private dining room. We won't be overheard in there."

Nell's heart skipped a beat as she followed Mr Ramsbottom into an elaborately decorated room, with a long rectangular table running the length of it.

"Please, take a seat."

Captain Robertson held out a chair for her while he spoke to Mr Ramsbottom.

"We wanted to tell you and Mrs Riley of the outcome of our investigation and ask for your help between here and New York. It must remain amongst ourselves, though. Is that clear?"

They both nodded.

"Splendid. I'll hand over to Mr Fothergill."

"Thank you, Captain." He got to his feet. "Today I've interviewed the people who saw or interacted with the Askwiths on the day in question, and I trust they all spoke with honesty. Reports matched up and supported each other, which was very pleasing. As a result, I can confirm that my suspicions were correct, and that Mrs Askwith is indeed our thief."

"*Mrs* Askwith!" Mr Ramsbottom's mouth fell open.

"Indeed, although I suspect Mr Askwith was aware of her activities, which is why he did his best to deflect attention from her."

"Well, I never. You'd think she'd have enough jewellery, her being a lady."

Nell shook her head. "When I first helped her dress, she told me she found it vulgar and never wore it."

"So, why steal Mrs Hampson's?" Mr Ramsbottom scratched his head.

Mr Fothergill interrupted them. "Because they're not Lord and Lady Askwith at all. They're a couple of chancers, who played the part for their own gain."

"You've proved that?" Nell's back straightened.

"Sadly not. Not definitively, at any rate. I'm convinced they made the whole thing up, though."

Nell cocked her head to one side. "When they first boarded, Mrs Askwith asked Captain Robertson if there were any members of the aristocracy on board. She gave the impression that she wanted to sit with other titled families, rather than the general passengers."

Mr Fothergill's eyes narrowed. "Was this before they *revealed* they were Lord and Lady Askwith?"

Nell pursed her lips as she cast her mind back ten days. "It would have been because we'd reached the stateroom when they mentioned the ancestral home. Do you remember that, Mr Ramsbottom?"

"I do. Mr Askwith was talking about money and mentioned they had an ancestral home to maintain, or something like that."

"That's very interesting." Mr Fothergill tapped his fingers on the table. "Perhaps the reason they asked wasn't to socialise with them, but to make sure there was no one on board who would realise their deception."

The captain looked at Mr Fothergill. "Does it change anything?"

Mr Fothergill paused. "Not at all."

"Very well." Captain Robertson stood up. "As things stand, the Askwiths have denied any involvement in the theft, and for the time being, we're going to let them think we believe them. It won't be for long, but I'd like to be closer to New York before we apprehend them. Until then, no one will be told the outcome of the enquiry." He glanced around the table. "The five of us, plus my wife, are the only ones who know, so if I hear that anyone else has been told of the decision, I'll know where to look. If anyone asks, tell them we haven't reached a verdict. Is that clear?"

"Yes, sir." Nell's voice was drowned out by Mr Ramsbottom's.

"Good." The captain turned to Mr Price. "Would you outline the change of duties for Mrs Riley and Mr Ramsbottom?"

"Sir." He looked across the table at the two of them. "Mrs Riley, it's clear you can't continue servicing the Askwiths' or Hampsons' staterooms. The easiest way is to do a straight swap, which will minimise the risk of you meeting either couple."

"Won't I still see them in the dining room or saloon?"

"There is that possibility, but if you serve the ladies' sections only, it should keep you out of contact with them. You won't need to serve at morning coffee or afternoon tea. Captain Robertson has asked that you spend more time with his wife."

Nell finally smiled. "I'd be delighted to."

Captain Robertson interrupted. "If you spend the time you'd normally be in the saloon with my wife, we'd both appreciate it."

"Yes, Captain."

Mr Price let his gaze fall on Mr Ramsbottom. "This whole incident has obviously had less of an impact on you and so we expect you to carry on with your normal routine."

"Even providing a valet service to Lord ... I mean, Mr Askwith?"

"Indeed, although with one difference. Whenever you're in their stateroom, try not to talk unless you're asked a question. We need you to listen. Ask questions yourself to get Mr Askwith talking. Most particularly, ask him what they'll be doing in New York. See if he lets anything slip."

The captain walked to the door and rested a hand on the doorknob. "Thank you, everyone. We need to prepare for dinner. And please, not a word to anyone."

# CHAPTER TWENTY-THREE

The ship had been passing the island of Nantucket that morning when Nell made her way across the deck, and she was hurrying to finish the guests' packing so she could go outside to glimpse Long Island before afternoon tea.

Mrs Turner watched as she packed the last of the hat boxes into her trunk and lowered the lid carefully.

"There we are. Let me check we've not left anything." Nell reached into the wardrobe but stopped as she felt a long, thin case. "Oh my, what's this? More jewellery?"

Mrs Turner put a hand to her mouth. "My hatpins."

"Goodness, it's a good job we found them."

"It is, although there's always one in my hat, and I carry a spare in my handbag. You can't be too careful."

Nell chuckled. "I'll take your word for it. I never have much need for them. This hat stays on by itself."

"Maybe one day, you'll develop a fondness for the more extravagant." Mrs Turner patted the floral creation on her head. "I'd be lost without mine."

"Perhaps I will." Nell checked the room. "That should do it. I'll tell the stewards they can collect the trunk when they're ready. I'd like to pop onto the deck before afternoon tea."

Mrs Turner reached into her bag. "I may do the same, but before you go, I wanted to give you this." She drew out her purse and handed Nell two crown coins.

"Thank you, that's very kind."

"It's no more than you deserve after the trouble you've been through. I hope the Hampsons apologised."

Nell creased the side of her lip. "They tried the other evening, but Mr Hampson was only saying what his wife told him to. I've kept out of their way ever since."

"Mrs Hampson's very upset about the way her husband dragged you into it."

"I don't doubt it." Nell glanced down at the coins and dropped them into her apron pocket. "Anyway, it's over now. Thank you again for this. I'll see you in the saloon."

She hurried to the foyer, relieved Mrs Swift was waiting for her by the outside door.

"Sorry I'm late."

"I've only been here a minute myself. I'll get our cloaks." Mrs Swift stepped into the cloakroom, but immediately reappeared as a screech pierced the air.

"What was that?"

"I don't know."

A second scream sounded, and they both darted towards the port-side staterooms, stopping as soon as they saw Captain Robertson and Mr Price with the Askwiths.

"They must have told them."

"Told them what?" Mrs Swift stared at her, but Nell put a finger to her lips as a crowd gathered.

"I'll tell you later."

They watched as the captain ushered the Askwiths into their stateroom, but once the door slammed behind them, Nell turned to leave.

"If we want to go on deck, we'd better go now. Service is in half an hour."


On the dot of seven, the Fothergills were the first to arrive for dinner and Nell smiled as they took their seats.

"Good evening. Are you all ready to leave?"

"We are." Mrs Fothergill smiled. "I hadn't realised how many dresses we'd squeezed into the wardrobe, but they're packed now."

Mr Fothergill put a napkin on his lap. "You may be interested to know that Captain Robertson has informed our couple about the results of our enquiries."

"I guessed as much. We heard Mrs Askwith screaming from the foyer."

"That was most unfortunate. We could have kept it quiet, but as it is, everyone wants to know what happened."

"They've only themselves to blame."

"Indeed. Now, enough of them. For our final night we'll have three champagne cocktails to toast a job well done."

"You deserve it, sir."

Mr Brennan looked up as Nell joined him. "Champagne?"

Nell grinned. "Three."

"Splendid. The daughter obviously changed his mind

over the week. It's quite something to move from Pimms to champagne cocktails."

"She looks much happier than she did when she arrived, so the Pimms must have done her good."

Mr Brennan polished the glasses. "Don't forget to encourage everyone to order an extra drink, with it being the last night. It makes them more generous."

"I'll try my best."

Dinner was ending as Nell and Mrs Swift stood by the galley.

"I hope they all want an early night, tonight." Nell glanced around the room. "Have you had many tips yet?"

"A few. What about you?"

Nell sighed. "I'm beginning to think all the rumours about me and the jewellery have put everyone off. Not only that, despite all the running around I did for the Askwiths, I won't get anything now."

"Nor from the Hampsons, I shouldn't wonder."

Nell groaned. "This will end up being the worst trip money-wise, and the one where I've had the most grief."

"It happens sometimes. Hopefully, you'll get more on the way home."

"I'd better. Shall we collect up the dessert dishes?"

They split up as Nell headed to the Fothergills' table.

"Are you all finished?"

"Thank you. It was lovely." Mrs Fothergill dabbed her lips with her napkin.

"I'll tell Chef. He always likes to hear when guests enjoy his food. Now, if you'd like to go up to the saloon, we're serving coffee and liqueurs until nine o'clock. There'll only be a basic breakfast in the morning, because many guests are keen to disembark."

"Won't we see you?" Mrs Fothergill's face dropped.

"I'll be serving the tea and coffee, but we don't do the usual service. Just porridge or toast."

Mr Fothergill stood up. "I'd better give you this now, then." He handed her an envelope.

"Oh, sir. You really didn't need to. You did more than enough as it was."

"Seeing justice done was as important to me as you. You deserve something for what you went through."

Nell gave a slight bow. "Well, thank you. I really do appreciate it."

Once the money was in her pocket, she gathered up the plates and headed to the galley. She was about to return to the tables when Mr Hampson approached with his wife close behind.

"Good evening, Mrs Riley."

Nell clasped her hands in front of her. "Mr Hampson."

He stood up straight with his hands in front of him. "I won't beat around the bush. I owe you an apology. I shouldn't have jumped to conclusions and I'm sorry."

"Thank you, sir. It hasn't been easy."

"I knew those Askwiths were up to no good. Rubbed me up the wrong way right from the start, he did."

"They had us all fooled."

"They did that. I hope the police are waiting for them when they leave the ship."

"I suspect they will be. Now, if you'll excuse me, I need to get these tables tidied."

"One minute." He reached into his inside pocket. "Please accept this by way of an apology, and a thank you for your service before all this nonsense started." He handed her a gold sovereign.

"That's very generous of you."

"It's the least I can do. Right, now I've said my piece, good evening, Mrs Riley."

The wind whipped around the deck as Nell stepped outside the following morning and she grabbed hold of her hat as she peered over the side of the ship. The port of New York looked bleak in the grey light of dusk, and she didn't dwell by the railings as spots of rain landed on her face. Mrs Swift was already ahead of her, and she hurried to keep up.

"I'm glad we won't be going outside today."

"You and me both."

They raced to first class, and Nell shuddered as she took off her cloak. Mr Price was in the foyer when they walked through.

"Good morning, ladies. Are you ready to bid farewell to our passengers?"

Nell smiled. "Most certainly." *Good riddance, more like.* "Has the captain made arrangements for escorting Mr and Mrs Askwith from the ship?"

"They'll stay in their stateroom until the rest of the first-class passengers have disembarked, then he'll escort them to the waiting police officers."

"Thank goodness for that."

"Quite. Captain has asked us to hurry breakfast for the rest of the passengers so he can hand them over."

"Yes, sir."

Mr Ross was in the galley when they arrived. "Morning, ladies."

"Good morning. Do you have Mrs Robertson's tray ready?"

"I do. You'd better be quick, though. The passengers will be arriving shortly."

Nell rolled her eyes. "I know." She picked up the tray and headed for the foyer. *Dare I go down the port-side corridor? It's quicker than going the other way round.* She pursed her lips. *Why not? The Hampsons have apologised and the Askwiths will be in their stateroom.*

The first of the guests had distracted Mr Price, and she turned right while he wasn't looking. *There. Nobody around.*

Mrs Robertson was still groggy when she arrived. "Leave the tray on the table. I hardly got a wink of sleep last night."

"Oh dear. Let me pour you a cup of tea before I go. I'm afraid you'll be like that until the baby arrives. It won't be long now, though." Nell kept her eyes on the teapot. "There we are. I'm sorry to rush off, but the passengers were already arriving when I left the dining room. I'll see you later."

Nell closed the door behind her at the same time as Mrs Turner stepped into the corridor.

"Good morning, madam. Are you ready to leave?"

"I am, thank you. A bowl of porridge and a pot of tea will be enough for this morning. My friend's husband is meeting me at ten o'clock and we'll have something to eat when I arrive at their house."

"How lovely." Nell stopped as Mr Price walked towards them carrying a large tray. He didn't smile.

"What are you doing in this corridor, Mrs Riley?"

"I ... erm ... I've just taken Mrs Robertson's tray, and it's quicker this way."

"Well, hurry up. I don't want the Askwiths seeing you."

"Yes, sir. Will you excuse me, Mrs Turner?"

"Certainly, dear. I'm afraid I can't rush at my age."

Breakfast was over by nine o'clock but as she stood in the foyer with Mrs Swift, Nell's heart was racing. *I don't know why I'm here. I could have stayed in the dining room to tidy up.*

Mrs Swift nudged her. "Cheer up. At least you won't have to see any of them again."

"I've got to stand here while everyone smirks at me, though. I'm sure half of them still think I took the jewellery."

"Nonsense. You'd be under lock and key instead of the Askwiths if you had."

"I just hope they stay locked up until I'm back downstairs. I've no desire to see them again."

"Well, you can relax for now." Mrs Swift nodded to the Fothergills.

"Mrs Riley." Mr Fothergill smiled as he approached. "I hope you have a more enjoyable return journey."

"Thank you, sir. I don't think it can be much worse. I hope you get chance to relax in New York."

"I'm sure we will." He put on his hat and Nell stared

after them as they left, almost missing the Hampsons as they scurried past on their way to the gangplank.

Mrs Swift grinned at her. "See. You needn't have worried. They looked more uncomfortable than you."

"We've not finished yet."

They smiled and bade farewell to the remaining passengers, until the crew were the only ones left in the foyer. Nell drew her eyebrows together.

"Did I miss Mrs Turner?"

"Now you mention it, she hasn't arrived. Did you tell her she had to be off the ship before ten?"

"I did. I wonder where she is. Should I ask the captain if he wants me to go and help her?"

Mrs Swift sniggered. "Anything to get you out of the way before the Askwiths arrive."

"It's nothing of the sort."

Captain Robertson was about to dismiss the first mate when she joined them.

"Excuse me, Captain, but I noticed that Mrs Turner hasn't left the ship yet. Would you like me to look for her?"

Captain Robertson sucked air through his teeth. "You'd better. We need everyone out of first class before we deal with the Askwiths. Be as quick as you can. I need to stay here until everyone's disembarked."

Nell hurried to Mrs Turner's stateroom and knocked on the door. "Mrs Turner, are you there?" When she got no answer, she popped her head inside. *Empty.* She tried the rooms on either side. *Where's she got to?* She scratched her head as she surveyed the corridor but stopped as six uniformed guards walked towards her.

"G-good afternoon, gentlemen. May I help?"

"The captain told us to wait outside room fifteen."

"Ah. That's just down there on the left." She stepped to the wall to let them pass but did a double take as Mr Ramsbottom brought up the rear.

"Have you seen the size of them? I wouldn't like to challenge any one of them, let alone all six."

"I'm not surprised. Why are you with them? I thought Captain Robertson wanted to hand the Askwiths over."

"I'm looking for you. Haven't you found Mrs Turner yet?"

Nell's cheeks flushed. "I don't know where she is. She's not in her stateroom."

"Have you checked the WCs?"

"Not yet. I'll do that now. Will you send my apologies to the captain?" She turned to walk to the far end of the corridor but hesitated as the men blocked the way. "Oh, actually ... would you escort me?"

His eyes sparkled. "It's always a pleasure. Stick with me."

Nell's right arm brushed against the wall as she followed Mr Ramsbottom past the guards, her heartbeat pounding in her ears as six pairs of eyes studied her. As soon as she turned the corner at the far end of the corridor, she paused for breath.

"I'm not going back that way."

"They didn't say anything."

Nell stared at him. "They didn't have to."

He tutted. "You shouldn't take any notice. Are you going to check the facilities now you're here?"

"Give me a minute." She straightened her uniform and walked to the first WC. "Mrs Turner, are you in there?" She gave a robust knock. "Mrs Turner." She waited a moment before pushing on the door. *Locked.* "Mrs Turner. Is it you in there?"

Mr Ramsbottom banged his fist on the door. "Mrs Turner. Stand away from the door, I'm coming in." He stepped back to take a run-up but before he moved, the door opened.

"Mrs Turner." Nell pushed through the door to keep it open. "Are you all right?"

"I'm sorry, dear. I was using the facilities."

"I'm afraid you needed to be off the ship a quarter of an hour ago."

Mrs Turner's cheeks flushed. "I didn't mean to cause any trouble. I was just hoping to see the Askwiths arrested while I was here."

Nell grimaced. "I'm afraid Captain Robertson can't escort them from the ship until all the passengers are off. He's waiting for you."

"Oh dear. I am sorry."

"Not to worry, we've found you now." Nell offered her an arm. "Shall we go?" She spoke to Mr Ramsbottom as they left. "I'll take her the other way."

He nodded. "I'll tell the captain you're on your way."

Nell tried to steer Mrs Turner to the starboard corridor, but was pulled in the opposite direction as Mrs Turner headed towards the Askwiths' stateroom.

"Are they the men who've come for them?"

"They are. They're waiting for Captain Robertson to unlock the room. We're going to walk the other way round."

"So, I'll miss all the fun?"

Nell tutted. "I'd hardly call it fun."

By the time they reached the foyer, only the first mate was waiting for them. "There you are, Mrs Turner. You had us worried."

"I'm sorry, Officer. I just needed to use the facilities. Has Captain Robertson disappeared?"

"I'm afraid he had some rather pressing business. Now, if you're suitably refreshed, perhaps I can escort you down the gangplank."

He offered her his arm, but they hadn't reached the door when there was a shout from behind them.

"Out of the way." One of the guards burst into the foyer immediately followed by Mr Askwith, who had his hands and feet shackled and his right arm bent up his back by a second guard.

He grimaced as he passed Nell and Mrs Turner but said nothing as a third guard followed him from the ship. A second later, another guard appeared, this time leading Mrs Askwith. She kicked and squirmed as her guard gripped her arms.

"Get off me, you brute. Do you know who I am?"

Mrs Turner sniggered. "I don't think he cares."

"You!" Mrs Askwith stared at Mrs Turner and then Nell. "And you. You should hang for this. You planted those jewels in my room."

Nell took a step back as the last guard looked her up and down. "I-I did no such thing."

"Well, it wasn't me, I'll get you..."

"You'll do no such thing." Mrs Turner stepped forward, staring Mrs Askwith in the eye. "You're the one who should hang." She stepped back as Mrs Askwith shrieked. "That's for Mrs Riley."

183

Mrs Askwith's legs crumpled. "What have you done? My leg, it won't work." Her guard yanked her to her feet.

"You can walk just fine."

She screamed as he twisted her arm. "Stop it, you're going to break it." She kicked out again, only for the chains to trip her up. "Get off me. You'll be hearing from my solicitor."

Nell stood by Mrs Turner and Mr Ramsbottom as Captain Robertson escorted the final guard from the ship. They followed them to the door to see two carriages waiting for them.

Nell turned to Mrs Turner. "What did you do to her?"

"Just a little prick in the leg as a reminder of her voyage." There was a glint in her eye as she reattached her hatpin to her hat. "It was no more than she deserved."

The first mate once again offered Mrs Turner his arm. "I'm going to pretend I didn't hear a word of that. Now, if you'll come with me, it really is time you were off the ship."

Mr Ramsbottom took a step closer to Nell as they watched the old lady leave. "What a to-do that was. She's a feisty lady, I'll give her that."

"She certainly is."

"You'll never guess what Mr Brennan told me, either."

She looked up at him. "What?"

"They didn't even pay their bar bill."

Nell's mouth fell open. "After all the whisky and cocktails?"

"Exactly. Mr Brennan's furious."

"How did they get away with that?"

Mr Ramsbottom shrugged. "They had no money, not

real money, anyway. They paid by bank draft, but it was a forgery."

"How do people have the nerve to do such things?"

"Your guess is as good as mine. It probably explains her dowdy clothes and lack of jewellery."

"I feel such a fool for believing her."

Mr Ramsbottom put an arm around her shoulder and guided her to the stairs. "Don't be too hard on yourself; a lot of us fell for it. Even the captain."

"That's true. Thank goodness we had Mr Fothergill on board. They'd have got away with it all if it hadn't been for him."

"And you'd have taken the blame. Come on, I think we deserve a cup of tea before we do any cleaning."

## CHAPTER TWENTY-FOUR

The two days in port had passed quickly, and Nell once again stood with Mrs Swift as they waited for Captain Robertson and the new passengers to arrive.

"I can't believe we've so many empty staterooms on this voyage. Maybe we'll get some time off."

Mrs Swift snorted. "I doubt it. They'll probably have us cleaning the ship from top to bottom ... and we won't even get any tips for it."

Nell sighed. "I'd forgotten about that. Still, you can't blame passengers for wanting to spend Christmas in New York rather than England. I know I would if I had the chance."

"I just want to get home quickly. My sister's letter may have said that Mother was feeling better, but I can't help worrying she won't be around for much longer."

"We've only two weeks to go."

Mrs Swift nodded as Captain Robertson arrived.

"Good morning, ladies and gentlemen. Are we all ready to welcome our new guests?" When he received a positive response, he clapped his hands together. "Splendid."

The first to arrive were all men, and although Nell watched the captain shake their hands, she paid little attention until a middle-aged woman with a shock of mousy brown hair stepped into the foyer ahead of a tall, thin man. He took off his hat as he approached the captain to reveal a balding head with a layer of hair combed over the top. Nell stepped closer to Mrs Swift and lowered her voice.

"Would you say they're married?"

"They don't look very well-suited."

"That's what I thought." Nell nodded towards the woman. "She's carrying her own bag. It looks heavy, too."

"They'd better not be married then." Mrs Swift smirked. "What's the point in having a husband if he doesn't carry the bags?"

Nell suppressed a chuckle. "I don't remember there being any single women ... ooh, I'm being summoned."

Captain Robertson extended an arm towards her. "Mrs Riley. This is Mr and Mrs Davenport. Mrs Davenport requires daily help in her stateroom."

Nell nodded. "Certainly, sir." She smiled at her new passengers. "If you'd like to walk this way." She checked the guest list on her way past. "Stateroom eleven. About halfway down the corridor. May I take your bag?"

Mrs Davenport pulled her arm away. "I can manage."

"Very well." *I hope it's not full of jewellery.* "What sort of service will you require, madam?"

"I'll be taking my meals in the stateroom."

"All of them?" Nell's eyes widened as she looked to Mr Davenport. "Both of you?"

"I'll dine with the rest of the passengers. My wife prefers to eat alone."

*How strange.* "That can be arranged easily enough."

"I'll join my husband for morning coffee and afternoon tea, so I won't trouble you for that. I do like a nice piece of meat at each meal, though. No fish."

"Not even the lobster? That really is delicious."

"No, thank you. I know what I like."

"As you wish." Nell opened the stateroom door and held it open as the Davenports followed her in.

"Very nice." Mrs Davenport glanced around the room, eying up the arrangement of the wardrobe and dresser on the wall opposite the door. After some deliberation, she placed the bag in the gap between the two. "I'll be here when you come in to clean. I don't want you touching that."

"There's no need for you to stay. I won't touch anything you don't want me to."

"I'd rather be here, but I want you here as soon as breakfast is over, so I can get on with my day."

"Yes, madam." Nell eyed the bag. "If that's all, I'll let you settle in."

Mrs Swift was missing when Nell returned to the foyer, and she waited while the captain spoke to a group of American men about the virtues of Liverpool. Mrs Swift distracted her when she reappeared.

"Where've you been?"

"Stateroom twelve. A Mr and Mrs Young. They're on their way home after visiting family in New York."

"You'd think they'd stay over Christmas, wouldn't you?" Nell watched as Mr Cooper led another group of gents away from the captain. "If I had family over here, they wouldn't get rid of me."

Mrs Swift nudged her. "Another couple."

Nell smiled at an elderly man and his wife as they shuffled towards the captain. "I imagine they'll need assistance."

"It must be Mr and Mrs Hunter. Everyone else has arrived."

"They'll be with you, then. It's as well, given I've got Mrs Davenport. I've a feeling she'll keep me busy."

Mrs Swift didn't have time to answer before Captain Robertson called her over. As she disappeared down the far corridor, Nell made her way to the saloon, where Mr Ramsbottom waited by the door.

"Have you got anyone interesting?"

"Not really. One eccentric woman, Mrs Davenport, who must have something valuable in her bag, because she won't leave it unattended. She wants to eat every meal in her cabin, too. In fact, I'd better tell Mr Ross she wants today's luncheon in there."

"She'll change her mind when she sees the dining room."

"I'm not sure she'll even get that far."

"You and Mrs Swift will be quiet, then. There are not many ladies on board."

"That's what we're hoping."

Mrs Davenport was sitting at the writing desk when Nell arrived with her luncheon.

"Ah, Mrs Riley. Splendid." She stood up as Nell put the tray on the table near the settee. "It is meat, isn't it?"

"A pork chop with mashed potato and carrots." Nell surveyed the still tidy room. "Do you need any help unpacking your trunk after luncheon?"

"Not at all. I'm perfectly capable. What time do we sail?"

"Not until four o'clock."

"Ah, so long."

"We need to board all the steerage passengers, not to mention the food and drinks for the voyage."

"Of course, I wasn't thinking."

Nell smiled. "If you'd care to go on deck after luncheon, there's a wonderful view of the port."

"I was going to wait until we sail away."

"It may be dark by then..."

"I'm sure I'll manage." Mrs Davenport ushered Nell to the door and pushed her into the corridor. "Thank you, Mrs Riley. I'll see you later."

Nell flinched as the door slammed behind her. *What a strange woman.*

With a shrug, she returned to the dining room where the Youngs and Hunters were waiting for Mrs Swift to deliver their drinks. *Will it be like this for the next two weeks? I'm glad I'll be taking Mrs Robertson her tray.*

Mr Ross was plating up the meals when Nell went into the galley. "Was she happy with the pork chop?"

"She seemed to be, although she didn't actually look at it. Such an unusual woman."

"As long as she doesn't complain, I'll be happy." He

sliced into a large tray of fish pie. "I'll have Mrs Robertson's ready for you in a minute."

"There's no rush."

Mrs Swift joined Nell as she waited. "This will be rather different from the last voyage. The Hunters only want a pot of tea and the Youngs are on sherry but have asked for cordial with their meal."

Nell tutted. "Mr Brennan won't be happy."

"He's not. The men aren't drinking much, either."

Mr Ross covered Mrs Robertson's plate. "We'll have to entertain ourselves, then. A sweepstake on how long it will be before Mrs Davenport visits the dining room, perhaps?"

Nell rolled her eyes. "It will take more than that."

## CHAPTER TWENTY-FIVE

Nell and Mrs Swift stood on the first-class promenade watching the crowds as men untied the ropes on the quay below.

"I wish I could stay out here for the sail-away." Nell sighed. "I don't know why Mrs Davenport wouldn't wait for afternoon tea."

Mrs Swift straightened up. "I'll come with you. This wind will stop the rest of them being out here for long, too."

"It will once the ship starts moving." Nell held open the outside door and hung up their cloaks before they walked over to the saloon. Mr and Mrs Davenport were already seated when they arrived, and she smiled as she approached them.

"Good afternoon. You're nice and early."

Mrs Davenport shifted in her seat. "My stomach's rumbling."

"Ah." Nell glanced at the clock. "We don't usually start serving until four o'clock, but I'll make an exception today. I can see the tea and sandwiches are here."

She didn't wait for a reply before she bustled over to Mrs Swift. "She's hungry already, and it's not long since she finished luncheon."

Mrs Swift chuckled. "We'll have to hope she doesn't eat all the sandwiches before everyone else arrives, then."

Nell picked up one of the platters. "There are plenty to go round."

Mrs Davenport's eyes were on Nell as she walked across the room, and she helped herself to a selection of sandwiches before her husband took his.

"They're so small."

"They're our usual size ... and there are cakes to follow."

"I should hope so."

Nell held onto the back of a chair as the ship jolted. "We must be moving."

"Excellent." Mrs Davenport's shoulders relaxed. "The sooner we're away from here, the better."

"Don't you like New York?"

"Oh, I didn't mean that. I'm just eager to get going."

"I'm sure you are." She turned to leave, but Mrs Davenport called her back.

"I'll take a couple more sandwiches before you go ... to save your legs."

Nell returned to Mrs Swift with her half-empty platter. "You weren't wrong about them eating everything."

"We needn't worry about running out. The Hunters didn't want much. I've just been to their table, and they only took two little triangles each."

Nell studied the elderly couple. "Mrs Hunter does look rather frail. I bet she'll enjoy the cakes."

Mrs Swift chuckled. "Don't they all. I'm just waiting for the Youngs now, and that's my lot."

"You'll still be busier than me." Nell studied the near empty saloon. "I need to take Mrs Robertson's tray. Would you serve the Davenports so I can go now? It will save you getting bored."

Mrs Swift picked up a platter of sandwiches as her last guests arrived. "I think I can manage that. Don't be too long, though. I'll need someone to talk to."

Mrs Robertson was sitting on the settee when Nell arrived with her tray.

"What are you doing out of bed?"

"I was bored and decided it couldn't do me any harm. I've not been anywhere else."

Nell put the tray on the table. "I hope Matron doesn't see you or I'll be in trouble."

Mrs Robertson sighed. "I'm tired of her shouting at everything I do. I know she means well, but I'm not a child."

"She's only doing her job." Nell took the hard-backed chair opposite and poured two cups of tea. "How are you feeling?"

"Other than being bored and uncomfortable, I'm fine. I'm glad we're finally on our way home, too. I'd rather not have the baby on the ship."

"Have you decided where you'll go when you get back to Liverpool?"

Mrs Robertson put a hand to her chest. "Thankfully, my husband contacted head office when we were in port and they're going to arrange a house for us."

"That's good of them."

"It is, but I'd like him to send another telegram when we reach Queenstown. I'd like to know that everything's arranged before we arrive in Liverpool."

"He should be able to do that. Queenstown's a lot closer to Liverpool than New York is."

Mrs Robertson stared into her cup. "That's what I'm hoping."

Afternoon tea was over by the time Nell got back to the saloon, and most of the tables had been cleared. She took Mrs Robertson's empty tray to the table where Mrs Swift was stacking the dirty plates.

"Did I miss anything?"

"Not really. Mrs Davenport had some more sandwiches before having several cakes."

"I don't know where she put it all. She's not exactly large."

Mrs Swift shrugged. "Who knows? Anyway, she wanted me to check you'd be prompt with her tray this evening."

"I'd better be. How were the Youngs?"

"Nice enough. Not that they said very much. I wondered if they'd argued before they came to the saloon, because I don't think I saw them utter a word to each other."

"Oh, dear. That's never a good sign..." Nell paused as Mr Ramsbottom arrived at her side.

"Mrs Riley. I was wondering where you were."

"For any particular reason?"

"Do you need to ask?" He grinned as Nell rolled her

eyes. "If you must know, I wondered if you'd both like to join us on deck to watch the sail-away. Mr Cooper and Mr Hancock have already gone."

Nell glanced around the room. "I wondered where everyone was."

"We've decided it's so quiet, we don't all need to be here."

"Has Mr Price agreed that?"

"Not only has he agreed, he said he'd stay and hold the fort." He placed the last stack of plates onto the dumb waiter and tapped the wall. "Shall we go?"

Dusk was falling as they walked onto the deck and the light was made worse as black smoke from the chimney billowed out above them. A small group of steerage passengers clustered around the back of the ship as they glided between the banks of the river. Mr Cunningham was supervising them, and Mr Ramsbottom waved as they strolled towards Mr Cooper and Mr Hancock.

*Thank goodness it isn't Mr Marsh over there.* She hung behind with Mrs Swift as Mr Ramsbottom joined his colleagues, but he turned and beckoned them forward.

"Don't be shy. It's not often we get to talk to each other about anything other than food and drink."

"Not that we should be." Mr Cooper bounced on the balls of his feet. "If it were down to me..."

"Well, it isn't." Mr Ramsbottom glared at his colleague. "I've told you to relax about these things."

"We're paid to keep passengers segregated..."

"Passengers, not crew, now enough."

Mr Hancock grinned at Nell. "Good afternoon, Mrs Riley. I've not seen much of you this voyage."

Nell shivered as the wind caught the bottom of her cloak. "I'm sorry I got you into trouble. I'd no idea Mr Marsh had seen us getting into the carriage ... or that he'd be back on the ship. Not that it gave him any right to be upset."

"It wasn't your fault."

"It was Mr Marsh's." Mr Cooper plunged his hands into his jacket pockets. "He's got a soft spot for you and doesn't like you talking to us."

"It's nothing to do with him." Nell's cheeks flushed.

"No, it's not." Mr Ramsbottom tucked a stray piece of hair under his hat. "At least he's back in steerage now."

"He should never have been brought into first class." Nell spoke through gritted teeth. "Do you know why he was?"

Mr Ramsbottom shrugged. "All I heard was that he'd had enough of being downstairs."

"It's hardly a good enough excuse to reorganise all the stewards and put Mr Hancock in charge of steerage. Was anything said to you, Mr Hancock?"

"Nothing. I thought it was strange, but I wasn't going to complain about getting a promotion."

"Didn't they give you an explanation?"

"No. Mr Marsh was in Mr Price's office for a long time when he came back, but I thought it was to discuss where he'd been and why he stormed off."

Nell pulled her cloak more tightly around her. "It may well have been, but given all that, why reward him with a move upstairs? There's something not right." She wandered to the side of the ship with Mrs Swift and looked over the water at the receding buildings.

"It's a grand view, isn't it?" Mr Ramsbottom joined them.

"It is. It's a shame we didn't get another visit."

Mr Hancock stood behind them. "Did you all go ashore?"

"We did, and it was wonderful." Nell smiled at him. "Have you been ashore yourself?"

"Not in New York. I got off in Boston once, when I did that route. It's a nice place but very busy."

Nell recalled one of Jack's letters from when he'd stopped there. "So I believe."

Mr Cooper's voice cut through the air behind them. "They should be inside by now." His stare was fixed on the steerage passengers. "Cunningham's too bothered about looking over here." He took out his pocket watch and waved it to the other steward.

"He's got his eyes on the ladies." Mr Ramsbottom stepped in front of Nell and Mrs Swift. "He won't be used to having them on board."

Mr Cooper ignored him as he continued to wave his watch. "Oi, Cunningham, have you seen the time?"

"We'll be gone in a minute. I'm waiting for Mr Marsh."

*Oh no.* Nell stepped out from behind Mr Ramsbottom. "I need to go. I don't want him seeing us together."

"Too late." Mr Cooper seemed to relish the appearance of Mr Marsh. "He won't be happy when we see him later."

"He's not happy now." Mr Ramsbottom smirked as he waved across the deck. "Don't worry, I'll look after her."

A tightening seized Nell's chest, and she coughed as she remembered to breathe. *Oh my goodness. He's coming over.*

"Are you all right?" Mrs Swift took her arm.

"I need to get inside."

"Mr Ramsbottom's only goading him."

"Well, I'd rather he didn't. Mr Marsh is bound to blame me for being out here."

"Don't be silly, we won't let him."

"That won't make any difference." She linked Mrs Swift's arm. "Will you escort me to the saloon? There'll still be land to see tomorrow."

# CHAPTER TWENTY-SIX

M r Brennan was preparing the bar when they went into the saloon, but with one look at Nell, he put down his tea towel.

"What's the matter?"

Nell shook her head. "Mr Ramsbottom and Mr Marsh. They were squaring up to each other on the deck."

"Over you?" He glanced at Mrs Swift. "Blimey. There'll be hell to pay when we get back to our bunks tonight."

Mrs Swift rested a hand on the table beside them. "Do they really argue?"

"They would if they could, but the rest of us usually tell them to be quiet. If Mr Marsh is in one of his sulks, though, it isn't pleasant."

"I've told her, the best thing to do is forget about them." Mrs Swift studied Nell.

"It's easy for you to say."

"Only because they know where they stand with me. I've told you often enough that you need to stop being so friendly."

"I try my best, but..." Nell paused as the stewards joined them. Mr Ramsbottom's face couldn't contain his grin.

"Why did you run away?"

"Because I didn't want to be involved."

"What happened?" Mr Brennan leaned over the bar, but Mr Ramsbottom's shoulders slumped.

"Nothing much in the end. As soon as Mrs Riley disappeared, he backed off."

"I knew he was coming over to chide me." Nell coughed as the pitch of her voice rose. "He'll think it was all my fault for being outside in the first place."

"You're allowed on the deck." Mr Ramsbottom cracked his knuckles. "I'll have a word with him tonight."

"Please don't cause any trouble." She turned to Mr Hancock. "You won't let him, will you?"

"I'm keeping out of it. I don't want to lose my job."

"It's not you who needs worry."


Mr and Mrs Davenport were first in the saloon, and they sat at a table near the bar.

"Good evening, madam." Nell smiled at them. "Are you planning to eat in the dining room tonight?"

"Gracious no. I'm here for a pre-dinner drink, then I'll go to the stateroom. I'll let you know when I leave so you can bring the tray straight up."

"Yes, madam. What would you like to drink?"

"A gin cocktail, please."

"And a whisky for me." Mr Davenport sat back in his chair. "No water."

"Very good, sir." She stepped to the bar. "Did you hear the Davenports' order?"

"I wasn't paying attention."

"Hopefully that means they can't hear us." She turned to check. "A gin cocktail and a whisky. I'll offer Mrs Davenport another drink to have with her dinner. She'll have it in the stateroom."

"Strange woman."

"She is, but don't be rude to her. I've a feeling she'll be back tonight. She seems to dislike eating in public."

His brow furrowed. "There's something not right there."

"I know. If I didn't eat with other people, I'd starve."

He added the curaçao to the gin cocktail and fastened the shaker. "You and me both." Once it was well shaken, he poured the cocktail into a glass and pushed the tray towards Nell.

"Don't rinse the shaker." She stepped to the Davenports' table and set down the glasses. "There we are. I hope it's to your liking."

Mrs Davenport licked her lips. "Very pleasant."

"Would you like our barman to take one to your room to have with your meal?"

Mrs Davenport beamed as her husband gave a slight nod. "What a splendid idea. I shan't need to sip this so slowly."

Mr Ross almost dropped the pan he was carrying as Nell dashed into the galley.

"You're early."

"Mrs Davenport wants her tray in five minutes."

"She'll be lucky. The beefsteaks haven't gone in the oven yet."

"Can you do hers ahead of everyone else's?"

"I will, but it will still take at least quarter of an hour. She won't want blood inside it."

Nell shuddered. "No, she won't. Will you do Mrs Robertson's at the same time, to save me waiting?"

"Give me a minute." He threw two steaks onto a metal tray.

"Thank you." Nell glanced over her shoulder as Mr Hancock joined them.

"Good evening."

Mr Ross stared at the clock on the wall. "Has that stopped and I've not noticed?"

Mr Hancock laughed. "Don't panic. They didn't need me in the saloon, so I've come to see if there are any trays."

"Not tonight."

"Oh well, it will give us more to do in the dining room."

"You should be thankful you're not in steerage." Mr Ross laid the rest of the beefsteaks on a large baking tray. "I had Mr Marsh up here earlier telling me how quiet it is down there."

"Mr Marsh was up here?" A shiver ran down Nell's spine.

"Not for long. He was looking for Mr Price."

Nell glanced at Mr Hancock.

"What have I missed?" Mr Ross's eyes flicked between the two of them.

"Nothing. Not much anyway." Mr Hancock ran a hand through his dark blond hair.

"What's that supposed to mean?"

Nell sighed. "A few of us were on the deck earlier taking a last look at New York and Mr Marsh saw us."

Mr Ross's eyes widened. "The two of you?"

"Not just us. Mrs Swift and Mr Cooper were with us." Nell gulped. "And Mr Ramsbottom."

Mr Ross stared at Mr Hancock. "And you weren't going to tell me?"

"I'd have mentioned it later, but it became rather awkward." Mr Hancock stared at the floor. "Mr Marsh looked ready to hit Mr Ramsbottom, but thankfully he backed off."

Mr Ross blew out his cheeks. "That explains it."

"Do you think he'll report us?"

"Who knows with Mr Marsh? He won't let it lie, though."

Nell held onto the counter as her head spun. "Will you excuse me?"

"Are you all right?" Mr Hancock put an arm around her as she stumbled to the door.

"I need to sit down."

"Let me help you." He led her to the dining room, but they hadn't reached the first table when there was a snort.

"Mr Marsh! What on earth...?" She flopped into the nearest chair as Mr Marsh stormed towards the door. "That won't have looked very good."

Mr Hancock took the seat next to her as her hands shook.

"Why does he always pick on me?"

"Let me get you a brandy. You look as if you could do with one."

"I can't drink while I'm working."

"You'll do as you're told. If I see Mr Price, I'll explain you were having a turn, and I was helping you. Mr Ross will vouch for us." He stood up to go to the bar. "As soon as you're feeling better, I'll go and find him."

The brandy was warm as it slid down Nell's throat. "That's better."

Mr Hancock hovered over her. "Will you be all right?"

Nell cradled the brandy glass. "I think so. Just find Mr Price before Mr Marsh does."

She watched him leave, but flinched as Mr Ross walked up behind her. "How are you doing?"

"I'll be all right." She took a deep breath and finished her drink. "This is good stuff."

Mr Ross laughed. "It certainly is." He helped her from the chair. "Try not to be too long with Mrs Davenport. We don't want Mrs Robertson's food spoiling."

Nell took several deep breaths as she stood outside the Davenports' stateroom. *It's not your fault you're late.* Summoning her courage, she knocked on the door.

"Come in." Mrs Davenport was sitting on the settee with her half-finished gin cocktail on the table in front of her.

"I'm sorry I'm late. The chef had to cook the meat while I waited."

"Put it on the table. I'll see to it once you've gone."

Nell straightened the tray. "Would you care for another drink?"

"Not yet. I'll have another in the saloon."

"Very well. Enjoy your food." Nell reached for the doorknob but stopped and turned around. "What was that?"

Mrs Davenport lifted the cloche from the tray and clanged it onto the table. "What was what?"

"That noise."

"I didn't hear anything." She replaced the cloche over the plate. "If you'll excuse me, I'd like to eat in peace."

Nell stepped into the corridor and was about to close the door when she heard it again. Mrs Davenport's face flushed as she popped her head back into the room.

"Did you hear it that time?"

"Mrs Riley, please. There was no noise. Now, if you don't mind."

"I'm sorry." She pulled the door closed and ran her hands over her face. *That brandy must have gone to my head.* She straightened up at the sound of footsteps behind her.

"Is everything all right, Mrs Riley?"

"Oh, Mr Hancock, you startled me."

"I'm sorry." He indicated for them to walk. "I spoke to Mr Price and explained what Mr Marsh saw."

"Did you tell him we were on the deck?"

"I told him we'd bumped into each other up there and Mr Marsh jumped to the wrong conclusion, as he had in the dining room."

"What did he say?"

"Not much. He just thanked me for letting him know."

Nell released her breath. "That's a relief. Thank you. I need to put it out of my mind now. Can you believe I imagined Mr Marsh was snarling at me when I was in Mrs Davenport's stateroom?"

Mr Hancock laughed. "We really would know he was following you if that happened."

Nell chuckled. "Unless he was hiding in the wardrobe."

They were still laughing as they turned into the foyer, but Nell's smile disappeared as Mr Marsh glared at her from his place by the door.

"Mrs Riley."

Nell took a step backwards. "What are you doing here?"

He strode towards her. "I'd hoped to talk to you, but it appears you have another suitor. Why am I not surprised?"

Nell retreated to the wall as he sneered at her. "It's not..."

"Actually, it is." Mr Hancock put himself between Nell and Mr Marsh. "I'll be acting as Mrs Riley's chaperone, and once we get to Liverpool, we'll be walking out together."

Mr Marsh glowered at Mr Hancock before he elbowed him aside and glared at Nell. "You and *him*?"

Nell's eyes widened, but Mr Hancock pushed him on the shoulder. "Yes, and I'd be obliged if you'd leave her alone."

"I most certainly will." Mr Marsh pulled down the front of his jacket. "You always were far too popular with the men for there to be anything innocent about it. I've tried to give you the benefit of the doubt on more than one occasion, but not any more. Good evening."

# CHAPTER TWENTY-SEVEN

Mrs Davenport's tray felt heavy as Nell trudged down the corridor the following morning. If she'd slept a wink last night, she didn't remember it. The stateroom door was ajar when she knocked, and Mrs Davenport called for her to enter.

"Good morning, madam."

"Ah, Mrs Riley. Put the tray on the table, and I'll get out of bed to eat."

Nell did as she was told. "I thought you'd like to know the weather's rather pleasant, if you'd care to go onto the deck."

"Perhaps I will. I didn't venture out yesterday. Good day, Mrs Riley."

Nell wandered to the door before stopping. "What was that? It sounded like scratching."

Mrs Davenport straightened the bedcovers over her lap. "It's probably the ship's rats."

"Rats!" Nell jumped backwards. "I do apologise, but

there shouldn't be any up here. I'll get someone to come and check."

"Pull yourself together. There's no need for that."

"Forgive me for disagreeing, but our first-class guests won't want to come across vermin." Nell scanned the floor, but suddenly stared at Mrs Davenport. "Doesn't it worry you?"

"They'll be in the pipework. They won't get out."

"You don't know that." Nell tensed as the scratching got louder. "It's coming from the wardrobe."

"Nonsense. It must be behind it."

Nell hesitated as she clung to the doorknob. "Whether it is or not, I'm getting someone up here." She yanked open the door, but Mrs Davenport called her back.

"Please don't."

"What was that?"

"What was what?"

"When you shouted then, it sounded like a bark." Nell ran to the wardrobe and pulled open the doors. "Do you have a dog in here?"

"No, I don't." Mrs Davenport climbed out of bed and slammed the doors closed.

"Where is it, then?"

"Please, Mrs Riley. Let me explain." The scratching increased until Mrs Davenport retrieved the bag from the side of the wardrobe.

"It's in there?"

Nell's heart pounded as Mrs Davenport opened the top of the bag.

"I couldn't tell you earlier, but this is Miss Tiddles. She's a cocker spaniel."

Nell gasped. "How did you get her on board without anyone noticing?"

"A spot of brandy in her milk." A smug smile settled on Mrs Davenport's face as she lifted the dog from the bag. "It usually sends her to sleep for a couple of hours. Long enough to get past any officials."

"You've done it before?"

"Not with Miss Tiddles. I've only had her for six months."

"But you can't bring dogs on the ship. I'll have to report you."

"Please don't." Mrs Davenport ran a hand over the dog's well-groomed coat.

"It's more than my job's worth if I don't."

"But what can the captain do about it? We're in the middle of the ocean. It would make no sense to turn back."

"We're less than a day from New York and still close to land." Nell raised her arms and let them fall again. "We could dock at any number of ports before we head across the sea."

"That makes it even more important that you don't tell him. Please, Mrs Riley, look at her." She shoved Miss Tiddles towards her. "I couldn't bear to leave her at home and she's perfectly well behaved. Nobody will know she's here."

"But she's a dog. What about the *mess*?"

"Everything's taken care of."

"Is that why you eat your meals in here?"

"She has to eat." She nestled her face into the dog's fur. "You liked your steak last night, didn't you? Shall we see what we have this morning?"

"It's ham and eggs." Nell's voice was stern as Mrs Davenport lifted the cloche. "You've put me in a very difficult position. By rights I need to tell Captain Robertson so we can remove her."

Mrs Davenport bustled to the dresser. "You'll be well rewarded if you keep it between us." She offered Nell a gold sovereign. "There'll be another one for you at the end of the voyage if nobody finds out. You won't get into trouble, trust me. Besides my husband, we're the only ones who know."

Nell's hand hesitated as she reached for the coin. "You won't let her out of the room ... or let her cause any damage?"

"Of course not, but you need to make sure you're the only one who brings my tray or services the room."

Nell nodded. "Very well, but if I see any damage, I'll have to tell Captain Robertson."

"There won't be any." She wrinkled her nose at the dog. "You're a good girl, aren't you?"

Nell cringed as it barked. "Stop that; someone will hear."

"It's only because you're here. She's been very well behaved, so far. Now, if you wouldn't mind, we'd like our breakfast."

Nell closed the stateroom door and leaned against the wall of the corridor, turning the coin in her fingers. *Have I done the right thing?*

Mr Ross made a point of looking at the clock when she went into the galley. "About time, too. Where've you been?"

"Oh ... Mrs Davenport wanted to talk. Is Mrs Robertson's tray ready?"

"Mrs Swift had to take it. The eggs would have been hard."

"I'm sorry, I wasn't thinking."

Mr Ross leaned forward. "Are you all right? You look a bit peaky."

"I'm fine. I just didn't sleep well." *And I doubt I will tonight, either.*

Mr Ross grinned at her. "I heard about your confrontation with Mr Marsh."

Nell groaned. "I bet everyone did."

"That Mr Hancock's a dark horse."

"He was only trying to help..."

Mr Ross burst out laughing. "Help what? He's got Mr Ramsbottom *and* Mr Marsh after him now. They've been chasing you all year, and he suddenly announces he's walking out with you. What were you thinking?"

"It's not like that..."

The door to the galley swung open, and Mr Ramsbottom joined them. "Look who's here." He stared down at her. "Do you enjoy leading us all on?"

"I don't lead anyone on. There's been a misunderstanding."

"A likely story. And as for Hancock..."

"It was his idea."

"You could have said no, like you have to everyone else..."

"I had no choice..."

Mr Ross put two bowls of porridge on a tray. "Leave her alone. Mrs Riley, take this porridge to the Hunters."

"They're Mrs Swift's passengers."

"And she's covering for you. Now, off you go." He pushed the tray towards her.

Mr Ramsbottom's nostrils flared as he stood to one side. *What a start to the day.*

Mr and Mrs Hunter looked up as she reached them.

"Good morning." Nell managed a smile. "I'm afraid Mrs Swift had to go on an errand. I'm Mrs Riley." She rested the tray on the edge of the table and served the porridge. "She won't be long, but is there anything else I can get you?"

"Our pot of tea didn't arrive."

"I do apologise. Let me fetch one now."

Mrs Swift was in the galley when Nell returned.

"How was Mrs Robertson?"

"Disappointed not to see you, but otherwise fine."

"That's all right then. I'll visit her in a few hours. I need to take the Hunters their tea. They haven't had it yet."

Mrs Swift banged a hand on her forehead. "I completely forgot. I came in here to get it, but Mr Ross asked me to take the tray instead." She pulled the nearest teapot towards her, but Nell picked it up.

"I'll take it."

"That was for me." Mr Ramsbottom stepped in front of her, but she dodged round him.

"You can have the next one. The Hunters have been waiting at least fifteen minutes."

"So have the Youngs." Mrs Swift grimaced. "You'll have to wait for the one after that."

A vein pulsed in Mr Ramsbottom's temple. "Don't come over all high and mighty with me."

"We're not. All we're trying to do is keep the guests happy." Nell puffed out her cheeks as she left the galley, only finding a smile for the Youngs as she passed their table. "Mrs Swift will be with you in a moment."

Mrs Young's jaw clenched. "If she's not arrived by the time you've delivered that breakfast, would you enquire about our pot of tea? We'd rather not be here for longer than necessary."

"Yes, of course, madam. I'll be as quick as I can." She hurried on to the Hunters' table. "Here you are. I'm sorry about that. We're rather hectic this morning."

"Take your time, dear." Mrs Hunter rested her spoon in her dish. "Life's not worth rushing."

"Not that we can at our age." Mr Hunter chuckled as he patted his wife's hand.

"And we don't want to."

"What a lovely attitude. I'll try to remember that. May I get you anything else?"

"We ordered some French toast..."

"I'll bring it as soon as it's ready." She turned back to the Youngs but gave a sigh of relief as Mrs Swift appeared from the galley. *Splendid. Now breathe.* She strolled back to the galley but hadn't reached the door when Mr Hancock bundled her to one side.

"Are you all right?"

Nell shook her head. "Not really."

"I'm sorry about last night. I thought I was helping to keep Mr Marsh away from you, but it looks like I've upset a few of the others."

"It's not your fault ... and it was very thoughtful, but, well ... things are never straightforward around here."

"I know that now. How do you want to deal with it?"

"We can't discuss it here. I can already feel Mr

Ramsbottom's eyes boring into me. Could we meet somewhere quieter later?"

Mr Hancock glanced around the room. "How did you know he was there?"

She shrugged. "Instinct. I'll be on the first-class promenade this afternoon after we've eaten. We can talk there."

Nell scraped the last of her ice cream from the bowl and set down her spoon.

"Have you found out what the problem is between Mr and Mrs Young yet?"

"Not exactly, but I think it's because they're going home. Mrs Young keeps making cutting comments about how nice it would be in New York, rather than on a ship with no interesting passengers."

"She has a point. What does he say?"

"Not a lot. I suspect he keeps his comments until I'm out of earshot."

"That's annoying." Nell grinned. "You'll have to slow down as you leave the table. Or pretend to forget something and go back."

Mrs Swift rolled her eyes. "Or signal to you when I'm about to leave so you can walk past the table. I'm clearly not at your level yet."

Nell laughed. "You're getting better."

"I noticed you talking to Mr Hancock earlier. What was that about? You'll get yourself into trouble if you're not careful."

"I'm already in trouble." Nell glanced over her shoulder. "Can you keep something to yourself?"

"I usually do."

"I'm not really walking out with him. He only said what he did to stop Mr Marsh pursuing me."

Mrs Swift grimaced. "I bet he regrets it now."

"Quite probably." Nell sighed. "The thing is, I don't know what to do about it. Should we carry on with the charade and hope it keeps Mr Marsh out of the way, or admit it was a hoax?"

"Won't Mr Hancock want the latter?"

"You'd think so, but he's such a gentleman it wouldn't surprise me if he's happy to keep it going."

Mrs Swift raised an eyebrow. "You could do worse than walk out with him. He's certainly handsome enough."

Nell chuckled. "The thought had crossed my mind, but I don't want to take advantage of him when he was only doing me a favour. We'll have to admit it was a lie and hope Mr Marsh stays downstairs for the rest of the voyage."

"I imagine he will. If word spreads that Mr Hancock only offered to walk out with you to protect you from him, it should make even him realise you want nothing to do with him."

"I hadn't thought of that." Nell groaned. "I hate being so mean."

"Does it matter? You've already been honest with him and it didn't work."

"Still." Nell pushed herself up from the table. "I said I'd meet Mr Hancock outside. Will you come with me?"

· · ·

Mr Hancock was waiting at the far end of the deck when they arrived, and Mrs Swift walked with Nell to within ten feet of him. Nell smiled as she approached.

"Where are the other stewards?"

"Still in the dining room. The atmosphere was rather tense, so I came away as soon as I'd eaten."

"Thank you."

"Have you decided what you want to do?"

She bit her lip. "I think we should tell them it was a jape. I don't like you bearing the brunt of everyone's anger."

"But what about you?"

"I'll be fine as long as Mr Marsh stays in steerage."

Mr Hancock nodded. "If you're sure."

She held his gaze. "I am, but thank you, anyway. I appreciate what you did."

"It was my pleasure."

Nell flinched as a group of passengers walked past. "Right ... well ... will you tell them?"

"I suppose so." He grinned. "It was fun while it lasted."

"I don't think that's the word I'd use." She glanced over her shoulder. "We'd better split up before any of them come outside."

Mrs Swift sidled up to Nell as Mr Hancock disappeared. "I couldn't decide if he was relieved or disappointed."

"I'm sure it was relief." Nell stared out at the flat mass of land ahead. "I can't believe they all turned against him."

"Will you finally put a scowl on your face to keep them away?"

She sighed. "The way things are going, I've no reason to smile."

The landscape didn't change as they stood in silence, watching it glide by, but Nell's fingers were numb when Mr Ramsbottom and Mr Cooper disturbed their peace.

"So, it was all a prank to get at Mr Marsh?"

Nell's cheeks reddened. "It wasn't meant to go any further than him."

"He wouldn't keep that to himself. Have you seen him today?"

"I don't want to see him again. He does nothing but get me into trouble."

Mr Cooper raised himself up onto the balls of his feet. "I've always said you ladies should keep to your own section..."

"It's not easy when we only have one galley and most of the passengers are male."

He held up his hands. "All right, there's no need to snap."

*Stop being so stupid, then.*

Mr Ramsbottom took out his pocket watch as an uneasy silence settled. "Have you seen the time? We'll need to prepare the saloon for afternoon tea soon."

Nell pushed herself away from the railings. "You can do it. I'm taking Mrs Robertson her tray."

# CHAPTER TWENTY-EIGHT

Nell was dead on her feet by the time she and Mrs Swift went to the dining room to serve dinner, but she managed a smile for Mr Ross.

"What do we have tonight?"

"The meat dish is roast chicken."

"That sounds nice, Miss Ti ... Mrs Davenport will like that."

"She should. I'll plate it up for you now."

Mrs Swift licked her lips. "I hope Mr Potter has some for us later."

"I'm not sure I'll be able to keep my eyes open long enough to eat it."

"You'll be fine once we step out onto the deck. The wind will wake you up."

Nell sighed. "I'd really rather it didn't."

"Here you are." Mr Ross returned with Mrs Davenport's tray and lifted the cloche. "She should be happy with that."

"I'm sure she will be." Nell picked up the tray but almost dropped it as Mr Hancock burst into the galley.

"Will one of you ladies come quickly? Mrs Hunter's not well. Mr Ramsbottom's gone for Matron, but she needs help now."

Mrs Swift looked to Nell. "Shall we both go?"

"If you want." Nell put the tray on the counter. *Miss Tiddles can wait.*

"I'll take it for you." Mr Hancock picked it up. "Mrs Davenport, isn't it?"

"No, leave it." Nell's cheeks coloured at the forcefulness of her voice. "I'm sorry. I didn't mean to shout, but she specifically asked me to take it. ... while she's on her own in the stateroom, you understand."

"Ah, yes. We'd better get to Mrs Hunter then."

Nell noticed the clock on the way out. "Matron's probably in our quarters. Mr Ramsbottom won't find her if she is."

Mr Hancock checked the time. "I'll fetch Dr Clarke, then. Will you be all right on your own?"

"We'll have to be."

Mrs Hunter was being propped up in her chair by Mrs Young when they arrived. Her husband held one of her hands.

"How is she?"

"Not very well." Mrs Young shifted her position on the floor as Nell placed a hand on Mrs Hunter's clammy forehead.

"Has she been like this for long, Mr Hunter?"

"Several hours, but we thought it was because she was

hungry." His voice croaked. "She hadn't wanted much to eat at afternoon tea, you see."

Mrs Hunter's breathing was laboured, and with her eyes closed, her face looked whiter than usual. "Let me get her a brandy, that might help."

Mr Brennan was shaking a cocktail when she arrived. "What's going on over there?"

"Mrs Hunter's not well. I need a brandy for her."

Mr Brennan put down the shaker. "There's not much this doesn't put right. Here you go."

Nell hurried to the table, but Mrs Hunter groaned as Mrs Young sat her up.

"Can you take a sip?" Nell held the woman's chin.

"She's in a lot of pain." Mr Hunter stroked his wife's hand. "Will the brandy help?"

"It won't do any harm, but we need Dr Clarke. He can give her some laudanum."

"Mr Ramsbottom should have found Matron or Dr Clarke by now." Mrs Swift scanned the room. "Let me check our quarters." She hitched up the front of her skirt as she headed for the door.

Mrs Hunter's breathing rattled in Nell's ear as she cradled her with one arm, while trying to get her to drink the brandy with the other.

"You can do it, Mrs Hunter. Dr Clarke will be here shortly. Take another sip." She put the glass down as the amber liquid dribbled from Mrs Hunter's mouth. "Is there a cloth anywhere?"

She wiped Mrs Hunter's face but looked up when she heard her name.

"What's going on here?" Mrs Davenport arrived at the table. "I've been expecting my tray."

"I'm sorry, madam. Mrs Hunter has taken ill and I'm waiting for Dr Clarke or Matron to arrive."

"Oh ... I'm sorry, although it would have been nice to be told."

"There wasn't time. I'll bring it when I can..." Nell froze as Mrs Hunter clutched her chest.

"We need to lie her down. Mrs Young, will you help me?" Nell glanced at the empty ladies' section. "We can settle her behind the screen."

"Please don't hurt her." Mr Hunter's hands shook as he held onto the chair and eased himself up.

Mrs Hunter was a dead weight as they carried her around the partition and lay her on the floor. Mr Cooper arrived with some towels to rest her head.

"Where's Dr Clarke? He should be here by now."

"I wish I knew." Nell held Mrs Hunter's hand as her breathing slowed. "Shall we pray for her?"

"Please." Mr Hunter stood beside his wife, his eyes not leaving her face.

Nell cleared her throat. "Heavenly Father. Look down on your servant..."

"Out the way." Dr Clarke raced towards them, causing Nell to fall backwards as he took her place. "What happened?"

Nell gave him the details as Mr Hunter struggled to speak.

He reached for his stethoscope. "It's her heart. Everyone, please leave us."

Nell ushered the passengers into the couples' section.

"Oh, Matron, you're here." She pointed to the screen. "Dr Clarke's with her now."

Matron bustled past without a word.

"All right, everyone. Mrs Hunter's in good hands now."

Mrs Young was shaking as she walked with Nell. "Might I have another drink before dinner? My nerves aren't up to eating at the moment."

"Certainly. I'll come and take your order in a minute."

"There's no need for that. A gin will do. As it comes. Just bring it as soon as you can."

Mrs Swift poured two brandies as they settled in their living room that evening.

"Get that down you."

Nell took a large gulp. "Thank you. At least Dr Clarke stabilised her, but why did it take so long to find him? He should always be available."

"I found him. And Matron."

Nell stared at her friend. "He was here?"

Mrs Swift nodded. "The pair of them sat here, on this settee, as cosy as you like."

"No!" Nell gasped. "What happened?"

"I've never seen two people move so quickly. Dr Clarke literally jumped to his feet."

"But that's not allowed. He should lose his job..."

"Only if the captain believes me over them. He could easily say that Matron was feeling unwell."

"He wouldn't..."

"He did. As we were racing across the deck, he said he was only there because Matron had a headache."

"She might have…"

"Whether she did or not is irrelevant. I saw them before they noticed me, and he wasn't giving her any medicine."

Nell drained her glass. "So, what do we do?"

"Not much. If we did, it would probably get us into trouble in the long run."

Nell nodded as she reached for the bottle. "I hope she doesn't arrive before we go to bed. I'd rather not face her tonight."

Mrs Swift pushed her glass towards Nell. "I doubt we'll see her. Or tomorrow morning, for that matter. She'll give Mrs Hunter most of her attention for the next few days, whether she needs it or not."

# CHAPTER TWENTY-NINE

There was no sign of Matron as Nell and Mrs Swift arrived for breakfast.

"Two days running."

Mrs Swift studied the table. "She clearly had a cup of tea, but not much else."

"She must have a guilty conscience." Nell settled into her seat.

"I'd say so. Not that it's troubling Dr Clarke. He was with Mrs Hunter when I was there yesterday and he acted as if nothing had happened."

"Because he knows it's your word against his, and Captain Robertson is more likely to believe him."

"We can keep it up our sleeves though, in case we ever need it, and at least he stopped Mrs Hunter from dying. She was actually quite chirpy yesterday."

"It might not have been so serious if the stewards had been able to find him sooner." Nell helped herself to some porridge. "I wonder how long it's been going on between the two of them. They could be down here every evening for all we know."

"After what I saw last night, it wouldn't surprise me. They looked quite relaxed with each other."

"It makes me think that when Matron was angry with Mr Ross the other week, it was because she was frightened the captain would find out." Nell took a mouthful of porridge. "It could have been going on all year."

"Why do you say that?"

"Remember when we went to New York. We all travelled together, but she and Dr Clarke took a carriage of their own. That may have been the start of it."

"They certainly know how to keep a secret, then. If it hadn't been for Mrs Hunter, they might have got away with it."

Nell sighed. "I suspect they will, anyway."

"We'll see. I'm hoping Matron will be with Mrs Hunter this morning. I'll see what she has to say for herself."

"You'd better get a move on, then. You know she always disappears before we get anywhere."


Mr Davenport was leaving the stateroom when Nell arrived, and he held the door open for her. "Good morning, Mrs Riley. I'll leave you to it."

Nell put the tray on the table. "I presume you'd like breakfast here."

"Please." Mrs Davenport climbed out of bed. "Let me see if the little lady's awake." She pulled open the bag to reveal a small box lined with layers of pink material. "There she is. Come to Mummy." She picked up the dog and cradled it like a baby. "Here we are, Miss Tiddles. This is Mrs Riley, the nice lady who brings your food."

The dog gazed at Nell, its huge dark eyes peering out from under a golden coat.

"She's only small."

"She's still a baby, not that she'll grow much bigger. I wanted a dog I could carry around easily." Mrs Davenport nuzzled her face into the side of the dog. "Would you like to stroke her?"

"Erm." Nell took a step backwards. "No, thank you. I've never had anything to do with dogs before."

"Oh, my dear, that's simply awful."

"I don't mind." Nell bent over to pour Mrs Davenport a cup of tea.

"Well, you must get to know Miss Tiddles." Mrs Davenport sat down and positioned the dog on her lap. "Would you cut the ham up for her? There's a bowl in the bottom of the wardrobe."

Nell did as she was told and showed the bowl to Mrs Davenport. "Do I put it on the floor?"

"Not at all. She likes to be fed. Don't you, my darling?" Mrs Davenport stroked the long fur before picking up several pieces of meat. "There you are."

"I'll leave you to it, then."

Mrs Davenport didn't look up as Nell left, but she had just shut the door when Mr Hancock appeared.

"Good grief, you startled me."

"My apologies. I've been delivering trays." He indicated for her to continue walking.

"Have the stewards been any friendlier over the last couple of days?"

He grimaced. "Some have, but I saw Mr Marsh last night."

Nell gulped. "How was he?"

"Very matter of fact, but he's obviously angry. Or upset."

"Don't say that. I already feel guilty enough."

Mr Hancock hung back as they reached the end of the corridor. "Do you want to go into the dining room first? We'd better not walk in together."

Nell smiled. "I will, thank you ... oh, Mr Price, I beg your pardon." She stepped backwards as he looked between them.

"So, the rumours are true?"

"No ... not at all." Nell's cheeks burned, but Mr Hancock remained calm.

"Mrs Riley was coming out of the Davenports' stateroom as I walked past."

Mr Price failed to look convinced. "You've already used that excuse."

"It's not an excuse..." Nell's voice squeaked, but a glare from Mr Price silenced her.

"Mrs Riley, go about your duties, but send a steward here before you do."

"Yes, sir." Without a backwards glance, she headed towards the galley.

"You took your time." Mrs Swift was about to leave with a pot of tea.

"I'm sorry, Mrs Davenport wanted to talk."

"Again? It's a good job I didn't do Mrs Robertson's eggs. You'll have to wait for them now."

Mr Hancock was still with Mr Price when Nell finally

left for Mrs Robertson's stateroom, but neither acknowledged her.

*What's taking them so long? I hope he's not in trouble.* She yelped as she rounded the corner and almost bumped into Mr Marsh.

"Good morning, Mrs Riley."

"Mr Marsh. What are you doing here?"

"You needn't worry. I've not come to trouble you. Mr Price wants to speak to me."

A lead weight settled in Nell's stomach. *I hope it's nothing to do with Mr Hancock.*

There had been no sign of Mr Hancock over luncheon and as afternoon tea approached, Nell kept an eye on the door as she unloaded the sandwiches from the dumb waiter. She carried them to the nearby table but froze as Mr Marsh appeared in the saloon and walked towards her.

"Might I have a word?" His face was stern and Nell struggled to breathe.

"What? Now? We ... erm ... the guests..."

"It will only take a minute."

Her heart pounded, but with no chance to object, she followed him across the room. His eyes bored into her as he stopped.

"I've come to tell you that Mr Price has insisted Mr Hancock and I swap roles. It wasn't my idea, but it seems your *friendship* is causing Mr Price some concerns."

"But..."

He held up his hands. "I don't need the details but I wanted you to know that I'll be keeping out of your way."

Nell's mouth was dry. "I-I'm sorry."

"It's rather too late for that." He turned and strode

across the room, but Nell stayed where she was until Mrs Swift joined her.

"What was that about?"

"Mr Price has made him and Mr Hancock swap roles, again."

"He doesn't look happy about it."

Nell sighed. "I'm not surprised. I've been horrible..."

"You only did what you had to." Mrs Swift linked her arm. "Why don't you take Mrs Robertson's tray and keep out of the way? I can manage here."

The captain's wife was dozing when Nell arrived with her afternoon tea.

"I do apologise, madam. Would you like me to come back?"

"Not at all. I must have been so bored waiting for you that I dropped off. You being able to stay is the highlight of the day."

Nell smiled. "That's nice of you to say."

Mrs Robertson ran a hand over her bump. "Not that it will be for much longer. The baby's been very restless, although I've no idea how it's going to come out. It feels so big."

Nell sighed. *I'm not getting into that.* "You'll have someone to help when the time comes."

Nell poured the tea and placed Mrs Robertson's cup on the table by the bed. "I've some Victoria sandwich cake this afternoon."

"How splendid." Mrs Robertson sat herself up but

studied Nell as she handed her a plate. "Is everything all right? You don't seem your usual self."

"It's nothing for you to worry about."

"That's obviously not true. Has my husband upset you again?"

Nell sat down. "No, not at all. It's Mr Price."

"What's he done?"

"I bumped into Mr Hancock this morning. We were only walking along the corridor after delivering our trays, but Mr Price wasn't very pleased when he saw us. He's sent Mr Hancock down to steerage and brought Mr Marsh up to first class, again."

"You're sure that's why Mr Price moved them?"

Nell nodded. "Mr Marsh made a point of telling me, in his usual superior way. He always assumes I'm in the wrong." She shuddered. "I hate being near him."

"Then he must go. I'll speak to my husband this evening and have him moved immediately."

"Would you?" Nell's posture straightened. "That would be such a relief."

"Consider it done." Mrs Robertson sliced into her cake. "And what about Mr Ramsbottom? Is he troubling you too?"

Nell put her plate down. "He is, but somehow it's different with him. He's always been overfamiliar, but even though we've had our misunderstandings, I never feel as if he's judging me. Do you know what I mean?"

"I think so. I've known Mr Ramsbottom for a couple of years, and he usually has a smile on his face. You can't be cross with him for long."

"That's exactly it. Not like Mr Marsh. He never smiles and always looks down his nose at me."

"Well, you needn't worry. Things will be back to normal by tomorrow."

Dinner was over early, and once the Youngs and Davenports moved to the saloon, Nell and Mrs Swift headed across the deck to their quarters.

"I wonder if we'll see Matron tonight."

Mrs Swift stopped. "What time was it when we left?"

"I didn't notice, but nearly eight o'clock, I think. Why?"

"We're not normally here before nine. We may find Dr Clarke here."

Nell shuddered. "Is that good or bad?"

"I don't know. It depends how guilty he feels."

"Well, I'm not hanging around in first class just in case. It's not often we get the chance to sit with our feet up for an hour."

"You're right. These are our quarters, and he can't stop us using them."

Mr Potter was tidying the galley when they arrived, and he jumped as they opened the door. "You gave me quite a start there, ladies. You're early."

"We are." Mrs Swift beamed. "We've hardly any passengers, so we thought we'd make the most of it."

He frowned. "I got some nice lamb chops from Mr Ross, but I haven't cooked them yet. I'll be another half an hour with your dinner. Shall I bring you a pot of tea first?"

"That would be lovely, thank you."

They continued to their sitting room, but Mrs Swift put a finger over her lips as they approached.

*Nothing.* Nell let out a sigh of relief, but gasped as she entered. "Matron."

"Mrs Riley! What are you doing here?"

"We finished early." Nell took her seat. "We've not seen you for a few days. What have you been doing?"

"Looking after passengers, what do you think?"

Mrs Swift sat in the chair opposite. "How's Mrs Hunter?"

"Managing nicely, thank you, although she's still very weak."

"It was quite a shock..."

"It was." Matron turned to Nell. "So was the news about you. If I'd had more time..."

"Me!" Nell squealed as Matron stared at her. "What did you hear?"

"About your relationship with Mr Hancock."

"There is no relationship. We only said there was to keep Mr Marsh away."

"That's not what Captain Robertson said."

Nell's eyes narrowed. "Captain Robertson? When?"

"Shortly before I came down here, he told me Mr Price had been forced to move Mr Hancock to steerage. Have you no shame? This isn't the first time..."

Nell floundered for words. "I've done nothing wrong. All I want is to be left alone ... besides, you've no room to talk..."

Matron's eyes bulged. "What's that supposed to mean?"

"You and Dr Clarke. From what I've heard, you've been more intimate with him than I've been with anyone on this ship."

Matron's face was like thunder as she glowered at Mrs Swift. "Is this your doing?"

"I only said that I'd found Dr Clarke in here when Mrs Hunter was ill. She might have died because nobody could find him and yet the pair of you are acting as if nothing's happened."

"That's because nothing did happen, and I'd thank you for keeping your opinions to yourself."

"It's no worse than you accusing Mrs Riley of wrongdoing when she's done nothing, either."

"It's not the same thing at all."

"Only because I've never given any encouragement to any of the stewards. Last week when Mr Ross told everyone how he'd seen you and Dr Clarke together in the dining room after service had finished, you were so angry, you made us all think it was because you were 'working', but it wasn't. You just didn't want to be found out. I've nothing to be found out about."

"How dare you! I'll have you removed from the ship..."

"Ladies." Mr Potter stood in the doorway. "I couldn't help overhearing..."

Matron's cheeks reddened. "You had no right to come down here, eavesdropping."

"Begging your pardon, Matron, I'm here to deliver some tea ... and to pass on a message."

"Who to?"

"You." Mr Potter put the tray on the table and retreated to the door. "I took the liberty of telling Dr Clarke that Mrs Swift and Mrs Riley were here early tonight. He said he's sorry he was late, but he'll see you tomorrow." He turned to leave. "I'll be back with your dinner shortly, ladies."

Mr Potter hadn't disappeared before Nell rounded on Matron. "He was coming here again, wasn't he? It's all very comfortable when we're not here."

Matron's cheeks were scarlet. "It's not what you think."

"Really? It's funny how nobody believes me when I say that."

Matron sank back on the settee and put her head in her hands. "All right, I can't deny that Dr Clarke visits me of an evening, but it's only ever for half an hour or so."

"That's all right then." Nell couldn't hide her sarcasm. "You're happy to believe the worst of me, no matter how many times I plead my innocence, but it's different for you."

"I have a working relationship with Dr Clarke..."

"And I do with the stewards, but it still doesn't make it right. It's about time someone reprimanded these men."

"I'd have thought that moving them to steerage was a suitable deterrent."

"But it isn't, when they're down there for a few weeks and then straight back to first class as if nothing's happened. It's so unfair."

"I'm afraid life's unfair, Mrs Riley." Matron pushed herself up from the table. "I'm turning in for the night, but if it's any help, I'll speak to Mr Price in the morning."

# CHAPTER THIRTY

M rs Davenport sat on the settee with Miss Tiddles on her lap as Nell finished dusting around the stateroom.

"That should do it for today. I need to get a move on. Morning coffee's in half an hour."

Mrs Davenport brushed the dog's coat. "I'll see you shortly then."

Once Nell had stored her cleaning equipment, she made her way to the saloon.

"Good morning, Mr Price."

"Ah, Mrs Riley, just the person. Might I have a word?"

"I suppose..."

He led her to a table in the ladies' section and offered her a chair before sitting opposite her. "You have friends in high places."

Nell smiled. "Matron, you mean."

"I was referring to Captain and Mrs Robertson, but yes, Matron as well. It seems you've done your best to undermine my authority, while I've tried to protect you from the stewards."

"Oh, no, sir. That was never my intention..."

"Well, that's what you've done. Captain Robertson asked me to reverse my decision about Mr Marsh."

Nell sighed. "I only mentioned it to Mrs Robertson yesterday, when she commented that I didn't look my usual self. I didn't mean to get you in trouble."

"What *is* your problem with Mr Marsh? It was months ago since you had your tantrum in New York. You should be over it by now."

Nell stared at the table as her cheeks burned.

"I wanted Mr Marsh up here, because I won't have you and Mr Hancock working together."

"All we've done is talk if we've met in the corridor."

"And announced that you'll be walking out together when you return to Liverpool."

"I told you, he only said that to stop Mr Marsh from troubling me. He's the real problem. And Mr Ramsbottom."

"Mr Ramsbottom?"

Nell shrugged. "He's been overfamiliar on occasions."

"And yet you've never reported it?"

"I didn't want to cause any trouble."

"Or was it because you didn't want to put him off?" Mr Price's eyes bored into her.

"Not at all, but..." Nell sighed. "You wouldn't understand."

"Why is it you who attracts all this attention? I've never had a problem with Mrs Swift. Not in terms of the stewards, at any rate."

"I don't know." Nell stared at her lap.

"It's about time you did. It's not my job to act as your guardian."

"No, sir."

"Now, because the captain's intervened, I've agreed to send Mr Marsh back to steerage, but I won't have Mr Hancock working up here. I suspect you're only protesting his innocence so you can see him again."

"But sir..."

"That's enough. To fill the gap, I've asked Mr Cunningham to move up here for the rest of the voyage. I presume you have no issue with him."

"We haven't met. Not properly, anyway."

"Splendid. Might I suggest you keep it that way? I don't want to hear any more allegations against you."

"No, sir."

Tears welled in Nell's eyes as she walked back to the serving table where Mrs Swift was waiting.

"What was that about?"

"Mr Marsh has gone back to steerage."

"So why do you look so miserable?"

"Because once again I'm the one being accused of leading them on."

Mrs Swift shook her head. "How many times do I have to tell you? Nothing will change until you stop being so friendly with them.

"But I don't want to be rude to them all."

"You don't need to be. Just let them know their place."

Nell wiped her eyes with the back of her hand. "I'll try."

Mrs Robertson's face was twisted in pain when Nell arrived with her afternoon tea.

"Oh, my! Are you all right?" Nell dropped the tray onto the table and hurried to the side of the bed.

"I'll be fine. I got a kick in the ribs, and it took the wind out of me."

"Thank goodness for that. I thought the baby might be coming."

"Why?"

Nell turned to retrieve the tray. "It can be a little painful."

Mrs Robertson's eyes widened. "How painful?"

"Nothing you can't cope with."

"I hope not." Mrs Robertson ran a hand over her belly as Nell showed her the plate of cakes.

"The scones are fresh today and there's some lovely strawberry jam. Would you like me to butter you one?"

The smile returned to Mrs Robertson's face. "You spoil me."

"It's the least I can do. Thank you for having Mr Marsh moved."

"He's gone, has he? Splendid. My husband seemed oblivious to all the goings-on."

"It's understandable. He's more important things to think about."

"He should still keep an eye on the crew, especially you and Mrs Swift. I've reminded him of that."

"And I'm very grateful." Nell put Mrs Robertson's scone and cup of tea on the table and collected her own before she sat down. "There was something else. May I ask you about Mr Price?"

"What about him?" Mrs Robertson took a large bite of scone.

"I'm not sure. I just can't make him out. When I first joined the ship, I had one or two disagreements with him, but since he's been head steward, he's much more cordial, and I always thought I could speak to him if there was an issue."

"But…" Mrs Robertson raised an eyebrow.

"He seems different on this voyage. For one, he knows the history between me and Mr Marsh, and yet he placed him in first class when we left Liverpool and refused to move him downstairs when I asked. Even when Mr Marsh volunteered to work in steerage, he moved him upstairs again. It's as if he's trying to upset me."

"Why would he do that?"

Nell shrugged. "I've no idea. That's why I wondered if you knew anything. Does he have any family problems?"

Mrs Robertson's brow creased. "Now you ask, I don't remember him talking about his home life."

"Even if there were problems, though, why should that affect me and Mr Marsh?" Nell paused, and stared at Mrs Robertson. "Thinking about it, the change started when Mr Marsh arrived back on the ship after going missing the month before. He insisted on working in first class, but rather than protecting me, which he's always done before, Mr Price agreed. Did Captain Robertson say anything about Mr Marsh reappearing?"

"Not in any detail. I remember he wasn't happy because he'd arranged for a new steward, and he had to transfer him to another ship."

"It doesn't explain why Mr Marsh ended up in first

class, though. Mr Price said that Mr Marsh is too good a steward to keep in steerage, but it hadn't bothered him for the six months before that."

"I'm afraid I can't help you. Shall I ask my husband?"

"Oh, gracious, no. I don't want Mr Price to find out I've been asking questions about him."

"Very well. I'll keep my ears open in case he says anything."

It was still light outside when Nell left Mrs Robertson and, rather than returning to the saloon, she grabbed her cloak and walked onto the deck.

A group of steerage passengers were still there, and she shuddered as Mr Hancock waved from the back of the ship. She gave a half-hearted wave. *I'd forgotten he might be out here.* She stayed near the first-class accommodation and peered out at the snow-covered landscape. She hadn't been there long when the door opened and Mrs Swift joined her.

"What are you doing here?"

"I needed some time to clear my head. Captain Robertson's going to ask soon whether we're rejoining next year, and after everything that's gone on this voyage, I don't think I can face it."

Mrs Swift sighed. "It's not been easy, but we've had a lot of decent trips this year. Don't let one voyage sway you unduly."

"I'll try not to, but it's not only that. I won't be popular at home if I come back. Especially not with Elenor. I hadn't realised how much it would upset her. What about you?"

"I'll be back as long as nothing's changed with Mother. We need the money."

"I suppose so. At least I have a choice, although that's part of the problem. When I get home, I want to be away and when I'm away..." She pushed herself from the railings. "Never mind, we'd better go in. They'll be serving pre-dinner drinks soon."

# CHAPTER THIRTY-ONE

Mrs Davenport waved as she and her husband walked into the saloon for morning coffee a couple of days later. Nell waited for them to take their seat before joining them with a plate of biscuits.

"Thank you, Mrs Riley." She helped herself to a shortbread. "I'm not nearly so hungry as I have been. What a wonderful idea to bring me some porridge with breakfast."

Nell smiled. "I don't know why I didn't think of it earlier. Would you like some extra bread at luncheon, too?"

"Oh, please ... and plenty of butter."

"I'll see what I can do." Nell moved to the Youngs' table.

"No Mrs Swift this morning?" Mrs Young took an oat biscuit before her husband helped himself to a selection.

"She'll bring the coffee. It seems silly her serving everything to one couple and me the other."

"I suppose so, although we've not seen much of you on this voyage."

"Mrs Robertson, the captain's wife, is rather indisposed at the moment, so I've been taking her a tray."

"That's a shame. I'd like to meet her. Talking of being unwell, do you know how Mrs Hunter is?"

Nell's face brightened. "Dr Clarke says she's improving."

"That's good. Such a nice lady. What about her husband?"

"Bless him. He's not left her side since the incident."

"Well, I hope he's looking after himself. If he's not eating properly, he'll be no help to her when they get home."

"Dr Clarke calls on them twice a day, and the stewards take them both trays each mealtime, so he should be fine."

"I'm glad. Will you tell him that if he wants company while his wife's asleep, he knows where we are?"

"That's very kind of you. I'll pass the message on."

Nell passed Mrs Swift on her way to the table, but groaned as Mr Cooper joined her. "I'm really not sure we need stewardesses when we're so quiet. We can deal with the couples."

"What would you have us do? Get off the ship in New York?"

"Of course not, but we used to manage perfectly well without you." He disappeared with a fresh pot of tea as Mrs Swift returned.

"Are you all right? You've gone very pale." Nell studied her friend.

"I don't know. I've just come over all peculiar."

Nell scanned the room. "Why don't you go to our quarters and have a sit- down? The two of us needn't be here. In fact, Mr Cooper doesn't want either of us."

"What's he said?"

Nell groaned. "He wants to go back to the days when women didn't travel on ships. He'd better be careful, though. If he says another word, I'll leave him to it."

"Are you sure you don't mind?"

"Not at all, as long as you do it for me, one day." Nell grinned. "I'll tell Mr Price you're ill if he says anything."

"Thank you. I'll ask Mr Potter to prepare us some luncheon. Don't be late."

Mrs Swift was in the sitting room with a pot of tea when Nell arrived, and she hadn't sat down before the sound of the crockery rattling in the corridor announced Mr Potter's arrival.

"Here we are, ladies. It's not often I get to serve you luncheon."

Nell smiled as he put the tray down. "It's an unusual voyage with so few passengers."

"It's the time of year. Everyone wants to start a new life, or spend Christmas in New York, so the trips are full going out but nearly empty on the return."

Nell lifted the cloche from her plate to reveal a beef stew. "I can't say I blame them."

"Well, enjoy your food. I'll see you later."

Mrs Swift's face brightened as Mr Potter left. "I overheard a rather interesting conversation when I was coming down here."

Nell didn't look up as she stabbed a piece of meat. "Who between?"

"Mr Potter and Mr Marsh."

"Mr Marsh?"

Mrs Swift had her full attention. "He works in steerage now so it's hardly surprising."

Nell grunted. "What was he saying?"

"Mr Potter asked why he was downstairs again."

Nell shrugged. "It's a reasonable question."

"It was, but Mr Marsh wasn't happy. He said that Mr Price had promised him he'd be upstairs but what could he do when Captain Robertson insisted he stay in steerage."

Nell's head whirred as her eyes widened. "Why would Mr Price do that?"

Mrs Swift raised an eyebrow. "It sounded like Mr Price wants to keep him happy."

"I wonder why."

Mrs Swift smirked. "Perhaps we should use our free time to find out what it was."

Nell tapped her fingers on the table as she stood in the saloon, waiting for Mrs Robertson's afternoon tea tray.

Mrs Swift arrived back with a platter of sandwiches. "Isn't it here yet?"

Nell sighed. "No. Mr Ross must have forgotten. I'll go downstairs and remind him."

She didn't hurry as she made her way to the dining room, but stopped when she reached the foyer and heard Mr Marsh talking to Mr Ross. *What's he doing here?*

She strained to make out what they were saying, but stepped back to the stairs as the voices got closer. *I need to go.*

Mrs Swift watched her walk across the saloon. "That was quick."

"I didn't get to the galley. Mr Marsh was talking to Mr Ross."

"Did they see you?"

"No, I heard them before I saw them and came straight back."

"What were they saying?"

"I couldn't make it out, but Mr Marsh wasn't happy. I'll ask Mr Ross later. You know how he loves to gossip."

Mrs Swift chuckled. "Doesn't he just."

Nell peered around the side of Mrs Swift as the dumb waiter moved. "Here's the tray now. Mr Marsh must have delayed it." She strolled to the corner and took it out. "I'll see you later."

She paused for breath before knocking on the stateroom door, but took a step backwards when Mrs Robertson opened it.

"Oh, Mrs Riley, I thought you'd never get here."

"I'm sorry, there was a delay with the tray, but what are you doing out of bed?"

"I've been so uncomfortable since you last called and walking seems to be the only way to relieve it."

"What sort of uncomfortable?" Nell's heart quickened as she put down the tray.

"I can't really describe it. It's like there's something tight around the baby, but thankfully it doesn't last long. It's not very pleasant."

"And this has been happening all afternoon?"

Mrs Robertson sat on the settee. "On and off. I've not felt it for a while now, but it was almost continuous after luncheon."

"I'd better fetch Matron."

Mrs Robertson sat up straight. "Do you think there's something wrong?"

"Not at all, but ... well, I wonder if the baby's on its way."

"Really?" A smile replaced the look of fear. "When?"

"I don't know, but you need to get back into bed." Nell poured a cup of tea. "You sit with this while I find her. Shall I tell Captain Robertson?"

"Oh gosh, no, not yet. He won't want to be worrying about me."

Nell reached for the door. "All right. I'll be as quick as I can." She took a deep breath as she stepped into the corridor. *Calm down. It could be hours yet.* Her heart pounded as she headed towards the bridge. *I hope I don't find her with Dr Clarke.*

Captain Robertson was leaving his office when Nell arrived. "Good afternoon, Mrs Riley. What brings you here?"

"I'm looking for Matron. Have you seen her?"

"Not recently. She was heading to steerage the last time I saw her."

"I'll ask a steward to go downstairs for me then."

"You do that. Do you have a guest under the weather?"

"Er ... yes." Nell bit her lip. "I'd better go." She raced down the corridor towards the foyer at the other end and paused outside the saloon. *Where now? The dining room.* She hurried down the stairs, relieved that the voices had gone, but even in the dim light, it was clear nobody was there. *I'll check our quarters in case she's in there.*

Mr Hancock was supervising a dozen or more steerage passengers on the deck when she went outside, and on impulse she raced across to him. His eyes glinted as she approached.

"Good afternoon, Mrs Riley."

"Mr Hancock. I'm sorry to disturb you, but have you seen Matron?"

"She's over there." He pointed to the opposite side of the ship where Matron sat huddled in a blanket.

"Oh, thank goodness." She paused as he held her gaze. "I'm sorry, for all the trouble I've caused you."

"You've done nothing wrong."

"Neither have you other than try to defend me." She shuddered as she glanced across to Matron. "I'm sorry. I hate to rush off, but I'd better go. Perhaps another time." She didn't wait for a reply before she headed towards Matron.

"Mrs Riley. What are you doing over here?"

"Looking for you. It's Mrs Robertson, I think her baby may be coming."

Matron huffed as she pushed herself up. "Very well."

"She's started getting tightening about her belly and I can't help her by myself."

"You'd better stay with me in case I need you." Matron marched across the deck as Nell chased after her.

Mrs Robertson was lying on her side when Matron let herself in and Nell closed the door behind them.

"Now then, Mrs Robertson, you don't need to lie like that yet."

"The bump went tight again, and this was the best way to ease it. It's passed now."

"Let me sit you up." Matron fluffed up the pillows and waited while Mrs Robertson made herself comfortable. "Let me feel." She rested her hands on Mrs

Robertson's belly. "It's still hard. How long ago did this happen?"

"Only a couple of minutes."

"And the pain disappeared when you lay on your side?"

"Yes."

"I'm going to have to examine you. Mrs Riley, will you bring me some towels?"

"What for?" Mrs Robertson looked between the two of them.

"In case the baby's ready to come out. Now, please, Mrs Riley, off you go while I do my examination."

"Yes, Matron." Nell darted from the room and along the corridor to the store cupboard but stopped when Captain Robertson walked towards her.

"Captain. Are you on your way to visit Mrs Robertson?"

"I thought I'd call in."

"Actually, Matron's with her. She had a bit of discomfort around the baby..."

"What sort of discomfort?"

"Oh, nothing unusual, but I wanted Matron in case the baby's ready to make an appearance."

"And is it?"

"We don't know yet."

The captain's face paled. "I'd better check."

"No!" Nell's cheeks flushed. "I'm sorry, I didn't mean to shout, but Matron was about to examine your wife, and..." Her cheeks were burning "...well, you probably shouldn't disturb them. I was on my way to get some towels ... in case Matron's wrong."

"She can't be. Dr Clarke said it wouldn't be born on this voyage."

"And it might not be, but..."

"I hope not. We're still days away from Queenstown and I won't know what's happening in Liverpool until we get there." He turned to leave. "You will keep me informed?"

"Yes, Captain."

"Carry on, then. Oh, and ask Matron to come and see me when she's finished. I'll be in my office."

After knocking loudly on the door, Nell averted her eyes as she carried a stack of towels into Mrs Robertson's stateroom.

"Have you finished?"

"Yes, yes, come in." Matron bustled towards her and took the towels. "We didn't need quite so many, but they'll keep."

"How is she?"

The captain's wife said nothing as she lay on the pillows, the bedcovers pulled up to her neck.

"As I thought. There's no sign of baby yet. It's a false alarm for now."

Nell breathed a sigh of relief. "Thank goodness. I bumped into Captain Robertson in the corridor and had to tell him you were here."

"You ... you told him ..." Mrs Robertson's eyes were wide.

"I said you'd felt some tightening."

"You'd no right to." Matron glared at her. "This is women's business."

"I'm sorry, but he was on his way here. I had to say

something to keep him out. Anyway, he asked if you'd go to his office once you're finished."

"I'll go when I'm good and ready. I've other patients who need attention."

"I was only passing on the message."

"Will you stay with me?" Mrs Robertson's voice was weak as she hid behind the sheet.

"For a little while, but I need to go to the saloon for pre-dinner drinks and take Mrs Davenport's tray."

"Mrs Swift can do that." Matron scowled at Nell. "You're quiet enough this week."

"I need to tell her."

"I'll do that."

"It should be me..."

Matron planted her hands on her hips. "What's the matter with you?"

"Nothing." Nell coughed as her voice shrieked. "You said you had other guests to see."

"And so I have, but I'm going that way. You stay here with Mrs Robertson. She needs you more than Mrs Davenport."

Nell's stomach fluttered as Matron opened the door. *Oh goodness. Miss Tiddles had better be in her box or I'm in trouble.*

# CHAPTER THIRTY-TWO

Nell suppressed a yawn as she stood outside Mrs Davenport's stateroom with her breakfast tray. The last few days had dragged, and she longed to be home. After taking a deep breath, she knocked on the door.

"One moment."

There was scuffling inside the room as she waited. *Mrs Swift would have said something if she'd seen Miss Tiddles.*

"Come in." Mrs Davenport put a hand to her chest as Nell walked in. "Oh, it's you."

She closed the door behind her. "I'm sorry about last night. I got caught up with Mrs Robertson. Did Mrs Swift see Miss Tiddles?"

Mrs Davenport collected the dog from the bag behind her. "Thankfully not. I'd put her in her box for a nap."

"Thank goodness for that. I couldn't warn you about it, but there's a chance Mrs Swift will bring the tray again over the next few days. I suggest you keep her in the bag whenever you expect a tray."

"Oh..." Mrs Davenport brought the dog towards her face. "You don't like being in there, do you, my darling?"

"It won't be for long and it will be better than her being found."


Mr Ramsbottom was with Mrs Swift when she arrived in the galley.

"Here she is. I've been waiting for you." He winked as he picked up a pot of tea.

"You needn't have bothered."

"And spoil my start to the day?"

Nell rolled her eyes. "I'm not even answering that. Now, I suggest you take that to your table before it stews."

"I'm going." Mr Ramsbottom grinned as he went through the door.

Mrs Swift patted her shoulder. "That's the spirit. You're learning."

"What have I missed?" Mr Ross appeared and picked up Mrs Swift's order as Nell groaned.

"Only Mr Ramsbottom up to his usual tricks."

"He's in high spirits this morning. I'm not sure why."

"He's not been promoted, has he?"

"What makes you say that?"

Nell shrugged. "It's the sort of thing that would cheer him up. Either that or someone's given him a tip."

"It's probably the second. There are enough chiefs around here as it is."

"What do you mean?" Nell's forehead creased as Mr Ross put two eggs into a pan of water.

"Mr Hancock and Mr Marsh are squabbling in steerage about who's in charge."

Mrs Swift rested her hand on the counter. "Who's winning?"

"Mr Marsh, although Mr Hancock hasn't given up the fight. He thinks Mr Marsh gave up the position when he left the ship and says that as he was in charge when we left Liverpool, it should be him."

"I'd have to agree." Nell crossed her arms. "The poor man's done nothing wrong, and it would serve Mr Marsh right for insisting on working upstairs."

Mr Ross stared at her. "Who told you that?"

"I ... well ..."

Mrs Swift straightened up. "I heard Mr Marsh saying that Mr Price wants to keep him happy. What do you know about it?"

Mr Ross checked over his shoulder and leaned across the counter. "There's not a lot to know. From what I heard, Mr Marsh saw Mr Price when we were last docked in Liverpool and Mr Price was up to something shady. Neither will say what, but Mr Price is rather embarrassed about it. He promised he could move back to first class if he kept quiet, but it's not worked out. The way things are looking, Mr Marsh will have to be made head steward to keep him upstairs."

The blood drained from Nell's face. "That's all we need."

"Well, you've no time to worry about it now." Mr Ross pushed a tray towards her. "Mrs Robertson will be waiting for this."

.  .  .

Breakfast was over by the time Nell returned to the dining room and once she'd taken her tray to the galley, she wandered over to Mrs Swift, who was setting the Youngs' table for luncheon.

"How was Mrs Robertson this morning?"

Nell grimaced. "She's still showing signs of being ready and wants me to stay with her when I take her luncheon tray."

Mrs Swift grimaced. "Rather you than me."

"I know. Matron's sure it's nothing to be worried about, but I don't want to be there on my own if she's wrong."

"At least I can help by taking Mrs Davenport's tray."

Nell passed her the glasses. "You will remember to knock, won't you ... and wait to be let in?"

"I will." Mrs Swift sighed. "It all seems so unnecessary."

Nell shrugged. "It's just the way she is. I might as well service her room before morning coffee. I'll see you later."

Mrs Davenport was reading a magazine with Miss Tiddles on her lap when Nell let herself in.

"It's only me."

"Oh, good. I was hoping I wouldn't have to stand up."

"It is for now, but I won't be able to bring your luncheon." Nell marched over to the beds and straightened the sheets on the first. "I've reminded Mrs Swift to knock, but I wonder if you should lock the door, to be on the safe side."

"That's a good idea. I'll speak to my husband during morning coffee. He insists on keeping the key with him."

Nell walked to the door to collect her carpet brush, but paused as she picked it up. "Are you expecting Mr Davenport back?"

"No, he usually goes to the saloon for a game of cards."

"I think you should put Miss Tiddles in her box. It sounds like someone's outside."

"They won't come in, surely?"

"It's better to be safe."

Mrs Davenport huffed as she stood up. "I really need to get that key."

A moment later, there was a knock on the door. "Mrs Riley, are you in there?"

*Mr Price.* Nell froze as Mrs Davenport struggled to get the dog in the bag.

"Mrs Riley." The doorknob twisted, but Nell clung onto it.

"Just a minute. Mrs Davenport's getting changed." She held her breath but suddenly yelped as Miss Tiddles barked.

"Mrs Riley. Are you all right?"

"I banged my elbow on the wall..."

With the dog finally hidden, Nell opened the door wide enough to see Mr Price with Mrs Swift. "Yes."

He tried to peer into the room.

"Did you want me?"

"It's Mrs Robertson. She's asking for you. Could you leave the room and Mrs Swift will take over from you?"

"There's no need. I'm finished now. Let me get my things."

"I'll get them." Mrs Swift stepped forward and pushed the door, but Mrs Davenport approached from the other side and slammed it shut.

"One moment, please." She leaned into Nell. "You can't let them in."

"I won't. You stand there while I get my things. I hope you don't mind that I've not finished."

"I don't mind at all, as long as they don't come in. You'd better be quick; Miss Tiddles isn't happy."

Nell glanced at the bag that bulged as the dog pawed to get out.

"I'm going. Will you open the door? They're less likely to want to come in if you open it."

Mrs Davenport nodded and opened it with a smile. "We're sorry to keep you. Mrs Riley's all yours."

Nell squeezed through the narrow gap. "Thank you, Mrs Davenport."

Nell's head nodded over her chest, and she woke with a start when someone knocked on Mrs Robertson's stateroom door. She jumped up and hurried to open it.

"Oh, it's you. What time is it?"

Mrs Swift followed her into the room. "It's nearly seven o'clock, so I brought Mrs Robertson's tray."

"She's asleep at the moment."

"Will you come to the dining room later?"

"I'll have to see how she is when she wakes up."

Mrs Swift nodded. "If you're not downstairs by the time I'm ready to leave, I'll come and get you. I'd rather not walk across the deck on my own."

"Me neither. Don't go without me."

Mrs Robertson stirred as the door closed behind Mrs Swift. "Who was that?"

"Mrs Swift. She brought your tray."

"Is it that time already?"

"It is. How are you feeling?"

Mrs Robertson ran a hand over her bump. "It doesn't feel as hard as it was earlier. Hopefully, that means we won't need Matron again. I hate it when she checks on me."

"I used to hate being checked on, too, but it won't be for much longer." Nell carried the tray over to the bed. "There you are. Do you mind if I wait and take the tray back to the galley when you're finished? I'll need to get back to my own cabin soon."

"Of course. I didn't mean to take up so much of your time. My husband should be visiting soon. You will come tomorrow?"

"As long as the baby isn't on the way."

"If Matron's to be trusted, it shouldn't be." She took a bite of bread. "Are we due in Queenstown tomorrow?"

"Not for a couple of days, unless Captain Robertson has found some extra speed."

"I hope he has. I need to know what's happening once we arrive in Liverpool."

"Try not to think about it. He'll send a telegram once we dock and I'm sure he'll let you know as soon as he hears anything."

# CHAPTER THIRTY-THREE

The clouds were dark grey and the air full of mist as Nell and Mrs Swift stepped out onto the deck and peered towards Queenstown cathedral as the ship left the dock.

"It feels like we've been away a long time."

"It does." Nell sighed as they continued walking. "I hope the captain sent his telegram. Mrs Robertson can't hold on for much longer."

"He will have done." Mrs Swift held open the door to the first-class area. "We should be in Liverpool this time tomorrow."

"Thank goodness."

Mr Price was in the foyer when they arrived. "Good morning, ladies. Are you ready for a busy day?"

"As ready as ever." Nell took a deep breath. "I've promised to help Mrs Davenport pack, so Mrs Robertson will have to manage on her own for an hour. Matron said she'd try to sit with her if she had time."

Mr Price looked at Mrs Swift. "The Hunters need assistance too. Can I leave that with you?"

Mrs Swift nodded. "I've already arranged it. If you'll excuse us, we'd better get on."

Mr Ross was waiting for them when they arrived. "It's nice to see you here."

Nell peered out of the door. "Why, where's everyone else?"

"I've no idea. They were all still in bed when I got up this morning, but they usually are."

"I might as well take my trays before they arrive, then." Nell glanced at the clock. "Are they nearly ready?"

"I'll have Mrs Davenport's with you in a second."

Nell watched as he scrambled some eggs over the heat. "Will you be leaving the ship in Liverpool, Mr Ross?"

"I will. My sister had another young whippersnapper before I left for this trip, and they've waited until I'm back to have the baptism."

"That's nice. My nephew's getting married next week, but it's on the day we're due to sail."

"That's a shame."

"I can live without it. One of the reasons I'm here is to get away from the bickering at home."

"I know what you mean." He tipped the eggs onto a plate beside two slices of ham. "There you go ... and the porridge as well."

Nell picked up the tray and headed out of the dining room, relieved to see several stewards arriving. Mr Price didn't seem to share her relief.

"Where on earth have you been? The guests will be here any minute and you've not taken your trays."

Mr Ramsbottom kicked at the carpet. "We didn't realise the time. We'll be as quick as we can." He headed towards the galley with the others close behind him.

*They were lucky to get away with that.*

The corridor was deserted when Nell knocked on Mrs Davenport's door, but as she turned the knob to let herself in, she almost dropped the tray. *Why's it locked?*

"Mrs Davenport, are you in there? It's Mrs Riley."

"One moment."

Nell's forehead creased. *What's she doing?* She put an ear to the door. *Is she moving the furniture?* She took a step backwards as the Youngs walked past.

"Good morning."

Mr Young raised his hat. "Good morning."

She waited until they reached the end of the corridor before knocking again.

"Mrs Davenport. I really need to put this tray down. May I come in?"

"I won't be long."

"I'll leave it outside, then." She was about to place it on the floor when the door opened.

"Ah, Mrs Riley. I'm sorry about that." Mr Davenport took the tray from her.

"Is everything all right, sir?"

"Nothing for you to worry about. Good day, Mrs Riley." He closed the door with a foot.

*What on earth...?*

Mr Ramsbottom grinned as he walked towards her. "You're taking your time."

"At least I was here for seven o'clock, which is more than can be said for you."

"I wasn't leaving the dormitory while Mr Marsh was in full flow. It's the best entertainment we've had all trip."

"What's he up to now?"

"Mr Hancock tried giving him some orders, and he didn't take kindly to it. Let's just say, the two of them shouldn't be working together."

"Mr Price already knows that. There's no reason for Mr Hancock to even be in steerage. If there's any trouble, Mr Price has only got himself to blame."

Mr Ramsbottom winked as he carried on walking. "In more ways than one."

Mrs Robertson was sitting up in bed when Nell arrived.

"Good morning, madam. How are you feeling today?"

"Rather deflated. I'd become quite excited thinking the baby was about to be born, but it's completely quietened down again."

"It's for the best. It will be difficult enough getting you off the ship and settled into your new home, without you having the baby to take care of, as well."

Mrs Robertson sighed. "I know, but I'm ready to meet it. I've had enough waiting."

Nell smiled as she handed her a cup of tea. "I remember thinking that, but it will happen soon enough. You catch up on your sleep. You'll be glad of it once the baby's here."

After arranging the tray across Mrs Robertson's legs, Nell made her way back to the dining room and stood near the galley with Mrs Swift.

"What a strange start to the day. Mrs Davenport wouldn't even let me into the stateroom this morning."

"What did you do with her breakfast?"

"I was about to leave it in the corridor, but her husband took it from me."

"She's a peculiar woman. I have to be in and out when I call. Do you know what's up with her?"

Nell shrugged. "I've no idea."

"According to Mr Cooper, they had quite a party in the saloon last night and she was in the thick of it. Much to his irritation."

"Perhaps she has a sore head after too many cocktails and didn't want me to see her."

"It's quite possible. Mr Brennan was very pleased with the way the evening went."

"I bet he was. I can't see us getting many tips, with so few passengers."

Mrs Swift shrugged. "It sometimes happens. You should be glad you put some of the money aside earlier this year. Not like my sister. She'll have spent it all."

"She won't stop you coming back next year, though. I've still got that decision to make."

"I hope you come back, otherwise the next trip together will be our last."

"It needs to be better than this one, then."

Captain Robertson was with his wife when Nell arrived with her afternoon tea.

"I do apologise, Captain. I didn't mean to interrupt."

"Not at all, Mrs Riley. It's me who's disturbing your routine. I've heard from head office and wanted to pass the news on." He patted Mrs Robertson's hand. "I know how much my wife's been fretting."

"Let me leave this here then." She put the tray on the table near the bed. "I still have Mrs Davenport's trunk to pack, and it's getting rather late. She's been feeling under the weather, which is why I've not done it sooner."

"Will you come back?" Mrs Robertson's eyes widened.

"I should be able to. I'll be as quick as I can."

The Davenports' stateroom was only a little further down the corridor and Nell knocked, but waited to be let in.

"It's only me, Mrs Davenport. I'm here to help with your trunk." She didn't wait long before a sheepish Mrs Davenport opened the door.

"What must you think of me? I'm sorry for the way things have been today, it's just that..." She extended her arm around the stateroom. "You'd better come in."

Nell's eyes widened. "Oh my goodness."

"Quite. Miss Tiddles didn't appreciate being left for so long last night. We've tried our best to patch things up, but there's not a lot we can do."

"Not with chunks taken out of the furniture." Nell stepped forward and ran her fingers over the hole in the settee.

"I don't even know where she got the strength to do so much damage."

Nell flinched at the two large eyes peeping out over the top of the bag. "She knows she's been naughty."

"Oh, she does. I was inconsolable last night when we got back from the saloon. I didn't sleep a wink."

"I don't suppose you did." Nell bent down to rub her

hand over the teeth marks on several chair legs. "I'm going to have to report it to Captain Robertson."

Mrs Davenport pulled a handkerchief from her sleeve and wiped her eyes. "Not yet, please. Will you wait until we leave Queenstown? He'll throw us off the ship and we'd never make it to Liverpool from here."

Nell sighed. "I will if you support me when I tell the captain I knew nothing of the dog. Can you tell him you hid her in the bag every time I called?"

Mrs Davenport stared at her. "I suppose..."

"And will you ask Mr Davenport to do the same? I could lose my job over this."

Mrs Davenport wiped her eyes. "He won't speak to the captain. He says it's all my fault and I should never have brought her."

"It won't matter what Mr Davenport wants. The captain will want to speak to him." Nell swayed as the ship lurched to one side. "We're moving again. Let's get this trunk packed and then I'll go and find him."

Nell stared down at the fully laden trunk. *How on earth do I get it into the corridor for collection?* She grabbed hold of a handle, but it barely moved. *No.*

She scratched her head as Mrs Davenport fussed the dog. "I'll have to get a steward to move this."

"But you can't!"

"What else can I do? I can't lift it and neither can you. Do you think Mr Davenport will be able to move it?"

"I'm sure he could. Would you fetch him? I can't leave Miss Tiddles again."

*I doubt she can do much more damage.* Nell took a deep breath. "Very well. I won't be long."

The saloon was quiet when Nell walked in, but Mr Davenport was sitting with a group of men in the corner of the men's section. *Trust him to have his back to me. Why are there no stewards?*

She returned to the foyer and started her descent to the dining room, but met Captain Robertson coming the other way.

"Oh, Captain." Her cheeks flushed.

"Were you looking for me, Mrs Riley?"

"Not really, but ... well, yes. I need to have a word with you, but I was looking for someone to speak to Mr Davenport for me."

"Where is he?"

"In the saloon, but there were no stewards."

"Was that all you wanted?"

"No, sir."

He continued walking up the stairs. "So, what is it?"

"It's the Davenports, sir. I told you earlier that they wouldn't let me into their stateroom. Well, I've found out why."

He raised an eyebrow as she struggled for the right words.

"The thing is, it appears they brought a dog on board and last night it did a lot of damage to their furniture."

Captain Robertson's face turned crimson, and he stormed into the saloon. "Davenport."

Mr Davenport didn't need any further prompting before he rushed out to join them. "Yes, Captain."

"Come with me."

Nell stood fixed to the spot, but a second later, Captain Robertson called her.

"You too, Mrs Riley."

Nell hurried to keep up as the captain marched Mr Davenport down the corridor and into the stateroom. He only took a moment to survey the damage.

"Explain yourselves."

Mrs Davenport sobbed. "I'm sorry, Captain. She's never done anything like this before."

Miss Tiddles once again cowered in the bag, but the captain stormed towards it and grabbed the handles. "Is this it?"

Mrs Davenport dived towards the bag. "Please don't hurt her. Look at her, I couldn't leave her at home."

"You had no right to bring her on the ship. Did you deliberately keep Mrs Riley out of here until we'd left Queenstown?"

"She already..."

Nell's heart skipped a beat as Mr Davenport stared at her, but his wife kicked his ankle.

"I didn't want to involve Mrs Riley."

Captain Robertson sucked air through his teeth. "If it wasn't for my wife's condition, I'd turn this ship around now and disembark the three of you."

"Please don't do that." Mrs Davenport clasped her hands in front of her chest. "My husband will pay for the damage..."

"I'm well aware of that." Captain Robertson spun on his heel to face Nell. "How did you not notice a dog when you've been in here five times a day for a fortnight?"

"I-I'm sorry..."

"Don't blame her, Captain. It's my fault." Mrs Davenport stood beside Nell. "I kept Miss Tiddles in the bag. Once she's had something to eat, she sleeps..."

Captain Robertson's eyes lingered on Nell. "Very well. Off you go."

Nell didn't wait to be told twice and scurried back to the saloon.

"What on earth's the matter with you?" Mr Brennan looked up from behind the bar where he was getting ready for pre-dinner drinks.

"I need a brandy." Her heart raced as she ran a hand over her face.

"While you're working?"

"I won't be for much longer, if you don't pour me one."

"You'll have to tell me what's happened."

Nell turned around to see Mrs Swift walking towards them. "Pour me that drink and I'll tell you both together."

# CHAPTER THIRTY-FOUR

The morning was still dark as Nell stood on the deck watching the ship glide up the River Mersey towards the landing stage. *Why am I so keen to leave when this is my favourite part of the trip?*

She didn't know how long she'd been there before Mrs Swift joined her.

"At least it's not raining."

Nell sniggered. "It's the first time in months that it hasn't been. Still, it can't always be wet."

"How are you feeling now?"

Nell sighed. "I didn't sleep very well, if that's what you mean."

"I doubt the Davenports did, either."

"They've only got themselves to blame. I was an innocent bystander."

"I don't understand how you didn't see the dog when you serviced the room. Didn't you ever move the bag?"

Nell shook her head. "Mrs Davenport wouldn't let me

touch it. She was always there when I was cleaning and said it had valuables in it."

"Well, we're home now. Imagine if it had happened when we were approaching New York."

Nell shuddered. "I'd rather not. As it is, I've Mrs Robertson to deal with this morning."

"At least she has somewhere to go, and staff to take care of her."

"Thank goodness. There was part of me that wondered if she'd ask me to be her companion."

"So, she hasn't?" Mrs Swift raised her eyebrows.

"No. The office has arranged everything. They must think highly of Captain Robertson. It's moving her that will be the problem. She shouldn't be travelling in her condition."

"It's better than giving birth on board."

"It is. Especially when I'm the one who would have had to do the running around after her."

The ship slowed as it arrived and once the ropes had been thrown ashore, Nell indicated to the door.

"Shall we get ourselves some breakfast? The passengers will be wanting breakfast shortly."

Mrs Robertson's tray was ready when Nell walked into the galley, and she lifted the cloche.

"Is she restricted to porridge and toast?"

"I'm afraid so. I don't have time for anything else this morning. The sooner this lot are off the ship, the better."

"I won't argue with that. I'll be as quick as I can."

Mrs Robertson was standing in front of the wardrobe when Nell carried her tray into the room.

"What are you doing?"

Mrs Robertson perched on the edge of the bed. "I've nothing to wear. I've not worn a corset for the best part of a month and every one of those dresses was tight when I last tried them on."

Nell groaned. "I hadn't even considered that. Do you have any with elasticated waists?"

"They're hardly the height of fashion."

"Maybe not, but you'd be able to get into them." Nell picked each dress out of the wardrobe until she came to a lilac two-piece. "What about this?"

"The skirt wouldn't fasten before we left Liverpool, let alone now."

"It may not, but if the top fits, it will sit over your waist. If we stitch you into the skirt with some cotton, the blouse will cover the gap. And you'll be wearing your cloak."

Mrs Robertson didn't look convinced. "Do you have any thread?"

"No, but Matron does. You eat your breakfast while I speak to her. I'll be back once the passengers have disembarked."

Mr and Mrs Davenport were walking into the dining room when Nell returned, and she ushered them to a table.

"I'm glad you could join us."

Mrs Davenport grimaced as she took her seat. "Thank you, my dear. I'm sorry I got you into trouble yesterday."

"Fortunately, I'm in Captain Robertson's good books at the moment, so I escaped the worst of it. I hope you weren't too distressed."

"I'm just thankful that he's in a hurry to get to Liverpool."

"You and me both." Nell smiled. "Now, I must get on. I can only offer you toast or porridge this morning."

"Tea and toast for both of us, please."

Mr Davenport nodded. "We're in a hurry ourselves. I need to go to work to pay for the confounded damage."

"I won't keep you then."

Nell darted into the galley. "Tea and toast for two, please. Where's Mrs Swift?"

Mr Ross put another teapot on the counter. "She's taken a tray to the Hunters. Mrs Hunter's still not well enough to walk by herself."

"It's going to make disembarking interesting. Do we have a bath chair she can use?"

He shrugged. "I've no idea. You'll have to ask Dr Clarke."

"I'd rather stay out of it. It's no concern of mine."


Mr and Mrs Davenport, along with Miss Tiddles, were the first to leave, and there was no warmth in Captain Robertson's farewell.

"You'll be hearing from the company over the next few days."

Mrs Davenport hugged the dog to her bosom. "It wasn't your fault, was it, my darling? Mummy shouldn't have left you."

Captain Robertson clicked his tongue on his teeth. "If you wouldn't mind moving along, we've other passengers to disembark."

"I'm sorry." Mrs Davenport nudged her husband and nodded towards Nell.

"Oh, right-o." He reached into his pocket to retrieve a coin. Mrs Davenport immediately took it from him and closed Nell's hand around it.

"I know none of this was your fault."

Nell clasped the coin as Mrs Swift's eyes bored into her. "Thank you. I'm sorry it had to end as it did."

"There'll be no lasting damage. It was nice to meet you, Mrs Riley."

Nell watched them disappear. "I might as well go and sort Mrs Robertson out."

Mrs Swift caught her arm as she left. "You knew about that dog, didn't you?"

"Of course not. And keep your voice down." She glanced over at the captain, who was with a group of gentlemen.

"That looked like 'thank you for keeping your mouth shut' money."

"Well, it wasn't. She just appreciated my help. Now, if you'll excuse me, Mrs Robertson has a carriage to catch."

She slipped away down the corridor and knocked on the door before letting herself in.

"I'm really not sure this is a good idea." Mrs Robertson stood in her lilac outfit, her hands holding up the skirt. "Look at the gap down the back."

Nell bustled over to her. "You'll be fine once I've put a few stitches in." She took some cotton from her pocket. "Have you seen Matron this morning?"

"She popped in while you were out. She's going to escort me to our new house and settle me in."

"That's good. Will Captain Robertson go with you?"

"He hasn't said, but probably not. He'll follow when he's ready."

Once Nell had secured the stitches, she pulled the blouse over the waistline.

"There, nobody will know. All you need to do is walk from the ship to the carriage and then from the carriage to the house." She flinched as Mrs Robertson threw her arms around her.

"What would I have done without you? Thank you so much."

"You're welcome. I've enjoyed your company. Perhaps I can call on you when the baby's born and you're receiving visitors."

"Oh, I'd like that. You must get the address from my husband. I don't actually know where we're going."

"I will indeed." Nell paused when there was a knock on the door and Matron let herself in.

"You're all ready?"

"Mrs Riley helped me." Mrs Robertson showed the back of her skirt. "You may have to help me out of it when we get to where we're going."

"We'll worry about that once we're there. Now, do you need anything else?"

"No, I'm all set. My husband will bring the bags."

"Let's get you settled then."

Nell followed them to the foyer, where Captain Robertson had dismissed the stewards. His face twisted when he saw his wife.

"Are you sure you're all right?"

"I'll be fine. You will join me as soon as you can?"

"I'll be with you this evening. Matron will look after you until then." He offered her an arm and led her to the door, but she stopped and waited for Nell to join them.

"Farewell, Mrs Riley. Thank you for everything."

"You're most welcome. I hope it all goes well." Nell wiped away a tear as Mrs Robertson followed her husband down the gangplank.

Mrs Swift joined her on the platform and watched until Mrs Robertson reached the carriage. "Shall we get our things?"

"I suppose so. I had hoped to speak to Mr Hancock before I left, but I doubt they'll let him out of steerage before we leave."

Mrs Swift linked her arm. "You'll see him next week."

"Not if Mr Price has anything to do with it. He'll have him in steerage before I arrive. I wish I knew why he's so keen to keep Mr Marsh happy. I wonder if it might help Mr Hancock."

"So you really like him then?"

Nell's cheeks flushed. "I feel responsible for what happened."

Mrs Swift raised an eyebrow. "Is that what it is?"

Half an hour later, Nell stepped onto the landing stage and surveyed the crowds. No Vernon. *Hopefully, it means he's working.*

"Are you waiting for someone?" Mr Ramsbottom grinned as he jumped from the bottom of the gangplank.

"I thought my nephew might be here to meet me, but I can't see him."

"I'm going in your direction. May I offer you a ride?"

Nell stared at him. "How can you be? You live in Birmingham."

"I want to make sure you get home safely. It will save you carrying your bag, too." His grin broadened. "What do you say?"

"I say, thank you, but..." She paused, sensing someone was watching her. A second later, she locked eyes with Mr Marsh, who was on the top deck, staring down at her. *Let's get rid of you, once and for all.* She turned back to Mr Ramsbottom. "I'd say, thank you. That would be most kind."

He yelped as a grin spread across his face, and he offered her an arm. "Walk this way. Your carriage awaits."

# CHAPTER THIRTY-FIVE

Nell leaned against the side of the carriage as they rounded the corner into Merlin Street and Mr Ramsbottom slid along the seat towards her.

"We're here." She peered through the window and gave a sigh of relief as the house came into view and Maria appeared in the street. "My sister's waiting." She sat forward and reached for her bag.

"At least I know where you are." There was a twinkle in his eyes. "Perhaps we could walk out tomorrow."

"Tomorrow! Er ... no. I've a wedding to attend. My nephew."

"That's a shame. What about the day after?"

"I..." Nell turned as the door opened and Maria poked her head inside.

"Where've you been? I was expecting you an hour ago." She stood Leah on the steps of the carriage. "Look who's here."

"Mama!"

"Look at you." Nell reached out and squeezed her

daughter's hand before turning back to Mr Ramsbottom. "I need to go. I'll see you on Thursday." She didn't wait for a reply before following Leah out of the carriage. "Have a nice few days."

Maria passed her daughter to her as the coachman closed the carriage door. "Do you have something to tell me?"

Nell shuddered. "No. I've just told him Sam's getting married tomorrow so he doesn't call. Isn't Elenor home?"

"In there." Leah pointed to the house.

She squeezed her daughter as she walked into the hall. "Have you been a good girl for Alice?"

Leah nodded, and Alice looked up with a smile as they joined her.

"They both have." She turned Elenor's head. "Aren't you going to speak to Mam?"

"No."

Nell put Leah on the floor and took off her cloak. "It's a good job Leah is, then."

"She doesn't miss you as much as me."

Nell crouched down on the rug. "If you miss me, you should be pleased to see me."

"Not if you go away again. Alice is my mam now."

Tears welled in Nell's eyes as Elenor flung her arms around her cousin's neck, but Alice unhooked them.

"No, I'm not. Now give Mam a hug or she might not want to come home again."

"Yes, I will." Nell reached for Elenor's hand. "I miss you, too, but I need to earn some money."

"Why? Aunty Ria says we have enough dresses."

"So we can buy some food and have a nice house. You wouldn't like to live on the streets."

Elenor stamped her foot. "Why does it have to be you? Why can't Aunty Ria go?"

The smug grin Nell had been ignoring on her sister's face disappeared.

"You'll go to your room if you carry on like that." Maria stomped to the kitchen and filled the kettle, but Nell stayed where she was.

"I'm home for nearly a week, so we can do lots of things together, and after one more trip I'll be here for a long time."

"How long?" Maria returned, carrying some cups and saucers.

"We'll talk about it later." Nell pushed herself up from the floor and sat in a chair by the fire, lifting Leah onto her knee. "What's been happening here? Has Vernon got himself some permanent work?"

"He has." Maria beamed. "He's ship-building again."

"What a relief. So, they're all working?"

"They are. Even Tom's got himself a job."

"That's wonderful. Making barrels?"

Maria snorted. "He's banned from that after the trouble he caused, but they've given him a position in a warehouse at the Albert Dock. He's not stopped moaning about it, but he knows better than to kick up a fuss."

"And Sam?"

"He's working, but he's more bothered about getting married." Maria went into the kitchen as the kettle boiled, but Nell called after her.

"Does that mean Sarah and Jane are talking to you?"

"They are now they want me to do some baking for the wedding. You can give me a hand while you're here."

"I will, but we can't do anything too soon. When are you expecting James home?"

"Not until Tuesday." Maria returned with the teapot and put it in the centre of the table. "As long as he's not delayed."

"I hope he's not." Nell's stomach churned. "I've not seen him for months. I'd hate to miss him by a day."

"You've no one but yourself to blame."

Nell rolled her eyes at Alice. *I asked for that.* "At least I'll have time to do other things. I need to visit Miss Ellis while I'm home."

"You'd better not be going today."

"I'm not. I'll call on Rebecca this afternoon and Miss Ellis on Monday."

"It would be nice if you could spend some time at home."

"I'll be here all day tomorrow and Sunday."

"You needn't spend all afternoon with Rebecca, either. You can make tea and give me a break. And don't forget George eats at half past four."

Nell sighed. *And she wonders why I don't want to stay.*


Rebecca was knitting when Nell arrived with Leah.

"You're home!" She dropped her needles onto the side table.

"I am." Nell sat Leah on the floor with her cousin Florrie. "How are you?"

"All the better for seeing you. Let me reboil the kettle."

She stepped into the kitchen. "Didn't Elenor want to come with you?"

"She's naughty." Leah followed Nell to the kitchen door and held onto her skirt before Nell picked her up.

"She is. Not like you."

"My good." Leah wrapped her arms around Nell's neck.

"Elenor won't even talk to me. I don't know what I'm going to do with her. I wish she was starting school after Christmas. That'd sort her out."

"Easter's only at the end of March, so not long to wait." Rebecca carried the cups and saucers to the living room.

"I suppose not. Anyway, what have you been up to?"

She sighed. "Nothing I haven't done a hundred times before. I'd rather hear about what you've been doing."

Nell took a seat and sat Leah on her knee. "You're not helping me with my decision. There are so many reasons to stay at home, but being stuck in the same rut as before isn't one of them."

"So you'll sign up for another year?"

"I've not decided yet."

George was in his usual seat by the fire when Nell walked into the living room, and he beamed as she joined him.

"You're home."

"I am. For six days."

"That's nice. She's got you cooking tea, though."

Nell peered into the empty kitchen. "It's only liver and onions, so it shouldn't take long." She took the seat opposite him. "Is she in the back?"

"She is. How was your trip?"

"I've had better. There was a bit of trouble with some stolen jewellery on the way out, but we were half empty on the return. I'm not sure which was worse."

"Did they blame you?"

Nell nodded. "They tried, but it turned out to be one of the passengers. We had a solicitor on board who helped sort it all out."

"I'm glad you had someone looking out for you."

Maria closed the back door as she joined them. "She's had another gentleman escorting her home. That's the second in two months."

Nell sighed. "It's not what it looks like. I was grateful not to have to carry my bag all this way."

George studied her. "You watch they don't expect anything in return."

"I-I'm sure they won't." Nell's cheeks flushed. "Oh my, look at the time. I'd better get your tea on."


As soon as George had left for work, Nell collected his dishes from the table.

"Is he never home at teatime?"

"No, he eats by himself every day except Sunday. That's the problem with alehouses opening for as many hours as they do."

"At least you see more of him than when he was at sea."

"I've got rather used to it, too." A smile settled on Maria's lips.

"So, you're happy?"

"As happy as you can be around here." The front door slammed. "That will be the boys."

"Evening." Vernon joined them and took a seat at the table before he noticed Nell. "When did you get home?"

"This morning. I hear you've found yourself a job."

"I have. More money too, so all the problems may have been worth it."

"No, they weren't." Maria scowled at him. "Don't even think of trying it again."

Billy took the seat next to his brother. "He won't. Dad'll see to that. I presume he's gone."

"Of course."

"We'll see him later." Vernon smirked. "It's handy having him behind the bar. We get faster service."

"He shouldn't be encouraging you to spend your money." Maria sliced into the extra sausage roll she'd made and handed it out.

"It's better than that. He doesn't always charge us. We're saving a fortune."

"You can give me some more then." Maria handed him a plate. "Your dad's not bringing home as much as he did."

"We're not saving that much." Billy nudged his brother. "It's him trying to show off."

"It's still good, though."

Maria huffed as she continued serving. "Just think how much money we'd save if there were no alehouses."

"And think how miserable we'd all be." Vernon took a large bite of bread as Billy accepted his plate.

"Stop worrying. You'll get some wages off James next week."

"Not before time, either." She divided the last piece of sausage roll between herself and Alice and disappeared into the kitchen. "Don't wait for me."

Nell leaned towards Billy. "Does James know what he's coming home to?"

"I doubt it."

"He's up to something." Vernon spoke despite his mouth being full.

"Like what?"

He shrugged. "We don't know, but he's been keeping out of Mam and Dad's way all summer. We hardly see him any more."

Nell turned to Alice. "Do you know what he's up to?"

She shook her head. "He doesn't trust me in case I tell Mam."

Nell stopped as Maria reappeared. *I don't like the sound of that.*

# CHAPTER THIRTY-SIX

The entrance to Sefton Park was quiet as Nell escorted Miss Ellis past the elaborate gateway. She took a deep breath as the lawns spread out before her.

"It's good to be back. It's one of the things I miss about being away."

"I've missed it, too. I never go out when you're not here." There was a skip in Miss Ellis's step as they walked. "Tell me more about Mr Marsh. Don't you think he'll be on the next voyage?"

"I hope not. If he was angry when he saw me with Mr Hancock, he'll have been furious that I accepted a ride from Mr Ramsbottom." Nell chuckled. "The only downside is that I'll have to watch myself with Mr Ramsbottom."

"You need to be careful."

"I will be. If I've learned one thing this year, it's how to look after myself. Besides, Mr Hancock will keep an eye out for me."

"And you won't mind?"

Nell's cheeks flushed. "He is rather nice."

"How exciting!" Miss Ellis clapped her hands, but suddenly stopped. "Does that mean you'll want to stay on the ship to be with him?"

Nell rolled her eyes. "I said he's nice. It doesn't mean I'll be marrying him."

Miss Ellis clutched her hands to her chest. "It would be romantic, though."

"Maria wouldn't be best pleased. Or Elenor. Or Rebecca."

"Or me, for that matter. Although I have something to occupy me next month." The smile returned to Miss Ellis's face.

"Don't tell me you're walking out with someone?"

"No, silly. Father wouldn't allow that, but... I've had a letter from Mr Hewitt."

"Really." Nell's eyes widened. "Is he coming to visit?"

"He is! With Mr Cavendish. They'll be here the week after next."

Nell's face fell. "How long are they staying for?"

"He didn't say. Several weeks I imagine."

Nell sighed. "I'll be away until the end of the month. The twenty something."

"He may stay that long. I can tell him you'd like to meet him again."

Nell shook her head. "He won't wait around for me. Not once he's finished his business."

Miss Ellis's shoulders sagged. "What a pity. I'd hoped we could all go for afternoon tea."

"I wish we could, but we both know I'm not in the same class as him."

"Me neither, but we had so much fun last time he was here. It's a shame you're away."

Nell grimaced. "It's almost enough to make me want to stay at home."

"But then you wouldn't see Mr Hancock."

"I only said I liked him, but there's no more future for us than there would be for me and Mr Hewitt."

"Why not?"

"Because he's a steward. His life's at sea, and after what happened to my husband, I couldn't go through that again."

"What a shame." Miss Ellis linked Nell's arm. "Do you remember last time you visited, and we took tea in the sitting room?"

"I do. It was lovely."

"I suggested we could walk out more often if you didn't go away next year."

"I remember, but I wasn't sure how much time I'd have, if I had to get another job."

"I've been thinking about that. Since we've started walking, I've realised that I need an official companion. Someone I can go out with whenever I want."

Nell stared along the gravel path. "Oh."

"Don't say 'Oh' like that. I was hoping it would be you."

"Me? But I wouldn't have time."

"Maybe you would if I paid you. I've spoken to Father, and now I'm getting more money from the publisher I could afford six shillings a week. I don't suppose it's as much as you get now, but at least you'd be at home..."

"Really?" Nell gasped. "That's very kind of you. I'd like to spend my afternoons doing this, but..."

"But what?"

"I'll need to check with Maria how she is for money. I should have done it already, but I keep putting it off because I know it will cause an argument. Can I let you know?"

"Only if you say you accept my offer. You're my friend now so we should spend more time together."

Nell smiled. "That's very sweet. I'll speak to her tonight and tell you next time I'm home."

Rebecca and Maria were in the front room when Nell arrived home. She popped her head through the door. "What are you doing in here?"

Rebecca grinned. "Waiting for you."

"And George was dozing by the fire in the other room." Maria stood up and closed the door.

"I thought he'd have gone to work by now."

"He has, but I lit the fire in here, so thought we might as well stay put until it burns out."

Nell took a seat near the window as Rebecca smirked at her.

"You had a visitor this afternoon."

Nell's forehead creased. "Who?"

"That's what we want to know. It looked like the man who brought you home on Friday."

"Mr Ramsbottom?" A tingle ran down Nell's spine. "What did you tell him?"

Maria shrugged. "That you were out."

"Did he say if he'd call again?"

"Do you want him to?" Rebecca's eyes brightened.

"No, I don't." She sighed. "I only accepted a lift from him to make Mr Marsh jealous."

Rebecca exchanged a glance with Maria. "You said last month that Mr Marsh had left the ship."

"He had, but he came back. He annoys me every time I see him and so I thought that if he saw me with Mr Ramsbottom, he'd leave again."

"And has he?"

Nell shrugged. "I won't know until the next voyage, but he watched us walking to the carriage, so I'm hopeful."

"Why didn't you tell us?" Maria stood up to pour Nell a cup of tea.

"I didn't want to worry you. I'm not interested in any of them, but ... well, they don't see many women on the ship, so we get a lot of attention."

"Nothing inappropriate, I hope."

"It's no more than a bit of banter."

"As long as that's all it is." Maria handed her the cup. "Why didn't James warn you?"

"He probably doesn't realise. It depends who he has as a stewardess."

"I still don't like you doing it."

"You're happy to have the money, though. You must admit, you'd have struggled this year without it."

Maria sighed. "It still doesn't make it right. You've seen how Elenor is with you. You can't keep going away and leaving them."

"Could you manage now, if I didn't?"

"We'd have to tighten our belts."

"The girls are growing up. They're only going to get more expensive, not less."

"We'll just have to deal with it."

Nell stared into her tea. "What about Alice?"

"What about her?"

"I won't be able to pay her to look after the girls any more. What will she do?"

"She can start making waistcoats again. You're not using her as an excuse to leave again."

Rebecca stood up. "Talking of Alice, I'd better get home. She was picking Isobel up from school and taking the girls to our house. I don't want Hugh getting home while she's there and I'm not. It would cause more trouble than it's worth."

## CHAPTER THIRTY-SEVEN

Nell bounced out of bed the following morning. James was due home and if Maria wanted her to make some cakes for Sam's wedding, they needed to be done before they went for a walk this afternoon.

They were already in the range when the front door opened, and Nell rushed to the hall.

"You're here!" She threw her arms around James' neck. "I've missed you."

"I've missed you, too." He laughed as he disentangled himself. "I tried not to get too excited in case you'd gone again." He hung up his hat and coat and followed her into the living room.

The girls carried on playing by the hearth as Alice gave her brother a hug. "Welcome home."

He peered into the kitchen. "Where's Mam?"

"At the shops. She won't be long."

"And Dad?"

"You've just missed him."

A smile split his face. "Splendid. I can have some peace with my two favourite girls."

"And us." Elenor looked up from her abacus.

"And you." He rubbed the girls' heads. "Is there any tea going?"

"There's a pot brewing." Alice jumped up to get him a cup while Nell sat opposite him by the fire.

"How are you?"

"All the better for seeing you. It's been a long time."

"Six months."

Alice handed him some bread and butter, covered in plum jam. "Tell Aunty Nell about going to New York."

Nell's eyes widened. "You've been again?"

He grinned. "In June. They let a group of us off the ship, but we only had a few hours. We didn't get much further than the immigrant houses, but it was still exciting."

"That's a shame. You'll get to Central Park one day."

"Maybe." He hesitated and took a bite of bread. "How long are you here for?"

"Until first thing on Thursday. What about you?"

"Until the Thursday after."

Nell cocked her head to one side. "That's a long break."

"I-I'm changing ships."

A lump settled in Nell's stomach. "You're not in trouble, are you?"

"No. Nothing like that. I thought it was time for a change. Anyway, tell me what's been happening here."

. . .

Maria had settled down for the afternoon before Nell took the last batch of cakes from the range and set them on the table.

"That should do it for now. What time is it?"

"Quarter past two." James jumped to his feet. "We need to go if we want to take a walk. Are you ready, Aunty Nell?"

Maria's face soured. "What about waiting to see your dad? He'll be home soon."

James reached into the hall for Nell's cloak. "I'll see him tonight. It will be too dark if we leave it much longer." He slung the cloak around Nell's shoulders, then plonked his hat on his head as he grabbed his coat. "We'll see you later."

Nell rolled her eyes as he closed the door and put on his coat.

"Don't look at me like that. I didn't realise the time."

"I'm not looking at you like anything. It's your mam. She should realise by now that you wouldn't wait for your dad."

"She chooses not to see it." He offered her his arm and pointed to his right. "We'd better go this way. I'd rather not bump into him yet." They walked at speed to the end of the road, only slowing down once they turned the corner.

"That should do it." He grinned at her. "Princes Park?"

"That would be nice. We might even meet Alice and Betty there. They've taken the girls to see the ducks."

He squeezed her arm. "I can't believe it's been six months. Are you still enjoying life on board?"

"Most of the time."

His brow furrowed. "What's that supposed to mean?"

"There are always issues, but nothing to worry about."

"What about that steward, Mr Marsh? Is he still keeping out of your way?"

Nell groaned. "Not on the last voyage."

"Why? What happened?"

"Our head steward, Mr Price, moved him back upstairs."

"Why would he do that?"

Nell creased the side of her mouth. "We don't know, but the rumour is, Mr Price did something *unsavoury* in port and Mr Marsh has threatened to report him."

James clicked his tongue. "It must have been something bad if he can hold that much sway over him."

"I don't doubt it, but at least the next voyage will be the last and I'm hoping he won't be with us."

"Why wouldn't he be?"

Nell sighed. "He doesn't like me talking to the other stewards, so I deliberately accepted a lift home with one of them on Friday, knowing he'd seen me. He left the ship last time it happened."

"Aunty Nell!"

She shrugged. "What else could I do? I'm not getting any support from Mr Price, so I decided I had to take things into my own hands."

"Would you like me to have a word with Mr Price?"

"What could you do? You've only met him once or twice."

"I don't know. I could talk to him, steward to steward. It might help."

"No, thank you. It could make matters worse and it won't be necessary if Mr Marsh isn't on board."

295

"Well, I hope your plan works. What will you do next year?"

"I've not decided. The last voyage wasn't the best, but there's still a part of me that would like to carry on. The trouble is, I feel guilty every time I leave home. Elenor's only just speaking to me, after me being here for five days."

"I imagine Mam's been having a go at you, too."

"She never stops. Sometimes I think it would be easier to give in, but then she'll have won."

"Would you get another job if you stayed here?"

She smiled as the gates to the park came into view. "I might already have one."

"What? Where?" His eyes widened.

"With Miss Ellis, the author I met on the ship. She's asked if I'll be her companion."

"So she'll pay you for taking afternoon tea?"

"Or going for walks." Her smile didn't last. "It sounds ideal, but she can only give me six shillings a week so I'm not sure."

"It's not to be sniffed at."

"I know, and I am tempted, but I'll see how this trip goes. What about you? What's all this with changing ships? Is it a promotion?"

"Not exactly. It's more that I need a change." He paused. "Don't say anything to Mam, but I've accepted a position on one of the Australian liners."

"Australia!" The colour drained from her cheeks. "Then you'll never be home."

"That's the point. Mam and Dad have been unbearable while you've been away, and I don't want to be here any more. No more than a couple of times a year, anyway."

"But your dad's hardly at home now he's working in the alehouse."

"He's in every afternoon, which is when I'm usually there, and he's behind the bar of an evening when I go out."

"Couldn't you go to a different local?"

"When all my friends are in that one? Why should I?"

"But going to Australia…"

"I have to try. If I earn enough money, I might be able to get a place of my own, which would make things easier."

Nell blinked back her tears as she stared out over the lake. "That will make it even worse if I stay at home."

"I'm sorry, Aunty Nell."

"Is it too late to change your mind?"

He nodded. "It's all arranged. The only thing I haven't done is tell Mam and Dad."

She wandered to a bench at the edge of the path. "Why do we let them frighten us so much? We're both adults. I'm a mam myself, for goodness' sake, and yet I can't make my own decisions."

"I suppose that's why I'm running away. It's the easy option."

"I'd do the same if it wasn't for the girls…" She sighed. "We really are a couple of misfits, aren't we?"

"We just want different things…" James paused as Alice rounded the corner with her cousin Betty and the girls.

"Here you are." Alice smiled. "I thought you might be here. We've been looking out for you."

Nell took Leah from the pram. "You can't have looked very hard; we've been here for the last half an hour. How are you, Betty?"

"Very well, thank you, Aunty Nell."

Alice beamed. "We've been planning Betty's wedding. Did you know I'm to be a bridesmaid?"

"Yes, I heard. Have you set a date yet?"

Betty's cheeks coloured. "June the eighth next year."

Nell looked up at Alice. "Did your dad agree to hold the wedding breakfast at home?"

"He did. Aunty Jane was very persuasive."

Nell raised an eyebrow to James. "I can imagine. Hopefully, I'll be here for the happy day."

Alice stroked the handle of the pram. "Do you think you'll go to sea next year?"

"I haven't decided yet. What would you do if I did?"

Alice shrugged. "Mam thinks I'll go back to making waistcoats, but..."

"You don't want to?"

Alice shook her head. "It's nice being paid to do something I enjoy."

"You'd better not say that in front of your mam. She'll blame you if I go away again."

"But you needn't go away. If you got a job round here, you'd need someone to take care of the girls."

"The problem is I couldn't afford to pay you with the wages I'd get here."

"Oh." Alice's shoulders drooped.

"Don't worry about it now. I'll add it to the list of things to consider. Once I decide what to do, you'll be the first to know."

# CHAPTER THIRTY-EIGHT

Nell hadn't got out of bed before the familiar stomach cramps that accompanied each farewell forced her to curl into a ball. *They're getting worse rather than better.* She wrapped an arm around Leah's small frame. *Five more minutes.*

Footsteps on the stairs roused her from her dozing and she planted a kiss on Leah's forehead before throwing off the bedcovers.

"Mama." Leah reached out to her.

"I'm going for breakfast; do you want to come?"

Leah pushed her dark curls from her face as she nodded.

"Stay there while I get dressed, then."

Maria was already at the table when they arrived downstairs. "Are you all ready?"

"I think so." Nell looked at Billy as she sat Leah on her knee. "Was James awake when you came down? He's walking me to the ship."

"If he wasn't, he will be once Vernon realises he's late. Again. He hasn't got used to the extra ten-minute walk."

As if on cue, Vernon burst into the room and grabbed two pieces of bread and butter. "I'll see you all tonight." He turned to leave, but Maria shouted him back.

"Aunty Nell won't be here later."

His eyes glazed. "Already? I thought you were here for a week."

"Six days."

"But ... oh, right. I'll see you next month." Without further delay, he headed down the hall, slamming the door behind him.

Maria stared at the ceiling. "Will he never learn? He'll have George awake now."

Billy stood up. "Time for me to go, too. Have a safe trip."

Nell forced down her bread as the front door slammed. "I hope Alice brings Elenor to wave me off. I only had my first hug from her last night."

"You know how to change that."

Nell bit her lip. "You don't need to keep reminding me."

By the time she was ready to leave, the rest of the family were downstairs, and Rebecca let herself in. Nell studied her sister's face.

"It looks like you didn't get much sleep."

"Florrie was awake for most of the night, and I had to keep her from waking Hugh."

"I'm sorry." She put a hand on her sister's shoulder. "Try not to let him get you down."

"It's easy for you to say. I know I shouldn't wish my life

away, but the next four weeks can't go quickly enough. Come home safely."

Alice joined them at the door with Leah. "Are you going to wave to Mam?"

Leah held out her arms to Nell. "My come, too."

"Not this time." She took hold of her daughter. "You be a good girl for Alice, and I'll be home soon."

"Tonight?"

"Soon." She kissed Leah on the forehead and handed her to Alice. "Where's Elenor?"

"She doesn't like waving you off."

A pang twisted Nell's stomach. "At least she gave me a hug when I told her this is the last trip for a while."

"What do you mean, for a while?" Maria glared at her.

"It depends how long the money lasts." Nell sighed and, with a final kiss for Leah, she stepped outside and took James' arm.

They set off towards Windsor Street and, as they approached the corner, she stopped to wave. "I wish Elenor would come and see me off."

"At least I don't have to worry about things like that. Does your friend Mrs Swift have children?"

"She's not married. It's just her, her mam and sister. She earns the money, and the sister looks after the house and the mother."

"There must be other women with families who work."

Nell sighed. "If they're on the ships, I don't know where they are."

. . .

Half an hour later, James set down Nell's bag at the top of the gangplank, and straightened up, a bittersweet smile on his face.

"This is it."

"It is." Nell choked back her tears. "You take care of yourself."

"And you." He wrapped his arms around her. "I should be home for Easter next year."

"It seems like such a long time away. We're not even close to Christmas yet."

"It will be here soon enough. And I'll write."

"I'll look forward to that." She wiped her eyes with a handkerchief, but turned at the sound of a discreet cough behind her. "Welcome back, Mrs Riley."

"Mr Cooper. Good morning." She indicated to James. "My nephew, Mr Atkin."

"Pleased to meet you." Mr Cooper offered James a hand. "It must seem strange dropping your aunt off for work. Most peculiar."

"Not really. I'm a steward myself and I've seen how our lady passengers value a stewardess."

"I see." Mr Cooper sucked in his cheeks. "Now, if you'll excuse us, we have a meeting in twenty minutes."

"I'm on my way."

Nell clung to James' arm. "Come home safe."

"I will."

Nell watched him walk down the gangplank, but as soon as he reached the bottom, Mr Cooper stepped inside.

"We need to go. Mrs Swift's already on board, and we're having our usual meeting at eight o'clock. Don't be late."

. . .

Mrs Swift had unpacked when Nell arrived at their cabin.

"You must have been early."

"I was. My sister's been driving me mad, so I couldn't wait to get away."

Nell grimaced. "Now you know how I feel. I take it your mam's better."

"She is, thank you." Mrs Swift paused as she studied her. "Have you been crying?"

"Not really, but it's my nephew, James. He's moving to an Australian liner. If I stay on the ship next year, I don't know if I'll see him again."

"So, will you leave?"

"I doubt it would make much difference. He'll only be home a couple of times a year." She hung her dress in the wardrobe and was reaching for her uniform when there was a knock on the door.

"Are you two in there?"

Mrs Swift stared at her. "Matron. What does she want?" She pulled open the door. "Good morning. Is everything all right?"

"I wanted to update you on Mrs Robertson before we went upstairs."

Nell fastened the button at the nape of her neck. "Has she had her baby?"

"Unfortunately not. I was with her until yesterday afternoon but had to pass her care to the local midwife."

"What a shame. Was she in good spirits?"

Matron shook her head. "She still couldn't understand why she had to stay in Liverpool. She'd have come with us if Captain Robertson had let her."

"I imagine she'll be quite lonely. Let's hope the baby arrives quickly. That will keep her occupied."

"It would be helpful if it arrived before we reach Queenstown. Captain Robertson will worry about her if it doesn't."

"It could be weeks before he hears, then. I remember it was like that for Jack. He was away for a couple of months after Elenor was born."

"It's what they sign up for. Now, we'd better get a move on. The men will be waiting for us."

Nell's face brightened as she scanned the stewards' side of the dining room. *No Mr Marsh. Splendid.* Her smile didn't last when Mr Ramsbottom waved to her. *He's rather eager.*

Mr Ross met them at their table. "Good morning, ladies. Did you have a pleasant break?"

"Yes, thank you. Did you?"

"Smashing." He rubbed his hands together. "Let me get you your tea."

Captain Robertson appeared subdued when he joined them. "Good morning, everyone. I hope you all had a good rest and you're ready for our last voyage. As usual, we're full to capacity on our way to New York, but will be rather quiet on the return. We'll use that time to clean the ship thoroughly, but more of that once we reach New York. For now, we only have one change of crew to tell you about."

Nell smiled as she waited for the announcement.

"Mr Hancock has left the ship and so Mr Marsh will once again be taking over in steerage…"

Nell's face fell. *That's the wrong way round.* She turned

to Mrs Swift, who was already looking at her. "Did I hear that right?"

Mrs Swift nodded towards the foyer, causing Nell's heart to skip a beat.

*Oh my goodness, he's still here... and he's forced Mr Hancock out.* "He's not supposed to be here."

"Why wouldn't he be?"

Nell couldn't speak. *I'll have Mr Ramsbottom to deal with, too.*

Mrs Swift leaned over. "Don't look so worried. Captain Robertson's already said he'll be in steerage."

*Mr Ramsbottom won't be, though. How do I keep out of his way?*

## CHAPTER THIRTY-NINE

B y ten o'clock the following morning, the staterooms were clean and ready for their next occupants. Nell was in her usual position in the foyer as the first of the guests arrived, but Mrs Swift edged closer to her.

"I've checked the passenger list and we've a number of ladies this voyage, several travelling on their own."

"That should keep us busy, especially if they've no one else to talk to."

"That's what I thought. Ooh, who's this?"

A middle-aged man, with a coat slung over his shoulders and a large hat covering his longer than fashionable hair, strode up to the captain.

Nell suppressed a cough. "What on earth's he wearing?"

"He must be from London."

"I don't doubt that. If he turned up at our house looking like that, George would send him on his way."

Mrs Swift laughed. "I wouldn't if he came to our door."

"I expect Mr Ross will find out all about him before

luncheon's ready. Or maybe not." Nell's shoulders slumped. "Mr Cooper's taking him to his stateroom. You know how much he disapproves of gossiping."

"When did that ever stop Mr Ross? Although he may have other things to think about." Mrs Swift nodded towards an elegant young woman with auburn hair and an exquisite bustle on the back of her dress. She offered Captain Robertson her hand.

"Mrs Phillips, how lovely to meet you. Did you have a pleasant journey here?"

"Very nice, thank you, although I've only travelled from the Adelphi. It's a marvellous place if you ever need somewhere to stay."

"So I believe." The captain signalled to Mrs Swift. "Would you take Mrs Phillips to her stateroom?"

Nell watched them disappear, but took a step backwards when Mr Ramsbottom winked and walked by a little too closely as he led an elderly couple from the foyer. *The lady's unsteady on her feet, and we've not left the dock yet.*

Several more gentlemen greeted the captain before another woman arrived, wearing a grey hat that matched her hair. *I imagine she'll be with me.* Nell waited for the captain to summon her.

"Will you show Mrs Everest to her stateroom?"

"Certainly. Would you walk this way?" Nell set off down the corridor but stopped when the woman failed to keep up. "Would you care to take my arm?"

"If you didn't walk so fast, there'd be no need."

"I'm sorry. There isn't far to go."

"I hope I won't have half the ship walking past my room

every evening. I'm a light sleeper and like to be in bed early."

"Not too many and passengers are usually considerate."

"They had better be or I'll be having a word with the captain."

Nell opened the stateroom door and stepped to one side as Mrs Everest walked past her. "I hope you'll find everything satisfactory. Your trunk should be with you soon."

"I should hope so. I don't want to wait all day for it."

"Would you like any help unpacking?"

"Certainly not. I'm not having the likes of you going through my personal property."

Nell bit her lip. "As you wish. Morning coffee is being served in the saloon, and luncheon will be at one o'clock." She didn't wait for a response and closed the door rather more forcibly than she intended. *I won't be coming back next year if things carry on like this.*

Nell stood near the galley as the stewards showed the guests to their seats for luncheon. She smiled as Mrs Phillips took her table.

"Good afternoon, madam. May I get you a drink?"

"A sherry, please." She studied Nell. "You're a stewardess, I presume. How many of you are there?"

"Only the two of us. You met Mrs Swift earlier."

"I did, and very helpful she was, too. Doesn't she serve at luncheon?"

"She does, but she must be delayed with another guest. I'll ask her to take over when she comes back."

"There's no need. I'm happy with either of you. It's nice having some female company." She studied the rest of the tables. "There don't seem to be many of us on our own."

"More ladies travel with their husbands than on their own, but they often sit together when they're in the saloon. I'm sure they'll be happy for you to join them."

The woman grimaced. "We'll see. Widows are not always welcome when husbands are nearby."

"You're a widow?"

"Is it such a surprise? My husband was twenty years my senior and I lost him several years ago."

"Oh, forgive me, but you look too young to have been on your own for any length of time. I see you're out of your mourning clothes."

"That ended earlier this year. Not that I minded wearing them. My acquaintances were far more accommodating when they didn't consider me a threat."

"I can imagine." Nell looked over her shoulders. "A word of warning, don't walk around outside by yourself, especially not after dark. The stewards..." She rolled her eyes. "They're in a particularly strange mood at the moment, too."

"I quite understand and thank you for the advice. Not that I intend to."

"Not now, but you might as we approach land." Nell hesitated as Mrs Everest took a seat close by. "Let me get your sherry."

Mr Brennan was already shaking a cocktail when she arrived at the bar.

"Good afternoon, Mr Brennan."

He grinned when he saw her. "Mrs Riley."

"Why are you smirking whenever I see you?"

He shrugged. "I don't know what you mean. I'm wondering if you've any drinkers for me?"

She huffed. "Not yet. Mrs Phillips would like a sherry."

"I noticed her. What's her husband thinking, letting her travel on her own?"

"She's a widow."

"Really." He raised an eyebrow as he stared over to her. "He must have left her a pretty penny."

"I couldn't say, but if I could take her drink."

"You see to the old woman next to her and I'll deliver the sherry."

"You'll do no such thing. I've already warned her about the stewards. I'll add your name to the list, if you carry on like that."

"Don't you dare." He continued to study her. "I'll wander over and introduce myself before luncheon's over."

"Then I'll definitely warn her."

Mrs Phillips and Mrs Everest were in conversation when Nell returned with the sherry.

"May I get you anything, Mrs Everest?"

The woman scowled. "You can stop interrupting, for one thing."

Nell backed away. "I do apologise. Let me know when you'd like to order."

"I may as well do it now. I'll try a sherry. Nothing too dry."

"Certainly."

Nell was at the bar when Mrs Swift joined her.

"Where've you been?"

"Helping Matron. Did you see an elderly couple arrive

earlier? Mr and Mrs Flanagan. She walked with a stick. She's had a fall in the stateroom and bruised her face and all down one side."

"Oh dear. Is she all right?"

"She's a bit shaken, but there's nothing broken. They're in one of Mr Ramsbottom's rooms, but she'll need you, as well."

"Why me?"

"She's on your corridor."

"I can't work with Mr Ramsbottom if he thinks I like him..."

Mrs Swift picked up the tray of drinks Mr Brennan had prepared for her. "Of course you can. You've put up with him for long enough. Unless you want to move down to steerage and work with Mr Marsh."

Nell glowered at her. "That's not even funny."

Nell's feet throbbed as she and Mrs Swift took their seats for luncheon.

"All the fetching and carrying from the last ten months must have caught up with me. I'll be glad for a longer break at Christmas."

Mrs Swift placed her napkin on her knee. "It could be the passengers. That Mrs Everest's a right moaner."

"You've noticed. It's a shame she's sitting next to Mrs Phillips. She's very pleasant, but there'll be no chance to talk to her with Mrs Everest there."

Mrs Swift smiled. "At least Mrs Phillips is on my side of the ship, so I may find out a bit about her."

"She's a widow, in case you're wondering. Her husband passed several years ago."

"You know that already?" Mrs Swift shook her head. "And have you found out about our flamboyant gentleman?"

"Hardly, when he's in the men's section. Here's someone who might know, though."

Mr Ross's eyes darted between them. "Might know what?"

Nell sat back while he set down a plate of fried halibut. "Anything about the *unusual* gentleman?"

Mr Ross laughed. "That's a good word for him. His name's Divine and rumour has it he's something to do with the theatre."

Mrs Swift clapped her hands together. "Is he an actor?"

"I've no idea. Mr Cooper prefers giving orders to asking questions. We may need to get one of you ladies on the case."

"I could do that." Mrs Swift's face lit up. "Mrs Riley could give me a few tips on what to ask."

Mr Ross chuckled as he turned to leave. "I'll bear that in mind."

"How exciting if he's an actor." Mrs Swift cut into her fish. "Do you ever go to see plays?"

"Don't be daft. I've heard some actors are famous, though."

Mrs Swift sighed as she gazed into space. "He's rather handsome, too."

Nell dropped her knife. "You're not serious..."

"Calm down." Mrs Swift tutted. "I only said he was handsome."

"It was the look on your face when you said it. I didn't think you wanted a husband."

"I don't, but you never know. If the right man came along..."

Nell took a drink of water. "You can't cause a scandal on our last voyage."

There was a twinkle in Mrs Swift's eyes. "That's the best time to cause one. We'll be getting off the ship in four weeks and needn't come back."

As soon as the guests were settled for the evening, Nell and Mrs Swift traipsed across the deck. Nell's feet were aching, and she collapsed onto the settee in their living room.

"That was an unexpectedly hard day."

"It happens sometimes. I've actually enjoyed it. Mrs Phillips is good company, so for once, I've done better out of the cabin selection than you."

Nell grimaced. "I'll swap you for Mrs Everest."

"No, thank you. I've seen enough of her already."

"At least she doesn't want any help from me. It's worse than having Maria shouting at me."

Mrs Swift grinned. "You'd better get used to it if you're staying at home next year."

Nell sighed. "Don't remind me. You know, if I had no one else to consider, I'd be on the same ship as James going to Australia."

"It sounds nice, but imagine what it would be like having the same passengers for two months, rather than two weeks." Mrs Swift shuddered. "I couldn't manage two months of Mrs Everest."

"I hadn't thought of that." Nell stopped as Mr Potter brought in their dinner tray.

"Here you are, ladies. An Irish stew to mark our stop in Queenstown tomorrow."

Nell sat up straight. "Thank you, that smells wonderful."

"Well, enjoy it. I'll see you in the morning." He raised an arm to wave, but Nell called him back.

"Before you go, may I ask you a question?"

"What is it?"

Her face flushed. "Did you hear why Mr Hancock left the ship?"

He grinned at her. "I'd have thought Mr Ramsbottom would have told you."

"Why would he?"

"Now that you're walking out together…"

Nell's mouth opened and closed several times. "We're doing nothing of the sort."

"That's not what he's been saying."

*Is that why the stewards have been behaving strangely?* Nell's pulse quickened. "What's he said?"

"He was boasting about walking you to the park, and how he'd met some of your family. Your sister and daughter."

"Was that the day we arrived in Liverpool?"

"No, although he was bad enough after he'd taken you home. I think it was the Monday that caused the trouble. After you'd agreed to walk out with him."

"I did no such thing. I didn't see him once he dropped me off. And what do you mean, trouble?"

"Ah." Mr Potter puffed out his cheeks. "When we got to our bunks that evening, he was determined to upset Mr Marsh. He told him you'd had a wonderful afternoon and that he was looking forward to doing it again."

"So why didn't Mr Marsh leave? Like he did the other month?"

Mr Potter shrugged. "He was too slow. He went to see Mr Price, but by the time he did, Mr Hancock had already spoken to Captain Robertson and agreed to change ships. Mr Price couldn't afford to lose the two of them at such short notice."

"Why would Mr Hancock do that?"

Mr Potter rolled his eyes. "He'd developed a soft spot for you, hadn't he? He didn't want to be around if you were with Mr Ramsbottom."

*He liked me?* Nell's heart sank. *What have I done?*

# CHAPTER FORTY

Queenstown was a distant memory when the bell sounded outside their cabin on the third morning. The room was dark, save for the glow from the night light, and Mrs Swift hadn't moved from the lower bunk.

Nell leaned over the side of the mattress. "Are you all right?"

"I am." She eased herself from the bed and lit the lamp on the wall. "I must have been more tired than I thought."

"Me too. I was fast asleep when the bell rang." Nell climbed out of bed and reached for her dress. "Let's hope the passengers want an early night, tonight."

The sky was still dark as they hurried across the deck, and Nell allowed herself a moment to admire the stars.

"They're so much brighter when we're at sea. I could stand and watch them for hours."

"Not now, you couldn't. Come on."

Mr Ramsbottom and Mr Cooper were in the foyer outside the dining room when they arrived.

"What a lovely way to start the day." Mr Ramsbottom's eyes sparkled, and he put an arm around Nell's waist to guide her through the door. "What's the weather like?"

Nell shrugged him off. "It's not raining, if that's what you mean."

"There's no need to be like that."

"If it makes you realise we're not walking out together, then I would say there is. You had no right to lie to everyone."

Mr Cooper grinned at her. "Is this another one of your japes?"

"No, it isn't. I didn't even see him when I was in Liverpool, let alone walk to the park with him. If you wouldn't mind telling the rest of the stewards, I'd be most obliged." She didn't wait for a reply as she stormed off.

Her heart was racing as Mrs Swift caught up with her in the galley. "Well done. It's about time you told him how you feel."

"I didn't have much choice. Fool of a man. I hope he'll leave me alone now."

Mrs Swift peered out into the dining room. "He's still in the foyer. Oh no..."

"What is it?"

"Mrs Everest's here."

Nell took a deep breath. "Mr Price should stick her with Mr Ramsbottom. Why does she get up so early when she doesn't have to?"

Mrs Swift smirked. "Why don't you ask her?"

Nell straightened her skirt and pushed through the galley door. "Good morning. You're bright and early."

"There's no point staying in bed when the waves make it impossible to sleep."

"Is this your first voyage?"

"First and last. I shall settle in the United States."

Nell's face brightened. "That's exciting. Do you have family out there?"

"A nephew suggested I join him and his family. I'd originally planned on returning home, but if I have another twelve nights like the last one, I'll be staying with them."

"You'll get used to the swaying. I don't notice it now."

"I hardly think you can compare the two of us." Mrs Everest tucked her chin into her chest. "Now, I'll have two poached eggs with two slices of bread and butter on the side, and a pot of tea."

"Certainly." Nell walked to the galley and plonked the order onto the counter.

"Oh, dear." Mr Ross chuckled as he picked up the piece of paper.

"It's that stupid woman. I was only trying to be friendly, but she can't help being rude. She can get her own breakfast if she's not happy."

"Steady on. I don't want her coming in here."

"Don't overcook the eggs then."

"Good morning, Mrs Riley. I'm glad you're here." Mr Price joined them in the galley and handed Mr Ross an order. "I've a request for a tray for Mrs Flanagan. She won't be able to come to the dining room this morning."

"That's a shame. Leave it with me."

Mr Ross studied the paper. "Give me five minutes."

Nell wandered into the dining room to check on the guests and watched as Mrs Swift spoke to Mrs Phillips.

Mrs Phillips wore an immaculate peacock blue dress and styled her hair in an updo. *I wish she was my passenger.* When no new diners arrived, she sauntered back to the galley.

"That was well timed." Mr Ross pushed a plate towards her. "For Mrs Everest. The tray will be ready when you've delivered that."

"You'd better be quick, then. I won't be hanging around to talk to her."

Mrs Flanagan's stateroom door was partially open when Nell arrived with her tray, and she gave a cursory knock before letting herself in.

"Good morning. We've not been introduced... Oh..." Nell's smile faltered as she approached the bed.

"It looks a mess, doesn't it?" Mrs Flanagan pulled up the bedcovers with a jerk. "How stupid. I shan't be able to leave the room for the whole of the trip."

"It must have been quite a fall." Nell placed the tray on her lap.

"I've had worse, but with the stateroom being so small, I banged my face on the ottoman. Usually, it's my arms that suffer."

Nell creased the corner of her lip. *I'd hardly call it small.* "I'm sure the other guests would be happy for you to join them."

"They might be, but I wouldn't."

"Well, if you change your mind, I'm happy to escort you."

"Thank you, but for now I'll take my meals on a tray."

She lifted the cloche covering her eggs. "You can service the room in an hour once I'm dressed."

Nell nodded and headed to the door. She was about to step into the corridor when Mr Divine charged past, his coat swinging from his shoulders.

"Oh! Excuse me." She shrieked louder than she expected, causing Mr Divine to stop and glare at her.

"I suggest you look where you're going, madam."

Nell's cheeks flushed. "I-I'm sorry. I wasn't expecting anyone to be in such a hurry."

"Then you shouldn't serve breakfast so early."

"The dining room doesn't close for another half an hour."

"Which is barely enough time to have a civilised meal. Now, if you'll excuse me." He tore off down the corridor.

*What a dreadful man.*

The dining room was busy when Nell returned, and Mrs Swift nodded towards Mr Divine as Nell joined her.

"Have you seen who's over there? With a companion, too, by the looks of it."

"Seen him? I nearly got knocked over by him."

"Did you speak to him?" Mrs Swift's eyes widened.

"Only to apologise."

"What for?"

"Because he accused me of not looking where I was going."

Mrs Swift hadn't taken her eyes from him. "So, you didn't find out anything else about him?"

Nell pulled on her friend's arm to distract her. "No, and I'm not likely to, either. He really wasn't pleasant. The best thing you can do is ignore him."

Mrs Swift stared at her. "That's rich coming from you."

Nell raised her arms in the air. "Suit yourself, but don't say I didn't warn you." She headed to Mrs Everest's table to clear the plates. "May I get you anything else?"

"Another pot of tea. This one's stewed. In future, I'll have a jug of hot water as well."

"Certainly. Would you like anything else while I'm here, Mrs Phillips?"

"No, I'm fine, thank you, although..." she lowered her voice "...could you tell me who the gentleman is, over there. He looks terribly familiar."

"The one with the long hair?"

"Yes."

"All I know is his name's Mr Divine, and he's an actor ... or something to do with the theatre."

"Ah! That explains it. I must have seen him onstage." Mrs Phillips dabbed her lips with her napkin. "I must congratulate him on his latest work. I don't suppose you know what it was."

"I'm sorry, I don't." Nell shook her head as she left. *What is it with these otherwise sensible women? He's not even handsome.*

Mrs Swift scowled at her as she returned. "What were you talking to Mrs Phillips about?"

"Don't worry, I didn't serve her. She thought Mr Divine looked familiar and asked who he was."

"And does she know him?"

"She said she might have seen him at the theatre."

"Humph." Mrs Swift flounced into the galley, leaving Nell to chase after her.

"What's up with you?"

"Nothing."

"I've known you long enough to know that's not true."

Mrs Swift clicked her tongue. "I'm tired. That's all."


Nell smiled as Mrs Swift joined her at the table for luncheon.

"Are you feeling any better?"

Mrs Swift shrugged. "Not really."

"I don't know why..." Nell paused as Mr Ross arrived.

"Here you are. Lamb cutlets today."

"Lovely." Nell picked up her knife and fork but stopped as Mr Ross took the seat opposite.

"Would you like to know more about Mr Divine...?"

"Yes! What?" Mrs Swift leaned forward.

"Well ... he's not an actor. He's a playwright. Apparently, he's written some famous plays for the theatres in London."

"Do you know which ones?"

"Not a clue." Mr Ross stood up. "I'll be back with your dessert."

Nell waited for him to leave. Why do you want to know that? You wouldn't recognise them, anyway."

"Why not? If Mrs Phillips can congratulate him, so can I."

"She clearly has as little idea about him as you. She was convinced she'd seen him onstage. Anyway, what makes you think he'll notice you? He left me in no doubt that he sees serving staff as insignificant."

"Just because I'm in this uniform doesn't make me invisible."

Nell sighed. "Earlier in the year when I liked Mr Hewitt, you spent weeks telling me there could never be anything between us. Well, it's the same now with you and Mr Divine."

"It's not the same at all. Mr Hewitt was the nephew of an earl."

"And Mr Divine is probably a well-known playwright with influential friends. What's got into you?"

"I happen to think he's rather attractive." Mrs Swift cut into her lamb chop. "You don't get men like that in Liverpool."

"Thank goodness."

Mrs Swift ignored her. "The problem is Mrs Phillips. How can I compete with her?"

"She may not like him if she has the chance to talk to him. He's very rude."

"I doubt he would be with her. Not if he thinks she's got money."

Nell shrugged. "She doesn't look like someone who'd want to give up her personal property."

"You're right." A smile crept onto Mrs Swift's lips. "That makes it even more important that he notices me."

# CHAPTER FORTY-ONE

The sea was calm as Nell and Mrs Swift stepped onto the promenade the following morning, but Nell shivered.

"I don't like it when it's still dark at this time. It's as if the day doesn't happen."

Mrs Swift looked up. "There are no stars this morning, either. I hope that doesn't mean storm clouds are gathering."

"Me too."

Mr Price was outside the dining room when they walked down the stairs. "Good morning, ladies. Did you see Matron before you came over?"

"No, we didn't." Nell looked at Mrs Swift. "She'd already left when we arrived for breakfast. Is there a problem?"

"I'm not sure. We had something of a medical emergency this morning and Dr Clarke sent me to fetch her, but I've not seen her since I woke her up."

"What sort of emergency?"

"That's what I don't know. It's nothing for you to worry

about. It was a passenger in steerage, but I'd hoped Matron might have told you what was going on."

"I expect we'll hear if it's anything important."

"Indeed." He stepped to one side to let them into the dining room. "If you do see her, will you send her my way?"

Nell slowed as they approached the galley. "I wonder what that was about."

Mrs Swift shrugged. "He's probably being nosy."

Mr Ross was stirring a pan of porridge when they walked into the galley.

"Morning, ladies."

"Good morning." Nell reached for the tray list. "It looks like it's just the one for Mrs Flanagan."

"It is. The weather's nice and calm, so they must all be feeling sociable."

Nell shuddered. "If I was Mrs Phillips, I'd stay in my room rather than sitting with Mrs Everest."

"The old bat may be more polite with her own kind." Mr Ross darted to the stove to take some bacon off the heat.

"You're probably right." Nell stepped back to the wall as Mr Ramsbottom and Mr Cooper squeezed past them to the counter.

"Ooh, it's nice and cosy in here." Mr Ramsbottom winked at her.

"A little too cosy." Nell pushed on the door. "I'll wait outside."

Mr Ramsbottom caught hold of her arm. "There's no need to be like that."

"There's every need." She unhooked her arm. "Mr Ross, will you call me when Mrs Flanagan's tray is ready?"

· · ·

Mrs Flanagan was sitting up in bed when Nell arrived.

"Good morning, madam. Did you sleep well?"

"Better than the previous night, thank you."

Nell studied the bruising as she placed the tray on her lap. "The blackness is going down."

"Not nearly enough, I shouldn't wonder."

"You might be surprised."

Mrs Flanagan flicked a hand. "I know you're only being polite. The swelling won't go down for a few days yet." She paused as Nell poured a cup of tea. "Am I missing anything by being in here?"

"Nothing in particular. Just being with your fellow guests."

"Is there anyone worth meeting?"

Nell shook her head. "Not that I've noticed. Certainly, no members of the aristocracy."

"That's a relief. I do hate missing out. You will tell me if you come across anything exciting. My husband's oblivious to a good bit of gossip."

Nell chuckled. "Aren't they all. I'll keep my eyes and ears open for you. Now, if that's all, I must be going."

She checked both ways before stepping into the corridor, and when she returned to the dining room, Mr Divine was at the table with a companion. *I wonder if he's famous, too.*

Mrs Everest was waiting to be served as Nell arrived at her table.

"Are you being seen to?"

"No, I'm not, and I've been here for over five minutes."

"I'm sorry. I had to take a tray to another passenger. Have you decided what you'd like?"

"The same as yesterday. In fact, I'll have the same every day. Two poached eggs, two rounds of bread and butter, and a pot of tea, with a jug of water."

"Yes, madam. I'll bring it as soon as I can."

Mr Ramsbottom was in the galley when Nell arrived. "Are you still here?"

"I do have tables to serve."

Mr Ross handed him two plates of kippers. "I've been asking him about Mr Divine's companion, too. Unfortunately, Mr Cooper's serving them, so we may not find anything out."

"I told you his name." He sneered at Nell. "It's Mr Robbins, in case you're smitten with Mr Divine, too."

"No, I'm not. I couldn't care less."

Mr Ramsbottom shrugged as he pushed open the door with a foot. "Suit yourself."


Once breakfast was over, Nell left the galley and walked towards Mrs Swift, who was with Matron on the far side of the room.

"You found her."

"I wasn't lost." Matron pulled Nell closer. "Are you finished in here?"

Nell nodded.

"Good. Captain Robertson wants to see you in his office."

Her heart sank. "What have I done now?"

"There's a problem in steerage."

"What's that got to do with us?" Nell stared at Mrs Swift, but Matron started walking.

"Captain Robertson will explain, so get a move on. He's going to be busy this morning."

Nell and Mrs Swift scurried after Matron until they reached the bridge. Captain Robertson was expecting them.

"Good morning, ladies. Please come in and take a seat."

"I won't if you don't mind, Captain." Matron hovered by the door as Nell and Mrs Swift went in. "I need to get back..."

"Of course. Let me know if there's anything I can do." He closed the door and waited while they sat at the table in the corner. "I'd be obliged if the information I'm about to impart doesn't go any further than this office."

Nell gulped as he paced the floor.

"We had some news late last night that means I need to reorganise your responsibilities." He paused as they both stared at him. "Unfortunately, a passenger in steerage died this morning."

Nell put a hand to her mouth. "Oh, goodness."

Captain Robertson nodded. "Quite, although I'm afraid the problem is bigger than that. The man in question died of an infectious disease, which has now passed to some of the other passengers."

Mrs Swift gasped. "Why are you telling us?"

"If the infection spreads, as Dr Clarke believes it will, he and Matron won't be able to manage. They need more hands to nurse the patients."

"Us?" Mrs Swift looked between Nell and the captain.

"I wouldn't move you if it wasn't necessary, but we must contain the spread."

Mrs Swift gasped. "What about the first-class passengers?"

"The stewards will take over your responsibilities."

"But the ladies ... Mrs Flanagan..." Nell struggled to speak. "We're not allowed in steerage ... the stewards should be downstairs..."

"I'm overruling those orders." Captain Robertson stood with his hands on the back of a chair. "Nursing is best done by women, and you are the only two I have."

"What do we tell our guests? And the stewards?" Mrs Swift had tears in her eyes.

"That will be taken care of. I'll take you downstairs now, so there'll be no need to speak to them. Once you're in steerage, you won't be coming into first class. We can't risk spreading the disease upstairs." Captain Robertson held open the door. "Mr Marsh is waiting for you."


Captain Robertson stopped at the bottom of the stairs and nodded to Mr Marsh, who stood with his hands behind his back.

"The help you were promised."

"Ladies." The grim expression stayed on Mr Marsh's face. "Matron is expecting you. If you'll follow me."

Captain Robertson clicked his heels together. "Thank you, Mr Marsh. I'll leave them in your capable hands."

A sour taste rose in Nell's throat as she watched the captain return to the stairs. *I can't do this.*

"Don't look so frightened, Mrs Riley. You'll report to Matron, and barring accidents, you won't see me." Mr Marsh set off down a dimly lit corridor and Nell held her breath as she followed him. The smell of sickness grew stronger the further they walked, and when they were halfway down the corridor, he poked his head through a door. A moment later, Matron appeared.

"You're here. Good. We don't have a lot of time."

"Will you excuse me? I need to go." Mr Marsh's face was grey in the dull light, but he didn't look at Nell as he hurried away.

*I've really upset him.*

"Mrs Riley. Are you listening?" Matron shook Nell's arm. "I said we've had another man die since I left you with Captain Robertson."

"Another one? What's causing it?"

Matron sighed. "Dr Clarke suspects cholera."

"Cholera!" Nell put a hand to her mouth. "How's that happened? We've not had it in England for years."

"The man who died was one of the Europeans."

"But everyone in steerage should have had a medical check before they boarded."

"And they did, but this man must have had hidden symptoms. We've been on board for four days, so he'll have had plenty of chance to pass it on, too."

"But the doctor and Captain Robertson do their daily sanitary inspections..." Mrs Swift looked from Nell to Matron.

"Something obviously went wrong, but unfortunately, we don't know what."

"Are we all going to die?" Nell's hands were clammy and her mouth dry.

"Don't be silly. Dr Clarke says you can't catch it by breathing the air."

"So why has it spread?"

Matron lowered her voice. "Those affected have very

loose bowel movements and they're making the dormitories and washrooms rather unpleasant. If we keep the men, the beds and the rooms clean, it should help."

"But we could still catch it?"

"Mrs Riley, these men need our help. It wouldn't do if we put ourselves first."

"But my children..."

"The chances are, you'll see them again. Now, stop arguing and follow me."

The stench hit Nell before they stepped into the large dormitory, and she put an arm over her nose as she ventured inside. "Don't they even have any portholes to let in some air?"

"You'll get used to it."

*I doubt it.* She peered at the bunk beds that ran along either side of the dormitory, but flinched as Matron clapped her hands. "Gentlemen. I've two helpers with me today. Mrs Swift and Mrs Riley. I expect you to treat them with the utmost courtesy."

Nell tried to smile as several sets of sunken eyes stared at them.

"Are they all ill?" Nell's voice sounded faint.

"Not yet, but we will be." A young man with dishevelled dark hair lay on his bunk. "It's only a matter of time."

"Nonsense." Matron bustled over to the passenger next to him. "You can't catch it through the air."

"You can if it smells as bad as this."

Matron tutted. "Take no notice of him. If you keep to your own bunks, you'll be fine."

"We can't stay where we are. When you've got to go..."

A man in the next bunk jumped to the floor, almost crashing into the row of tables that ran down the middle. He hadn't reached the door when a trail of fluid leaked from his trouser legs, but he kept going.

"Is that what...?" Nell gagged as she pointed to the rivers of liquid on the floor.

"We have to get the place cleaned up. And the men. We need more chamber pots, too."

"Can't Dr Clarke do anything to help?"

"He'll be here shortly to give all who need it a dose of laudanum. It should stop the bowel movements."

Mrs Swift ran her eyes around the room. "Shouldn't we move those who are still well, so they don't have to put up with all this?"

"Where to?" Matron shot her a glance. "We're fully booked down here. We can't have everyone swapping beds." She pointed to a water jug at the far end of the table. "That needs to be topped up so the men have enough to moisten their mouths. Don't give them too much, though. It passes straight through them and makes matters worse."

Mrs Swift headed for the jug. "I'll do that."

"Before you go, we need to make sure they're all lying down and if anyone has a fever, use a wet towel to keep them cool. If they have pains in their stomachs, offer them one soaked in hot water. Holding it on the belly can relieve the discomfort."

"It doesn't work." An older man with a gruff voice rolled over on his lower mattress. "I've been doing that all morning and it's made no difference."

"I don't like the sound of that." Matron turned him over,

and Nell shuddered at the hollow cheeks and pallid skin. "As I thought. We need Dr Clarke." She hurried to the door. "You start on getting the place cleaned up."

# CHAPTER FORTY-TWO

Nell wiped up the last of the soap from the dormitory floor and stood up to survey the wet floorboards. How long will that stay clean? Mrs Swift was ahead of her and Nell followed her from the room.

"It would be nice if it could dry while it was still clean."

"It would, but we need some fresh buckets of water in case it doesn't."

"I'll get some clean towels, too."

Mrs Swift went to change her water while Nell rifled through several cupboards. She eventually found them and took out a stack, but dropped them as Mr Ramsbottom came up behind her.

"What a pleasant surprise." He grinned as he picked them up for her. "I wondered what had happened to you after breakfast."

"What are you doing here?" She snatched the towels from him.

"Don't be like that. If we've all got new jobs down here, we need to get along with each other."

"After what you said…"

Mr Ramsbottom held up his hands. "I was trying to wind Marshy up, that's all. I thought you'd be pleased."

"Why did you have to do it in front of everyone?"

"Why not? Nobody else seemed bothered."

"Except Mr Hancock…"

Nell's cheeks flushed as he stared at her.

"Is that what this is all about? Were you really going to walk out with him?"

"N-no, I wasn't … but he shouldn't have had to change ships because of your banter."

"Well, I'm sorry to spoil your little flirtation." He turned to leave. "At least I know where I stand."

The afternoon was a constant cycle of wiping the men's brows, giving them mouthfuls of water and washing the floor, and by the time the evening meal was due, Nell was exhausted.

Several stewards she hadn't met before brought in some large soup tureens, but before they could lift the lids, Dr Clarke joined them.

"How many cases do we have in here?"

Nell shrugged. "About half of them."

He surveyed the bunks. "Put the food on this end table. We can't give anything to those who are ill. It will only make them worse. I'll do a quick round of the room, to determine who can eat."

Mrs Swift ladled some soup into a bowl for those passed fit, but he'd only cleared five men before he called Nell over.

"This man's burning up. He needs a cold towel on his face."

"Yes, sir." She darted to the towel cupboard. *The last one. That's all we need.*

Two men rushed to the lavatories while she was at the sink, and with tears in her eyes, she made a dash for the door. *I didn't sign up for this.* She turned into the corridor, but slid to a halt as a pair of legs spread out across the floor.

"Mr Marsh!" His crumpled body lay slumped against the wall and Nell bent down to shake his shoulder. "What's the matter?"

His legs twitched, but his laboured breaths were the only sound he made. *I need Dr Clarke.* She scurried into the dormitory where he was leaning over a passenger.

"Dr Clarke, you must come quickly?"

He looked up with some indifference. "What is it?"

"Mr Marsh. He's collapsed..." She hurried to the door, but Dr Clarke showed no sense of urgency. "Please. Hurry..."

She held open the door and peered down the corridor while she waited. "He's not moving."

"Where is he?"

"Over there." Nell followed Dr Clarke as he hastened towards him.

"How long's he been like this?"

Nell shook her head. "It can't be long because he wasn't here when you sent me for this cloth."

"We need to move him to one of the hospital beds. He can't go to the stewards' quarters. Wait with him while I get a stretcher."

Nell's heart raced as she stared down at Mr Marsh's

unrecognisable features. *What on earth happened? He was fine...*

Mrs Swift ran towards her. "What's the matter?"

"I don't know." Nell's voice squeaked. "Dr Clarke says he has to go to the hospital room."

"Is it cholera?"

Nell shrugged. "Look at the way his cheeks have sunken into his face and his skin's all wrinkled. Isn't that what some passengers look like?"

"Only those who are very ill." Mrs Swift crossed herself. "The man you got the cloth for has died and he looked rather like this."

"Oh, my. I'd completely forgotten about him..." She put a hand to her mouth.

"I doubt you could have done anything that would have made any difference."

Dr Clarke reappeared around the corner. "Out of the way. We need to get him to a hospital bed now. We've no time to lose."

Nell and Mrs Swift were finishing their evening meal when Matron shuffled into the sitting room.

Nell stood up and offered her a seat. "We thought you'd already gone to bed."

"I'm afraid not. I wanted to call on Mr Marsh before I came back here."

"How is he?"

"Not well. I suspect it's only a matter of time."

"The poor man." Nell sat down and pushed away the last of her dinner. "It's all my fault."

Matron stared at her. "Don't talk nonsense."

"I'm not. I was the one who insisted he work in steerage…"

"You can't think like that." Mrs Swift patted her hand. "If it wasn't Mr Marsh in steerage, it would have been someone else."

"That doesn't make it right. How did nobody notice?"

Matron shrugged. "I hadn't seen him for a couple of days and according to Dr Clarke, he hadn't, either. We've both been too busy."

"And he always was rather thin around the face. It probably wasn't obvious."

Nell closed her eyes and gulped down some tears. "Assuming he's still alive, do you think Dr Clarke will let me visit him in the morning? I need to apologise."

"Whatever for?" Mrs Swift glared at her.

"For overreacting and being rude. He didn't deserve it. I'd like him to know that … before the end."

"It was hardly overreacting. He upset you every time he spoke to you."

"It was probably me being unreasonable."

Mrs Swift rolled her eyes. "I've heard it all now…"

Matron put down her cup. "I don't know what happened between you, but if you want to visit him, perhaps I could offer your services to nurse all the men who are up there."

"I can't work up there on my own…"

"It's no more or less than you've been doing today and it would mean you'd get to see Mr Marsh."

"I don't need to see that much of him..." Nell rubbed her hands over her face. "I'm going for a bath."

"Now?" Mrs Swift's eyes widened.

"I can't stand this smell any longer. I want to wash every inch of me. I'd wash my clothes, too, if I could get them dry again."

"Is there any point if we'll be straight back into it tomorrow?"

Nell took a deep breath. "It will give me a chance to sleep without this stench in my nostrils."

Nell lay awake, waiting for the morning bell, and as soon as it sounded, she swung her legs over the edge of the bed.

"You're up early." Mrs Swift peered at her from the bottom bunk.

"I need to get to the hospital room. I've not stopped worrying about Mr Marsh. What if he died overnight?"

"You couldn't have done anything about it."

"It was me who forced him to work down here."

"It's not your fault you didn't want to walk out with him; there's nothing wrong with that."

"It's my fault I was so mean to him. He didn't deserve that. Now, are you getting out of bed? I want to be quick."

Matron was about to leave the sitting room as they crossed the corridor, and Nell gasped as she bumped into her

"Goodness, you must have been up before the bell."

"I'm afraid I didn't sleep, and I wanted to know how things were before you arrived. Don't rush upstairs."

"But..." Nell hesitated. "I'd hoped to visit Mr Marsh."

"Let me speak to Dr Clarke first. Meet me in steerage in about twenty minutes."

Nell helped herself to a bowl of porridge, but ate little of it before the clock struck seven. "Time to go. Are you ready?"

"I am." Mrs Swift finished her cup of tea. "I hate walking through the boiler room by myself."

"Me too, but it's the only way to get there without going near first class. These ships really should have been designed better."


Matron was in the dormitory when they arrived, and Nell glanced around at the growing number of empty bunks.

"How many more have we lost?"

"Two. A couple more are in the hospital room."

Nell bit down on her lip. "H-how's Mr Marsh?"

A smile flitted across Matron's face. "I'm pleased to say he's still with us..."

Nell released her breath. "That's a relief."

"Before you get too excited, he's unconscious, and his pulse is very weak."

"Will he recover?"

"We don't know, but Dr Clarke has said you can visit for five minutes."

"Thank you." She bit her lip. "Was anything said about working on the ward?"

"Dr Clarke wants to keep an eye on them himself with them being so poorly."

"May I still go and visit?"

"You may, but not yet. I need you here first."

Most of the men were groggy from the previous evening's laudanum, but Nell washed each of their faces before offering them some water.

"Many of them want more than a mouthful."

"I'm afraid we can't allow it. We mustn't let them eat or drink anything for at least one day and night after the symptoms have disappeared. The water is only to stop their mouths from being dry. It sounds cruel, but it's for their own good. And ours. The beds would be in more of a mess if we let them drink more."

"I suppose so. I do feel mean, though."

"You'll get used to it." Matron wandered out of the room to check the time. "Nine o'clock. Dr Clarke will be down any minute and then I'll take you upstairs. Ah, here he is now."

He smiled at them. "Matron, Mrs Riley. How are they?"

"We've a couple who've started with restless legs, but several seem to have picked up. You can tell who's who."

"Splendid." He peered at Nell. "Matron tells me you'd like to visit Mr Marsh."

"Yes, sir."

"You'll be pleased to know he's still fighting. You can go up now if you like, but he won't be talking."

Nell nodded. "Thank you. I'll try not to disturb him."

Once they got upstairs, Matron led the way to a small room with four beds sticking out into the middle.

Nell ran her eyes over them. "Where is he?"

"In the far-right corner."

The room was dimly lit, with the only light coming from the small porthole opposite the door. She crept to the side of the bed and stared at the seemingly lifeless body as Mr

Marsh lay with his arms resting on top of a grey blanket, his usually immaculate hair dishevelled on the pillow.

Matron checked the other beds. "Dr Clarke has given them some laudanum, so they'll sleep for a good few hours. You may stay for five minutes while I call on the bridge, but I need you downstairs."

"Yes, Matron." Nell waited for her to leave the room before she pulled the solitary chair and sat down. "Mr Marsh. It's Mrs Riley. Can you hear me?" She kept her voice low, and when she got no response, she took hold of his hand.

"Mr Marsh..." Her pulse raced. "I don't know what to say, except ... I'm sorry. You didn't deserve to be in steerage because you asked me to walk to the park..." Her voice broke as tears welled in her eyes. "I didn't mean for you to end up like this." *He only wanted a friend ... and now look at him.* She took a deep breath. "If we both make it to Liverpool, I promise we'll take that walk. We'll take as many walks as you like. I don't want you to die."

She closed her eyes, but froze as Mr Marsh's fingers tightened around her hand. "Mr Marsh?" *Did I imagine that?* "Can you hear me?"

His fingers twitched as she continued to hold them. "If you can, please get well. I'd never forgive myself if you didn't." Nell looked up as the door opened.

"That's enough for now, Mrs Riley." Matron wandered to the bed.

"He moved. I held his hand, and he squeezed it."

They both stared at his fingers as they moved again, but Matron sighed. "Don't build up your hopes. It isn't a good sign."

"But he squeezed my fingers…"

"Come along. I'll be back later to check on him. We need to focus on the men who have a chance of recovering."

"One moment." She stepped to the washstand in the corner and wet the flannel that rested on the side before wiping his face. "It may help."

# CHAPTER FORTY-THREE

Mr Potter was delivering breakfast the following morning when Nell hurried into the sitting room. He straightened up as she took a seat.

"You're early. Don't you have Mrs Swift with you?"

"She wasn't ready to get up, but I want to go to the hospital room before I start."

Mr Potter sighed. "It's a bad outbreak, that's for sure. I've never known one like it."

"You mean you've seen cholera on a ship before?"

"It was a long time ago, and there weren't many passengers, but yes. We didn't know what to do with them. They couldn't eat, but they were thirsty, so we gave them plenty to drink. Lots of brandy, too."

"Matron says that would go straight through them."

"We knew no better." Mr Potter stared at the wall. "We had no doctor on board, so we just kept them comfortable until they recovered."

Nell sighed. "I wish we could give them more, but we're out of clean linen as it is."

Mr Potter patted her on the shoulder. "I don't envy you. We've got off lightly with far fewer passengers to feed. Most of them are women too, so they don't eat so much."

"Well, make the most of it." Nell sat down and helped herself to some porridge. "I'd better get a move on if I'm to finish before Matron arrives."

The cup of tea she'd poured for herself was still hot when Matron arrived and sat beside her.

"Couldn't you sleep?"

"I was so exhausted, I dropped off well enough, but I woke early. I want to visit Mr Marsh before I start."

Matron helped herself to the porridge. "I called in to see him late last night and was amazed he's still with us. He's a fighter for sure."

"I didn't think he looked well. Is there nothing else Dr Clarke can do?"

"I'm afraid not. Laudanum's the best thing we have, but we'll be running out of that soon the way things are going. It's more important than ever to stop the spread. Since we've been isolating the infected men, there have been fewer cases, so we're hopeful."

"That's a relief. Some of those who were ill even seem to be on the mend."

"It's encouraging when they want something to eat. There are several we'll feed later. Hopefully, they'll be able to keep it in."

"I hope so." Nell sighed. "Does that mean we're allowed on deck again? That early morning walk to first class doesn't seem so bad after being stuck down here."

"I don't know when you'll have the time, but there's no reason you can't go onto the deck at the back of the ship.

345

The steerage passengers are being kept in their rooms, so it should be clear."

Nell smiled for the first time in what felt like days. "That would be wonderful, even if it's only for five minutes." She finished the last of her porridge. "If you don't mind, I'll nip upstairs now. I'll see you later."

The lamp on the wall of the hospital room flickered in the draught from the door as Nell pushed it closed behind her. The room was quiet, with nothing but the sound of waves to mask her footsteps as she approached the bed. Mr Marsh was in his usual position as she stared down at him.

She took her usual seat and reached for his hand. "Good morning, Mr Marsh. How are you feeling today?" She gazed over to the porthole. "It looks like it will be a nice day, and I'm hoping we'll catch sight of land. Do you remember when we were in New York? I've been thinking about it a lot lately." She paused. *That might upset him. Change the subject.* "Some of the men are on the mend. Hopefully, that will be you soon..."

Movement from the bed behind startled her.

"Do you have to come in here with all that muttering? Some of us are trying to sleep."

"Oh, I'm sorry. I thought you were all... Well, you know."

"We're not all as bad as him, if that's what you mean."

"But you were."

The man turned his head to face her. "As you said, some of us are on the mend. As you're here, you can pass me some water."

"Oh, yes." She read the piece of paper on the end of the bed. "I can't give you much, Mr Ashworth. Only a mouthful."

He watched as she filled a cup. "He's your beau, is he?"

"Oh, no..." Nell's cheeks coloured as she checked Mr Marsh was still asleep. "He's a colleague and I don't like seeing him ill."

"No one else has been to visit."

*Because it's no one else's fault he's here.* "They're ... erm ... not allowed."

"What about him?" He nodded to the bed opposite. "Mr Wood's a steward, too. Are you here to visit him, as well?"

"I-I didn't know he was here. I've not met him before."

"So, Mr Marsh gets you all to himself?"

"I have passengers to deal with, too." She took the glass from him, but as she turned to go to the washstand, she bumped into the end of Mr Marsh's bed. "Ow." She bent to rub her shin, but stared as Mr Marsh licked his lips and settled again.

"He moved!" She edged further up the bed. "Mr Marsh. Are you awake?"

He ran his tongue over his lips again.

"Would you like some water?"

"Of course he would." Mr Ashworth gave a brusque reply, but her heart raced as she refilled the cup.

"Here, let me help you." She sat on the edge of the bed and lifted his head enough to get the water to his lips. "That's it, well done." She poured it until it ran down his chin. "I'm sorry." She placed his head on the pillow and found a cloth to wipe his face. *I hope I didn't give him too much.*

"What's going on here?"

Nell flinched as Matron strode into the room. "Thank goodness you're here. It's Mr Marsh, he moved."

"I'm not surprised, with you manhandling him."

"It wasn't like that..."

"What precisely did he do?" Matron stood at the foot of the bed, her hands on her hips.

"He licked his lips ... twice, so I gave him a mouthful of water."

"You had no right to. Dr Clarke specifically told you not to."

"I'm sorry, but they're so thirsty..."

"You might have set the whole process off again. His stomach isn't ready for anything. Look at the mess you've made, too." Matron pulled on the wet blanket.

"I can change that..."

"See that you do, then I expect you downstairs where you'll do as you're told." Matron stomped to the door, but Mr Ashworth stopped her.

"Aren't you going to check on the rest of us? Some breakfast wouldn't go amiss here."

"I'll be back when Mrs Riley has finished."

Once they were alone, Nell gave him a weak smile. "I'm sorry. She knew I was coming up here. I'll try to get you something if I can."

"She doesn't like you using your initiative, that's what it is."

Nell pulled back the blanket, thankful that the sheet

underneath was still dry. She folded the covers over the top of the bed and tucked in the edges. "That should do."

"Garghh..."

The gasp was barely audible, and Nell bent her head towards Mr Marsh's mouth. "Did you say something?"

The same whispered sound came from his lips.

"He needs some more water." Mr Ashworth didn't take his eyes off Mr Marsh. "He's parched."

"But Matron said..."

"I know what she said, but trust me."

Nell nodded. "Very well. You won't tell her, will you?"

"Not a word. We'll blame that first mouthful if he gets worse."

*Gets worse? That's not possible.* Nell refilled the cup and once again sat beside Mr Marsh as she lifted his head from the pillow. "Slowly this time." She held the cup to his lips and watched as his tongue dipped into the water. "He's moving."

"I told you." The man looked pleased with himself.

"I can't give him too much, though." She moved the cup away, but jumped as he caught hold of her wrist and pulled it back. *"Oh, goodness."* Her cheeks flushed as she gazed down at his tousled brown hair. He looked so different somehow, less stern. *Please let him be all right.*

Nell wasn't sure how long they stayed locked together, but finally he released her hand and she settled him onto the pillow.

"You sleep now, Mr Marsh. I'll call again later."

"Don't forget my breakfast." Mr Ashworth kept his eyes on her. "I'll have another drink too, before you go."

"But Matron..."

"What did we say? I won't tell if you don't."

"Very well, but what if it makes you worse?"

"I could drink all the water in that jug and more besides, so a cupful won't hurt." He raised an eyebrow at her. "Would you top the jug up on the way out?"

Once the morning was over and they'd had something to eat, the afternoon continued with much the same monotony. Finally, with the men settled for the night, and the floor once again clean, Nell slipped into the corridor. She didn't remember when she had last seen Mrs Swift, but when there was no sign of her, she hurried to the stairs. *She'll know where I am.*

The sun had long since set and, with only a dull light from the one wall lamp, she crept to Mr Marsh's bedside.

"Mr Marsh, can you hear me?" Her voice was so quiet, she could hardly hear herself, so she rested a hand on his. "Are you awake?"

Nothing. She sighed. *I imagine Dr Clarke's already given them their laudanum.*

She stood up to leave, but as she passed the adjacent bed, a low voice groaned at her. "More water."

"Mr Ashworth. Shouldn't you be asleep?"

"I will be, but my mouth's too dry. Just a sip..."

"Very well. I'm surprised Dr Clarke didn't give you any." She handed him a cup. "Are you feeling any better?"

"Much. If you could find some breakfast again tomorrow, that would be smashing."

She took the cup from him. "I can't promise, but I'll try."

She glanced over to Mr Marsh. "Have you seen any movement from him since this morning?"

"He's been moving, but not opened his eyes."

She gave a weary smile. "It's better than nothing."

She left the room and hurried down the stairs. *I hope Mrs Swift waited for me.* She popped her head into each of the rooms, but when she wasn't around, she headed to the boiler room. *She must have got fed up of waiting.*

Matron was still eating when she arrived in the sitting room, but Nell's brow creased as she sat down.

"Have you seen Mrs Swift?"

"Not tonight. I'd assumed she'd be with you?"

Nell stared at Matron. "I couldn't find her and thought she'd come back without me. Where else would she be?"

Matron's lips were thin. "That's a very good question. If she's not here when you've eaten, we'll have to look for her."

Nell pulled her already cooling dinner plate towards her as Matron watched.

"Have you been to check on Mr Marsh?"

"I popped in when I'd finished, but he was asleep. The man in the next bed said he'd moved today, but not opened his eyes."

Matron nodded. "I called in myself this afternoon. He's doing remarkably well, given how ill he's been. Perhaps there's a chance for him yet."

Nell sighed. "I hope so. I still feel guilty about him being there."

"You never did tell me why."

Nell swallowed her mouthful. "It all seems so petty now...." She stopped as Mrs Swift appeared in the doorway.

"Matron, you're still up."

"And wondering where you are. We were about to come looking for you."

Mrs Swift gave a half-hearted laugh. "You don't need to worry about me. I went outside for some air."

Nell stared at her. "By yourself? Why didn't you tell me you were going?"

"I ... erm ... I couldn't find you. Did you go to the hospital room?"

"I did, but only after you'd disappeared."

"Ah ... I stopped to use the facilities."

"Well, I'm very glad you're here." Matron stood up. "I wasn't looking forward to searching the ship at this time of night. I'll see you in the morning."

Nell waited until she heard the click of the latch on Matron's door. "What were you doing on the deck by yourself?"

"Nothing."

"Nonsense. You wouldn't go up there without a reason."

Mrs Swift sighed and put down her knife and fork. "If you must know, I went to see Mr Divine."

"What! Are you mad?"

"I didn't go in. Well, not far. Mr Ramsbottom had told me he was reciting one of his plays and I wanted to listen. It was wonderful..."

Nell gabbled her words. "You may have infected the whole of first class."

"Stop worrying. I wasn't near anyone." She took a mouthful of liver.

"And a good job too, but what if someone saw you?"

Mrs Swift rolled her eyes. "I'm not that daft."

# CHAPTER FORTY-FOUR

The days in steerage had become a blur, but she smiled as she stepped onto the deck and saw the familiar landscape of softly undulating hills bathed in the dawn light. She sighed as she rested her elbows on the railing.

"I'd forgotten what fresh air was like."

Mrs Swift rubbed her hands together. "I'd forgotten how cold it would be."

"It's worth it though, given we've only got five minutes."

They stood in companionable silence until Nell pushed herself away. "We'd better go. Matron will be wondering where we are."

Mrs Swift stayed where she was but stared towards the first-class accommodation. "You go; I'll catch you up."

"Mr Divine won't be coming out at this time in the morning. If he's any sense, he'll still be asleep."

"He may not be."

"When he told me we served breakfast too early?"

Mrs Swift groaned as she left the railings. "I hate it when you're right."

Nell waited for her by the door. "I can't believe we'll be on our last journey home by this time next week. We should try to come out again this afternoon when the doctor's done his visits."

"Won't you be visiting Mr Marsh then?"

"I'll go up to the room, but not for long. I always give him a drink of water, but he's not shown any improvement for days. Mr Ashworth's been discharged now, so I've no one to talk to."

"Is that other steward not improving either?"

"Mr Wood? Yes, he's woken up. I could talk to him. We had another passenger admitted yesterday, though. He's very poorly, so it wouldn't surprise me if he's not with us long." Nell let out a deep sigh. "What a horrible disease."

Mrs Swift led the way downstairs and found Matron ushering several patients along the corridor.

"What's going on?"

"We've sent all those without symptoms out onto the deck to give them some fresh air. It will let us change the beds now we have some clean bedding."

"Do you want one of us to go with them?"

Matron shook her head. "I need you both down here. Mr Ramsbottom will supervise them."

Nell sighed. *It's all right for him.*


The three of them worked together in the empty dormitory, but stopped at midday when Dr Clarke and the captain joined them.

A frown settled on the captain's face. "No passengers?"

"The healthy ones are upstairs so we can give the room

a good clean."

Dr Clarke took a deep breath. "Splendid. There's nothing better than a thorough wash with carbolic soap to get rid of the smell."

"I thought that." Matron smirked. "I also thought that while the healthy ones are outside, we'll move the ill ones in here and do the others, too."

*She didn't mention that to us.* Nell ran a hand over her forehead. *We'll be here for hours.*

"Excellent. Well done, Matron." The doctor glanced around the room. "I'll examine the men next door before I send them in here. We'll keep the sick ones together and hope they do no more damage."

Mr Cooper half-escorted, half-carried the new patients into the dormitory, and it was nearly four o'clock by the time he brought in the last one. "I'll go upstairs and tell Mr Ramsbottom he can bring the passengers inside."

Nell nodded. "As you like. I'm moving next door." She didn't wait for him to leave before she picked up her bucket. *I need clean water.*

She was on her way back to the dormitory, but stopped when someone called her name.

"Mr Ashworth. It's good to see you up and about again. Has the doctor given you a clean bill of health?"

"He has." He grinned as he leaned forward. "The water did me no harm after all."

"Keep your voice down!" She straightened her apron. "We're about to serve some tea and biscuits."

He rubbed his hands together. "I won't say no. It's freezing on that deck. We'll catch our death of cold if they send us out there too often."

"If it's a choice between being down here with the sick patients or being up there, I know which I'd prefer."

"You're not wrong."

Nell smiled as she escorted him to the dormitory. "Is this your first visit to America?"

"First and last. I've a brother who made the journey a couple of years ago and we're hoping to settle close to him."

"That's nice. Who are you with?"

"I've a wife and daughter, not that I've seen them since we boarded. Is it right that they've had no illness in the women's section?"

"It is, and long may it stay that way." Nell stayed in the corridor as Mr Ramsbottom ushered the last of the passengers into the dormitory.

"That should do it. Is Mr Cunningham in there?"

Nell shook her head. "I didn't see him."

"I don't know where he's got to. He's supposed to be helping me, but I've not seen him since this morning."

Nell shrugged. "He may have moved to another room."

"Possibly. I'll keep looking for him, but will you send him my way if you find him?"

"I can manage that." She set off to her own dormitory, but before she arrived, Dr Clarke joined her.

"Mrs Riley, I'm glad I've caught you. I wanted to tell you that Mr Marsh is showing signs of recovery and so if you'd like to spend longer than five minutes with him, you may."

"He's awake? That's ... wonderful."

"He's still weak and not ready for anything to eat or drink, but it's a start."

"It is." Nell forced a smile. "I'll call once I've finished

here."

Mrs Swift approached as Dr Clarke left. "Did he say that Mr Marsh was getting better?"

Nell nodded.

"You don't seem very pleased. I thought that was what you wanted."

"It is ... and I am, but, well, it means I'll have to talk to him. While he was asleep, it was different."

"Did you want him to stay unconscious forever?"

She sighed. "I can't explain it. I didn't want him to die, but now he's likely to recover, I'd rather things were how they used to be."

"They will be, soon enough. There are only another four days until we reach New York, and all these passengers will get off."

"Mr Marsh won't be leaving."

"No, but we should be allowed back upstairs."

Nell broke into a broad smile. "What a wonderful thought."

It was turned seven o'clock before Nell arrived in the hospital room and her heart pounded as she peered through the door. It was already dark, but she could see Mr Marsh propped up on some pillows. She took a deep breath as she crept towards him. "Good evening, Mr Marsh."

His eyes flickered as he turned to face her. "Mrs Riley. You came." His smile was weak, and he ran a finger over his cracked lips. "May I have...?"

"Some water? Of course." She half-filled a cup and held it to his mouth as he steadied her hand.

Once it was empty, he settled on the pillows and watched as she took her seat. "Dr Clarke said I'd been in here for most of the week, and that you've been to see me every day."

"I have." Her voice squeaked, but a smile crossed his face.

"I dreamt of you."

"You did?"

"You promised we'd take that walk..."

Nell caught her breath. *He heard me.*

"I wanted to believe it was true, but then I woke up." His face fell, and Nell studied his sunken eyes.

"I'll tell you what. If you're well enough when we get to Liverpool, we'll take a walk."

"Really?" He licked his lips. "I'd like that."

"We've all been worried about you."

He sank lower on the pillows. "I'm sorry."

"What for?"

"For this. I'm here to do a job and I've let you down. Someone will have had to cover my position, which will have left you short upstairs."

"We've not been..." Nell paused. *He's forgotten we've been moved to steerage.* "Actually, the passengers have been very understanding."

"That's a relief."

Nell placed a hand on his. "Why don't I leave you to get some sleep?"

"You'll come again tomorrow?"

"I will." The chair scraped across the floor as she stood up. "Would you like some more water before I go?"

He nodded as he stared at the water jug.

"All right." She helped him with the cup, but the water spilled as he struggled to lift his head. "Be careful. If Matron sees this..."

He gripped her hand, only letting go when the cup was empty. "More."

"I can't give you any more. You shouldn't have had so much as it is."

"Please." His eyes pleaded with her, causing her heart to skip a beat.

"Very well, but don't blame me if you're ill again. I'll deny all knowledge of this."

He drank the second cupful as quickly as the first, but relaxed into the pillows when it was empty.

"All done." Nell hesitated. "I'll see you tomorrow."

She was about to leave when the man in the opposite corner tried to sit up.

"Mr Wood." She bent over the bed. "It's Mrs Riley, one of the stewardesses."

"Water." His voice croaked as he spoke, and she hurried to the washstand and back. "Here we are." She held an arm around his shoulders as he drank. "I hope this doesn't have you rushing to the lavatory again."

"Not rushing ... anywhere."

"I don't suppose you are." *Which is why Dr Clarke doesn't want you to have anything.*

He emptied the glass before Nell settled him onto the pillows.

"Dr Clarke ... he's cruel."

"I'm sure he's not. He's trying his best for you."

With what looked like a great effort, Mr Wood shook his head. "No."

# CHAPTER FORTY-FIVE

Nell took a deep breath as she stepped out onto the deck the following afternoon.

"How lovely to get outside in the daylight for a change."

"It's even nicer that the men are more settled today. Hopefully, we've stopped the spread." Mrs Swift joined her by the railings. "I hope we'll be in first class for the return journey."

"That would be nice."

"It's typical that we were sent downstairs when there's a passenger I like."

"It may have done you a favour."

"I don't know how. Not that I've been able to talk to him. He's never without that companion, Mr Robbins."

Nell nodded. "He's a strange chap."

"I imagine he only stays with him to keep the ladies away."

"Well, it was working when we were still up there." Nell straightened up. "Shall we go?"

Mr Ramsbottom was in the corridor when they arrived.

"Ah, ladies, here you are. Matron's looking for you. We've had a couple of cases of cholera amongst the ladies."

"How's that happened?" Mrs Swift's voice was shrill.

He shrugged. "Don't ask me. Anyway, Mr Cooper's with them at the moment. Much to his discomfort." Mr Ramsbottom sniggered as he left. "I'll see you later."

They hadn't reached the dormitories when Matron bustled out of one and headed towards them.

"Where've you been?"

Nell shuddered. "We didn't think you needed us and so we went onto the deck for five minutes."

"You're on this ship to work, not sightsee." Matron glared at them. "While you've been away, we've had some cases reported in the women's area. We'll need to move one of you over there."

Mrs Swift's stare was thunderous. "Keeping everyone segregated was supposed to stop it spreading."

"It was. Dr Clarke's furious about the whole affair. When we find out who's responsible, there'll be trouble."

Nell put an arm between the two of them. "How many are affected?"

"Six so far. Thankfully, the ladies' dormitory isn't full, so we've moved them all to one end."

"That's something." Nell looked at Mrs Swift. "Would you mind going rather than me ... so I can carry on in the hospital room..."

"Only if it helps us get back to first class quicker."

Matron planted her hands on her hips. "Mrs Swift. Nobody will be going to first class until we dock in New

York. Have you any idea how it would look if the infection spreads upstairs? We'd never attract first-class passengers again. Now, if you've finished complaining, finish your work here and start preparing for your move to the ladies' section tomorrow."

Once the men were settled in their rooms for the night, Nell hurried upstairs. The hospital room was dimly lit, but she smiled at Mr Wood and Mr Marsh, who were propped up on their pillows.

"Good evening, gentlemen. This is a pleasant surprise. Are you both feeling better?"

Mr Wood's voice croaked. "I'd be better if he'd feed us. He won't even give us any water."

"Who? Dr Clarke?" She filled up a cup. "He must have forgotten."

Mr Wood struggled to sit up straight, but he grasped the cup and guzzled down the water before flopping onto the pillows. "He hasn't, he's just heartless. He won't give us anything."

Nell looked over to Mr Marsh. "Is that the same for you?"

"I'm afraid so. He can see I'm feeling much better, but he won't budge. He seems to take great delight in saying no."

"That doesn't sound like him."

"You'd be surprised." Mr Marsh licked his cracked lips. "What I wouldn't do for a cup of tea, but he's having none of it."

"I can't bring you tea, but you can have more water." She offered him the refilled cup.

Mr Marsh took hold of it with both hands. "I fear that if it wasn't for your kindness, Dr Clarke would let us perish in here."

Nell took the chair by his bed. "Hasn't Matron been in?"

"She's as bad. She won't do anything without him telling her to."

"I'd assumed you were being well cared for. I know they stopped the food and drink to relieve the symptoms, but now you're improving, they should bring you something soon."

"I hope so, or I'll be going to the galley myself."

Nell tutted as she took the cup from him. "There's no need for that. I'll pop up more often if that helps."

The twinkle returned to Mr Marsh's eyes. "That would certainly help. Seeing you is better than any tonic."

Nell was thankful the darkness covered her blushes. "Please, Mr Marsh..."

"I don't mean to embarrass you, but while I've been here, you're the only thing that's kept me going."

Nell gulped. "That's nice."

He lowered his voice. "I hope you don't mind me telling you this, but I've liked you since the first time we met. I'm sorry I was angry when I saw you with your nephews. I wasted so much time by assuming the worst."

Nell's heart pounded. "I'm sorry too, for the way I behaved in New York. I wasn't ready to walk out with anyone then."

"I realise that now." His eyes searched her face. "May we start again?"

She bit her lip. "If that's what you'd like."

Mr Cunningham was wandering the corridor when Nell returned to steerage. "I thought you'd long gone."

"I've been to see Mr Marsh. I'm pleased to say, he's a lot better."

"That's good news. Will he be at work soon?"

"I doubt it. He's still very weak. Have you seen Mrs Swift recently?"

His brow furrowed. "I can't say I have. Hasn't she moved to the ladies' section?"

"Not yet. She's starting there tomorrow."

"She must have gone on ahead, then."

"Never mind. Goodnight, Mr Cunningham." She made her way to the stairs and took a deep breath as she descended to the boiler room. *I wish she'd wait for me.*

She crept down to the corridor and, after checking both ways, turned right and hurried towards the end, where she barged through the door. She came to a halt when it hit something on the other side.

"Mrs Swift! What on earth...?"

"Leave me alone."

"What's going on?"

"Nothing. You go, I'll follow you."

"But..."

"Leave me..." Mrs Swift buried her face in her hands and after a moment's hesitation, Nell climbed the stairs, glancing down at the huddled-up shape of Mrs Swift when she reached the top.

"I'll be back in five minutes if you don't follow me."

Matron was still in the sitting room when Nell arrived, and she greeted her with a frown. "Have you lost Mrs Swift again?"

"She'll be here shortly." Nell settled into her chair. "I called into the hospital room before I came here, and the men there seem to be making a good recovery. They wondered if they might be allowed something to eat."

"I hope you didn't give them anything?"

"I had nothing to give other than water."

"And you gave it to them?" Matron's face turned red. "Dr Clarke specifically told us they weren't to have anything. You'll give them another attack."

"But they're so much better for it..."

"They may now, but what about overnight? If I find the beds soiled in the morning, I'll be coming for you to change them."

"But you can't starve them. They've eaten nothing for days."

"That, Mrs Riley, is a decision for Dr Clarke, not a stewardess. Now, if you'll excuse me, it's time I was in bed. It sounds like there'll be extra duties for me in the morning."

Nell waited for Matron's cabin door to close before she sank onto the settee. *What was all that about?* She pulled a tray towards her and uncovered a plate of sausage with mashed potatoes smothered in congealed butter. *Mr Potter must have been early tonight.*

She was about finished when Mrs Swift joined her, the rims of her eyes still red.

"Come and sit down."

Mrs Swift did as she was told without speaking.

"What's the matter?"

"I've been upstairs to see Mr Divine."

Nell's mouth opened and closed several times before any words came out. "What were you thinking? Did he see you?"

"No ... but Mrs Phillips did."

Nell gasped.

"I was only there for a minute. I wanted to see him again."

"You've been into first class? You could have infected them."

Mrs Swift put her head in her hands. "I didn't mean to. And I wasn't close to anyone."

"But you still might have carried it with you. Our clothes must stink of the disease. Did anyone else see you?"

"I don't think so."

"It's to be hoped Mrs Phillips doesn't mention it to anyone, then."

"She said she was going to tell Captain Robertson." Mrs Swift wiped her eyes with the back of a hand. "She knew about the cholera..."

"How could she? I thought it was being kept quiet?"

Mrs Swift shrugged but looked up as Nell dropped her knife and fork.

"You've not been into the women's section of steerage, too?"

"Why would I? I'm not due there until tomorrow."

"Not officially, but someone passed cholera to the

women. If the captain finds out you've been up to first class, he might assume it was you."

Mrs Swift gasped. "But I didn't; I had no reason to. I just thought..."

"...that you'd pop upstairs and stare at Mr Divine from a distance?" Nell shook her head. "No one will believe that."

"But it's true..."

"Even if it is, you shouldn't have been up there. You need to come up with a better explanation, before Captain Robertson comes looking for you."

# CHAPTER FORTY-SIX

Matron sat at the breakfast table, her lips pursed as Mrs Swift sobbed into her hands.

"Can you imagine how foolish I felt when Captain Robertson arrived down here to tell me what you'd been up to? You could lose your job over this."

Nell glanced at Mrs Swift as she squirmed in her seat.

"I didn't go into the women's section. Why would I?"

"That's a very good question, but we've had three ladies die because of your actions. The captain wants to see you in his office at nine o'clock sharp."

"No!" Mrs Swift's eyes widened as she stared at Matron. "Has anyone in first class caught it?"

"Not yet, but Dr Clarke now has to do extra medical checks on them all to make sure they're well enough to leave the ship."

Mrs Swift gave a loud sniff as she wiped her nose. "I'm sorry."

"It's too late for that. Mrs Phillips has been terribly frightened since she saw you and wants the stewards to give the foyer and corridor a thorough clean. We've not got enough staff upstairs to be doing that. You'd better pray she doesn't go down with it." Matron stood up to leave. "Don't forget. Nine o'clock."

Nell pushed a cup of tea across the table. "What will you say to Captain Robertson?"

Mrs Swift shrugged. "Tell him the truth, and hope he believes me."

Nell leaned back in her chair. "He's always been very lenient with me."

"You've not put the health of half the ship at risk." Mrs Swift shook her head. "What was I thinking?"

"You weren't."

"No." She took a slurp of her tea. "Do you think they'll move me to another ship?"

"Quite possibly. A lot of stewards get moved."

"I know." Mrs Swift studied her. "Will you still be here next year?"

"No. I'm not coming back."

"You're not?" Mrs Swift's mouth fell open. "When did you decide that?"

"I think I've known for weeks, but this voyage has been the final straw. Even when we were in first class, the passengers were miserable. I've made enough money this year to last me for a while, and if I ever need to be a stewardess again, I'll do it once the cholera's gone."

"But this is a one-off. You can't base your decision on one trip."

"It's not just this voyage. It's the stewards, too. I've had enough of them."

Mrs Swift's shoulders slumped. "There's no point

pleading to stay on this ship then if you won't be here."

Nell gave a wry smile. "Perhaps that's for the best."

Nell spent the morning with the passengers who were still ill, and by the time she'd finished, her back ached. *I wonder if Mrs Swift will come here or go straight to the women's dormitory. I hope she comes here.* She stepped into the corridor as Mr Cunningham walked past.

"Mrs Riley. Are you all done in there?"

"I am. Have you seen Mrs Swift lately?"

"I can't say I have, but I've been dealing with passengers in dormitory two for the last half an hour, and I'm still not finished. I need to get on."

"I'd better, too." She picked up her bucket and carried it down the corridor, but stopped at the sound of crying further down the corridor. *Mrs Swift?* She followed the noise and pulled her friend into the linen cupboard.

"What's the matter?"

Mrs Swift struggled to speak. "I've lost my job."

Nell's brow creased. "But you knew you were likely to be moved...."

She shook her head. "He's not moved me. I can't work on any ship in the Guion Line, and he won't give me a reference."

"No!" Nell's eyes widened.

"I didn't stand a chance. Dr Clarke had told the captain I was responsible for the three women dying..."

"Are you sure you're not?"

"Positive. I've never been to the women's dormitory. And I'm not going now. Someone else can do it."

Nell studied her friend. "Who else would have gone there?"

"I've no idea."

Nell clicked her tongue. "Me neither, but it must be someone. We can't let you take the blame."

"I'd still be in trouble for going into first class, and I can't deny that."

"Would that be enough for you to lose your job, though?" Nell stood up and put an arm around Mrs Swift's shoulders. "Come on. Stop crying. We'll find out who's responsible for this and clear your name."

Nell held a hand to her neck and rolled her head, relieving the stiffness that had come from tending to so many passengers. *Do I really need to go upstairs tonight?* She straightened up and wandered over to Mrs Swift. "I'd better go."

Mrs Swift looked up from mopping the floor. "Where to?"

"To visit Mr Marsh. I'd rather not, but he looks forward to it. I'll only stay for five minutes."

"Go now then, and I'll wait for you."

Most of the men were asleep when she arrived, but Mr Marsh was sitting up in bed and he waved as she opened the door. "I hoped you'd come."

Nell sighed and flopped onto the chair. "You're lucky I did. It's been a difficult day. How are you feeling?"

"Other than hungry, much better, thank you. The doctor was in an hour ago to give everyone a sleeping draught, but I told him I didn't need one. He wasn't easy to convince, but, as you can see–" He pointed to himself.

"He likes giving everyone laudanum. It serves so many purposes. Mostly good."

"It does, but I wonder if he's using too much of it. Mr Wood didn't want any, either, but Dr Clarke forced it into his mouth. He said that if he wanted something to eat tomorrow, he had to take it."

"I suppose he knows best." Nell fidgeted in her chair as Mr Marsh watched her.

"You said you've had a hard day. Was it anything in particular?"

Nell gulped. "Unfortunately, several female passengers have contracted cholera, even though they're separated from the men. We don't know how it happened, but Mrs Swift's been blamed for it. She's lost her job."

"No!" Mr Marsh's mouth fell open. "Why would they blame her?"

Nell sighed. "She was daft enough to go into first class last night and a passenger reported her. The captain and Dr Clarke have decided that if she was foolish enough to go upstairs, she must be the one who slipped into the women's dormitory, too."

"But she didn't?"

"No. She's adamant about it, and I must say I believe her. She had no reason to go in there."

"And she had a reason to go upstairs?"

Nell sighed. "Not a very good one, but yes. She wanted

to see someone. The problem is, three of the women in steerage died, and she's being blamed for it."

Mr Marsh leaned back on his pillows and closed his eyes, causing Nell to stand up.

"I'm sorry, you're tired. I'll call again tomorrow."

He bolted upright. "Not at all. Please stay. I was only thinking."

Nell retook her seat. "What about?"

"Who may have gone into the women's section. The obvious person would be Matron but also Dr Clarke, or even the captain himself. They'd all do their daily inspections."

"But they wouldn't make anyone ill..."

"Not deliberately, but the doctor and Matron have been working with the sick for this last week or so, so why shouldn't it be them who caused the problem?"

"I hadn't thought of that, but..." Nell twisted her fingers "...if that was the case, why blame Mrs Swift?"

"So they don't lose *their* jobs. I imagine either would be happier for Mrs Swift to take the blame."

"But that's horrible. Mrs Swift needs the money for her sister and mother. As far as I'm aware, neither Matron nor the doctor have any family ties."

"Maybe not, but the ship's their life. Their home."

"But it's not right, is it?" Her shoulders slumped. "Do you think I should tell the captain?"

"Not yet." His face stiffened. "We need proof."

"But how do we get that?"

Mr Marsh blew out through his lips. "Who's nursing the women who are ill?"

"Only Matron at the moment, plus the usual stewards who work on that side of the ship."

"You should get yourself over there. If you can nurse those women, you can speak to them. Ask them who's been in."

"That's a good idea. I'll ask Matron before she goes to bed." She smiled down at Mr Marsh as she stood up. "Thank you, you've been very helpful. Would you like some water before I go?"

"I thought you'd never offer."

Mrs Swift was waiting when Nell returned to steerage. "I don't want to go anywhere on my own any more."

Nell rested a hand on her friend's arm. "Don't worry. We're going to sort this out."

"How?"

They made their way down to the boiler room and the familiar sound of men loading coal into the furnaces. When there was no one in the corridor, Nell carried on to the door and held it open.

"Someone else must have gone between the men's and women's sections, the three most obvious being Captain Robertson, Dr Clarke and Matron. We have to find out if any of them could have passed it on."

"How do we do that?"

"Leave it to me." Nell raced to the sitting room but stopped and threw her hands in the air. "She's gone."

Mrs Swift caught her up. "That's no surprise. We're late."

Nell huffed as she sat down and pulled the waiting tray

towards her. "I was going to suggest I work in the women's section of steerage to ask if anyone saw anything."

"You've not got long. It's our last day before New York tomorrow."

"That's why I wanted to speak to Matron tonight. I'll need to be up early in the morning now."

# CHAPTER FORTY-SEVEN

The sitting room was empty the next morning when Nell walked across the corridor. She stared at the table. *No Matron or breakfast.*

Mr Potter disturbed her as he arrived with the tray. "You're early if you've beaten Matron."

"I am. I imagine she'll be here in a minute."

"She may have overslept. She's been very busy this last week."

Nell nodded. "I'll check on her shortly if she's still not here."

"Well, say good morning to her from me." He set off down the corridor with a wave.

Mrs Swift joined her five minutes later. "On your own?"

"For now. I think we should knock on Matron's door to make sure she's awake."

"She could have been called away."

Nell poured Mrs Swift a cup of tea. "She could, but I'll check, anyway."

"I need something to eat first. I hardly ate a thing yesterday."

"Did you sleep all right?"

"Better than you'd think. I'm clearly expecting you to sort this whole mess out."

"I'm glad you have so much faith in me!" Nell crossed the corridor and knocked on Matron's door. "Matron, are you awake?" When there was no answer, she knocked again. "Matron."

Nothing.

She reached for the doorknob, twisting it slowly before she stepped inside. "Matron, are you in here?"

There was a soft groan from the lower bunk. "Fetch Dr Clarke."

Nell fumbled with the night light as she lit the wall lamp. "Oh, gracious. You're ill."

"I need Dr Clarke..."

"It's all right, leave it with me." She raced across the corridor. "Will you find a clean chamber pot for Matron while I find Dr Clarke? She's got cholera."

Nell didn't wait for a reply before she headed towards the steerage rooms. *He won't be here yet. I'll try the hospital room.* She carried on up the next flight of stairs. *Please let him be here.*

The room was in darkness when she popped her head in, and it looked as if the men were still asleep. She was about to leave when footsteps marched up behind her.

"Mrs Riley. What are you doing here at this time of day?"

"Oh, Dr Clarke, thank goodness." She put a hand to her

chest. "Matron's got cholera. She asked me to fetch you. She said she needs some laudanum."

Dr Clarke ran his eyes around the room, then took out his pocket watch. "Tell her I'll be with her shortly. I need to deal with the men first."

"They were both very hungry when I looked in on them last night. Would you mind if I brought them a light breakfast?"

"Mrs Riley. How can I do my job when women like you keep interfering? I need to know the best way to deal with these patients and giving them nil by mouth is an option I'm trialling on them."

"But they're desperate..."

"It's a small price to pay if I save their lives. Now, if you'll excuse me."


Mrs Swift had finished breakfast by the time Nell got back, but she poured herself a cup of tea.

"Isn't Dr Clarke with you?"

"He wanted to check the men in the hospital room first." Nell shook her head. "I don't know what he's doing to them, but they'll be starving to death if he doesn't let them have something to eat soon."

"Let's hope he treats Matron better."

"I wouldn't bank on it. Have you been in to see her?"

Mrs Swift nodded. "About ten minutes ago. She's not well but she's panicking about Dr Clarke seeing her as she is. One of the downsides of her being so friendly with him."

"She's no one to blame but herself for that."

They were ready to leave the sitting room when the

doctor arrived, and they waited for him to tend to Matron. Nell looked up as he joined them.

"How is she?"

"Poorly. I've given her a dose of laudanum, which should settle her stomach and help her sleep. I'll call again this afternoon."

"Is there any need for anyone to stay with her?"

"Not at the moment." He checked his pocket watch. "You should be in steerage by now."

"We're going, but..." Nell glanced at Mrs Swift "...I'm not sure if Matron told you, but she wanted me to go to the women's dormitory today, to help with the outbreak there."

"She hadn't, but it makes sense. Once you're there, you're to have no more contact with the men's section."

"Yes, sir."

"I'll take you there now and hand you over to one of the stewards." Dr Clarke glared at Mrs Swift. "You, about your business."

She turned on her heel and hurried towards the boiler room, while Nell followed the doctor down the corridor, between several long storage rooms. Once out into another foyer, he went through a door.

"It's an easier journey getting back and forth." He marched to a door on the left-hand side. "Mr Cooper. Mrs Riley for you. I believe you were expecting her."

"I was hoping for one of them. She should make life easier."

*How fortunate we're still on the ship, then.* Nell took a deep breath as Mr Cooper showed her to a dormitory similar to the men's, with bunks along either side and a long table down the centre.

"All the patients are in here." He gave a disparaging glance around the room. "Just keep them clean and comfortable. They don't need much. Mr Cunningham will help you if you have any questions." Without waiting for an answer, he strode from the room.

Nell gazed at the women in the bunks. Those closest to the door had the familiar sunken eyes and cheeks, except for one young girl. *She doesn't look ill. What's she doing in here?*

The child cowered against the wall as Nell smiled at her.

"I'm Mrs Riley. One of the stewardesses. What's your name?"

"Ruth, miss."

"There's no need to be frightened, Ruth. I'll be taking care of you. Are you ill?"

The girl's eyes flashed to the next bunk.

"Is this your mam?" Nell nodded to the woman in the next bunk.

"I'm Mrs Ashworth, and she's not ill, but I have been. Thankfully, it was only mild and I'm on the mend, but she didn't want to leave me."

*Ashworth?* Nell tilted her head to one side. "Are you travelling with your husband?"

"Yes, why?" The woman shot the girl a glance.

"There's no need to worry. I saw him earlier this week in the hospital room. He's had cholera, too, but you'll be pleased to hear that he's over it."

The woman's eyes filled with tears. "Praise the Lord. I knew he'd been ill, but the doctor wouldn't tell me what had happened. I thought he was dead."

"Well, I can assure you he's fine. If you'd like to send a

message to him, my colleague Mrs Swift is working in the men's dormitories. I'll see her later if you want to write a note."

"There are two stewardesses on the ship and we get stewards looking after us?" A woman sat up on one of the lower bunks. "Why are you both seeing to the men?"

"We normally work in first class, but when the cholera was discovered, they moved us down here to help. Matron's ill herself now, which is why I'm here."

"Another perk of being a toff." The woman flopped on her pillow. "I hate them all."

Nell hesitated. "Most of them are nice, Mrs..."

"Topham."

"Right, yes."

Mrs Ashworth smiled. "While you're here, may we have a drink?" Her eyes pleaded with her, and Nell nodded.

"Let me top up the water jug."

Once the ladies were clean and settled, Nell headed to her own quarters. *How do I get to the hospital room?* She shrugged. *I either have to go through the men's section or first class.* She turned to the left. *It had better be steerage.*

She raced through the boiler room to the stairs, where she slowed to a crawl, listening for voices. With a quick check of the steerage foyer, she skirted around it to the stairs and ran straight up to the hospital room.

She knocked on the door before going in.

"Mrs Riley." Mr Marsh smiled as she entered. "I was hoping you'd come. Dr Clarke's discharged me, so I won't be here tonight."

"He has? What prompted that?"

He grinned as she took her seat. "You did. I overheard you talking to him this morning and told him he'd have questions to answer if we die of starvation, rather than cholera."

"You said that?"

He shrugged. "What did I have to lose? Mr Wood backed me up, and shortly afterwards, a steward brought me breakfast."

"Not Mr Wood?"

"No. I think that was the compromise. Mr Wood is a couple of days behind me in his recovery, so Dr Clarke was able to save face. We're both being allowed luncheon, though."

"I am glad." She stared at Mr Wood's bed. "Where is he?"

"Using the facilities ... but without the need to rush."

"That's a relief. I worried that I'd make you worse by giving you as much water as I did."

"Not at all. In fact, quite the contrary. It really perked us up."

"That's a relief."

Concern crossed his face. "Have you made any progress with Mrs Swift's job?"

She shook her head. "Only that I'm now working in the ladies' section. They all confirmed they've never seen Mrs Swift before and were quite angry to find out there are stewardesses on board when they're only provided with stewards."

"At least it's a start."

"It is. The problem now is that Matron has gone down with cholera, and so I'll need to keep an eye on her, too."

"Oh, dear." Deeply etched lines appeared on his face. "How is she?"

"Not very well. Dr Clarke called this morning and gave her some laudanum. I'll have to hope it will sort her out."

# CHAPTER FORTY-EIGHT

The sun was sinking behind the distant hills as Nell stood on the deck, looking out over Long Island. Those healthy enough had been allowed outside, and Nell was acting as their chaperone. *I've certainly had worse jobs this week.*

The sky was red as the light faded, but Nell pulled her cloak tightly around her. The November air in New York was no warmer than in Liverpool.

*It will be strange not seeing Mr Marsh tonight. At least he's alive.*

Mrs Ashworth walked up beside her. "A penny for your thoughts."

Nell smiled. "One of my colleagues has been in the hospital room for the last week, but was discharged earlier today. I was thinking how strange it would be not to visit him."

"Is that one of the stewards?"

"Yes. Mr Marsh. He worked in steerage, so you may have met him before the outbreak."

Mrs Ashworth's forehead creased. "Is he tall with greased-back hair and a moustache?"

"That's him. He was only down here because I'd insisted on it after falling out with him, so when he caught cholera, I felt very guilty."

"He's rather handsome, if I remember rightly. Not the sort of man I'd have fallen out with." There was a smile in her voice, but Nell's eyes remained fixed on the horizon.

"I didn't notice until he was in hospital."

"They must be working you too hard if you missed that."

"Perhaps..." She focussed on a group of trees on the land. "It's funny how we see things differently. Anyway, how are you enjoying your first trip outside?"

"It's wonderful. Thanks to you, Ruth is finally smiling again." She watched her daughter playing with another young girl. "It was such a weight off both our minds, hearing that my husband was safe. The thought of arriving in a new country with only a child for company was something I didn't dare consider."

"I'm not surprised. It's horrible knowing you're on your own." Nell felt Mrs Ashworth's eyes on her. "I'm a widow, which is why I'm here."

"I'm sorry." Mrs Ashworth paused. "Will you get off the ship in New York?"

"I doubt it. I did once, earlier this year, but we'll need to clean the place from top to bottom once you disembark. We still have several members of the crew with cholera, so that won't help."

"Do you enjoy the work?"

Nell snorted. "That's a question. I didn't, and then I

did, but now? Not this trip. It's my last, too. I'm not coming back next year."

"That's a shame. You're good at what you do. Better than some of those stewards. Mr Cooper's all right, but that Mr Cunningham always annoys me, flitting in and out whenever he likes and using our facilities."

"I don't know him very well, because he's been down in steerage, but I saw him when he was in the men's..." Nell's voice trailed off. "How long's he been working in your section?"

Mrs Ashworth shrugged. "All the time."

"Earlier this week?"

"Yes. I didn't see so much of him when I was ill, but I'd seen plenty of him before that. In fact, he was the one who told me my husband was in the hospital room."

Nell spoke to herself. "He was in the men's section when I was there."

Mrs Ashworth put a hand on her arm. "Are you all right?"

Nell's lips curled up. "I am. We've been wondering who could have transferred the illness from the men to the women, and you may have given us our answer. Do you remember the names of any other stewards who've worked in your dormitory?"

She put a finger to her chin. "Mr Marsh did, before he was ill, and another chap. Mr Price. He would walk round with the doctor and captain when they did their inspections. I didn't have much to do with him, though."

"What about a Mr Wood?"

"Yes, but not for a while."

"He's in hospital now, too. He was there at the same time as your husband."

Mrs Ashworth frowned. "How is he?"

"A lot better. Dr Clarke should discharge him for the return journey."

Once the passengers were in their dormitories for the evening, Nell slipped away to her own quarters. As soon as she arrived, she knocked on Matron's door and let herself in. "Are you awake?" When there was no answer, she stepped further into the room.

"Matron."

The older woman lay flat on her back with her eyes shut and mouth open. *She looks peaceful enough.* She glanced at the chamber pot. Still empty. *That's a good sign.*

Mrs Swift was in the corridor as Nell closed the cabin door.

"That was well timed. How is she?"

"Sleeping like a baby."

"It's strange without her." Mrs Swift took her seat. "How's your day been with the ladies?"

"Rather pleasant, actually. They're a lot less demanding than the men, and there are fewer of them."

"Did you find out anything of interest?"

Nell sat down with a smirk on her face. "I think I've discovered the person who spread the infection."

Mrs Swift's eyes widened. "Who?"

"Mr Cunningham."

Mrs Swift frowned. "He's allowed to be in the ladies' section. Dr Clarke sent him there this morning."

"He wasn't while he was in the men's dormitories. One of the ladies said he'd been in their section from the beginning and even used their facilities."

Mrs Swift gasped. "The scoundrel! He knew they'd blamed me, too." Her eyes narrowed. "Will Captain Robertson believe the women, though, if it's their word against his?"

Nell clicked her tongue. "That's what I don't know. There's another thing in your favour, though. When I mentioned you to the women, they were all amazed there were stewardesses on board. They'd clearly never seen you."

A smile settled on Mrs Swift's lips. "You really are good at this."

Nell was awake early the next morning, a smile already on her face as she climbed from the top bunk and lit the wall lamp. Mrs Swift was still in bed.

"You're eager."

"I want to see the back of these passengers and get the ship cleaned. The sooner we start, the sooner we'll finish."

"We need to check on Matron first."

"I'll do it. In fact, let me get dressed and I'll go straight away."

Matron was restless when Nell arrived and crouched beside the bed.

"How are you feeling?"

"Terrible. My stomach and legs keep going into spasm. I couldn't stand up if I tried."

"Stay where you are, then. Hopefully, Dr Clarke will visit before we start disembarking the passengers."

"Is it Friday already?"

"It is, but don't worry yourself. We'll do whatever needs doing. I'll bring you some water to rinse your mouth."

Mrs Swift was in the sitting room with the breakfast tray when Nell joined her.

"How is she?"

"She's awake, but not well. I hope Dr Clarke isn't too busy to visit."

Mrs Swift helped herself to some bread. "I wonder what we do with the passengers in steerage this morning. They can't leave the ship until those in first class have disembarked, so presumably we give them breakfast and tell them to wait."

"I imagine so. The stewards will put us right soon enough if we do anything wrong."

Nell hadn't finished her second cup of tea, when there was a knock on the door and Mr Price walked in.

"Good morning, ladies. I'm sorry to disturb you, but the captain would like to speak to everyone at nine o'clock in the dining room."

"In first class? Are we allowed up there?"

"All the first-class passengers will be off the ship by then."

"What about those down here?"

"I'm afraid they'll have to wait. The captain has an urgent message. Could you help with breakfast in steerage and then come straight up?"

. . .

Mr Price was waiting for them at the entrance to the dining room when they arrived, and he ushered them to their usual table.

"The stewards from steerage will join you. We want to keep you all separate from the first-class crew."

Mr Ramsbottom winked at Nell as he took a seat at an adjacent table with Mr Cooper and Mr Cunningham.

Mrs Swift leaned over to them. "Have you heard what this is about?"

Mr Ramsbottom shook his head. "Not a word. I reckon it's serious, though."

"Do you think they'll tell us who spread the cholera to the ladies' section?"

"I thought it was you."

"Well, it wasn't. I might have taken the blame for it, but I've never set foot in there."

Mr Cunningham smirked. "A likely story."

"You've no right to look so pleased with yourself..." Mrs Swift was about to get to her feet, but Mr Price rang the bell and called for silence.

"Captain Robertson would like your attention."

The captain strolled to the centre of the room, his face stern. "Good morning, ladies and gentlemen. I'm sorry to disturb your usual routine, but I'm afraid I've some rather difficult news." He paused as all eyes turned to him. "I've spoken to the port authorities this morning, and because of the cholera outbreak, they want to do a full inspection of the ship before they let the steerage passengers disembark."

Mrs Swift stared at Nell as the room erupted with noise. "What does that mean?"

"I don't know."

The captain clapped his hands. "Gentlemen, please. If I could continue. Until we hear the outcome of the inspection, the steerage passengers are to stay where they are."

Mr Cooper raised his hand. "Will this delay our return journey?"

"I'm hoping not, but it's too early to say." Captain Robertson's shoulders sagged. "We should know more by luncheon, so we need you to carry on as best you can. Mr Price will give you the details of what we've arranged." He strode from the room with Dr Clarke close behind, while Mr Price sounded the bell again.

"If I could have one more minute. Those who've been working in first class should make a start cleaning the staterooms. Those from steerage are to clean the dining room before moving up to the saloon. We need to keep you separate as best we can. If I need anyone in steerage, I'll come and find you."

Nell held her stomach as Mr Price ushered the first-class stewards from the room. "I hope it doesn't delay us; I've had enough of this voyage."

"We didn't get any tips, either ... and I didn't get to say goodbye to Mr Divine." Mrs Swift's bottom lip jutted out as Nell did a double take.

"You didn't speak to him at all."

"He smiled at me."

Nell shook her head. "Don't fool yourself. He was probably smiling at someone behind you. Now, are we going to get started? Hopefully, we'll have some news sooner rather than later."

# CHAPTER FORTY-NINE

Nell's stomach rumbled as she and Mrs Swift went down the stairs to the dining room. It was already filling up when they arrived, and Nell nudged her friend and pointed to the far side of the room.

"Captain Robertson."

"Do you think he has some news for us?"

Nell studied him. "I hope not, he doesn't look very happy."

Mr Ramsbottom remained silent as Mr Cooper stood up and offered them both a seat.

"We don't think it's good news."

"What have you heard?"

"Nothing, but the officials who came on board this morning didn't look very impressed." Mr Cooper retook his seat. "There's no sign of the steerage passengers moving, either, and Captain Robertson will want them off as soon as they give him permission."

A wave of nausea washed over her. "We're going to be delayed, aren't we?"

"It might be more serious than that. It wouldn't surprise me if the captain's in trouble."

Mr Cunningham turned round in his seat. "Here we go."

At the sound of the bell, the stewards settled down.

"Ladies and gentlemen. Thank you for your patience and hard work this morning. As you know, the outbound journey from Liverpool was fraught with difficulties, but I'm afraid it doesn't end here. The inspector who boarded the ship has given me a verbal update of the report he intends to file. In summary, because of the outbreak, the Port Authority is not prepared to grant entry to our steerage passengers."

Nell gasped as everyone spoke at once. "They can't disembark? What does that mean?"

Mr Price rang the bell to quieten the noise. "Gentlemen, please."

Captain Robertson cleared his throat. "I know this is a shock, and you'll have many questions, but I'd like to answer some of the most pressing. Firstly, we'll leave New York this afternoon, once fresh provisions have been loaded. The authority won't allow us to stay in dock while the passengers are contagious, so we need to make our way back to Liverpool and hope they've recovered by the time we arrive."

"At least that's something." Nell exhaled, but immediately gasped again. "Will they let us off in Liverpool?"

Mrs Swift shrugged. "I've no idea."

The captain raised his voice to compete with the

murmuring. "Because of that, we won't be able to take any new passengers for the return journey."

"Not even in first class?" Mr Cooper spoke for those around him.

"I'm afraid not. The risk of infection is too great."

A steward from the other side of the room raised his hand. "What will the first-class stewards do with no guests?"

Captain Robertson grimaced. "There'll still be plenty to do, but before we do anything else, Dr Clarke and I need to explain to the passengers what's happening. The chefs have been told to prepare them something to eat and after that, Dr Clarke will assess them all so we can fully segregate those who are sick from those who are well. We'll work on further arrangements this afternoon and speak to you again once we leave port. Take over, Mr Price."

Mr Price waited for the captain and Dr Clarke to leave. "Once luncheon is over, those who've been serving in first class will give a thorough clean to every part of the ship that isn't occupied by passengers. Those in steerage should return to their dormitories and continue as if it was a normal day at sea."

Nell waited for Mr Price to follow the captain from the room before she turned to Mrs Swift. "Captain Robertson looks like he has the weight of the world on his shoulders."

"I imagine he'll be in trouble with Mr Guion. How much money will they lose by not taking any first-class passengers?" Mrs Swift stared after him. "If he'd bothered to find out how this infection spread rather than blaming the first person he saw, he might have done a better job."

Nell patted her hand but held her tongue as several

chefs appeared carrying trays of food. The last to appear was Mr Ross.

"Welcome back, ladies." He beamed at them as he placed their plates on the table. "We've missed you. How's steerage?"

"Not as good as up here, that's for sure." Mrs Swift picked up her knife and fork. "I'm surprised you're allowed to serve us."

He shrugged. "Someone has to do it. I believe Matron has it now. How is she?"

Nell's jaw dropped. "We should have gone to check on her. I don't suppose Dr Clarke visited this morning with everything else that's been going on."

Mrs Swift blanched. "He won't have done. We'd better call as soon as we've finished this."

Once she'd finished eating, Nell stood up to leave. "I'll call and see Matron on my way to steerage. I'll see you later." She smiled at the stewards as she walked past their table, but Mr Ramsbottom caught hold of her wrist.

"What's all this about you and Mr Marsh?"

"What about us?"

"Don't act so innocent. Mr Marsh has been telling anyone who'll listen that you're the only reason he's still alive."

Nell's cheeks coloured. "I'm sure he's exaggerating. I only visited a couple of times because I felt guilty about him being ill."

"According to him, it was more than that. He said you'll be walking out together when we're back in Liverpool."

"I offered to walk to the park with him. That's all."

"Was that a guilt offering too?"

"That's none of your business. Now, if you'll excuse me, I need to check on Matron." She hurried from the room, not slowing until she reached the deck. It was empty when she stepped outside, but she hadn't taken half a dozen steps when Captain Robertson approached her from the back of the ship.

"Mrs Riley?"

"Captain."

"How's morale amongst the crew?"

She fidgeted with her fingers. "We're here to do a job. We'll carry on as before."

"Splendid." He smiled down at her. "I'm glad I caught you. On top of everything else that's happened today, there was a telegram waiting for me when we docked. Mrs Robertson was delivered of a baby girl ten days ago."

A smile brightened Nell's face. "That's wonderful. Congratulations."

"Thank you. I can't tell you how glad I am that I forbade her from coming on this voyage. She wanted to, but could you imagine?"

"No, sir. I couldn't. Will you send her my best wishes when you see her?"

"I will. Now, I must get on."

"Before you go..." She hesitated as Captain Robertson stared at her. "Might I mention Mrs Swift?"

He rubbed the back of his neck. "What about her?"

"I've been talking to the ladies in steerage, and they were amazed that there are two stewardesses on the ship. They knew nothing about either of us."

He cocked his head to one side. "What are you saying?"

"With respect, sir. If the ladies had never seen or heard of us before, it's highly unlikely that Mrs Swift could have spread the cholera to them."

"But she was in first class."

"She hasn't denied that, but that doesn't mean she visited the ladies' dormitory. Why would she?"

"Why would she go into first class when she'd been specifically told not to? It seems clear to me she has no regard for rules."

Nell sighed. "She was rather infatuated with Mr Divine and hoped to catch a glimpse of him."

"She risked our passengers' safety so she could see someone?"

"She knows how foolish she was, but she's adamant she didn't visit the women's steerage section ... and I believe her."

"Well, somebody did, and until I'm told evidence to the contrary, I have to suspect her. We wouldn't be in the mess we're in today if the infection hadn't spread."

Nell pursed her lips as she took a breath. "There were other people who visited both the men's and women's sections."

"Who?" The captain's dark eyes bored into her.

"Well, Dr Clarke and Matron. And Mr Price, when he was with you and Dr Clarke."

"I hope you're not implying..."

"I'm not saying anything, just pointing out that other people could have spread the disease. Then there's Mr Cunningham..."

"Mr Cunningham?"

"One of the ladies commented on him being a regular visitor to their section and even said he used their lavatories."

"I wasn't told of that." The captain's face coloured. "Thank you, Mrs Riley. Leave it with me."

# CHAPTER FIFTY

By the time Nell and Mrs Swift returned to their sitting room that evening, the ship had left port and was moving at speed up the coast of America.

"We'd better check on Matron before we sit down." Mrs Swift knocked on the door. "She was out cold when I visited earlier."

Matron's eyes flicked open as they went into the cabin.

"You're awake." Nell rested a hand on the older woman's forehead. "How are you feeling?"

Her voice croaked. "I need water."

Mrs Swift poured a mouthful into the cup and handed it to her. "You know what Dr Clarke says, only enough to wet your mouth."

Matron emptied the glass in one gulp. "He's wrong. More."

"We can't do that. You told us so yourself."

Nell noticed a trace of tears running onto the pillow. "We don't want you getting worse."

"But I need to drink."

Nell took a deep breath and pulled Mrs Swift away from the bed. "What do we do? She reprimanded me for giving the passengers too much water. Do you think she's checking up on us?"

"She could be." Mrs Swift peered out into the corridor. "Why don't we fill the cup but leave it by the bed. If she wants any more, she'll have to help herself. That way she won't be able to blame us."

Nell nodded. "I'll tell her what we're doing, while you pour it."


Mr Potter was delivering their trays when they arrived in the sitting room, and he smiled as they joined him.

"Here you are. How's Matron?"

Nell sighed. "I think she's getting better. When we were leaving, she said she didn't need to see Dr Clarke again. Not that he's likely to call at this hour."

"He's had a tough day for sure. I heard those officials having a stern word with him earlier. It sounds like they blame him for what's happened rather than the captain."

Nell's forehead creased. "I thought Captain Robertson would take overall responsibility."

"He should, but they said the doctor should have spotted the cholera before the passengers boarded or contained it when he confirmed the first case." Mr Potter hovered near the door. "It wouldn't surprise me if they both lose their jobs over this. I'll see you tomorrow."

Mrs Swift sat down and lifted the lid on her plate. "It will serve them right if they do."

"It wouldn't be fair to Captain Robertson, though. He

couldn't tell whether a patient had cholera. Besides, he can't afford to be out of a job. Mrs Robertson had her baby ten days ago."

Mrs Swift stopped with her fork in mid-air. "How do you know that?"

"I bumped into Captain Robertson when I came back here earlier."

"Had a nice cosy chat, did you?"

"Don't be like that. I told him you've never been into the ladies' dormitory, and that the passengers could confirm it. I also mentioned that there were other people who might have spread the infection, including Mr Cunningham."

Mrs Swift snorted. "I bet he took no notice of you."

Nell stabbed a piece of beef. "I think he did. We'll just have to wait and see what he does about it."

Nell was awake early the following morning and was about to knock on Matron's door when Dr Clarke rounded the corner, his Gladstone bag in his hand.

"Mrs Riley."

"Good morning, Doctor. Are you here to see the patient?"

"I am indeed."

"She was feeling better last night..."

"I'm pleased to hear it." He paused outside the cabin. "I've a message for you and Mrs Swift. Mr Price has reassigned your duties and wants to see you upstairs at eight o'clock."

Nell grimaced. "We need to get a move on, then. Tell Matron I'll call and see her later."

There was no time to study the landscape as they hurried across the deck, but as soon as they entered the dining room foyer, Nell stopped.

"Mr Marsh."

He gave a slight bow. "At your service, madam."

"What are you doing here? You should be recovering."

"I'm much better, thank you."

Nell studied him. "You still look rather peaky."

He smiled. "I'll manage. I've been told to sit down if I need to. May I escort you to your table?"

"If it's not too much trouble."

"It's no trouble at all." He walked beside her and held out a chair for her and Mrs Swift before he joined the table with Mr Ramsbottom and Mr Cooper.

"You're sitting with us now, are you?" Mr Ramsbottom glared across to Mr Marsh, but Nell interrupted.

"Please. Can we call a truce? Where's Mr Cunningham?"

Mr Ramsbottom shrugged. "I've not seen him this morning."

Nell raised an eyebrow but held her tongue as Mr Price rang the bell and waited for silence.

"If you'd take your seats." He paused as the noise subsided. "Thank you for your promptness. I won't keep you long, but I have the arrangements for our journey to Liverpool. Dr Clarke's done a thorough assessment of the passengers, and he and Captain Robertson have decided that families with no signs of infection will move to the first-class staterooms. There will be one stateroom for each family, which means there'll be ten families upstairs, including forty men, women and children."

"Children in first class." Mrs Swift grimaced.

"There are also several unchaperoned women who will be put into the maids' rooms. Mrs Riley will move upstairs to support them. Mr Marsh and Mr Ramsbottom will also join us in first class."

*Oh, gracious.* Nell's stomach churned. *He should know better than putting them together.*

"Mrs Swift, you'll go to the ladies' section of steerage and deal with the sick passengers. Mr Cooper, Mr Cunningham and Mr Wood will also remain downstairs."

"Mr Wood?" Nell looked at Mr Marsh.

"He was discharged from the hospital yesterday, so he should be ready for work tomorrow."

Nell smiled. "That's good."

"It might be, but why do you always get the best jobs?" Mrs Swift spoke through gritted teeth.

"Perhaps because I already know some of them."

"Or because she's not been fired." Mr Ramsbottom sneered at Mrs Swift, but she scowled back.

"Through no fault of my own."

Mr Price continued to run through the duties for the remaining stewards before dismissing those working in steerage. "If the rest of you could wait, we'll discuss which passengers will be coming upstairs."


At eleven o'clock that morning, Nell escorted the Ashworths into their designated stateroom.

"Oh my, how the other half live." Mrs Ashworth turned in a full circle in the middle of the room.

"They pay a lot for the privilege." Nell indicated to a

stack of blankets on the settee. "These are for Ruth. She should be comfortable enough."

"She better had be." Mr Ashworth frowned at his daughter. "If she's not, she'll be going downstairs on her own."

"I will be." Ruth clung to her mother. "It's much nicer here."

"It is, and she'll be fine. Thank you, Mrs Riley."

"You're welcome. Now, if you'll excuse me." Nell hurried back to steerage to collect Mrs Topham. "If you'll follow me, your husband is waiting outside."

Once they found Mr Topham, Nell led them up the stairs and along the corridor past the Ashworths' room. "You'll be in here. You should be more comfortable."

"We'd better be." Mr Topham's ruddy face didn't lose its scowl. "We shouldn't even be here. Who's going to pay for us to make the journey again? That was our future they forced us to turn our backs on."

"I'm sorry. Maybe something can be sorted out. In the meantime, I hope being in here will make up for some of your disappointment."

"I'll say." Mrs Topham ran her fingers over the furniture. "To think there were passengers travelling like this while we were crammed in downstairs."

"Some people have got more money than they know what to do with. This sort of accommodation shouldn't be allowed."

"Would you rather move back to your bunk, sir?"

"No, he wouldn't." Mrs Topham shot her husband a glance. "We'll be very happy here, won't we?"

"It's still indecent. You could fit another three beds in here and be comfortable."

Mrs Topham gritted her teeth. "Stop giving them ideas."

"I'm not, I'm just saying."

Nell gave Mrs Topham a sympathetic smile. "If there's anything you need, let me know. Otherwise, I'll leave you to settle in."

Luncheon was about to start when Mr Ramsbottom joined Nell at the entrance to the dining room. He gave her a curt smile. "You'll stand with me now, will you?"

"We both have jobs to do." Nell kept her eyes on the far side of the foyer. "It wouldn't do to squabble in public."

"It's only because of you we're arguing in the first place."

Nell's heart raced, and she stepped back to the wall as he wandered to her side of the entrance.

"Still, it's nice to see passengers appreciating what they have. Not like the usual lot who expect the earth."

Nell grimaced. "It is for most of them, but I'd send Mr Topham back to steerage if I had the chance. He's done nothing but moan."

"There's always one. You'd think they'd be glad of a bit of pampering."

Nell lowered her voice. "They're here."

Mr Ramsbottom rubbed his hands together as he strode back to his own side. "Good afternoon, sir, madam. If you'd care to take a seat in the middle section..." He extended an arm towards the centre of the room.

"I hope we don't get any fancy stuff to eat." Mr

Topham's voice boomed into the room. "Pie and mash will do me."

Mr Ramsbottom fixed a smile. "Shall I arrange for you to eat in steerage, sir?"

"Not likely. You can give us some decent stuff up here. A strong pot of tea wouldn't go amiss, either. None of that watery rubbish we had earlier." He half-led, half-pulled his wife to the table as Mr Ramsbottom returned to Nell's side.

"Leave it with me. I'll have him back in steerage before the end of the week."

Nell had no chance to reply before Mr and Mrs Ashworth rounded the corner. "Good afternoon. Are you all settled in?"

"We are, thank you." Mrs Ashworth smiled. "It's so nice to sit in a comfortable chair and relax."

"I'm pleased. Did you find the shelf in the saloon with games and playing cards?"

"We did, but we're saving that for tonight. It's such a treat, even Mr Ashworth's been smiling."

He nodded as he walked into the dining room. "I can't complain. Now, where's this food?"

Mr Ramsbottom gestured to the middle section. "Let me show you."

Once the last of the guests had arrived, Nell carried out plates of trout on thinly sliced potatoes. She smiled at the Ashworths as she put theirs down.

"I hope you enjoy it. I've brought a piece of cod for Ruth. It will be easier for her."

"That's very considerate." Mrs Ashworth picked up her knife and fork. "Do you get this sort of food, too?"

"We do. It's a perk of the job."

"How wonderful. I'm sure you deserve it."

"We try."

Mr Ross was waiting for her when she returned to the galley. "It's a lot quicker serving them all the same thing rather than giving them a choice."

"Most of them seem to be enjoying it, too. Do you have four more for the young ladies?"

He turned and peered along the counter. "They're coming. Desserts are ready too when they're finished."

Mr Price arrived in the galley as she waited. "Mrs Riley."

"Mr Price."

He hesitated. "Before you say anything about Mr Marsh being upstairs, may I say that I only agreed to it because he told me the two of you had put your differences to one side."

Nell nodded. "We have, although you might have mentioned it to me first. It's rather awkward having him working alongside Mr Ramsbottom."

Mr Price put a hand to his head. "I hadn't thought of that. I can't move either of them now, but if there's any trouble, let me know."

"If there's any trouble, I'm sure you won't need me to tell you."


Matron looked to be asleep when Nell called on her after luncheon, but she opened her eyes as she crept into the room.

"May I have a drink?"

Nell filled a cup. "Here you are."

"I need more." She emptied the cup and passed it back.

"I can't..."

Matron shook her head. "Dr Clarke's wrong. We need water ... not laudanum."

"But he's the doctor..."

"He's never had cholera. I know the rules make sense, but since I've been ill, I've lost so much fluid. We need to replace it."

"So, you won't reprimand me?"

"No, and if there are any men left in the hospital room, you must give them more, too."

"I can't. I'm in first class, now with the healthy passengers."

"Somebody has to. I can't visit for a few more days, at least."

# CHAPTER FIFTY-ONE

The last glimpse of land disappeared from view as Nell stood at the end of the deck, the wind whipping her cloak around her legs. *At least we're on our way home.* She flinched at the sound of a voice behind her.

"You look cold."

She turned as Mr Marsh joined her at the rail. "I am, but it's worth it. I doubt I'll see America again."

His face dropped. "You're not coming back?"

"No. This voyage has made me realise I need to spend time with my daughters."

He pursed his lips. "I thought they managed well enough without you."

"Not really." She sighed. "If I carry on as I am, I fear they'll grow up not knowing who I am."

"I should be grateful I've no ties."

"It's different for men, as I'm constantly told when I mention my work in the same breath as my nephew's. My sister's done nothing but criticise me since I took the job, so it will make a change for her to be happy with me."

He stared out towards the horizon. "Nobody misses me when I'm away. I've nieces and nephews, but I see them so infrequently I may as well not exist."

"That's sad."

He shrugged. "I'm used to it. I suppose I could have settled down and had a family, but ... well, the right woman didn't come along."

"It comes with the job. You're hardly likely to meet anyone on these voyages."

"I thought the same for years, but sometimes things take you by surprise." He smiled down at her. "I'd like to get to know you better, Mrs Riley."

Nell gulped. "There's not much to know. I'm a widow with two small daughters, and I live with my sister and her family. That's about it."

"You're also a woman who left all that behind to become a stewardess. Not many women do that."

"It's not that unusual."

"I've never met anyone like you." His eyes searched hers, but Nell turned away.

"I wouldn't be here if I hadn't been widowed."

"We all have our reasons for signing up. Would you allow me to spend more time with you?"

Nell's pulse raced as she scanned the horizon for something to distract her. "I expect we will over the coming week. What will you do next year?"

He sighed. "I'm doing one more trip on the *Wyoming* after this, but then it depends."

"On what?"

His gaze returned to the sea. "You."

"Me?" Her voice squeaked. "What's it got to do with me?"

"I'm looking forward to walking out with you when we get back."

"I doubt it will affect your future..."

He looked down and placed an arm around her shoulders. "Let me get you inside. You're frozen."

Mr Price was at the door to the saloon when they arrived. "Ah, Mrs Riley. I've been looking for you. Captain Robertson would like a word."

"With me?" Her stomach spasmed. *What have I done now?*

"Don't be so worried. I'll walk there with you. Would you excuse us, Mr Marsh?"


The captain looked up from a pile of papers when they went in, and he offered Nell a seat.

"Thank you for coming. It's nothing to worry about. I'm just working my way through the crew to find out who'll be rejoining us next year."

*This is it.* She sighed. "I'm afraid I won't be. It's not been an easy decision, but this voyage has been too much."

"It has for many of us. I sincerely hope we won't have another one like this. We'll vet the passengers more thoroughly before they board, in future."

"I'm sure you will, but that's not the only reason. I'd like to spend some time with my daughters."

Captain Robertson stared into space. "I wish I could do the same, for a few weeks at least, but I fear most of my shore leave will be taken up with sorting out the events of this trip." He shook his head. "We'll be sorry to see you go, Mrs Riley, but I'll arrange to have a reference typed up in case you need to find a job in the future."

Nell was the first in the sitting room that evening and she collapsed onto the settee. She closed her eyes for what felt like a minute, but woke with a start when Mrs Swift sat down beside her.

"Were you asleep?"

"I must have been." She sat up, startled by the tray on the table. "I didn't even hear Mr Potter bring this."

"It's supposed to be easier in first class. Why are you so tired?"

"I'm just weary of it all. Captain Robertson wanted to see me earlier, and I told him I wasn't coming back. He was very good about it and said he'd give me a reference in case I changed my mind..."

"Did he mention anything about me?"

Nell gasped and put a hand to her mouth. "I forgot to ask. He said he was going to speak to everyone, though."

"He won't bother with me. He already knows the answer."

"Do you want me to have another word with him?"

Mrs Swift shook her head. "I don't want him to think I'm begging."

"You're entitled to..." Nell paused and cocked an ear to the corridor.

"Did you hear that?"

Mrs Swift didn't have a chance to answer before Matron appeared in the doorway.

"You're out of bed. And dressed." Mrs Swift jumped up and offered her a seat. "Are you feeling better?"

Matron's smile was weak. "A lot better, thank you. I could do with something to eat, though."

"Will Dr Clarke let you...?" Nell was cut short when Matron held up a hand.

"I don't care what he says. I know what I need more than he does."

"But he's the ship's doctor..."

"He's the ship's *surgeon*. I've realised while I've been lying in bed that they won't teach them about things like cholera. They've no need to since it's not a problem in England."

"Don't you think he knows what he's doing?"

Matron sighed. "He's trying his best, but ... no. That's probably why it spread so quickly."

"Gracious. I wonder if Captain Robertson knows."

"Probably not."

Nell hesitated as she stood up. "Let me find you something to eat. Mr Potter should still be around."

She hurried up the stairs and along the corridor, but stopped as Mr Ramsbottom came out from the galley.

"Mrs Riley." He looked her up and down.

"What are you doing on this side of the ship?" She took a step backwards as he rolled his eyes at her.

"Trying to sort out something to eat for Mr Topham. You'd think he'd be happy to be served roast duck, but he did nothing but complain. I've asked Mr Potter if he can save a portion of meat and potato pie for him tomorrow. See how he likes that."

"You said you were going to get him sent back to steerage."

"I was, but I'd feel mean to Mrs Topham. We've knocked the rough edges off her and she's quite happy to try new things."

"I'd noticed. Perhaps we could send Mr Topham to eat down here, and Mrs Topham could sit with the other single ladies."

"It's a thought. I'll see how he is tomorrow." A glint developed in Mr Ramsbottom's eyes. "Do you fancy going out on deck later? You and me?"

"Erm, I can't. I'm on an errand..."

"At this time of night?"

Nell took another step backwards. "Matron's got out of bed and wants something to eat. I need to catch Mr Potter before he disappears."

"Oh." His smile disappeared, but he stood against the wall to let her pass. "Another time then?"

"I really don't think so..."

"Go on. You know you want to." His face lit up again. "I'll look out for you after luncheon tomorrow."

# CHAPTER FIFTY-TWO

The dining room was emptying out after luncheon as Nell collected up the dirty plates and carried them to the galley. Mr Ross took them to the sink but stopped as she hesitated.

"What's the matter with you?"

"Nothing." She flinched as someone in the back dropped a tray.

"It doesn't look like nothing. Who are you hiding from?"

"What makes you think that?"

"Skulking behind the door, for one thing. Who is it? Mr Marsh."

"No."

"Mr Ramsbottom then. He's been in a good mood today. Is that because of you?"

Nell took a deep breath but said nothing.

"If you don't want anything to do with him, tell him."

"As if that works. He's not been talking to me since New York, but he's back again..." She jumped backwards as the door opened.

"Good afternoon, Mrs Riley." Mr Marsh smiled at her. "You seem rather distracted today."

"I'm fine, thank you. I'm not used to working without Mrs Swift, that's all. Have you finished your section?"

Mr Marsh reached for a cloth. "I need to wipe the tables."

"Me too. Perhaps I'll wait for you. If you don't mind."

Mr Ross nodded towards her. "She needs a protector."

"I didn't say that."

He smirked. "You didn't need to."

"Who do you need protecting from?" Mr Marsh's features stiffened.

"Nobody. I'm just being silly. Will you excuse me?" She straightened her back and pushed through the door, but shrieked as she walked straight into Mr Ramsbottom.

"Here you are." There was a glint in his eyes as he caught hold of her arm. "I've been looking for you."

"And she's been hiding from you." Mr Marsh edged him out of the way. "Can't you see she's not interested?"

"Says who? She's never been interested in you…"

"That's where you're wrong." Mr Marsh stood toe to toe with Mr Ramsbottom.

"Stop, please." She turned to Mr Ross, who had followed them out. "Tell them."

"Gentlemen, come on now. No fighting." He put a hand between them. "We don't want you losing your jobs."

"Well, he should leave her alone." Mr Marsh glared down at Mr Ramsbottom, who shoved him to the wall.

"It's not me…"

"Stop, both of you." Nell's voice was shrill. "I don't want any attention. I want to do my job for another week and then go home. Is that too much to ask?" She scurried to the far side of the dining room, but stopped and stared at the table. *I didn't bring a cloth with me.* Tears stung her eyes. *Now what? I can't go back.* She used her hands to brush the crumbs to one end of the table, but squeezed her eyes tight when one of them ran through some spilled tea. *That was stupid.* She wiped it on her apron but sank onto a chair as tears ran down her cheeks. *What's happening to me?* She jumped up as footsteps approached.

"Here you are." Mr Ross handed her a cloth.

"I'm sorry. I should be able to deal with them by now, but I can't." She took it from him, but couldn't stop the tears. "Why does Mrs Swift have to be downstairs?"

"Sit down." Mr Ross sat beside her. "While she's not here, I'll be your chaperone. They didn't realise they'd upset you."

"I've told Mr Ramsbottom enough times..." She wiped her eyes on her sleeve. "All I want is to be left alone. Is that so hard to understand?"

When Mr Ross stayed silent, Nell glanced over his shoulder. "Have they gone?"

"I suggested they start preparing the saloon for afternoon tea."

"Thank you." She stood up to wipe the table. "I'd better get a move on here, but they'll have to manage without me upstairs."

"Where will you go?"

Nell's voice cracked again. "I've no idea. I can't even visit the hospital ward now I'm in first class. Mrs Swift is doing that."

"What about Matron? Is she still poorly?"

417

"She is. I'll pay her a visit." She rubbed a hand across her face. "Thank you, Mr Ross. I appreciate it."

Matron was nowhere to be seen when Nell arrived at their quarters. *Where on earth is she?* She glanced up and down the corridor. *Now what do I do? I'm not going on deck by myself.*

She took a seat in the sitting room and let out a deep sigh. *I've another five days of this.* She rested her head on the back of the settee, but flinched as a nearby door closed.

*Who's that?*

She crept across the room and peered out. "Matron?" When she got no reply, she checked her cabin. *Nothing. I must have imagined it.*

She retook her seat, but jumped up as a lavatory flushed. *What on earth...?* She poked her head into the corridor as Mr Cunningham appeared from the bathroom and disappeared towards the stairs. *He was using our facilities. He can't do that.*

She sat down and scratched her head. *I need to tell Matron, but I've no idea where she'll be. Mr Potter may have seen her. I'll go and ask him.*

Mr Potter was mashing the largest pan of potatoes Nell had ever seen when she went into the galley, but he stopped when he saw her.

"I didn't think you were in steerage any more."

"I'm not, I'm looking for Matron. Have you seen her?"

He sucked air through his teeth. "I can't say I have. Not since I collected the breakfast tray this morning."

"What time was that?"

"It had turned nine o'clock because we'd finished serving breakfast. Have you checked her room?"

"She's not there."

"I expect she's gone to see Dr Clarke, then. She was looking a lot better, so I imagine she'll want to get back to work."

"You're probably right. Thank you, Mr Potter."

Nell hesitated as she stepped out onto the upper decking, but her shoulders relaxed when she realised she was alone. *The others must have decided not to come out. Or gone on the first-class promenade.* She pulled the hood of her cloak over her head as she leaned against the railings. *Deep breaths.* The rhythmic swell of the waves as the ship cut through them sent her into a trance and she didn't hear Mrs Swift walk up behind her.

"What are you doing here? Shouldn't you be working?"

A broad smile split Nell's face. "I could say the same about you."

"We've just finished luncheon, and I needed some air. We've had another three cases this morning."

Nell shook her head. "Will there be no end to it? I was hoping you'd be able to come back upstairs."

"So was I. What have I missed?"

"I've been hiding from Mr Ramsbottom for the last hour."

"I thought he wasn't speaking to you."

"He's changed his mind. I need to find Matron too, but I can't go to the hospital room. You haven't seen her, have you?"

"She was in steerage a short while ago. She may be in one of the other dormitories for all I know."

"Would you check for me? In fact, could you try to persuade her to come up here? We've had an intruder in our quarters and I don't know who else to tell."

Mrs Swift's eyes widened. "Who?"

"Mr Cunningham. He was using our lavatory."

"No! He can't do that."

"Precisely, but thinking about it, if he thought Matron was working again, he would assume nobody would be around."

Mrs Swift turned on her heel. "You wait here and I'll find her. I'm not taking the blame for him."

Nell wrapped her hands in her cloak and leaned her back against the railing. *I need to keep my wits about me.*

Her teeth were chattering by the time the two women joined her.

Matron scowled at her. "What are you doing out here? We'll catch our deaths of cold."

"I'm sorry, I didn't think. Shall we go to our sitting room?"

"We haven't time. Mrs Swift told me about Mr Cunningham. Are you sure you saw him?"

"I'm certain. I'd gone to visit you, but when you weren't there, I went into the sitting room. It was shortly afterwards that I heard the lavatory flush and watched him leaving."

"That's quite unacceptable. He should only ever use the facilities nearest to him to stop the spread of the disease. I need to speak to Mr Price about this."

"This isn't the first time it's happened, though. When I moved to the ladies' section of steerage, Mrs Ashworth commented that she didn't like him using their facilities, but he was working in the men's quarters at the time. I wondered if he could be the one who spread the cholera to the ladies."

"And you didn't report it?" Matron glared at her.

"Not to you because it was when you were ill, but I told Captain Robertson. He mustn't have believed me, though, because nothing's happened."

Matron shook her head. "Fool of a man."

Nell and Mrs Swift exchanged glances.

"Not Captain Robertson, I mean Dr Clarke. He was the one who insisted Mrs Swift must have transferred the disease." Matron shuddered as she paused for breath. "Leave it with me. I'll speak to Captain Robertson as soon as I can."

# CHAPTER FIFTY-THREE

Matron looked exhausted when Nell and Mrs Swift joined her for breakfast the following morning.

"Are you all right?" Nell took the seat beside her.

"I did too much yesterday and I'm not sleeping well without the laudanum."

"Could you ask Dr Clarke for some more?" Mrs Swift helped herself to a piece of toast.

"I don't want any more. It causes more harm than good." Matron shuddered. "I'll be fine in a day or two."

"Did you speak to Captain Robertson?"

"No, I didn't. It's the one thing I hope to do this morning. If Mr Cunningham's spreading cholera around the ship, he needs to be stopped."

"And I want my job back." Mrs Swift stirred some sugar into her tea. "I swear I didn't go near the ladies' section before I was officially sent there. Mrs Riley will tell you."

Matron sighed. "You've both already told me, but all I can say is that I'll do my best. It would be nice if I had a little more energy, but this can't wait until I'm feeling better."

"Well, I wish you luck." Nell bit into her toast. "We need to hurry with this. The passengers will be arriving for breakfast shortly."

Mr Marsh was waiting outside the dining room when Nell arrived and her stride faltered as she saw him.

"Mr Marsh."

"Good morning, Mrs Riley." He tried to smile, but his voice was shaky. "I want to apologise for yesterday."

Nell raised her arms and let them drop back by her sides. "It wasn't your fault."

"I shouldn't have squared up to Mr Ramsbottom." He lowered his voice. "I didn't mean to make you cry. Will you forgive me?"

She nodded as their eyes met. "It was all rather unfortunate."

"It was more than that. I've thought of nothing else all night." He studied his feet as they shuffled on the carpet. "It won't stop you taking that walk with me, will it?"

"Not if you don't want it to."

He let out a deep sigh. "Oh, thank you. I was so worried last night. I thought I'd upset you for good. I promise I won't do anything like that again."

"It wasn't you who upset me. Perhaps I could ask you a favour, though?"

"Certainly. What is it?"

"Will you keep a watch on Mr Ramsbottom to make sure he doesn't pester me again?"

A smile transformed his face. "It will be my pleasure. I've hated the way he looks at you ever since I joined the ship." He extended his arm into the dining room. "Let me walk you to the galley."

Nell kept her head down until they arrived and she looked up to see a row of teapots lined up on the counter. Mr Marsh picked two up.

"Are these ready to go, Mr Ross?"

"They'll be stewed if you don't get them served quickly. I don't know where everyone is this morning."

"I'm on my way." He smiled at her. "I'll see you later."

Nell waited for him to leave before she picked up her own. She was about to follow him out when Mr Ross grinned at her.

"You two have made up, then?"

"It looks like it, not that I was angry with him. It was Mr Ramsbottom. Has he arrived yet?"

"He's been in and out. Not that he looks very happy."

"Well, he's no one but himself to blame. Thank you for being there, yesterday."

"I don't like to see ladies upset."

Nell's shoulders slumped. "I'll try not to do it again. At least there's not long to go now."

"What about next year?" Mr Ross raised an eyebrow at her.

"I'm not coming back; this trip has been too much. I've already told Captain Robertson."

Mr Ross grimaced. "This cholera's got a lot to answer for."

Nell nodded. "It has." She left the galley and headed to the Ashworths' table.

"I'm sorry to keep you. Did you sleep well?"

Mrs Ashworth smiled. "Like a top. The beds are so comfortable. Do you think the captain will let us stay on board and take us to New York on the next trip?"

Nell's heart skipped a beat as Mrs Ashworth stared up at her. "The ship isn't sailing again this year. It's staying in Liverpool for some repairs and a thorough clean."

"What are we supposed to do, then?" Mr Ashworth plonked three lumps of sugar into his tea. "We'll have nowhere to live when we get back. We were banking on it."

Nell's face dropped. "I'm sorry..."

Mrs Ashworth took a deep breath. "We sold everything when we left England and new tenants were moving into the house the day after we left. We don't know what to do."

Nell's eyes flicked to Ruth as she sat close to her mother. "Do you have family you could stay with?"

Mrs Ashworth shook her head. "Not for more than a day or two. We'll have to take it in turns to use the beds."

"There are usually houses in Toxteth to rent. You could probably move in quite quickly if you have the money."

"We have no money after this." Mr Ashworth's raised voice caused many of the passengers to look in their direction. "We spent everything we had paying for this trip, and the little we saved to settle us in New York, we begged from family and friends. Until I find work, we won't be able to afford a room, so what do we do in the meantime?"

"I-I don't know..."

"We're not the only ones, either."

Nell gulped as several sets of eyes stared at her. "Have you spoken to Captain Robertson about this?"

"We've not seen him since we left New York." Mr

Topham's voice carried down the table. "If he thinks he can fob us off with a fancy bedroom and then get rid of us without a second thought, he can think again. We've been talking and we're not getting off this ship until we reach New York."

"I don't know what to say." Her lips moved, but no words came out. "Let me speak to him. Not that I can promise anything."

"Would you?" There were tears in Mrs Ashworth's eyes. "Unless he can get us to New York, we spent all our money for nothing."

"I understand." Nell scurried to the galley to collect the rest of the breakfast. *I hadn't even considered that. I don't suppose the captain has, either.*

Luncheon was over before Nell could look for Captain Robertson, and the corridors were unusually quiet. She made her way to the bridge, but when she arrived, he was about to leave.

"Good afternoon, Mrs Riley. Are you looking for me?"

"Yes, sir." She took a deep breath. "Several families in first class have asked if they can stay on the ship once we get to Liverpool."

"I'm afraid that's not possible. Not for the healthy ones at any rate."

"I told them that, but they've nowhere else to go. When we left Liverpool, many were leaving for good and they sold everything to make the trip. They'll be on the streets when we get back to Liverpool."

"I'm afraid I can't do much about that."

Nell fidgeted with her fingers. "The thing is, some are threatening to stay on the ship when we arrive in Liverpool and say they won't leave unless they get free passage to New York."

Captain Robertson said nothing as he ushered Nell into his office. She watched him pace the floor.

"Might you be able to help them?"

"I could speak to someone in the office when we arrive in Liverpool, assuming the Port Authority will let us dock."

Nell gasped. "You mean they might not?"

The captain creased the side of his lip. "There's a chance, but as it's our base, it's highly unlikely. How many passengers are we talking about?"

"I'm not certain, sir, but Mr Topham seems to be the ringleader. Would you like me to ask?"

"Do it discreetly. I need to know how much of a problem it is, but don't go giving anyone ideas."

Matron was waiting for her when she arrived in the saloon foyer. "Here you are. Where've you been?"

"I needed to speak to the captain."

"I said I was doing that."

"It was about something else. What did he say about Mr Cunningham?"

"That's what I need to tell you. He wants you to write down what you saw and get Mrs Ashworth to do the same. He says he can't dismiss a steward on the hearsay of women and he'll need proof of any wrongdoing before he challenges Mr Cunningham."

"He dismissed Mrs Swift easily enough on nothing more than Dr Clarke's say-so."

Matron sighed. "You know as well as I do that's different. The only thing we can do is get the accusations written down and hand them to him."

Nell leaned against the wall. "There's no point then. Even if he's found to be the one spreading the disease, he'll only get a reprimand."

"There's every point, because unless he's confirmed to be the culprit, Mrs Swift will lose her job. Now, I've put some writing paper in our sitting room, so I suggest you go over there as soon as you can and get it done. He wants a report from me, too, so I'll be over there once I've spoken to Mrs Ashworth."

Nell sighed. "I may as well do it now. I've an hour before we serve afternoon tea."

Nell blotted the writing paper and folded the letter in half before pushing it into an envelope.

"I hope that's good enough." She wrote the captain's name on the front and handed it to Matron.

"I hope so, too."

"Did you speak to Mrs Ashworth?"

"I did and I'll collect her letter in the morning." Matron stood up from the table in their sitting room. "I'm rather tired now, so if you don't mind, I'll speak to Captain Robertson in the morning."

"Will you stay with him when he reads them?"

Matron huffed. "I have to be careful. It can't look as if I've seen the testimonies or helped to influence them."

"It's so silly. Why can't he just believe us?"

"I'm hoping he will. I suspect he's feeling rather shaken after everything that's happened. Not that he'd admit it. Now, you need to get back upstairs, before anyone misses you."

## CHAPTER FIFTY-FOUR

Nell hadn't seen Matron all day, but she had no time to think about it as she rushed into the saloon to serve afternoon tea. Quite where the days went now she was on her own, she didn't know, and she groaned as several passengers were already waiting to be served. She wandered to the dumb waiter and took out a tray of milk jugs and sugar bowls, but flinched as she placed them on the table.

"Mrs Riley. On your own too." Mr Ramsbottom grinned at her. "It makes a change to see you without Marshy in tow."

She glanced around. "We have passengers."

"They can wait. I'm more bothered about Mr Marsh. Since he's had cholera, he never leaves you alone. Shall I have a word with him?"

"No! I mean, thank you, but it's fine. I can deal with him, but I'd like to be left alone, as I've mentioned several times before."

"You don't mean me."

"I do. My husband only died last year, and I've no intention of settling down with anyone else at the moment."

He nudged closer to her. "We needn't settle down. Just keep each other company…"

"Mr Ramsbottom! What sort of woman do you think I am?" She straightened her uniform as she backed towards the wall. "Now, if you'll excuse me, I need to get on and you should be in your own place."

"All right, calm down." He smoothed down a stray piece of hair. "I'm only being friendly."

"A polite conversation is quite enough, thank you." She stepped away from the table, but recoiled as Mr Marsh walked across the saloon.

"What's going on here?"

Mr Ramsbottom glared at him. "Nothing. I'm going."

Mr Marsh didn't acknowledge him as he gazed at Nell. "Are you all right?"

"I'm fine. He only wanted to talk."

"It didn't look…"

"Please, Mr Marsh."

He adjusted his necktie. "I'm sorry. May I help here?"

"There's not much to do. I'm waiting for the tea and coffee. You should probably get ready to greet the rest of the passengers."

He sighed. "You're right. I'll see you later."

Nell had no sooner placed the teapots on the table than Mr and Mrs Ashworth arrived with the Tophams.

"Good afternoon." Nell kept her tone light as they took the seats closest to her, but there was no smile on Mr Topham's face.

431

"Captain Robertson came to talk to us this morning about getting off the ship in Liverpool."

"That's good ... isn't it?" She glanced round at four dejected faces.

Mr Topham shrugged. "You tell us."

"Well, it shows he's interested. Has he agreed to take you to New York?"

"No. That's why we wanted a word with you. He said he'd speak to Mr Guion when we get to Liverpool, but we need you to put in a good word for us. We've been agreeable passengers after all."

"Well ... yes, but I don't have any influence with Mr Guion ... or even the captain."

Mr Topham leaned forward. "Do your best. We're relying on you."

"I doubt I can say any more than you already have..." Nell stopped as he glared at her "...but I'll try. Now, why don't you help yourselves to some cake while I pour the tea?"

She turned to leave the table when a middle-aged man she hadn't met before grabbed her arm.

"Did I hear you say you'd be arranging a free trip to New York for those passengers?" He nodded at the Tophams.

"Not at all." Nell's cheeks flushed. "They spoke to the captain this morning, that's all."

"Why weren't we given the chance to speak to him?"

"I ... erm ... well, Mr Ashworth had asked me to pass a message to him, which I did."

The man glared at her. "It shouldn't be one rule for

them and another for the rest of us. If they get free passage to New York, we all should."

"I..." Nell's voice squeaked. "I can't promise."

"But you can try. We all talk to each other, you know."

Nell pulled her arm free. "Were you planning to settle in New York, too?"

"It doesn't matter what we were doing, it still cost a lot of money. Either we get free transport on another trip, or we want our money back. Isn't that right, everyone?"

"Yes." Voices clamoured for attention and Nell retreated as several passengers stepped towards her.

"Very well, I'll let the captain know."

Mrs Swift was already in their sitting room that evening when Nell got back.

"You're early."

Mrs Swift's face lit up. "I've been to see the captain, and he believed our testimonies."

"That's wonderful!" Nell clapped her hands. "Has he given you your job back?"

Mrs Swift sighed. "Yes and no. He agreed not to sack me, but he won't get rid of Mr Cunningham."

"Why not? He was the one responsible."

"It clearly wasn't as serious for him to spread the disease as it was for me. Anyway, I told him that if Mr Cunningham was still on the ship, I wanted a move."

"Why?"

"Because I don't want to see him again. Captain Robertson was happy to get rid of me without any evidence, but even with proof, all Mr Cunningham gets is a reprimand."

"Did you tell him that?"

Mrs Swift snorted. "There'd be no point. It wouldn't change anything. Anyway, he said he'd arrange a transfer to the *Wyoming* for next year, so at least I won't be out of work."

"The *Wyoming*? Mr Marsh used to work there and he's doing the next voyage with them. He should be able to tell you something about the captain and staff."

"If I ever see him again." Mrs Swift huffed. "He's not allowed in steerage and I can't come upstairs. You'll have to ask him for me."

Nell shuddered. "He'll think I'm chasing him with all these questions."

Mrs Swift studied her. "And what's wrong with that? You don't look too unhappy about it."

# CHAPTER FIFTY-FIVE

Nell lay in bed and pulled the covers over her head as the bell rang in the corridor. *It can't be morning already.*

Mrs Swift rocked the bed as she climbed from the lower bunk. "Come along, sleepy. Only one full day to go."

"That's one too many."

"What's up with you?"

Nell waited for Mrs Swift to light the lamp before she sat up and swung her legs over the edge of the bunk. "I've still not spoken to Captain Robertson to tell him the rest of the passengers want a free return trip to New York or their money back."

"Why's that put you in such a bad mood? We can't just speak to him whenever we want."

"Because they were complaining to me yesterday, and they're likely to be worse today."

"You should be all right this morning. They'll all be on deck trying to catch the first glimpse of land."

"I doubt it." Nell snorted as she climbed down from the bed. "Half of them never wanted to see the United Kingdom again. They're not likely to be excited. If anything, it will make them madder."

Mrs Swift sighed. "I hadn't thought of that. We'll be passing Mizen Head today, too."

"Thank you for reminding me. It's days like this I wish I could stay in bed."

"Come on, I don't want to hear talk like that. Hurry up and get dressed while I pour the tea."

Mrs Swift and Matron were both halfway through their porridge when she arrived in the sitting room.

"Is there any left?"

"Of course." Mrs Swift pushed a bowl towards her. "Hopefully, you'll feel better when you've had that."

Matron looked up. "What's the matter with you?"

"Nothing."

"Come on, out with it."

Nell sighed. "If you must know, the passengers in first class are angry that they've spent all their money on emigrating, but have ended up back where they started. Some have already spoken to the captain about how they'll manage when they're in Liverpool, but now they want me to talk to him about letting them travel to New York for free."

"You'll do no such thing." Matron scowled at her. "Poor Captain Robertson's got enough to worry about."

"It's all right for him. He'll be back on the ship soon enough and go again. Many of these people have used their life savings to make this trip and they've said that if they don't get free travel to New York, they want their money refunded."

"It's not as easy as that."

Mrs Swift's forehead creased. "Why not?"

"In case you haven't realised, both the captain and Dr Clarke are fighting for their jobs, so I don't think the passengers will be their top priority."

"So even if he wanted to, Captain Robertson couldn't offer them another voyage." Nell bit on her lip. "He still needs to know what they're saying."

"Well, not today ... and not before he gets a chance to talk to the clerks in the office. This voyage will have cost Mr Guion a lot of money. He won't be happy as it is, let alone giving free passage to half the passengers."

Nell's shoulders slumped. "It's not that many, but that makes it even more important that I speak to him today."

"No." Matron held up a hand. "He has enough on his plate. We dock in Queenstown in the next couple of hours and officials are coming aboard to inspect the ship to confirm we can disembark in Liverpool."

"They might stop us?" A shiver ran down Nell's spine. "Can they do that?"

"I'm afraid so."

"But what will happen to us? I have to go home."

"I don't know. I'm not even sure the captain does, so if you see him, don't be giving him more problems. Right, I need to leave you." Matron finished her tea. "We've still a couple of patients in the hospital room that we need to be awake by the time the officials call."

Once Matron had gone, Nell pushed her empty bowl

into the middle of the table. "I need to go myself. If you get the chance, come onto the deck when we're in Queenstown."

"I'll try my best. I imagine we'll have to work extra fast this morning to make the place clean enough for the officials."

"We'd better get a move on, then."

Mr Marsh was waiting by the door to the dining room when Nell arrived at breakfast and she smiled when she saw him.

"Three days running?"

"You asked me to be your chaperone and I take the role very seriously." He gave a mock bow. "Besides, I can't think of a better way to start the day."

Nell blushed as he led her across the room. "I'm pleased to say the chaperoning seems to be working. I've not had any trouble with Mr Ramsbottom for the last few days."

"I'm delighted to hear it. He's given me a wide berth in our quarters, too."

"You're together?" Nell raised an eyebrow at him.

"There are six of us in each section, so I'm rarely on my own with him. He has the occasional snide remark, but I rise above it."

"I'm glad about that. Did you know we have officials coming aboard to inspect the ship when we reach Queenstown?"

"No." Mr Marsh's brow furrowed. "Where did you hear that?"

"From Matron. I need to speak to the captain about another matter, but she said he'd be too busy today."

"Is there a problem?" He pursed his lips as he stopped to study her.

"Nothing for you to worry about."

"Are you sure? It's not Mr Ramsbottom again?"

Nell shook her head. "It's nothing like that. It's an issue with some of the passengers. They want free passage to America and have told me to tell him they'll be filing a complaint if they don't get one."

"You shouldn't be speaking to the captain about things like that."

Nell shrugged. "Who else is there? Besides, he hasn't visited the first-class area since we left New York and with the cholera restrictions, they can't go looking for him."

"But they shouldn't expect you to do it."

Nell smiled. "I'm on reasonably good terms with Captain Robertson, so I'll speak to him once we leave Queenstown."

"If you're sure..." Mr Marsh held open the galley door. "I don't want you getting into trouble."

The cathedral of Queenstown looked as majestic as ever when Nell stepped out onto the deck after luncheon, but with no sign of Mrs Swift, she wandered to the far end of the ship to rest on the railings. She shuddered as a cold gust of wind swept over her and she pulled her cloak tight. *At least the sun's shining.*

"Do you mind if I join you?" Mr Marsh appeared by her side.

"Not at all, although I doubt I'll be here long with this

wind." She studied Mr Marsh with only his suit jacket for warmth. "Don't you feel the cold?"

"Sometimes, but not today. It may be the last chance I get to spend time with you before we leave the ship."

"I suppose so. We'll be busy tonight."

He smiled down at her. "I wanted to thank you for making this journey so much more bearable than it might otherwise have been."

"It was the least I could do. I felt so guilty about you being so ill."

"Well, if that's what made you look favourably on me, it was worth it." He gazed at the small cluster of houses around the cathedral. "I'm sorry we didn't get off to the best of starts."

She studied the hills behind the buildings. "I didn't know what I'd done wrong given you were so pleasant to Mrs Swift..."

"I was a fool." He shook his head. "I've told myself time and again not to jump to conclusions, but I'm afraid it's one of my many failings."

"It's easy to do. I've done it myself."

"You'll forgive me then? For thinking the worst of you?"

Her heart fluttered as his dark eyes held her gaze. "It's all in the past. There's nothing to forgive."

"Thank you." Mr Marsh's shoulders relaxed. "And we'll take that walk to the park once we're in Liverpool?"

Nell grimaced. "As long as they let us off the ship. Do you know if the officials are still on board?"

"I've not seen them, but they shouldn't be much longer if they are. I expect they'll be with the captain and Dr Clarke."

Nell nodded. "I wouldn't like to be in their shoes."

"Me neither. Especially not Dr Clarke. He has to take most of the blame for what's happened."

"I hope Captain Robertson doesn't get into trouble. He's been very kind to me." Nell glanced up at Mr Marsh, whose gaze had settled on the land. "How many days' shore leave do you have before your next voyage?"

"Assuming we dock in Liverpool on time, five. I don't know what I'll do if we're delayed."

"Would they put you on another ship?"

"They might, although with Christmas approaching, there won't be so many options."

"You'll find lodgings in Liverpool easily enough."

He stared down at her. "I'm not used to being on land for Christmas, but if you'd show me around the city, it would make it worthwhile."

Nell's cheeks flushed, and she diverted her eyes.

"It really is peaceful here, isn't it?"

She nodded. "It's lovely, but why would anyone want to disembark here? It doesn't look like there's much to do."

"It's mainly mail that leaves the ship, although somebody must live here. It's a lot quieter than New York. Remember how busy it was there?"

Nell smiled. "I do. That was my favourite day this year, being in Central Park after I'd waited for so long. It's a shame we couldn't go again."

He raised an eyebrow at her. "Perhaps we could if you sign up again for next year."

She shook her head. "It's out of the question. Besides, I've already told Captain Robertson I'm not coming back."

"That's a pity. I like having you on board." He fixed his

stare on a spot in the distance. "Tell me, did you take Mr Hewitt around Liverpool after we'd brought him home from New York?"

"Mr Hewitt?" Nell's brow creased. "That was months ago."

"I know, and I realise it has nothing to do with me, but..." he turned his head, his eyes searching hers "...did you?"

"I met with him when he visited Miss Ellis and we went for afternoon tea at the Adelphi, but that was all. I only had two days at home that month."

He kept his face straight as Nell's smile faded.

"He visited Miss Ellis a couple more times when I was at sea, so he'll have seen enough of Liverpool."

"How do you know?"

"I visit Miss Ellis whenever I'm home. She doesn't live far from me and we walk together in the park."

"That's nice. I often wondered what had happened to them all. Send her my regards if you see her again."

"I will. I'll actually be seeing a lot more of her next year. She's asked me to be her companion."

"Really..."

Footsteps striding across the deck caused them both to turn.

"This all looks very cosy."

"Mr Ramsbottom!" Nell gasped at the look on his face.

"Is he troubling you?" He indicated to Mr Marsh.

"Not at all. We're just taking the air..."

"Yet you wouldn't do that with me."

"We were only talking."

"So I suggest you leave her alone." Mr Marsh stepped forward.

"I've not touched her."

"Maybe not today, but you do most other days. Don't think I've not seen you. Haven't you got the message that she doesn't want your advances?"

"I'm not taking orders from you. You're the one she's been trying to get away from for the last year, not me."

"That's where you're wrong. I'm protecting her from you."

Mr Ramsbottom stared at Nell. "Is this another one of your japes? Can't you see he has designs on you? That's why he won't let anyone else near you."

"It's not like that."

"I think it is, and if you can't see it, you must be blind."

"That's enough." Mr Marsh stepped towards him, but Mr Ramsbottom grabbed Mr Marsh's arms and forced him against the railings.

"I'm sick of you coming over all high and mighty when I've as much right to speak to her as you."

"Mr Ramsbottom, stop it." Nell pulled on his arm, but he pushed her away, hurling her backwards into the rear mast where she landed on the deck. "Argh!!"

Mr Marsh dashed to her side. "Are you all right?" He helped her sit up as Mr Ramsbottom knelt down by her other side.

"Are you hurt?"

"My arm..." Her voice squeaked as her left arm rested limply on her lap.

"It was an accident..." Mr Ramsbottom shifted his position as Mr Marsh glowered at him.

"Don't just sit there, man. Go and fetch Dr Clarke."

"You go…"

"Stop it!" Nell gritted her teeth. "Mr Ramsbottom, please. You've done enough damage…"

"I didn't mean…"

"Whether you did or not, find either Dr Clarke or Matron." Mr Marsh spat out his words. "Mrs Riley's in a great deal of pain thanks to you."

"Yes … I'm sorry." Mr Ramsbottom jumped up and scurried to the door leading to steerage, but stopped abruptly as it swung towards him and Mrs Swift appeared.

"What's going on here?" She hurried to Nell's side and crouched beside her.

"There's been an accident." Mr Marsh stood up. "She slipped on the decking and hurt her arm."

Mrs Swift reached to take hold of it.

"Ow!"

"I'm sorry. Has anyone gone for the doctor?"

Mr Marsh nodded. "That's where Mr Ramsbottom's gone."

"It was all his fault." Nell sobbed as she wiped her good arm over her face.

"Whose? Mr Ramsbottom's?"

"He pushed me and I lost my footing. I was about to go inside too." Nell shivered as the wind ruffled her cloak. "Will you take me to our sitting room?"

"Let me help you." Mr Marsh offered her an arm and wrapped his other around her waist as he lifted her up. "Can you walk?"

Nell tentatively put her weight on each foot. "Yes."

"That's good." He released his hold and passed her good

arm to Mrs Swift. "You take her to your quarters, and I'll wait here for the doctor and ask him to follow you."

Mrs Swift nodded and led Nell to the door. "Come on, it's over now. If Mr Ramsbottom caused this, I can't see him getting away with it."

# CHAPTER FIFTY-SIX

The walls of the sitting room faded in and out of focus as Nell leaned against the back of the settee. The only thing that held her attention was the throbbing in her wrist.

"I can't move my fingers." She screwed up her face as Matron lifted her hand.

"I'd say you've broken a bone. I'll get Dr Clarke. He'll know how to set it."

"Will it hurt?"

"No more than it does now. Let me go and find him."

Nell turned to Mrs Swift as Matron left. "I've no one but myself to blame."

"It wasn't your fault. All you were doing was talking to Mr Marsh. You didn't ask for Mr Ramsbottom to interrupt."

"But if I'd been more forceful with him..."

"Stop this. You've told him often enough that you didn't want his attention. I doubt he'll keep his job after this ... and don't you dare blame yourself for that."

Nell rolled her head and stared at the ceiling. "What a mess. I didn't even get to speak to the captain about the passengers. Do you think he'll know whether we can go home?"

Mrs Swift sighed. "Who knows? We've not started moving yet, so the officials could still be on board. Or they've stopped us from leaving."

"I want to go home. I can't work with a broken arm ... and I certainly don't want to see Mr Ramsbottom again."

Mrs Swift patted her good hand and poured two glasses of brandy from the bottle Mr Potter had delivered earlier. "Here, drink this. Mr Marsh won't let Mr Ramsbottom near you. Don't think I didn't notice how concerned he was for you."

"He's been very sweet. He's kept Mr Ramsbottom away from me for most of this week ... although that could have been part of the problem today."

"You may need him again then if we can't dock in Liverpool." Mrs Swift paused as Matron appeared with Dr Clarke.

"Here she is, Doctor."

Dr Clarke peered down at her. "Been causing more trouble, Mrs Riley?"

"It wasn't me." She struggled to sit up straight. "I was pushed."

"For good reason, I imagine. Now, let me look."

Nell shrieked as he took her hand.

"All right. It's clearly a break." He moved each finger in turn. "I'll give you a dose of laudanum and get it set."

Nell's frame stiffened. "You can't put me to sleep."

"It will ease the pain and allow me to set it properly, so

if you'll let me do my job..." He took a measure from his bag and filled it. "Here, drink this."

Nell closed her eyes as she drank the bitter liquid. *I hope it works.*

"Good. We'll give it a few minutes to work, and you'll need several doses over the next few days. Your arm will still be painful once it's set."

She watched as the doctor took a selection of bandages from his bag, along with a container and dish, which he laid out neatly on the table. He looked over at Mrs Swift.

"I need some water."

Mrs Swift scurried off, but by the time she returned, Nell was struggling to keep her eyes open. Darkness closed in on her until a pain shot through her arm.

"No!" Her eyes shot open as she sat up straight.

"Calm down, Mrs Riley. This shouldn't hurt."

"Well, it does..."

"Nonsense." Dr Clarke wrapped the wet bandage around her wrist. "I'll be done shortly. Once the plaster's dried, you'll need your arm in a sling. Matron will fix it for you."

Nell clenched every muscle as the doctor worked on it, only relaxing when he'd finished. "May I go to sleep now?"

The ship was moving when she woke up, but the light was dim and she was alone in the sitting room. *What happened?* She moved to sit up, but the weight on her arm stopped her. *Oh yes.* She glanced at the clock. *Mrs Swift should be back shortly.*

She returned to her doze, but promptly sat up again at the sound of footsteps in the corridor. "Who's there?"

"It's only me." Matron studied her as she walked in. "How are you feeling?"

"Drowsy, and my arm hurts, but otherwise, I'm fine. Have you spoken to the captain?"

"Just. He looks exhausted." Matron took the seat opposite.

"Did he say what's happening. Are we being allowed to dock in Liverpool?"

"We are. He said it was touch and go, but the officials were happy that we're over the worst of it. Those who are still infected need to stay on the ship until they get the all-clear."

Nell smiled. "That's good news. Will we be home in the morning?"

"We'll arrive later than usual because we didn't leave Queenstown until six o'clock, but yes. You'll be home by this time tomorrow."

"What a relief." She settled back again, but her eyes sprang open. "What about the passengers who aren't sick? Will they have to disembark? I said I'd speak to the captain..."

"Mrs Riley, relax. Captain Robertson hasn't had a minute today and after this fiasco, he has Mr Ramsbottom to deal with too."

"You told him?"

Matron shook her head. "Not me, Mr Marsh. He's very concerned about you."

Nell nodded. "I can imagine. Do you know what the captain said about Mr Ramsbottom?"

"Not yet. He wants to speak to him once dinner's over." Matron paused as Mr Potter appeared at the door with a tray.

"Are you ready for this, ladies?"

Matron stood up to help him. "Yes, please. Mrs Swift will be here shortly."

He stared down at Nell's arm. "I heard you got into a spot of bother."

"What did you hear?"

He shrugged. "Nothing much, only that Mr Marsh and Mr Ramsbottom were fighting, and you got in the way."

"I was trying to stop them."

"You certainly did that. Mr Marsh was asking after you earlier."

Nell smiled. "That's nice. If you see him again, you can tell him I'm fine."

"I will. I told him I'd be bringing a tray, so he'll be back. Right, I'd better be going in case he's waiting."

Nell looked at Matron as Mr Potter left. "Do you know, Mr Marsh really isn't as bad as I made him out to be."

"I never understood why you took such a dislike to him."

"It's complicated, but at least we've made up now." Nell sat up as Matron pushed a plate of steak and kidney pie towards her.

"See if you can eat some of that."

Nell stared down at her hand. "It won't be easy holding my fork in the wrong hand and not having a knife."

"Would you like me to cut anything up for you?"

"If I pretend I'm using a cake fork, I might be able to manage. I'll have to learn how to do it."

She sliced through her first piece of pastry as Mrs Swift joined them.

"Sorry I'm late."

"It's not a problem." Nell raised her good hand. "I'm likely to be rather slow eating like this. Where've you been?"

"Nowhere. I came via the galley and bumped into Mr Marsh."

Nell paused between mouthfuls. "Mr Potter said he'd asked after me. Did you tell him I was all right?"

"I told him you were asleep, because the last time I saw you, you were." Mrs Swift pulled a plate towards her. "He sent a message for you, too."

Nell raised an eyebrow. "What about?"

"He said he'd spoken to the captain about the passengers who want to be taken to New York."

"Oh, what a relief." Nell's face broke into a grin. "Did he say how he'd got on?"

"No, just that Captain Robertson would deal with it."

Nell looked over to Matron, who was halfway through her dinner. "Will you be seeing him before we reach Liverpool?"

"Not until the morning."

"Can you ask if he's going to let the passengers stay on the ship and take them to New York when the ship sails again?"

"Neither of us will have time for that. The captain has to prepare for docking and decide what to do about those who are still sick. I need to help Dr Clarke assess them, and the crew won't be allowed off the ship while passengers are still on board."

Nell's mouth fell open. "None of us?"

"You will be. You can't work with a broken wrist."

Nell's chin quivered. "But will you both have to stay on?"

"That's what we don't know. Captain Robertson has called a meeting for tomorrow morning to tell us what's happening. It depends on how many passengers we're left with."

"At least I'll be able to speak to him then."

Matron let out a loud sigh. "Mrs Riley. Do I have to spell it out? The meeting won't be for you. You'll be getting off the ship no matter what, so there's no need for you to attend. Besides, the captain asked that you're kept down here to avoid the rest of the stewards seeing your arm in a sling. He wants no more gossip."

"Oh." Nell's shoulders fell. "Won't I be able to say farewell to everyone?"

"I'm afraid not. Now, go to bed and you can pack your bag in the morning while you wait for someone to escort you from the ship."

# CHAPTER FIFTY-SEVEN

The ship was still sailing when the bell rang the following morning, and Nell groaned as she momentarily forgot about the plaster on her arm.

"You stay where you are." Mrs Swift climbed out of bed and lit the wall lamp.

"I still need to get up for breakfast. I may need help putting my dress on, too."

"I hadn't thought of that. You'd better get a move on then."

Matron was already in the sitting room when they arrived, and she smiled as they joined her.

"I was thinking, this will be our last meal together. We've been through quite a lot this year."

"We have." Nell shuffled round to the far side of the table. "And it's not all been bad. What time's your meeting?"

"Eight o'clock."

"Do you think the stewards will know what happened yesterday?"

Matron sighed. "I hope not."

"I don't know who'd have told them." Mrs Swift poured the tea. "I've not said anything and I'm fairly sure Mr Marsh and Mr Ramsbottom won't have, either."

"Won't everyone wonder where I am this morning?"

"We're going to tell them you're feeling unwell."

Nell's eyes widened. "Don't let them think I've got cholera. They'll wonder why I'm not being kept on the ship."

Matron rolled her eyes. "I'm not that foolish."

"I'll miss you both when I move." Mrs Swift buttered a piece of bread for Nell. "I hope the *Wyoming* has two stewardesses. I've got rather fond of having a companion."

"They should. It is the sister ship after all, so the staff numbers should be similar."

"I hope so. I don't suppose you asked Mr Marsh."

Nell gasped. "I'm sorry, I didn't. I'm not sure whether I'll see him again before I leave the ship, either."

"Don't worry, there's not much I can do about it now."

Nell suddenly brightened. "You could speak to him, if he's in your meeting this morning."

Mrs Swift smiled. "I'd forgotten that. All this isolating passengers and crew has been hard work. I'll be glad to see the back of it."

Nell hesitated as she fidgeted with a teaspoon. "I wonder, could you ask him when he might like to take the walk in the park? I promised him we'd go while he's onshore but we've not had chance to make any arrangements."

Matron nodded at her arm. "You won't be going very far with that."

"I can still walk."

"Maybe you can, but it'll take it out of you. You need to rest if you want it to heal."

"And I will, but I'm sure I can manage an hour in the park. I can't let him down again."

Mrs Swift looked at Nell with a twinkle in her eye. "Are you finally going to return his affections?"

Nell's cheeks coloured. "I haven't decided yet."


Nell was sure Matron wouldn't approve of her leaving their quarters, but she took a deep breath of sea air as she leaned against the railings of the deck and gazed at the shoreline as they made their final approach into Liverpool.

This was her tenth voyage, but it was the first time she'd seen this view. Certainly in daylight. Why the ship always docked so early in the morning, while everyone was asleep, she didn't know.

The sky was grey as they approached and the docks filled the landscape rather than the fields of America, but she didn't care. She didn't even mind that there was rain in the air. *I'm nearly home.* Tears welled in her eyes as she imagined the welcome she'd get. *There'll be no arguments about me going away again and I'll be home in time for stir-up Sunday.* She let out a gentle sob. *I'll be able to help Elenor make a Christmas pudding.*

She flinched at the sound of footsteps on the decking and looked to her right. "Mr Marsh."

"I thought it was you." He settled beside her on the railings. "I'd hoped to see you at the meeting, but when you weren't there, I nipped out to see if you needed anything."

"That's very kind of you, but I'm afraid Matron

wouldn't let me join you. She doesn't want anyone seeing my sling and wants me off the ship as soon as possible. Do the stewards know what happened?"

"They do now. If I was in charge, I wouldn't have said anything, but Captain Robertson told everyone that Mr Ramsbottom's been moved to a male-only ship, and they wanted to know why."

"I imagine I got the blame."

"Not at all. That was all placed on me and Mr Ramsbottom."

"You?" Nell straightened up and stared at him.

"I'm afraid so. Mr Ramsbottom was adamant it was my fault for harassing you."

"But you weren't. Do you want me to have a word with him?"

"Thank you, but there's no need. In fact, he may have done me a favour. Mrs Swift and most of the stewards will be staying on board to clean the ship and deal with the sick passengers, but the captain wants me and Mr Ramsbottom off as soon as those who are healthy have disembarked."

"So the others are still in the meeting?"

"Those who are staying. Mr Ward and Mr Cooper are changing ship, so they're packing."

Nell glanced over his shoulder towards the door. "Did Mrs Swift pass you my message about when to take our walk?"

"She did, but I've a better idea ... if you don't mind."

Nell cocked her head to one side as he cleared his throat.

"As we both have to leave the ship at the earliest

opportunity, would you allow me to escort you home? I'll arrange a carriage..."

"Well ... I suppose so. Unless any of my nephews are waiting for me."

"Won't they be at work at this time on a Friday?"

"Actually, yes, they should be." *As long as there's been no more trouble.*

A grin almost split his face. "Splendid. I imagine Mr Price will walk you from the ship, so I'll wait for you at the bottom of the gangplank."

Nell's stomach fluttered. "I'll look forward to it."

THE NEXT INSTALLMENT...

**The Companion's Secret**

**Nell's new job sees her welcomed into a more prestigious social circle.
But she comes to realise that not all friendships are what they seem...**

*November 1882*: Scarred by the events of her last voyage, Nell is ready for a change, and being offered a role as lady's companion is too good an opportunity to miss.

It should be no more than taking walks and afternoon tea, but Miss Ellis's life isn't her own.

Surrounded by people wanting to control her every move, she longs to make her own choices, but when an old adversary arrives on her doorstep, her dreams are shattered.

Not prepared to give up hope, Nell is determined to help, but when she gets more involved than she expects, the outcome has far-reaching consequences...

To get your copy visit my website at:
https://valmcbeath.com/windsor-street/

If you're enjoying the series, why not sign up to my newsletter?

Visit: https://www.subscribepage.com/fsorganic

You'll receive details of new releases, special offers and information relating to *The Windsor Street Family Saga,* and my other series, The *Ambition & Destiny* Series. Occasionally, you'll also receive details of other offers relating to historical fiction.

# AUTHOR'S NOTE AND ACKNOWLEDGEMENTS

At the end of the last book, I mentioned that I'd found a website giving fabulous insights into life on board for first-class guests during the early days of transatlantic travel. It provided inspiration for most of the passengers in *The Stewardess's Journey* and I continued to use the site to develop the characters for this book. I'm sure you'll recognise some of them from the descriptions below.

One thing it said was that there was a lot of snobbery on board about who people were prepared to talk to, and that people preferred to stick to their own social circle. This meant people would actively avoid anyone they thought was beneath them.

Not that you would necessarily know who suitable companions were, given the limited information on the guest list.

On top of that, it wasn't uncommon for passengers to lie about their social status. Passports were still in their infancy and once guests had boarded, there was no way for anyone

461

to check up on them. People would often 'make up' their fortunes and nobody would be any the wiser (unless they accidentally bumped into someone they knew). It was an attractive thing to do, because of the benefits it could bring. One of those things was an invitation to sit at the captain's table. It could help to build reputations and many aspired to receive an invitation. Guests pretending to be someone they weren't, however, had to know how to behave, otherwise they could find their humbler origins exposed.

Another group of passengers worthy of mention were widows. Irrespective of their circumstances, other guests always considered them to be wealthy. Why would they be on a liner otherwise? They were, however, a prime target for gossip and scandal to be conjured around them.

Regarding the storyline in Liverpool, most of it was fictitious. The only bits that were true were that Nell ended her time at sea in November 1882 and subsequently stayed at home with Maria, George and the family.

As Miss Ellis had been a popular character in *The Stewardess's Journey*, I thought it would be interesting to continue that friendship. I actually became so involved with the characters myself that Miss Ellis plays a big part in the story line of the next book. *The Companion's Secret*.

If you'd like to find out how the story develops once Nell gives up going to sea, you can get your copy of *The Companion's Secret* by visiting:

https://books2read.com/TCS2

As ever, thanks must go to my husband Stuart and

friend Rachel for providing feedback on my early drafts. I'd also like to thank my editor Susan Cunningham.

Finally, thank you to you for reading.

Best wishes

Val

# ABOUT THE AUTHOR

Val started researching her family tree back in 2008. At that time, she had no idea what she would find or where it would lead. By 2010, she had discovered a story so compelling she was inspired to turn it into a novel.

This first foray into writing turned into The *Ambition & Destiny* Series. A story of the trials, tragedies, and triumphs of some of her ancestors as they sought their fortune in Victorian-era England.

By the time the series was complete, Val had developed a taste for writing and turned her hand to writing Agatha Christie style mysteries. These novels form part of the *Eliza Thomson Investigates* series and currently consists of five standalone books and two novella's.

Although writing the mysteries was great fun, the pull of researching other branches of the family was strong and Val continued to look for other stories worth telling.

Back in 2018, she discovered a previously unknown fact about one of her great, great grandmothers, Nell. *The Windsor Street Family Saga* is a fictitious account of that discovery. Further details of all series can be found on Val's website at: www.vlmcbeath.com.

Prior to writing, Val trained as a scientist and has worked in the pharmaceutical industry for many years. In 2012, she set up her own consultancy business, and currently splits her time between business and writing.

Born and raised in Liverpool (UK), Val now lives in Cheshire with her husband, Stuart. She has two daughters, the younger of which, Sarah, now helps with the publishing side of the business.

In addition to family history, her interests include rock music and Liverpool Football Club.

# ALSO BY VL MCBEATH

**The *Windsor Street Family Saga***

**The full series:**

Part 1: *The Sailor's Promise*

(*an introductory novella*)

Part 2: *The Wife's Dilemma*

Part 3: *The Stewardess's Journey*

Part 4: *The Captain's Order*

Part 5: *The Companion's Secret*

Part 6: *The Mother's Confession*

Part 7: *The Daughter's Defiance*

**The *Ambition & Destiny* Series**

**The full series:**

Short Story Prequel: *Condemned by Fate*

Part 1: *Hooks & Eyes*

Part 2: *Less Than Equals*

Part 3: *When Time Runs Out*

Part 4: *Only One Winner*

Part 5: *Different World*

A standalone novel: *The Young Widow*

***Eliza Thomson Investigates***

*A Deadly Tonic (A Novella)*

*Murder in Moreton*

*Death of an Honourable Gent*

*Dying for a Garden Party*

*A Scottish Fling*

*The Palace Murder*

*Death by the Sea*

*A Christmas Murder*

**To find out more about visit VL McBeath's website at:**

**https://www.valmcbeath.com/**

FOLLOW ME

Printed in Great Britain
by Amazon

30261701R00270